A TURN FOR HOME

Also by Gregg Clemmer

Valor in Gray:
The Recipients of the Confederate Medal of Honor

Old Alleghany:
The Life and Wars of General Ed Johnson

Winner of the Douglas Southall Freeman Book Prize

A TURN FOR HOME

GREGG CLEMMER

The Hearthside Publishing Company
Staunton, Virginia

The Hearthside Publishing Company
180 Vista Lane
Staunton, Virginia 24401
www.thehearthsidepublishing.com

ISBN 978-0-965-0987-4-8

Library of Congress Control Number 2012914042

First Edition

10 9 8 7 6 5 4 3 2 1

ISBN: 0965098796

ISBN 13: 9780965098793

For Daniel...

who I pray never knows the horror of war

And in memory of Charlie...

who did

BOOK ONE

BOOK ONE

That which is, already has been;
that which is to be, already has been;
and God seeks what has been driven away.

ECCLESIASTES 3:15

Prologue

Saratoga County, New York, Fall 1857

The stone, palm-sized and polished, had never been touched. Fractured and wrenched from geology's grasp, it had tumbled for an eon in a long-forgotten, frozen lapidary of compressed ice and grinding grit, captured in the crushing slow dance of the earth's dynamic crust. So sculptured, with edges honed, the stone emerged unheralded from a buried, jumbled stratigraphy during a spring freshet, dumped with six tons of collapsing, cobbled creek bank. There it lay in the American wilderness, washed clean by the waters yet captured in an endless cycle of weather—gripped in winter's freeze, baked under summer's sun—until buried by another spring's sodden slide centuries later.

The stream—and gravity of course—undid matters again and again, season after season...pushing and scraping the stone in its relentless journey to the lake. And in all this, time had no measure.

It was a child's hand that finally touched the stone and changed matters. But destiny required eager purpose to grip this particular stone on this fall morning. Indeed, keen in judgment, perceptive in observations, the youngster's first glimpse of it there at the water's edge conjured promise. Then again, the stone could be just one more

1

among countless thousands. Already on this morning the child had sent plenty just like it skipping across the lake. Most bounced against the water a half-dozen times or so before sinking from sight. A few fared better, skating a path of graceful, curving sputter. But these too, always died in the crossing.

The challenge was to get one to the other side. Make a wish and skip a stone to the far shore, so the legend went, and your dream would come true.

Hundreds had tried—hadn't everybody?—hoping to get their particular stone flying above and against the pull of the earth long enough to reach sanctuary in the gravel beach on the other side of the lake.

But no one had ever done such a thing. At least no one in these parts knew anyone who had. It was just too far. Yet legend hinted that back in '77, a strong-armed Continental had somehow skipped a perfect stone across...and a week later the world witnessed the seemingly miraculous American victory over the Redcoats at nearby Saratoga.

So teamsters and masons, preachers and drunks, widows and fishermen, and kids on a lark all skipped a stone for good luck when they visited the lake. Could it be, they wondered, that somewhere along this shore, another stone—another perfect stone—awaited destiny's call?

One more time, the youngster thrust fingers into sand...and grasped the underside of this particular cobble, feeling for just the right shape, the ideal contour. It was an intuitive thing.

The child washed the stone at the water's edge, rubbing a thumb over it to get the last of the mud from its smooth, weathered surface. It fit comfortably in the palm. Curling forefinger around one edge, the skipper judged the weight proper, the angle precise, and the tilt accurate. A scalloped hollowness coursed one side of the stone and this in particular whetted the youngster's expectations.

A heavy morning mist lay upon the lake. Autumn's crispness sharpened the air. The sun had yet to burn through the lofty, fog-shrouded hemlocks that cloaked the hills. Water lapped along the shore, slapping a gentle, indifferent cadence. No wake from a fisherman's boat. No morning hikers. No one to impress. Hardly another soul it seemed, venturing the lake for fish, frolic, or fortune this quiet hour. Not even the loon's lonely call broke the approaching spell.

The lake's mine. Let's see what this one does!

But someone was watching, secreted in the boulders banking the far shore.

"Lad's about to try his luck again? Hah! Nary made a quarter the way with two dozen stones this day."

The old woman eyed the heavens as the heavy mist crept across a splendid but now vanishing field of view. She often spied on visitors here, a voyeuress captured by human curiosity and drawn to the water's deep allure of scenery, lore, and mystery.

"Just as well," she shrugged as the kid on the opposite shore melted into the descending fog. "Enough of this."

Humming to herself, she trudged down to the lake's edge. Despite her bent figure from hard years of outdoor living, she picked her way along the narrow, rocky shore with practiced ease. At the edge of the trees, a winding path led a half mile to her stone cottage in the forest glen. If anyone had been watching, she seemed to glide as she moved, a stodgy, yet spectral figure of the mist.

The child across the lake liked the rock, but gathering fog suggested rain.

Shucks, this'll have to be the last one.

Gripping the stone precisely—curved and contoured, balanced and tilted just so—the youngster raised hand above head and paused. Swooping down with an underhand motion of surprising rapidity, the thrower ground to an abrupt halt, the stone still firmly gripped.

Felt good! But again. And faster!

Gauging personal agility, the youngster repeated the movement, sweeping through a powerful submarine only to again thrust to a sudden, frozen stop, tracking the stone's imaginary trajectory like a revered statue gazing into the memory of a long ago triumph.

This one might really sail!

Scribing the downward arc a third time, the releasing hand blurred in its sweep and the stone sped away with a sharp, clockwise spin. It sailed hard and true from the first, cutting a long horizontal streak above the water before dipping to kiss the lake's surface. Deflected upwards, it came down some distance away, only to soar again. Little splash accompanied the stone's brief touch with the water.

This IS a good stone!

Indeed, the rock's bullet-straight path zipped a spellbinding, fluid elegance. For instead of slowing and skimming to a final splash like all the others, this stone stayed true, skipping again and again, hardly even daring to slow...! *Can't be! But it is! And maybe...maybe...!*

Wide-eyed, the youngster watched the stone speed toward magic, only to cry out when it vanished into the shrouded far shore.

The old woman turned and watched the water lap across her fresh boot prints in the sand. "Here one moment, gone the next. Like so much in this life."

Hunched and sore, she eyed the sky. "Weather's coming."

To explore her world, she walked. Everywhere.

To pound out the demons, to grip the truth, she trudged her trails.

Not pacing back and forth, for there was no journey in that. Pounding up and down the same path mired one's thinking as much as it rutted life's road. But walks were different. They implied purpose. Not a place necessarily, but a result, consuming nervousness, settling the mind, and funneling rhythm. Along the way, one encountered new faces with fresh smiles and hopefully, a few good words.

And discoveries. Who knew what lay 'round the next bend? Didn't interweaving destinies power the world?

Yep, walking brought concentration, a bit of solitude, and hours of inner peace, not to mention a sharpened appetite and a good night's sleep. She often relied on the lake and forest trail to sort her thoughts and *get things right*. But of late, tangles and strings of dread clouded her quiet.

By the second hour past dawn, she had trekked across three miles of countryside. She stopped and pressed her hands together.

"Yeah, old girl, worries cramp this world, stabbin' in like the penetrating damp of this gloomy day. And nailing my knobby old fingers with these hurts."

Yet how many times had she come down this path? How many hours had she pondered a problem...then found its solution in a simple walk through the woods...or along the cliff face...or by the water? A smile of cynical recollection cracked her weathered face, her one gold tooth gleaming from a gray cavern of decay.

Some salesman traveling the shore road or perhaps an angler after a morning's catch would have thought her odd, certainly ugly, and possibly preternatural in her way along the water. In the town, strangers paid no attention to her bent, ancient figure shuffling along the street. But seeing her hold a sparkling quartz to the sun, or hearing her break into rhyme without warning or sense, these peculiar habits turned heads and set her apart.

That's why the locals gave her wide berth on the sidewalk, scurrying their bug-eyed children from her approach with whispered warnings not to stare. Wintertime dares often brought boys sneaking close to her stone cottage to put their breath on a window pane while the bravest carved their enemies' initials into the posts of her front porch. The rest, too timid to approach her clearing, tormented her army of cats with rocks and rotten apples.

But there were others who quietly sought her counsel. More than a few—mothers and babes—owed their very existence to her mastery of midwifery. Young girls consulted her on matters of the heart. And those confronting the ultimate mystery gasped to her their deathbed confessions. Anonymous pilgrims, by horse, buggy, or on foot, sought her forest cottage where a tap on her door with a quarter dollar bought a confidential reading of their future. What did it matter if she divined from the palm of a hand, prophesied from chimney smoke curling to the heavens, or saw visions in her quartz on a sundrenched afternoon? The old woman seemed to know things.

She paused to engage the lake one last time in her morning walk, to listen to its language, absorb its aura, and marvel in its riddles. Mysteries abounded everywhere and people sought her to fathom such things. But here, near the water's edge, she sensed something had changed.

Or was about to.

The lake this morning reflected more than its usual quiet and solitude. The blanketing mist cloaked a secret. Of that she was certain.

5

But just as the morning chill would vanish as the shroud of vapor lifted, so too, might this veil of mystery.

Humming softly, she hunched her shawl closer about her shoulders and trudged on, musing to herself. Images pulsed in bursts as they always did, at first unrelated and colorless, but on this morning, vivid and haunting. Even profound. The words would be hard. But she would get them down.

"But how will I know? I can hear the phrases, but to whom do they go? And what do they portend? Whose destiny will..."

SPACK.....SPACK....SPACK...SPACK!

A gray blur...a spinning top in the gravel, just beyond the water's grasp. She puzzled on it, blank.

An ordinary stone, gray, hard...perhaps laced with feldspar, smooth, cool, and wet. Now motionless with all the others. One of thousands in the sand.

Then, with a gasp, she knew!

"NO! How can this be? No one could! But here it is, out of the mist...a stone from the other side! And someone—that boy, of course!—has done it!"

The old woman stared into the fog. Only gray met her gaze...no hint of the *where* or *what* or *who* of this. She bent toward the sand—the stiff ache in her spine always there—and lifted the slick cob of granite from its journey's end, smoothing it in her palm, coveting it like a rare gem.

"Had I not seen this myself, no one would ever know!"

But she had seen. And such things did exist.

A perfect stone!

Temperatures plummeted that night. In the darkness, a stiff wind lashed hemlock and oak against each other. Shrill, harsh noises hurtled from the forest. Bending, creaking, and breaking trees splintered sounds sinister and surreal. Inside her cottage, the old woman's face reflected the dying embers of her hearth. She brooded, amazed at what she'd witnessed this day.

"And such legends herald great wonders," she mumbled. "Something amazing, yet frightful...something born of purpose, but ominous...something unsettled, yet promised." She grasped at the emptiness overhead as if to pluck some intangible truth from the air.

"And a wish comes true!"

Foolscap lay on the table beside a single lit candle. She always had ink and paper ready for her quill. For when she saw things, she wrote them out... words to white, a prophecy read, a destiny revealed.

She scratched a line...then scribbled it through. She started again, only to ball up the paper.

She tipped a fresh candle to the burning wick. A single flame jumped to two. A third candle brightened better.

And then, midst the raging storm, she saw forward. And penned it to paper.

"But whose words are these?"

Weary but home, she closed her eyes, knowing clarity swirled just out of reach.

Let the tempest abate. Truth always follows a cleansing storm.

Chapter One

Keswick, Virginia, October 1957

W rink-les!" Ginny McGill cooed the word, playing the syllables into each other like the block letters she stacked on the table at the foot of her bed.

"Wrink-les!" Glee filled her voice. And comprehension. The triumph of a newly learned word!

Carefully, the little girl traced the lines in Grandie's forehead with her fingers, exploring the fleshy furrows around her great-grandfather's closed eyes with soft, intent deliberation, breathing close and serious as she counted, "Eight...nine...ten..."

Her touch carried a delicious tingle, teasing the old man from his nap.

Eyes kept closed, Charlie Harrison savored her touches. *But these tingles...tickled!*

"Fourteen...eighteen...thirteen...sixteen..."

Ginny's pudgy digit pushed the grooves in the old man's mug with each announced tally. As Princess of the Wrinkle People, she kept right to her work, mapping her Grandie's weathered face, counting its rough, palpable valleys.

"Nineteen...fifteen...seventeen...."

He felt her index finger—a warm little sausage—challenge the gray grain of his two-day stubble.

"Scratchy," she pronounced, wedging the bristle back and forth. There was much she might discover here. But this part of Grandie's face...

Ginny slid her palm down his left cheek. "UGH!"

NOW!

Like a frog's tongue sticking a marsh fly, Charlie Harrison mouthed the girl's exploring digit in a wet, blitzkrieg "mmwaaaaahhh," then swept her up in his arms with more slurpy kisses.

The awakened monster rampaged!

"Grandie! Grandie! Scratchy face, scratchy face!"

Ginny squealed and wriggled to free herself from the monster's clutches and sandpaper countenance. But Charlie bussed her again, tossing her into the air and catching her breathless, all the while roaring and hissing like some fire-breathing dragon rousted from its cave. Then, at the perfect time, he let her squirm free.

She darted to her mother's open arms, to Mommie who had heard the ruckus and magically appeared in the doorway.

"Ohhh, Ginny! Is that Tickle Monster in here?"

Charlie Harrison swung his legs to the sofa's edge, but slow enough to let his great-granddaughter know that her mother's arms guaranteed true security. Feigning dejection, he grimaced one of those "OK, you-escaped-my-lair-this-time" looks, while Ginny clawed knots in her mother's skirt.

Yet on dancing eyes and cherubic cheeks, so beamed between cornered dimples, the little girl grinned her own childhood triumph: *You didn't get me!*

For Ginny McGill loved every second. Magic always purred around her Grandie!

And happiness. For nothing brought the old man more pleasure than these moments with this child. She stretched his imagination to the future. He nodded in approving silence as Laura McGill, his only granddaughter, hoisted her daughter.

"OK. Nap time, young lady! Say beddie-bye to Grandie."

"Noooooooooo!" Ginny whined, squirming for another chance to tempt her favorite dragon.

But Mommie had other ideas, and despite Ginny's twistings and wiggles, she found herself out of the room.

"See you later, sweetie," he waved, savoring her peeking, unblinking blue eyes. Then she was down the hall and behind a shutting door.

Baby days. The old man sighed. *Oh well, time for lunch.*

In the kitchen, he pondered his autumn afternoon. *Happiness. Contentment. The love of my family. That's all I've ever wanted.*

Or so he'd tell himself.

Whatever time I have before a yawning grave claims me... Well, hardly matters a whit now. Aren't these the twilight years? Those who've made a difference leave their mark behind. The rest of us...are just marking time.

Charlie Harrison understood such things now at the end. They tugged at him, sometimes burning an ache behind his breastbone. As far as he knew, he'd leave no mark behind.

But I loved a good woman, raised our daughter, raised her daughter, and doctored this community. That's pretty OK.

But that wasn't what bothered him. Sure, old age muddled short-term memory and pained his knees when it rained. Yesterday's street corner conversation might blur with who'd waited on him in the bank or last cut his hair. And despite what Laura had told him, he couldn't quite recall where her husband Harney was stationed these days.

Yet his childhood memories stayed sharp, not unusual for octogenarians. Still for Charlie Harrison, something seemed unfinished. He couldn't pull it up exactly, generate that burning image, or hear a voice, but a Nameless Something hovered out there...waiting.

And now there's this Sputnik.

The night before, Charlie and half the village had spotted the Russian satellite blink its way across the constellations. All America was agog. The world had changed in a single sunset.

And I need to change with it.

He plopped down on the sun porch sofa...

Yet some things endure.

...and scrolled his left thumb across his forefinger.

Like the softness of a little girl's cheek...

Or the grizzle of an old man's beard.

He almost grinned.

But after all these years, what could it be?

He had no answer, but one question did loom above all the others. *How will Ginny remember me?*

But that wasn't it. *WILL Ginny remember me?*

That mattered. A lot. It gnawed like a hungry dog howling on an empty night.

He'd certainly never forgotten. The old times, that is. He often found himself going back, wondering. After all, who was it that said, 'Old men confronting time, often wonder about the past? Or wandered about...in the past?'

God, don't let me die like that.

T he crackling wood stove, flue-roaring on a winter morning. The hurried swish of Mama's cotton dress, a splash of flour across her blue apron. Crockery on the countertop. Spoons and forks dug from the drawer. And a little boy discovering the pulling aroma of bacon and buttermilk pancakes.

These earliest images of Charlie's childhood presented as detached portraits now, so many loose pictures...jumbled in a scrapbook. Longevity tended to do such things, freezing the oldest memories in chiseled granite, while yesterday's conversations faded into the setting sun.

Yes, Charlie could still recall the sound of his mother's voice...a soothing, R-less, Boston twang. Certain phrases, especially song lyrics, triggered the aura. And when he closed his eyes during thunderstorms, she could be there, calming him with the delicate confidence of her words, the caress of her fingers.

Such things he still had of her. And vignettes of the farm.

Playing in the dirt under the broad-boughed pecan tree. Or digging up the old bricks buried in the weed field behind it, discovering them like small pirate chests, which when stacked just so, made a grand fort. Such labors guaranteed "grandma's black beads"—that stenciled reward of necklaced grime and bejeweled sweat connecting his collarbones at the sultry end of a summer's afternoon.

In Charlie's memory, the rabbit path still snaked through the blackberry thicket, winding its way into the Big Woods. Beyond lay The Ruins—a fallen down brick chimney—where he hid his treasures and knew they were safe from the skullduggery of his imaginary playmates.

Peeking out from the thicket, he had often spied into the broad expanse of the East Meadow, pastured ground bordered round by a whitewashed, five-paling fence.

Lush, soft grass carpeted the East Meadow, nourished by the Water Cress Spring which split the field as a happy, gurgling brook staked in cattails and shoe-sucking mud, snarled in honeysuckle and brush piles ideal for marauding pirates. On hot days, he had splashed in the cool, shaded waters of the brook, sniffed and chewed the spearmint that flourished on its marshy bank, and opened his hand to the mules and work horses shaded at the fence, eager for his sneaked sugar. Papa took visitors to the meadow, men who would lean over the rails and stare at the animals, spit black juice on the ground, and talk loud if they had a mind to. They squinted into the sun, waved and laughed and pulled things from their pockets, sometimes saying bad words and pointing across the field. Papa smiled, but often shook his head.

And then Papa would nod to the West Meadow...

Charlie cherished an afternoon's reverie—like this sun porch moment now—to go back to the old times. Just closing his eyes let him feel the rough, broken bricks in the cool dirt...savor Mama's pancakes and maple syrup before a roaring stove on a winter morning... and listen to the war stories of Papa's friends.

He could always go home, to the East Meadow, to the Water Cress Spring, to the Big Woods, to the memories.

But never to the West Meadow!

Jolted awake, Charlie stared wide-eyed into the backyard. Sweat beaded his brow. *Who are You? Tell me! Show Yourself!*

The nagging, out-of-focus Presence that hovered in the cobwebbed memories of his childhood lurked vague and sinister.

Never have I been able to summon it...to confront it. Never!

But he had always sensed it, waiting, dark and powerful, eager and terrible. *Something was in the West Meadow.*

And it would seize him when his hour approached.

Weren't such things just a matter of time?

C ould you go in and give her a kiss?" Laura leaned against the door, her eyes smiling. "She's got a question for you."

Charlie blinked, fumbled with his cane, and eased himself out of the lounge chair, feeling the twinge in his knee that now never left.

"Story?"

"More of a question. I told her you're the best one to ask."

"About?"

Laura just patted his shoulder. "Don't be long. Nap time, you know."

Down the hall, Charlie tapped on the door, waited, then poked in his head. "Who's giving out free kisses in here?"

Ginny giggled and squirreled deeper into her blankets.

The Wrinkle Monster entered and sat down on her bed, his hand close but not daring to touch her wiggling form.

"Grandie...Grandie...?" She stilled, signaling the end of their game...that her bed was "base"...and that he couldn't "get her."

"Right here, sweetie. Had a good time, didn't we?"

"Yeaaaahhh!" she gushed, reaching up to touch his cheek.

"Don't know if my old scratchy face should kiss such a pretty little princess."

Ginny beamed but Charlie leaned over and kissed her anyway, to which she giggled again as his grizzle grazed her.

Shades pulled, the room settled into a lazy softness.

But he could feel her eyes searching. *Wrinkles? Sure. But does my old mug still convey love?*

"Grandie?"

"Yes, sweetie?"

"Your...Mommie?"

The question caught him and he replayed the sound of her voice. "Your Mommie? Pretty?"

Charlie cleared his throat with a "Well," but Ginny's eyes kept asking. "Sweetie, my Mommie...lived a long time ago."

"Wrink-les?"

He chuckled. "Oh, no...none that I recall!"

"Your DaDa?"

"Oh, yes. Now he had wrinkles."

The little girl looked to her great-grandfather, then away as if to gather these discoveries into a single bundle.

"In fact, honey, my Mommie was almost as pretty as you!"

She smiled and wormed deeper into her blankets.

"Her hair was lighter than yours...more *sunshine* than your beautiful *sunset*, but she did have some of your freckles and I think I see her two dimples...right here...and...here!" He touched her cheek...just so...and so, eliciting more giggles.

"Can I see her picture?"

"Oh sweetie, my Mommie and Daddy died years ago."

Patience. There was much he might say, but...

Ginny looked up at him, yawning, settling in, snuggling to find sleep in just the right place. Eyes closed, she yawned again, drifted, and after a time grew still.

What a marvelous miracle, the innocence of a sleeping child.

And then one more time, Charlie Harrison leaned forward and kissed his great-granddaughter. Slowly, silently, he stood and made his way to the door. Turning, he looked to his little cherub, angelic in her afternoon nap.

"Oh, how they would have loved you."

Chapter Two

*O*h, *how they would have loved you.*
Two weeks had passed and still the words haunted him. Little Ginny's curiosity about the old times, about his parents, had stirred Charlie back to his boyhood. As the last of the Chesterfield Harrisons, only he remembered life on the farm.

And time's certainly replowed that field.

Of course his great-granddaughter had no real sense of any of this. At three years of age, Ginny McGill's world bounced with rubber balls and stuffed animals on a backdrop of crayons and coloring books.

But what she wants to know, old boy, is, "Who are you to me?"

Charlie closed his eyes. *Well, I'm her mommie's...mommie's...daddy. And when she's older, I'll be...*

He blinked, staring into his backyard. His eight plus decades simply ticketed him a tired, old man now. *What's a life anyway but one complete harvest of the field?*

Father Time no longer smiled; he beckoned.

So when Ginny gets older...I won't be here.

Still, he had a treasure trove of memories...and a talent for telling stories...

Oh, how they would have loved you.

Charlie often savored the notion of going back. *If only I could.*

16

He toyed with the fantasy...like some call from an enticing siren. *I just close my eyes and there's Mama's kitchen, the stable, the meadow, Papa's log office. Nothing's changed...*

Yet...

Ginny, if I could, I'd take you there! If only for a day. Then you could see it for yourself.

But Dr. Charles Harrison, just one more soul facing life's sunset, also craved his share of answers. Memories, it seemed, always wrenched forth more questions.

And fears. Like the dark West Meadow dream that haunted him. Two times in September, first on Labor Day, then again two weeks later, it had awakened him gasping and wide-eyed.

The blurred images of happy, joyous people, with Mama close and smiling ...wrecked in all that light and noise. And the sickening, pit-of-the-stomach sense of falling...crashing into stabbing pain...and the choke-swallowing, airless sensation of being smothered...

Charlie wiped his glistening brow. *I must banish this!*

And Ginny?

Stay as sweet as you are, honey. Your Mommie and I love you oodles. As does your Daddy, too, who's just away right now keeping us protected.

Still the little girl's curiosity bedeviled him. Since that afternoon, he'd returned to his youth a hundred times by a score of trails, hop skipping into "the eighteen hundreds" as Laura styled it.

Once upon a time, she too had sat on my knee.

But to Laura, Charlie had tempered his tellings. Sure, she thrilled to his earthy accounts of fishing for "shiners," monkey-swinging on the grapevine down in the Big Woods, and skinny dipping in the branch on a hot summer's afternoon.

Some day I'll tell Ginny all that...

Yet the home place outside Richmond was long gone, burned to the ground by a candle-laden Christmas tree in 1899. Flames had consumed the plantation house in minutes, sparing only the outbuildings and new stables his father had erected after the war.

Papa never got over that.

Charlie could still see the whitewashed, five paling fence that girded the front pasture along the Midlothian Turnpike. Now a busy parking lot fronted a garish strip mall housing a barber shop, liquor store, convenience mart, laudromat, real estate office and taxidermist.

A filling station crowded the north corner. Towed-in wrecks, parts cars, and a few rusting dump trucks—shoe-horned around a rundown body shop—cluttered the southern side. Beyond a flimsy, dilapidated palisade fence meant to hide the garage, single-family homes stretched for eight blocks, thrown up after the war.

Papa's meadows...now houses since the 40s. Nothing left I'd recognize 'cept perhaps the old pit where the icehouse stood...and that's filled with brush and yard clippings as I recall.

Mixed feelings had roiled him the day of his last visit. Mildred Blake, his cousin from Saratoga Springs, New York, had just lost her husband. Charlie urged her to come down for a family reunion in Chesterfield County.

"It'll be swell," he promised.

Charlie, Laura and her new husband Harney met Mildred at Richmond's Byrd Field and drove her around the county for old time's sake.

But Charlie found little he recognized. Two thousand cars an hour roared up and down the Turnpike's three lanes. Subdivisions obliterated the East Meadow and chewed choice building lots out of the Big Woods. Commercial development metastasized from every intersection including a sprawling shopping mall that had paved over most of the West Meadow. A barrier fence erected on the warnings of litigation lawyers kept kids out of the Water Cress Spring. Only Harney McGill had nudged the day into positive territory.

Charlie had had little chance to meet the groom at Laura's wedding the year before, but at this reunion, he'd warmed to her USAF pilot-husband on temporary assignment as a training/liaison officer to the Naval Air Station at Virginia Beach.

Never saw Laura so happy.

And he had beamed with joy and kissed her when she told him they were expecting. *Ah, good memories.*

Charlie settled his gaze to the familiar contours of the distant Blue Ridge. *Snow's coming.*

He closed his eyes.

But I don't really need to go back. Keswick's home.

He diverted his eyes to the backyard.

Still here, Nell, aren't we?"

Yet he wondered.

I'd love to share things with Ginny. But how?

Just tell the stories, echoed a warming voice inside.

Yet his soft smile of remembrance vanished when he thought it through.

If I do, I'll have to confront it. 'Cause it's still out there.

T he discovery came a week later and it all started with another simple question.

"Your Mommie?" Ginny sought him with round, asking eyes. "Picture, Grandie?"

"Oh Ginny, we lost them a long time ago."

The little girl thought on this for a moment. "Let's look."

"Ginny? Didn't you hear Grandie? Everything was lost."

"It's OK, Laura." Charlie winked. "I'm sorry sweetie. Just don't have much from when I was a little boy. Maybe in the attic. But I haven't been up there in years..."

"Let's look!"

"Now Ginny, Grandie told you..."

"Sure, sweetie," Charlie smiled. "Papa's old Saratoga trunk...you know the one, Laura? Beside the chimney? Papa stored it out in the stable loft before the fire. I moved it up here after Nell..." He glanced into the backyard. *Has it really been almost forty years?*

Laura hugged an arm around her grandfather.

"Guess the old times edge a bit closer these days, huh, Laura?"

"Let's look, Grandie!" The little girl tugged on the old man's pants.

T he recon launched after lunch while Ginny napped. Charlie slogged his way up the steps, but the last flight of stairs—steep and narrow—presented a robust challenge.

"Haven't been up here in a coon's age," he gasped, eyes darting. "Kinda forget things after a time."

Laura turned the brass knob and shoved open the attic door. Gable windows at either end admitted the only light into the attic's musty aura.

"Light switch's over there, my dear." Charlie watched his breath drift across the cold.

Laura flipped on two bare 100 watt light bulbs dangling just below hand-hewn oak rafters. Stacked boxes lined either side of a narrow path down the random-width pine flooring, little of which was visible in the clutter. An early Singer sewing machine lay in pieces to one side. Old window screens, empty picture frames, and a long neglected, dented Conn trombone leaned behind it. A pile of bent and twisted window blinds lay in a heap beside a jumbled assortment of old paint cans, Christmas decorations, and a child's hobby horse. A half dozen boxes of *National Geographic*, a few old calendars and an incomplete set of Compton's encyclopedias stood next to a spiraling pile of magazine—*Life* and *The Saturday Evening Post* mostly—poised to cascade across the floor. A near empty keg of 10-penny nails, a wooden step ladder, and a heap of old sweaters, coats, shirts, and other forgotten hand-me-downs—all stuffed into cardboard boxes and exuding the faint waft of mothballs—rose to the rafters. Beside the ladder and half buried behind the magazines, an old trunk buttressed the brick chimney, a draped, soiled quilt almost hiding the chest from view.

Laura nodded toward the chimney.

"That's it. All Papa saved from the fire."

Laura tugged at the quilt, bringing up a dust swirl when it yanked free. She folded the quilt across her arm and lay it aside. The trunk's twisted lock appeared broken.

Charlie raised the domed lid and leaned it against the chimney, exposing an upper tray. A jumble of loose papers, two ribbon-tied bundles of old letters, an inkwell, several bulging manila envelopes, two hunks of broken white chalk and a small, flat, gutta-percha box lay in a heap.

"Not much." He lifted the tray. "Just a bunch of blankets here." He pushed his fingers into the folds, finding a black tasseled riding crop and a matching pair of dark leather gloves. "Probably bed covers the rest of the way down."

Laura picked up the gutta-percha box, nicely decorated with little bouquets and fruits. "There's a hook clasp here, Grandie."

"Oh." Charlie froze. "I totally forgot..."

Laura fingered the hook and popped open the box. "Goodness!"

Inside lay the gold framed daguerreotype of a young woman. Her soft smile, unseen these many years, exuded warmth and friendship.

"She's beautiful, Grandie. Who is she?"

The old man returned the gloves and riding crop to the trunk. Taking the photo case from his granddaughter, he walked over to the first gable window, away from the glare of the light bulbs and tilted the image to catch the sun's rays just so.

"Grandie?"

Charlie turned to Laura, his face serene but his eyes in marvel. "Never thought..." He daubed at his cheek and turned back toward the window, quivering the black case to the light. "I forgot you were up here."

"Who?"

"Mama...ah, your great-grandma, Laura."

"Grandie! She's your mother? She seems so...alive. I feel like I could talk to her. And look at the detail. Her hair, her clear eyes that seem to look right through you. She's stunning!"

Another tear coursed down Charlie's cheek. "Ginny was right, you know."

"About what?"

"About looking."

"She was just being her typically impatient little self, Grandie."

"Perhaps. But she's the one who got us to come up here."

Charlie closed the daguerreotype and handed it to his granddaughter. "We'll show it to her after her nap. Think she'll remember?"

"Are you kidding? I rather think she's expecting it!"

S ee?" Ginny beamed.

Charlie beamed back. *You knew it was up there, didn't you, honey?*

He placed the daguerreotype into a glass cabinet case atop the small table beside his easy chair in the den, displaying the image of his mother at an open ninety degrees.

"There, sweetie. Now you two can visit anytime you want. But we need to be very careful with old-timey things. My Mommie's picture is made of glass and we don't want to break or scratch her, do we?"

Ginny nodded, all serious. "Your DaDa?"

"This was the only picture we found."

The little girl peered again at the image of her great-great grandmother. "Pretty."

"Well, I think I see your nose," said Charlie, looking into the glass case while tugging Ginny's left ear.

She giggled and pulled back as her mother entered the room.

"We need to get going, young lady." Laura grabbed her car keys off the coffee table. "Remember, Emily invited you over today."

"Oh, yeah!" said Ginny.

"Don't forget your pink Play-Doh. Emily's only got blue."

"Gone long?" asked Charlie.

"I'm taking her to the Stewart's, then it's into town to the grocery store...the cleaners...and the bank. That should do it." Laura looked at her watch. "Calling for snow tonight. You gonna be OK?"

"Sure. Just stiff. This cold weather's hard on my joints. No walk for me today. Think I'll stay by the fire."

Laura bundled Ginny into her car coat, then kissed her grandfather.

As the front door shut, Charlie settled into his recliner, crushing the morning newspaper.

Mighty nice to have 'em here while Harney's deployed in Hawaii. At least I think that's where he is. Sure miss that fellow.

Charlie leaned forward and tugged at the paper beneath his butt... tearing off a ragged corner of the Metro section. *Damn shoulder's stiff as a board and the small of my back throbs like a bass drum.*

Again he yanked at the morning news, getting only a wad of mangled newsprint. *Lot of good this is.*

Charlie tossed the newspaper aside. *So much for all this crap about living the glorious "Golden Years."*

He picked up the daguerreotype.

You told me you'd just graduated from music school when this was made. Or was it after you married Papa?

The portrait survived in remarkable condition, especially the sharp clarity of the image itself.

Wish you could know our Ginny. Yet I guess these things aren't meant to be. Charlie cradled the image in both hands.

Ironic, isn't it? You loved me when I was so small...but never got to see me grow up. And now Ginny and I are fated for the same thing.

His fingers caressed the gutta-percha frame.

What was it like...back then? You and Papa never said much...

Chapter Three

D r. Charles Harrison made his home in the village of Keswick, east of Charlottesville. Folks in that section of Virginia's Albemarle County trusted him in their sicknesses. For half a century, he'd been there. Caring, competent, and consoling. Doc Harrison's door was always open.

At five feet eight inches, Charlie carried a solid build. He combed a full head of white hair, sported an ever-present bow tie, and when needed, mustered a voice of calming assurance. Iconic minus intent, Doc Harrison with his black bag...looked a doctor, if a bit old fashioned.

He ran his office from his home, formerly an 18th century clapboard tavern and inn known as Macon's Ordinary. A recognized landmark, the old roadhouse stood hard by the south side of Route 22, west of Keswick's center.

The building dripped history. Literally.

Thomas Jefferson had sometimes stopped by for "refreshment" in his travels to and from Monticello. After the Blue and the Gray battled at nearby Trevilians Station decades later, Confederate surgeons converted the tavern into a make-shift hospital. Charlie kept hand-knit rugs in three rooms to hide the bloodstained planking.

Over the years, colleagues had offered Dr. Harrison a number of opportunities to expand or modify his practice. He could have joined Dr. LeGrand Brewster in Gordonsville, but he knew Brewster was a drunk. His alma mater, the University of Virginia Medical School, had him in several times as a guest lecturer on the challenges of rural obstetrics. And during World War One, a prominent Charlottesville family practice almost talked him into a full partnership.

But Charlie liked it where he was.

Although just a few miles north of US Route 250, Keswick endured as a serene niche off the rat race to Richmond. Locals marked lunch by the C & O's 12:10 freighter rumbling down the tracks east of the village. Charlie's neighbors were mostly the landed gentry and the tenant farmers employed by them. These large estates owned or controlled most of the sweeping, pastoral countryside in eastern Albemarle County, proprietors with extensive interests in cattle and sheep and horses.

So life stayed simple in Keswick. Still, Charlie might have moved his practice elsewhere, but he could never leave Nell.

They'd married in the summer of 1903 after his graduation from medical school. In those days, a newly-minted doctor simply hung out his shingle. Nell's father had done just that thirty years earlier. Seeing the dilapidated old tavern for sale, Dr. Thomas Blankenship bought Macon's Ordinary and began restoration. Three months later he moved in his family and opened an office. With the War Between the States a decade in the past, Keswick seemed "up-and-coming."

"I could use a younger set of hands," Dr. Blankenship hinted the month before Charlie graduated. "Really need to slow down. I just don't have the stamina for twelve-hour days anymore. What do you say, Charles? Be great experience for you. Join me?"

His wife Ruth also urged them to stay. "You know your father needs to cut back, Nell. Think maybe Charles might go in with him for a while?"

He did. Charlie and Nell moved into a two-bedroom bungalow on the north end of the village. When he walked home at night, Nell had supper waiting, and in winter, a fire in the fireplace. They made passionate love in an antique canopied bed, then cuddled through the night, adrift in the other's arms. Life got cozy. Dr. Blankenship's practice grew. Five years passed. And then two things happened.

Nell got pregnant.

And 23 days after the little girl's arrival, Dr. Blankenship dropped dead of a heart attack.

Swirling joy into grief, Charlie and Nell christened their daughter Amanda Parker Harrison: Amanda after Dr. Blankenship's mother; Parker for Charlie's mother's maiden name.

And Keswick reverted to a single doctor.

It was then Charlie considered going to Richmond. Surely Virginia's capital held more lucrative opportunities. He and Nell discussed the possibilities. But weeks edged into months. And well, he couldn't just up and leave the good folks he'd gotten to know.

So they stayed, selling their bungalow and moving into Macon's Ordinary with Grandma Ruth. Charlie kept busy tending the growing stream of patients knocking on his door, his black bag and ubiquitous bow tie signaling that "the doctor is in." Nell busied herself upgrading the tavern, crafting the landmark into a real showplace while nurturing a colorful flower garden in the backyard. And little Amanda started first grade.

They tried for more children, but nature said no. When Grandma Ruth died three years later, Charlie and Nell revisited the idea of leaving. But they couldn't. Keswick was home.

Whenever Laura quizzed her grandfather about these early years, Charlie would always recall the little time he had to call his own.

"Sort of a blur." But when he said this, Laura noticed he always smiled. *Those were the good years.*

"I was on the go all the time, Laura. Ran my office out of that horse and buggy. Plodded down miles of muddy, bottomless country lanes. Did everything from delivering babies to diming dead men's eyes. Then I got that Tin Lizzie. Bought 'er right before the war. Shiny brass radiator and all!"

The Great War, of course, changed everything. Henry Ford's affordable Model T sped up American life. And instead of Charlie spending his day navigating Albemarle's back country roads, more patients began coming to him.

People limped in kicked by horses and mules, bit by snakes and dogs, and stung by bees and nettles. He treated everything from simple fractures, food poisoning, and hemorrhoids to kidney stones, impetigo, and arthritis, with the occasional case of lockjaw or venereal disease presenting to keep things interesting. Cancer, heart ailments, tuberculosis, and liquor of course, loomed as deadly scourges, but pneumonia killed the most.

Charlie stayed and his practice flourished. And by spending more of his hours tending the sick instead of traveling to them, he could do more good.

That changed in January of 1919 when Sgt. Harry Hobson drove his mother to Macon's Ordinary. Hobson had just returned from France, a seasoned veteran of the Western Front.

The sergeant reported he'd just gotten over "a darn bad cold." He confessed he'd rarely been so sick, spitting up blood, suffering debilitating body aches, and spiking 103 degree temperatures, while fighting some heavy chest congestion. But with time and his mother's nursing, he'd gotten better. Now she'd apparently come down with the same thing.

Only Alma Hobson wasn't getting better.

Charlie examined her and discovered an exhausted, dehydrated woman, wracked by chills and fever, flush in the face, and as he noted in her file, "suffering from intense, viscous congestion of the nose, pharynx, larynx, trachea, and upper respiratory tract with an unproductive, hacking cough."

Yet it was her gray, bluing lips—and especially her darkening nail beds—that stabbed him cold. *Cyanosis!*

Viscous congestion throughout her respiratory tract kept her lungs from transferring oxygen into her blood. Even as Charlie struggled frantically to help her breathe, she waxed toward purple.

"Mahogany spots" dotted her cheeks. Into the evening, Alma Hobson languished in and out of consciousness. Nothing worked and Sgt. Hobson's mother died that night in Macon's Ordinary.

Charlie had never seen such a case.

Plague? The Great Black Death? Can't be. But what else could it be?

He soon found out. *An unknown, deadly strain of influenza. Brought back by returning soldiers. Spanish flu, they call it.*

A similar case presented in his office the next day, along with two desperate notes to please visit neighbors too sick to travel. Over the next week, eight more people in Keswick came down with this pestilence. Three died, turning blue just like Alma Hobson.

Then Nell began to cough.

Having assisted her husband in his desperate struggle to help others, she too had contracted the deadly influenza. With four deaths, the Virginia Department of Health quarantined Keswick. Officials blocked all roads into the village. No one knew where this pestilence would strike next.

More sickened and Charlie, working now behind a gauze face mask, battled eighteen hours a day to save the few who made it to Macon's Ordinary or languished in sick beds at home. But big Jake Brady died on Thursday. Angie Thorpe, Prentiss Shoemaker's colored cook, passed away the next day. And the following Monday, Deputy Sheriff Arnold Ewell, coughing up blood and bits of lung, breathed his last.

By then, Nell seemed on the way to recovery.

Ten-year old Amanda, banished by her father to the attic and ordered to wear a gauze mask at all times, came down to tend her mother. Perhaps the crisis had passed.

It had not. The girl soon developed a fever and dry cough. She quit eating and complained of aches all over her body. Her eyes and throat burned red-hot. So her recuperating mother, though feeble, nursed her.

Charlie remained unscathed despite daily visits to all of Keswick's bedridden. A miracle some would later call it.

And Doc Harrison, a hero.

But he missed Nell's relapse. And this time it wasn't flu.

Instead, when Charlie examined Nell, he stared into the face of medicine's oldest adversary, opportunistic pneumonia.

Charlie was helpless. In pneumonia, normally spongy lung tissue fills with an inflamed mix of enzymes, mucus, cell debris, and fluids. Solidifying and losing their elasticity—consolidation, doctors call it—the lungs begin to fail in their job of oxygenating the blood and removing carbon dioxide. If the trend is not reversed, the patient slowly suffocates.

So in the winter of 1919, with the advent of antibiotics still more than a decade in the future, Nell Harrison faded. A day later, despite his every effort, Charlie lost the love of his life to medicine's greatest killer. She simply drifted into a deep sleep. And then grew cold.

He and Amanda buried Nell in her wonderful garden behind the tavern, marking the grave with a modest stone and bordering it with a white picket fence. As long as he stayed in Keswick, he would always have her close.

So that rather decided it. But now what would he do? How could Dr. Charlie Harrison possibly raise his motherless young daughter?

Chapter Four

L osing Nell plunged Charlie into the depths of despair. He had often confronted death in his practice, but hers he could not fathom. How could he possibly go on? His love for her still burned bright; true love always did. But Nell's warming candle would shine no more.

Charlie visited the garden every evening, staring at her stone, focused into the finality of inscribed birth and death dates.

We were supposed to grow old together.

And Keswick was home. So he stayed...to be with his Nell.

Two epic snows buried February. March gusted in on Arctic air and still the lonely father kept his evening graveside vigil. Only when Nell's garden gloried in May's full bloom did Charlie finally lift his eyes to the dark, starred heavens.

Where are you, love?

And that's when he saw Mizar. Yes, it was just a star to anyone else. But up there in the Big Dipper, second sparkle in the handle, Charlie Harrison refound his Nell. She shone to his every question, confident and reliable. He posed his fears, his concerns, his hopes. And the twinkling replied with reassurance, a modicum of inner peace...and continuance, for thanks to latitude, reliable Mizar never missed a Virginia night. *I need you to help me here, love...to keep shining your candle.*

Young Amanda recovered from the deadly influenza that had claimed her mother and more than half a million other Americans. In time, this so-called Spanish flu would ravage mankind as the deadliest plague in all of human history, killing more than fifty million people around the world. But for the widowed physician and his daughter in Keswick, Virginia, this pandemic was tragedy enough in claiming a wife and mother. At forty-five, Charlie confronted the reality of raising his ten-year-old daughter alone.

Empty days followed. He advertised for a live-in domestic. Word-of-mouth brought half a dozen applicants to his door. None suited.

But number seven, Sadie Levels, snatched his attention. At age fifty-six, this widow, grandmother, and ex-slave strode into Macon's Ordinary with the stark confidence of a door-knocking salesman.

"My man's dead in the ground and I need a roof o'er my head. All due respect, sir, I'll scrub, wash, and sew for you. And I'll tell you now nobody gets thin that visits my cookin'. Just so you know, folks over in Louisa'll swear—straight up now—that I do the best Brunswick stew in these here parts." A big-toothed, confident cackle boosted her boast.

Sadie Levels paused to let her potential employer mull matters. Seeing the doctor's cautious nod, she pushed to the heart of things.

"I see you got a young missus growing up on you. Well sir, all due respect, sir, I'm sorry for your recent b'reavement. But I raised three daughters myself, all good mothers now."

She dabbled another moment. *Men folk need to grasp these things.*

"So I knows what I'm doing here." She bore down beeline straight.

And Charlie nodded again.

"Ain't gonna find no better," she summarized. "All due respect, sir."

That rather decided it.

Aunt Sadie—as Amanda came to call her—proved true to her word. Over the next decade, she instilled order and a degree of normalcy—if such can be for a widower—to the Harrison household. Throughout the Roarin' Twenties, she kept Macon's Ordinary tidy and clean. Indeed, working for a country doctor demanded everything from washing mud tromped-in on the parlor waiting room floor to soothing scared children with a friendly pat on the head and a ginger cookie. Patients came to know Aunt Sadie's kind words and genuine smile as the fuzzy warm welcome mat to Doc Harrison's bedside manner and medical skills.

In time, Charlie began having her help him in the office. She proved an adept assistant, mastering skills in everything from sterilization techniques to aiding in gynecological exams. When mothers-to-be went into labor in the middle of the night, she jumped in the car with him.

And yes, her Brunswick stew *was* the best Charlie Harrison had ever tasted.

Amanda took to Sadie right away. The black woman taught her to knit, guiding the girl to stockings and doll clothes first, then letting her graduate to sweaters and pillow cases and even small throw rugs. Embroidery lessons followed. Hours in the kitchen honed Amanda's baking skills, with her father enjoying scrumptious dividends in tarts, cakes, and pies, especially sour cherry. Access to the Brunswick stew secrets beckoned.

Yet while the former slave could never substitute as Amanda's mother, Aunt Sadie did skill the girl in the domestic duties of running a household. Despite the pervasive racial barriers of the time, Amanda Harrison respected Sadie Levels as a friend and mentor, and eventually as a trusted confidante.

That's why Charlie figured his hired domestic knew all about Harry Hobson before he did.

Amanda had first noticed the former sergeant that awful day in the winter of 1919. Hobson was lucky to be alive himself, having survived mustard gas horrors in the Argonne Forest the previous autumn. Six weeks intensive care in Washington's Walter Reed Hospital followed. Harry Hobson would live, his doctors said, but his lungs were scarred for life. It had been all the ex-sergeant could do to carry his mother up the steps of Macon's Ordinary.

But he'd been in uniform that day.

And that's what Amanda remembered.

With the Allied victory in Europe, the aura and sweep of such a man would impress any woman. Not to mention wide-eyed ten year olds.

Losing her mother to the same scourge established a common grief bond between them. Each comforted and sought solace in the other. Everyone in Keswick who had lost a loved one did. But with Harry twelve years senior, no one figured on romance blossoming between the recovering veteran and Doc Harrison's little girl.

So a few years passed. Harry got into the automobile business and opened a service station down on Route 250. His garage did repairs and sold gas and tires. He traded used cars on the side. Business prospered.

Amanda advanced into young womanhood and by age 16, blossomed as a petite brunette fascinated by spit curls and Rudolph Valentino. Boys her own age found her athletic, full of charm, and stunning in the saddle.

Charlie didn't fool much with horses. True, his father had owned one of the finest thoroughbreds in Virginia before the war.

The Civil War.

Papa used to go on and on about him. What...oh what was his name. Doesn't matter now. That war was a lifetime ago, a decade before I came along, and what the Confederates didn't requisition, the Yankees stole.

Yet when people asked him about Morton's Ford, Doc Harrison would shrug and smile. Yeah, he'd heard the legend.

And Papa had said it was true.

But instead of horses, Charlie's *thing* was science, specifically medicine. That was the future he deemed bright and boundless. He'd pursue pestilence and save lives, and where passion had pushed his father to seek the fastest horse, Doc Harrison labored to defeat death.

But no man should lose the love of his life.

Yet perhaps his father's love for horses had only skipped a generation. Amanda spent much of her spare time in Oak Manor's well-kept stables, the Clarke family estate two miles south of Keswick.

And if that meant mucking out the stalls, lugging buckets of water, spreading fresh straw, or grooming a mount after a summer's ride, so be it.

"You got this horse business honest, my dear," Charlie told her when she turned fourteen. "But straight from my Papa."

And that's all Charlie really ever said for Amanda never pressed him for more. On her sixteenth birthday, her father bought her a fine gelding she named Champion, telling her that Shelby Clarke had offered to board the horse at Oak Manor as long as she continued to help out in the stables.

And Harry Hobson?

To Amanda he was just that quiet, lean mechanic who fixed cars down on Route 250.

Then came Armistice Day of 1928.

On the morning of November 11th Charlie drove his daughter into Charlottesville for the veterans' parade at 11 a.m. Ten years of world peace merited a marking. As they passed Jackson Park, he pointed toward the equestrian statue of Stonewall Jackson. "Sam, Papa's younger brother served under Old Stonewall. But listen! That's Sousa."

The Stonewall Brigade Band, harkening back to its origins with Jackson himself, turned onto High Street. Spectators waved and cheered, energized by the jaunty beat of John Philip Sousa's *Sabre and Spurs March*.

"Well, glory be..."

"What, Dad?"

"Rebels!" said Charlie, waving at a bent, shuffling waif of a man. "That's Ernie Lockhart, Amanda. Ninety years if he's a day."

Lockhart's ex-Confederate companions flashed toothless grins and plodded along, half aided by their canes. Soldiers of the Spanish-American War followed, two dozen middle-aged men dispensing their own smiles and waves under flags floating above. Twenty yards to the rear, surged more than a hundred younger men, many in uniform, in line and in step. Veterans of the Great War.

"Dad! There's Harry. He's carrying Virginia's flag!"

Amanda beamed as 32-year-old former Sgt. Harry Hobson, 116th Regiment, 29th Division, AEF, neared, focused once again on duty. No car mechanic this day, Harry had only the ghosts of fallen comrades before him.

Buried these ten years in the fields of France.

Jaws taut, eyes ahead, the ex-sergeant passed her by. The thin, solemn soldier who had so comforted Amanda in that terrible winter of 1919, never glanced her way.

"Harry! Harry!" she shouted.

But the flag bearer kept to his task, bound by duty, patriotism and remembrance...yet marking the moment with a voice from the crowd.

Harry Hobson never really recovered from his Argonne injuries. Few men did. Initially stricken with severe lung congestion, conjunctivitis, and bleeding gums, he soon developed large blisters on his hands, back, neck and scrotum. In the worst cases, these turned gangrenous. The conjunctivitis could ulcerate and blind and the lung congestion might explode into a debilitating, fatal pneumonia.

Somehow Harry Hobson recovered.

But mustard gas could inflict an insidious, progressive pathology. Army physicians who examined him every April detected chronic bronchitis, corneal opacities in both eyes, and by 1925, the ominous onset of emphysema.

The proprietor of Hobson's Automobile Service didn't complain and customers paid little notice to the magnifying glass Harry kept on his desk or to the cupped, little cough that punctuated his small talk. If he needed a doctor, he knew a good one just up the road.

So when Harry let a wrench slip while taking out a manifold on a 1925 Star Model F Touring and broke his right index finger, he wrapped his injured hand and visited Doc Harrison. Six months later, food poisoning after a church social brought him back again, bent and retching.

Each time Amanda met him at the door, made him comfortable, and went for her father. Aunt Sadie, usually alert for such duties, quietly noted Amanda's new found zeal for nursing. On a bright Sunday afternoon a week later, when a recovering Harry pulled up outside Macon's Ordinary in his 1927 LaSalle Series 303 roadster, Sadie realized Amanda's new interests involved more than aiding the sick.

The romance flourished. Sunday afternoon picnics gave way to dinners in Charlottesville and drives in the country. Aunt Sadie knew enough to keep her mouth shut. The good doctor would learn in good time his daughter was "aflutterin' in the heart."

And soon enough, Harry Hobson came to Charlie Harrison with the question. Despite the age difference between his daughter and her suitor, Charlie respected the Great War veteran and successful car mechanic. The match seemed a sound one.

All of Keswick turned out for the joining. Amanda wore her mother's white lace wedding dress, preserved for a generation up in the tavern's attic. She briefly entertained certain designs for Harry, but even as the little girl in her wanted him to wear his old Army uniform, she knew better. Never would she ask him to revisit the terrors of the trench war.

But unbeknownst to her, the Argonne war ticked in his chest.

Harry had lived alone in the house in which he'd been born, and friends agreed his new bride brought a woman's much needed touch to the place. Amanda began by scrubbing the floors, first then second, room by room.

Harry helped out in the evenings, painting the kitchen and bedrooms, then wallpapering the center hall and parlor. Charlie gave the couple a new walnut dining table with four carved chairs. A month later, he presented his daughter and son-in-law five knit rugs. New curtains and a kitchen countertop followed. Remembering her mother, Amanda planted pansies—those wonderful Johnny Jump Ups—down the walkway, and stitched small lemon jonquils in the soil around the porch. Harry repaired the roof and contracted to put a bathroom with porcelain fixtures and running water in the house.

Privies were past.

After six months, the Hobson residence stood transformed. But Amanda sensed something amiss. When Harry came home after battling flat tires, chewed gears, and dead batteries, he more and more sought the sofa and napped. At first Amanda thought nothing of it. *Work's getting him down.*

But the naps soon filled the evening and when she woke him for dinner, he seemed groggy, listless, out of sorts. If asked why, he waved her off. He had no pains, no complaints, he said. But Amanda noticed his afternoon fatigue and his shortness of breath on mild exertion. Harry ignored it...and her. And she got scared and he got worse.

Finally she convinced him to see her father. Charlie found the veteran's weight down. Harry confessed that his appetite "was off," joking that perhaps Amanda's cooking was to blame. But Charlie didn't laugh. The warning signs were everywhere. Harry's long medical history worried him. His son-in-law's "color" was bad. And that progressive, hacking cough that cracked Harry's every sentence had deepened. Charlie ordered tests in Charlottesville.

A dozen years after the Great War, several thousand cases among returning veterans affirmed that exposure to mustard gas skyrocketed the incidence of cancer later in life. Leukemia and lung cancer topped the list.

Charlie learned the worst on a gray March Wednesday. X-rays revealed extensive, white lobular shadows in Harry's lower right lung. Even without a biopsy, the radiologist believed they were malignant. Two colleagues in town, both thoracic surgeons, declared the tumors "inoperable."

Charlie agonized in silence for two days. On Friday, Amanda showed up at noon, lugging lunch. Charlie thought she looked happy, but tired.

Whipping that old bachelor quarters into a home has taken its toll.

But he knew there was more.

She wants to ask. And she's scared.

Amanda bubbled on about house decorating dreams, about her new flower gardens, and how nice the drapes looked, even how wonderful life was without chamber pots. And Harry had promised to get a new mail box. But he'd been too tired of late to dig a post hole at the front gate.

She's asking now. She wants to know.

"Dad?"

"Yes, sweetie?"

"I...ah.." Amanda giggled.

Charlie eyed his daughter, anxious.

"Ah, Dad. I'm very late."

Her father turned his head and squinted.

"You know, Dad. Late. As in L-A-T-E!"

Charlie mouthed the word, clueless.

"I'm expecting, Dad!"

A freeze frame girded the doctor's face. "You're serious? You're sure?"

Amanda nodded, eager, grinning, and waiting.

And then Charlie saw her glow. *God in heaven, what do I say now?*

He kissed her, embraced her, then smoothed his hands through her hair, hugging her close. *I'm going to be a grandpa!*

"Do you have a doctor, my dear?"

"Only the best." She leaned up and returned his kiss.

To celebrate, Amanda produced a cherry pie out of her hamper and sliced it. Charlie called in Aunt Sadie to share both news and dessert.

"Heaven's news, Miss Amanda!" The old woman cackled, smacking her lips. "This pie's out of this world, too!"

With a practiced hand, Aunt Sadie cupped an open palm to Amanda's tummy. "A girl, if you ask me..." She moved her fingers up, then slowly to one side. "Yep. Gotta get back to my dustin', but mark my words: you got a little missus in there." She hugged Amanda and smooched her forehead. "Know the good Lord's done blessed you, chile!"

Charlie waited until it was just the two of them. "She's been a godsend, you know. Don't know how I would have..."

"Dad..." Amanda turned to the garden. "Mom knows."

Again they hugged.

"Did you want me as a boy or a girl?" She had never asked.

Charlie held her close, shutting his eyes to get back a full generation. "We...only wanted you to be healthy."

Amanda nestled closer, hoping to garner a nugget of wisdom with the warmth.

"You sound so serious, Dad."

"A child should get every opportunity life offers."

"But?" Amanda sensed more. *His words pulse fear.*

"We go with what we're dealt, my dear."

"What do you mean?" Her voice quickened.

"I need to tell you..." Charlie's eyes filled.

"Dad? What...about Harry?"

"He's..." Charlie exhaled. "...got a mass in his right lung."

Amanda sagged into her father's arms.

"We'll get him the best care possible. You know that."

"He's going to die, isn't he? He's never going to see our baby," Amanda sobbed, draining Charlie of words.

How do I tell her he hardly has another three months?

H arry survived seven weeks. The white-hard bleeding cancer that knifed and twisted through his right lung spread to his left and then metastasized to his liver and brain. The University Hospital staff made the car mechanic as comfortable as possible and when the pain became unbearable, put him on a morphine drip. In one of his last conscious acts, Harry Hobson willed his body to science.

Charlie fixed Amanda's due date for early October. He moved her into Macon's Ordinary. Aunt Sadie prepared a nursery. And despite her grief, Amanda exited the second trimester with few complications. The baby seemed to thrive, active inside her mother at all hours.

But stress and sadness can extract their own toll. In August, Amanda's blood pressure soared. Charlie ordered Sadie to keep his daughter on strict bed rest. The days inched into autumn, but Amanda, hands and ankles swollen, fared no better. Then Charlie discovered the baby had shifted to breech.

With these risk factors facing his daughter and future grandchild, Charlie consulted an old classmate, Dr. Mitchell Woods, Charlottesville's leading obstetrician. *Amanda has protein in her urine,* Mitch told him. *Get her in here now! A home delivery's no place for a pre-eclamptic breech baby.*

But Amanda went into labor that night. Charlie phoned Mitch, then with Sadie tending his daughter in the backseat, stomped the pedal to Charlottesville.

Woods met them in Admitting. "Don't even think of scrubbing, Charlie."

"Look here, Mitch..."

"You know protocol, my friend." Dr. Woods glared to make his point, then patted Charlie on the shoulder. "Make yourself comfortable. I'll be back when I know something."

The night seemed to never end. Charlie paced the halls, oblivious to acquaintances and friends on staff. He stepped into the chapel a few times, but found no words to soothe his fears. Aunt Sadie went through two boxes of tissues, weeping one moment, then trading recipes with two friends in housekeeping the next. An hour past dawn, Mitch appeared, shoulders sagging.

"You have a healthy little girl, Charlie. Going to be fine."

"Amanda?"

"Her baby, Charlie. The baby's fine."

"Amanda?"

"Your daughter...she had a rough time. Had to do a C-section. she...ah..., she lost a lot of blood, Charlie. She..."

"Tell me, Mitch."

"Amanda lost a lot of blood, Charlie...a lot." Dr. Woods' voice broke. "Too much. We fought...for more than an hour...after the baby came...but...she...God, old friend, I'm sorry!"

On a glorious autumn afternoon, Charlie buried Amanda beside her mother. He'd lost his wife. Now his only child. All the love lanterns in his world had gone dark.

Aunt Sadie proved a tower of strength. She battled her own grief by staying busy, cooking and doing laundry, keeping the tavern neat and clean, assisting Charlie with patients, and offering all a kind word, and when necessary, one of those ginger cookies.

But Charlie went wooden, now with little to say, a lonely man stumbling through the mechanics of a daily routine. For a month Sadie left him alone. She secured a wet nurse for the baby and otherwise gave the infant her every attention.

But I can only do so much. That chile needs her Grandie.

Then two days before Thanksgiving, as she brought him lunch in his office, she spoke her mind.

"Sure's a bright afternoon, sir. Don't you think?"

Charlie continued writing.

"I'm so glad time shines a new light on every day."

Her employer put down his pen and looked up.

She met him square. "Don't be eyeing me. I ain't no new light."

The baby's cry broke from upstairs.

"But I know where you can find one." She grinned toward the steps.

A new light indeed, illuminated Charlie Harrison's world. *My beautiful granddaughter, Laura Marie Hobson. Amanda loved that name.*

"Yes, Aunt Sadie, you're right." He patted her shoulder as he started up to the nursery.

"Remember, time's a'wasting, sir. You got a young missus growing up on you."

*U**pwards! In the West Meadow!*

In the dream, Charlie neither soared or floated, nor was he yanked skyward like a weed wrenched rootless. The warm hands that gathered him and hefted him aloft always accompanied those gleeful voices that egged him on.

But to what?

It had never made any sense, this precipitous, reoccurring vision... or his lifelong fear of the West Meadow.

But did it matter?

In it, Charlie felt himself moving, settling, getting comfortable amid the cheers, yet he never smelled fear. Not then, anyway. In fast, frozen time, he would glimpse his mother's sweet smiles, her loving, yet urgent glances. *But what Mama, what?*

That's when she always faded behind the timeless mask of cooing voices.

Were you trying to warn me? Were any of you? All you happy people?

The dream never changed. Clamoring, saluting, faceless voices regaled him until everything blurred brilliant in a tumult of whirling thrashes and primeval poundings. The ambush pitched him headlong into a sickening grasp at nothingness, enveloping him in pain and smothering claustrophobia.

And this...is how I will die?

Rearing its head in the dark times, the Nameless Something thundered and wrenched, then always dragged him away into the velvet night.

The contentment of rocking his granddaughter to sleep in the nursery's quiet had never thwarted this. Death, his sworn foe, had taken his wife.

And daughter.

No more in this world would he know their love.

Death.

Hurled into the West Meadow's dream-clawing abyss, then jarred awake, breathless and sweating and wide-eyed, he knew this dream scribed his own end.

Death. That's it.

Just a matter of time.

And then away...and into that velvet night...

Chapter Five

Old Faithful Inn
Yellowstone National Park
June 1952

arney McGill hailed from Montana. That, welded to his confident bearing and rich baritone voice, had caught Laura's attention the first time she met her future husband. The rustic, storied ambiance of Yellowstone's Old Faithful Inn didn't hurt either. Yet when she thought back on it, the real magic came packaged in his friendly face of freckles and that flaming red hair.

"Inn's always a cozy place for dinner, Ma'am." McGill motioned to the massive stone fireplace and soaring beams of lodge pole pine. "Sure can't beat it." His eyes caught hers, then her green-bordered name tag:

Laura
Virginia

"Back east, huh?"

"Yours from the Old Dominion. You?" Although only two weeks into her summer job of waiting tables in the Old Faithful Inn's dining room, Laura was already polishing banter with restaurant patrons. She dug a pencil from her apron pocket and dished him her best *may-I-serve-you-please* smile.

"Harney McGill. Montana. Glad to make your acquaintance, Ma'am. You know, your Virginia's one gorgeous fly over."

"Fly over?"

"Air Force, Ma'am. Headed home on leave. Taking the scenic route."

"Oh...you're in the service." *That explains this Ma'am thing.*

Laura eyed him again. *Mr. Spit and Polish for sure, but definitely the rugged type. Cute, too.*

"But you're out of uniform."

"Ma'am, you don't have to tell the whole world," Harney whispered with a grin. "Course if you don't believe me, I could take you flying sometime...Laura. May I call you Laura?"

She drew a deep breath, twirling pencil between thumb and forefinger. *Go up in an airplane? Just like that! This guy really pushes the envelope. Careful girl, you've got a live one here.*

"Can't say I've had many invites to go soaring off into the wild blue yonder." Her head toss on the word *soaring* spun her ponytail with a zesty bounce. *The old confidence move.*

"Wild blue yonder?" McGill sported a devilish grin, savoring the flush in Laura's cheeks. "Why stop there? I'd rather go to the moon. But for now, let's just say I'd be honored if you'd take me up...on me taking you up."

Ohhhh...so cocksure, yet a wordsmith to boot!

"Well, I'm sure good pilots don't fly on empty stomachs," she said, getting back to business. "And...ah...as for tonight's menu...I'd recommend the grilled chicken breast. An Old Faithful favorite." She widened her eyes to emphasize how delicious it was, then leaned over and whispered, "We glaze it with honey...lemoned...and buttered."

I can do the whisper stuff too, big guy.

McGill started to say something, but settled for a sage nod and a grinning face of freckles.

"Then there's the filet, a house specialty, plus tonight we're offering fresh mountain trout." Laura could feel the burn of his gaze; she waited with her sweetest smile.

"OK, Laura. That chicken sounds like a winner. But I've got two friends outside waiting on Old Faithful." He looked at his watch. "Due...right...about...now. Gawking tourists, you know. Give 'em a couple of minutes?"

"Sure. Something to drink in the meantime?"

Twenty minutes later, after Old Faithful awed the early evening crowd gathered in Yellowstone's Upper Geyser Basin, Laura took three orders for the grilled chicken. Harney McGill's recommendation to go poultry, especially when he described the *honey-lemoned butter* in a whisper did the trick. When she returned with the salads, one of his friends was going on and on about the geyser.

"So much fuss over a hot splash of water," shrugged Harney. "Can you believe it, Laura?"

"I think it's spectacular! Course I'm not from around here."

McGill had watched Old Faithful spew a hundred times, mostly during the summer he'd worked the Park as a "seasonal." He and his father had done a major dust-up on that one.

"Your future's here, boy," Sean McGill had declared with a wave across his herd. "If you don't think so, git out and find out on your own."

Growing up on a small cattle ranch south of Missoula, Harney knew by fourth grade how to ride a horse, rope a steer, and appreciate a dollar. As the son of a cowboy, he knew that *being* a cowboy meant enduring all-day grime, raw saddle sores, and some rather epic body odors. All while working from *can't see to can't see.*

Coming of age in Big Sky Country made the days he could call his own all the more special. Because Harney loved sports, especially baseball, and he could swing for the fences. Yet Ravalli County, like most of Montana, had little money for high school athletics. Still, if he hitchhiked to Missoula on a Saturday, he could always find a summer sandlot game.

That left the mountains. Harney loved hiking and with his two older brothers Matt and Elmer, he often roamed deep into the Bitterroots. On overnight treks, the brothers backpacked their way through miles of towering Ponderosa pine to fish the high mountain streams for cutthroat trout and sift river gravel for native sapphires. In the evenings, their catch secured, they spread camp under the stars, ending their day around a crackling fire, belting out ballads and bawdy rhymes but with trigger fingers ready for bear.

Growing up in wildness could challenge and bring forth the best in a boy. It wouldn't teach him much about music or elocution, but the Methodists in Hamilton sure savored Harney McGill's rich contributions to their choir. Yet to him, *America the Beautiful, Amazing Grace,* and *Onward Christian Soldiers* resonated best up in the narrow canyons of the Bitterroots.

When he looked back on his youth, he considered himself lucky to call Montana home. Out there in those mountain bivouacs, in those last moments before sleep came, when he stared up into the far flung stars sparkling the dark western sky or marveled at the ghostly glow of the Northern Lights shimmering overhead, he knew he wanted more. The world was bigger than Montana. And up there among those stars and Big Sky moon, Harney McGill burned to see that world. And touch it. All of it.

Across those spacious skies. From sea to shining sea.

Yet a year after graduating high school 3rd in his class of 27, Harney Brodnax McGill appeared locked to a dusty life of breaking horses and branding cattle. Or cutting timber. Or mining silver. He had no money for college, much less flying lessons.

But in the spring of 1949 he heard that a bush pilot contracted by the National Park Service down in Yellowstone needed a good mechanic. With no qualifications except high school shop and some knuckle busting repairs on his father's John Deere, he drove to Mammoth Hot Springs and applied.

He didn't get the job, of course, but Slack Gibson, the bush pilot who interviewed him was impressed by Harney's mechanical savvy and outdoor experience. He recommended him for seasonal work clearing trails and rebuilding boardwalks in the geyser basins. And by the way, if he wanted to spend his free time helping out around the hanger, sure, fine, said Gibson.

Just stop by.

Harney did. Long, unpaid hours first as Gibson's grease monkey eventually got him time aloft.

Summer's end brought a few lessons and some supervised flying time. At the end of September, his seasonal job over, Harney McGill went back to roping steers. But Montana, the Treasure State, had always shed gold and silver and sapphires and agates. And ambitious sons and daughters eager for fortunes beyond Big Sky Country.

So the next spring on his 20th birthday, with zero notice to his parents, he went into Missoula and joined the Air Force. No ROTC. No OCS. Not yet, anyway. Just a stubborn, passionate kid headed for basic training. With a dream to get his wings. Somehow. All he needed was the opportunity.

A month later, Communist North Korea invaded the non-Communist South.

After twenty months in uniform, expedited by wartime needs and battlefield promotions, 1st Lieutenant Harney McGill earned his wings, honing his skills in helicopters, especially the agile Sikorsky H-5. Nicknamed the *Dragonfly,* the four-seat, light utility chopper proved a real work horse in combat rescue operations.

Headquartered in Japan with the 3rd Air Rescue, Harney flew 47 hot missions in the H-5. He ranged up and down the Korean peninsula, picking up downed pilots or wounded personnel in the last year of the Korean War. He came home unscathed with four Air Medals and the Silver Star. He came home resolved to make the Air Force his career. And he came home with a box of worn, oft-read letters signed "Laura, from Virginia."

Yes, he'd written her. Gotten her summer address on the back of a napkin that evening in Yellowstone. She'd been surprised to hear from him, then again, three days later.

But his words carried a zest for life. And an urgency.

So she wrote back. And was glad she did, only to gasp when his third letter revealed he had been ordered to Japan. He wrote her thereafter twice a week. She doubled his count and love bloomed in their words.

And when Harney McGill returned, he sought out his Laura from Virginia. Kept his promise and took her flying. Proposed at 12,000 feet. And asked her grandfather to give her away.

Spry and lean at eighty, Charlie Harrison still cut a distinguished figure. Yet when he escorted his granddaughter down the aisle, he did so holding dear the love candles of his Nell and

Amanda. But on this wonderful day, he didn't let past grief darken his glowing happiness. Friends and family noticed the old fellow sported a curious twinkle and a hearty laugh when he wowed 'em all in a dapper dance with the bride. Yeah, Charlie Harrison's people heralded from solid stock.

And Ginny's happy arrival brought him unbounded joy. He'd watched the little girl grow and blossom through Laura's letters and those first Christmas visits. He lived for such days.

Chapter Six

Keswick, Virginia, July 1961

It wasn't the big story on Monday's front page that got Laura's attention. No, she found herself drawn instead to a local item in the State Section. She scanned the article, then reread it to make sure.

I'll fold the paper so he'll be sure to see it. There, beside the OJ.

"Breakfast!" she announced, as her grandfather shuffled into the kitchen. "How are you this morning, Grandie?"

"A bit rugged today, my dear. Knee's barking at me again. Didn't sleep worth a tinker's hoot last night."

"Sorry you don't feel well." Laura put her arm around his shoulder and produced a plate from behind her back. "Maybe these'll help?"

"Blueberry pancakes! Ah, you sweetie."

Charlie knew how fortunate he was. Having Laura and Ginny down for the summer meant far more than home-cooked meals and getting his laundry done. With Harney on active duty in Southeast Asia, their visit was...well, just what the doctor ordered.

"These cakes go beyond the call of duty, Laura."

His granddaughter turned, handing him a smaller plate rolling three link sausages.

"Whatever...are you talking about, suh?" she asked in her prissiest voice.

"Done died and gone to heaven!"

"Not yet. We're just taking care of you, Grandie. Like you're putting up with us while Harney's away."

"Putting up with? Laura, my dear, you've brought more zap into this house than the power company. You and Little Miss Live Wire have coiled some major spring into my step...even with this bum knee!"

"Grandie, it's worked for all of us. Ginny's being around you—and hearing all your tales—well, who can top that?"

Where's that kid, anyway?

"Ohhhhhh, Ginny? Grandie's eating his bunnies! You better march in here before the last one hops away!"

Scrambling footsteps down the hall confirmed message received.

Charlie picked up the morning paper, folding it back to the front page, reading as he chewed. "Remarkable time to be alive."

"How so, Grandie?" Laura asked as Ginny skipped into the kitchen. "Take your seat beside Grandie, young lady. Here's your bunny rabbit pancake with the big blue eyes, big blue nose, and wide blue mouth."

"Goodie! Look, Grandie? How many bunnies did Mommie make for you?"

"All gone, Ginny! He and his sister are way down here." Charlie patted his stomach and grinned his big smiley face. Both adults practiced the art of multiple conversations when the rambunctious roamed near. "Goodness, Laura, see this?"

"Not that rocket ship thing?"

"Rocket ship thing! Laura, space exploration's going to change our world!" Charlie fisted his orange juice. "Alan Shepard's suborbital shot back in May, and this upcoming flight..."

Surely she sees the epic importance of this?

Laura began rinsing dishes in the sink.

"We blundered big time when we let the Russians get the jump on us. Mark my words! At least Kennedy's on it. He'll put a man on the moon!"

"I know you like to stargaze..."

"Stargaze? Laura, have you any idea how fast these rockets go? How high they travel? What all this means for our future?" Charlie paused, watching his great-granddaughter devour her bunny rabbit pancake. "For her future?"

Laura shrugged. "Women on the moon?"

"Mommie, can I have more juice?"

"I didn't hear the magic word, young lady."

"*Pleeeeease!* Can I have some more juice?"

"*May* I have some more juice, Ginny. Not *can*."

Ginny scrunched her nose and thrust her plastic cup at her mother.

"Look! Shepard's *Freedom 7* soared 115 miles above the earth at speeds exceeding 5,000 miles per hour. Who knows how far Grissom will go."

"Well, that's all fine Grandie, but I thought you might want to see a civil war battle re-enactment this coming weekend. There's an article about it...let's see, page twelve. Yeah, here it is."

Laura unfolded the paper and smoothed it flat.

Charlie glanced at the headline: BATTLE OF MANASSAS TO BE RE-ENACTED.

Re-enact? The Civil War?

"I'll fix a picnic. It's only a few hours away. And it would do you good to get out of the house."

"A picnic, Mommie? Yippee!"

"Maybe so, Ginny. With lots of old timey soldiers. But only if Grandie feels up to going."

"Soldiers? You mean like Daddy?"

"No, not quite like your Daddy, sweetie." She ogled her grandfather. "See what I mean?"

"I don't know, Laura. In this heat. Says here, the Park Service expects more than 50,000."

That war? Has it been a hundred years?

"Well, it's something different. Go down there and urge the Rebels on to victory. I mean your father actually fought for the South." Laura stopped scrubbing. "You know Grandie, there aren't many people left who can say their father fought in the Civil War."

"You make it sound like a baseball game, Laura. Don't forget Mama's older brother fought on the other side."

51

"Just thought we'd take a little day outing. See some history."

"There's nothing back there to celebrate, Laura." His words zapped an unexpected sting.

"I know, Grandie. But...Ginny might like...I mean..."

"That war tore my folks apart, Laura..."

"I didn't mean to push, Grandie." She bent silent over the sink.

Charlie folded the paper and closed his eyes. *I've done it now. Run off my mouth again without thinking, just like the crotchety old fart I am.*

Ginny finished her pancake. Two inches of cupped OJ languished.

Well, say something. I hate these awkward silences.

"Can't we picnic, Grandie?"

Charlie smiled. *Now how do I answer that?*

"Grandie's thinking about it, Ginny. Now finish up that juice."

Ginny did as she was told, also making sure to lick the last syrup smear off her plate, but only when her mother turned to scrub the kitchen countertop. Charlie went back to the front page. But the Blue and Gray kept fighting Gus Grissom's Redstone rocket.

History's going to be made this week...and history's going to be revisited. But whatever YOU think about 'em old boy, doesn't really matter.

Charlie glanced at his great-granddaughter.

But they will to you, my sweet.

"A whole century." He spun the soft words over, not so much in surprise, as in resignation to Father Time's relentless advance. *I almost go back THAT far. Ginny knows nothing of what I've seen.*

"Laura, perhaps I... You know Papa rarely talked about it."

"You've said that before."

"Well, the war took nearly everything he had. Wasn't really bitter, but it changed him." Charlie smoothed the newspaper.

"Even growing up, I heard plenty of men swear and say hard things about Yankees. I remember 'em sitting on the courthouse steps on Saturdays. Old man Benton who helped out at Jewett's mercantile in Midlothian only had one arm. He was always telling us boys about the fighting. Lost his arm at Manassas...second time they fought there. Actually seemed kind of proud of it."

"Two battles at Manassas, Grandie?"

"Yeah, year apart. Second far deadlier than the first. But we...er...ah, the South won 'em both." *Here I go again with the history lesson. I should shut up.*

Laura picked up her grandfather's plate. *Some days his fires burn red hot. Today, only the embers glow.*

"We don't have to go..."

"It's not about me, Laura. Now that I think about it, Manassas is a great idea. I mean really..."

The little girl pushed her plate to the center of the table. "Done."

"And what do you say, young lady?"

"May I be excused?"

"Yes, you may."

Ginny jumped down and ran back to her dollies in the den.

Laura finished scrubbing the countertop. "I guess a lot went on back then we'll never know."

Charlie sipped the last of his orange juice.

Probably best that way.

By mid-Saturday morning, northbound traffic on US Route 29 a mile beyond Gainesville, Virginia, had slowed to a crawl. Everyone it seemed was headed for the Manassas National Battlefield Park to witness the spectacle of another "engagement" along Virginia's Bull Run.

With a scorcher in the forecast, Laura had the top down on Grandie's 1958 Chrysler Imperial convertible. A few minutes before ten, she inched into Route 29's intersection with the Sudley Ford Road and turned right up the hill toward the battlefield's Visitor's Center entrance.

"Look at all the cars! Laura, who would have thought..."

A sprawling parking lot stretched across the fields away from the battle staging area with a "FULL" sign blocking the entrance. A tall man waved a red flag. "More parking ahead," he barked. "Keep 'er moving, please."

Cars jammed the road, inching at a creep. A beige Ford station wagon three vehicles ahead boasted a pair of snappy Confederate battle flags as crossed hood ornaments. Among the blaring car horns, one to the rear kept tooting a raucous version of *Dixie*. Pedestrians, including musket-shouldering re-enactors in Blue and Gray, jammed the sides of the roads, trudging their way to the battle site beyond the Visitor's Center.

"I'm hungry, Mommie."

"Patience, sweetie. We're almost there." A motorcyclist zoomed by on the shoulder, backfiring when he braked for a dozen oncoming rebels.

"Never in my born days..."

"I know, Grandie. Where are they going to put all these people?"

"Mommie, I'm thirsty, too."

"Just a bit longer, honey. Mommie's going to get us out of this first."

Inching cars stretched over the next hill and out of sight. The battle was slated "to start" in less than an hour.

"Laura, take a right. At that Chinn Ridge sign. I see some trees."

"I'm really hungry, Mommie!"

"Soon, Ginny. Mommie's got us a nice spot down this road."

"Is this part of the battlefield, Grandie?" Laura removed her sunglasses and wiped her brow.

"Think so. Yeah. See that marker over there?"

Laura guided the Imperial into the shade of a large basswood at a roadside pull off and turned off the ignition. "Don't see any picnic tables, but at least we're here. Blanket?"

Charlie stepped out of the car. *Sure feels good to stretch.*

"I'll have tomato sandwiches in no time...and peanut butter and jelly for you, big girl. Grandie, let's spread the blanket on that grassy spot under the tree. Here're some chips, Ginny."

After lunch, Charlie walked over to the monument. "There was a big fight here, Ginny. A long time ago. Two battles actually."

"Was your daddy here?"

"Only in the second one. His youngest brother joined at the beginning... but...something happened. I'm not sure."

Two sharp concussions shook the woods.

"Goodness, Grandie, is it starting?" Laura ducked as three more blasts jarred the ground.

"MOMMIE!" Ginny pointed north. White smoke billowed above the tree line like an exploding flour mill.

"Let's go stand on that big rock."

A peppered staccato of massed musketry hit the landscape like a thousand hammering drumheads, studded by thundering salvos of cannon belching fire from the Henry House. The restored home actually post-dated the battle, the original having been shredded in a shower of bullets and shrapnel.

"Mommie! It's scary!"

"It's just pretend, Ginny. And way over there."

Volley after volley swept the hills above Bull Run, pummeling a raw yet entrancing rhythm, hauntingly entertaining to anyone waiting on a war. Faint yells and cheers, back and forth, echoed the waxing or waning fortunes of the pseudo combatants.

Charlie found a smooth area on the rock and lay down. Torrid humidity beaded his lined forehead, sliding off into the moss and lichens. *Wonder if it was this close back then.*

"More lemonade, Grandie?"

"Sold." Charlie blinked. Glare, then sweat. "Stifling, isn't it? Those fellas must be broiling in those wool uniforms."

"Are they still fighting, Mommie?"

"No, sweetie. It's just a show battle. Nobody's getting hurt."

"Then, why are they doing it?"

"Well, a hundred years ago, there was a real battle...right here. And today, people are remembering the sacrifice of those who died that day."

Ginny jerked north then back to her mother, still not sure what to make of this booming, acrid, smoke-drifting ruckus.

"Come here sweetie. I've got a story."

The little girl leaned into her great-grandfather, hurting for a hug.

Charlie smoothed his fingers through her red curls. "Did I ever tell you...how when I was a little boy, I loved to dig in the dirt?"

Ginny shook her head, darting looks at the trees, then at her Grandie.

"Well, especially on hot summer days, I had this secret spot where I'd dig up things. Old bricks, nails, hinges, bits of pottery. But I always hoped I'd find a pirate's chest!"

"Really?" She whirled, eyes into the ground, then at him.

"Yep. And dirt's always cool in the summer."

"Yeah."

"Well, I had Papa's shovel and my pocket knife. Even used a stick if the ground was really soft."

Ginny picked up a short, jagged tree branch. "Like this one?"

"Sure. That'll do."

"Show me, Grandie."

Charlie shoved the stick's sharp end into the sod and turned up a corner, then pushed down along one side. Slowly, he pried the grass back with his fingers. "See?"

Ginny palmed the raw earth. "It IS cool."

"Now my Mama always made me take a bath after I played in the dirt. Said I had Grandma's black beads. Your Mommie knows what they are."

"Ugly sweat and dirt balls around your neck, Ginny. Grandie thinks they're cute. I think they're yuckie."

Ginny giggled, the sham battle no longer a concern. "Let's dig!"

"No messes, young lady! Hear me?"

Charlie watched the little girl gouge the ground. "Don't fret, Laura. We're looking for pirate treasure."

She scraped free a small stone, then pushed and pried the stick deeper.

"I think you're stuck in the roots, Ginny."

"What's this, Grandie." Ginny's pudgy fingers picked up a dirty white, but perfect sphere. For a moment, Charlie drew a blank, then grinned.

"That's a musket ball! A real civil war bullet!"

"Honey, give it to Grandie."

"The odds of finding..." The old physician shook his head. "This is really neat, Ginny!"

Charlie rolled the .69 calibre lead ball in the palm of his hand and described how soldiers during the Civil War loaded muskets with such ammunition. *Hate to get hit by this.*

Resounding gunfire and the sharp smell of black powder smoke drifted out of the woods. The sham battle swelled to its roaring climax.

"A hundred years ago, these things ripped through everything," Charlie said, holding up the musket ball between thumb and forefinger. "Even whole sections of forest. Today, they're using blanks and will conclude with handshakes. Progress, huh?"

"Thank God for that," said Laura.

Charlie closed his fist over the bullet. *Yeah. But wasn't the same God here a hundred years ago?*

The public as a whole embraced the first major reenactment of America's Civil War Centennial. Thousands mobbed the rolling, open fields northwest of Manassas, Virginia, gawking in thrilled amazement as 4,000 Blue and Gray would-be warriors charged and counter-charged. Suburban America had rarely witnessed a more bizarre stab at pseudo-realism and yet, as one newspaper reporter admitted, the whole spectacle "left a catch in the throat."

Still problems abounded. Spectators exceeded 100,000 souls, doubling the National Park Service's pre-event estimate. Traffic congestion and crowd control thwarted the preparations of event planners, law enforcement, and park personnel. Temperatures soared to 101 degrees Fahrenheit. Despite Army aid stations stocking ice, water, and 10,000 salt tablets, heat exhaustion dropped a hundred people. Sunburns, upset stomachs, and bee stings kept first-aid crews hopping. A dog bit a nine-year-old Texas girl. A cardiac emergency required a helicopter evacuation. And authorities returned two dozen children to their parents.

It was to be expected that people would get sick, children would get lost, and accidents would happen. And rotten weather is a fact of life at any outdoor public event. But the nation's Civil War Centennial Commission had not reckoned on the carnival atmosphere that pervaded the mock battle scenes.

From the start, planners had treated the event like a sporting event. Temporary bleachers grabbed choice venues with seating for nearly 20,000 spectators, reserving special sections for governors, senators, congressmen and other VIPs. Crowd control fences snaked across historic fields. Hot dog vendors and concession stands crowded the actual ground where the immortal Jackson and his brigade had "stood like a stone wall."

To heighten the realism, organizers hid the Visitor's Center and all battlefield monuments, including Stonewall Jackson's equestrian statue under tarps and army gun netting. Field dummies littered the ground as "battle casualties." So all might follow history on the field, an announcer chronicled the unfolding battle like a football game on a blaring PA system. Adding to the drama, a small spectator plane crashed on takeoff from a nearby airstrip, plowing across both lanes of Rt. 234, injuring the pilot, and blocking traffic for miles.

The Director of the National Park Service had reminded all that "this is not a pageant...It is a presentation designed to enable us to better understand our history." But after this day, the U. S. Civil War Centennial Commission wanted no more sham battles on hallowed ground. To them, the Manassas spectacle bordered on farce. Even the obscene. The event had been more about cheap commercialism and entertainment than commemoration and documented history. Said one official report, the re-enactment was an "affront to good taste."

Yet, among those who attended, one aged son of a Confederate veteran pondered the legacy bestowed on him from another time.

Mama and Papa did the best they could after the South lost. But I should've asked more about what happened. I tell myself I'd never go back...

Charlie fingered Ginny's lead bullet.

...but I wish I knew more. At least no one died here this time.

Chapter Seven

Keswick, Virginia, October 1962

Now who in blazes can that be?" Charlie eased his feet to the floor and shuffled over to the phone. *Don't they know I'm retired?*

"Dr. Harrison? Grandie? You there?"

"I hope so. My God, what time is it...and who's this, anyway?"

"Harney, Dr. Harrison. It's Harney!"

"Christ, Harney, you picked a devil of a time to dial me out of bed." Charlie yawned, rubbing his eyes, then scratched his neck. "Everybody, OK?"

"Just work. I need to send the girls down for a few days. It's a little hectic up here and, well, I'd feel better if they were with you."

You're calling me at o'dark thirty? For this?

Charlie pawed his forehead and yawned again. Sleep still cobwebbed his thinking. Blinking eased his mind into gear.

Laura's usually the one who calls.

He mashed the phone to his ear, suddenly wide awake. "What's wrong?"

"I just need them to visit you for a few days." Major Harney McGill, USAF, never lied.

59

The chilling, stunning discovery of offensive based Soviet SS-4 medium range ballistic missiles in Cuba by an American U-2 plane was still a closely guarded military secret when Harney McGill phoned Charlie Harrison that October Saturday night.

Harney kept it that way. Despite a Top Secret clearance, he already knew too much. Newly transferred to Air Force Intelligence, he'd been assigned to one of several teams examining raw U-2 imagery shot over Cuba. The job was taxing enough. But in the past week, he'd seen changes to the terrain of Castro's communist state: fresh, patterned excavations; dozens of parked trailers with canopied, elongated loads; and finally the unmistakable images of nuclear missiles being readied for launch.

The old man doesn't need this on his plate right now.

With Harney "working late," Laura knew her grandfather's door was always open. *Ginny just needs to realize we're not going to the circus.*

Two days later John F. Kennedy went on national television to detail the threat to the American people. Although some senior military analysts and Senate leaders urged immediate air strikes, JFK ordered a naval blockade of the island, a military quarantine as he styled it. The Strategic Air Command went to DEFCON 3; two days later, they ramped it to DEFCON 2. The Cuban Missile Crisis, as history would know it, had pushed the world to the brink of nuclear war.

Charlie watched the President's Monday night address on TV. *Washington's in Russia's crosshairs! And Harney's in the middle.*

"Why are you sad, Grandie?"

"Oh, Ginny. Things'll be fine in a few days."

I pray to God they will.

"Bath time, dear." Laura reached for her daughter, her eyes darting and scared. "Not even a hint," she said under her breath as Ginny squeezed her dollie. "Nothing. Harney sent us down here...knowing...this."

"He's doing his duty, Laura. You know he can't..." *She needs reassuring. But what do I say?*

"Bubble bath, Mommy?"

"If the bottle's not empty, Ginny. Maybe Grandie will tell you a bedtime story?"

"I've got just the one." Fatigue lined the old man's face as he leaned down for a hug. "But only if you get squeaky clean."

Charlie walked into his darkened kitchen, hearing Ginny chatter on as her mother filled the tub. Through the open back window, he lifted his eyes to the Big Dipper, to Mizar.

War robbed Papa. And it took you from me. So tell me, Nell, why does history come back at us?

The star sparkled from the October night.

Love, I keep doing the best I can. But maybe...I've lived too long?

Charlie Harrison sucked in the evening air...then let it go.

How much longer Lord? How much longer?

Chapter Eight

Stars awed Charlie Harrison. He took in the night sky whenever he could, be it the Perseid Meteor Shower in mid-August or, bundled against January's cold, a shimmering glimpse of the *aurora borealis*. After Amanda's death, he had ordered a 3-inch Broadhurst Clarkson refractor with the deluxe 40x, 120x and 180x eyepieces. Seeking solace, he marveled at the harvest moon's craters, Jupiter's swirling Red Spot, and Saturn's mysterious rings. Yet he always made time for Mizar.

Nell, how are you tonight? Let me tell you about my day.

Charlie expected no answers, of course. A star was, after all, just a star. But dependable Mizar seemed to pulse her photons, and his new telescope confirmed it. The light was actually two stars, Mizar and Alcor—the Arabs' ancient rider and horse, an early test of visual acuity.

Second from the end in the Big Dipper's handle, this double became Charlie Harrison's constant. Because Mizar's and Alcor's sparkle spurred his imagination. A single light speck sourced from two stars. *Nell and Amanda, together. The essence of eternity.*

His eyepiece capturing the light of rider and horse warmed him to a wife and daughter lost. All that was mortal of Nell and Amanda lay at peace in his flower garden. But this dual beacon, light-years away, beamed him a peace of his own.

Aunt Sadie soon joined him in the yard after sunset, escaping the heat of the kitchen to sip her sweet tea.

"Peekin' into heaven again, suh?" she'd ask, after giving little Laura a bath and putting her to bed.

Charlie would nod, a quiet gesture Aunt Sadie respected. She knew his time alone with the Lord's heaven brought an inner calm. *Just what the doctor ordered.*

The summer after third grade, Laura got to join Grandie and his telescope. He introduced her to the major planets and their nightly trek across the sky, to the phases of the moon, and of course, to the meteors that slid fire overhead.

But sometimes when their conversations quieted and drifted from astronomy, Laura would ask her grandfather about the old times.

When he was a boy.

Doing what he liked to do.

And wonder about his mother and father.

"That was such a long time ago," he'd begin. But if Laura persisted, and she was pretty good at that, Charlie would open up, telling her about her grandmother and what a good cook she was, about her mother and how she loved gardening and flowers and horses. He'd burnish stories about his days in medical school, about his first baby delivery and—fascinating this—his first autopsy. He'd relate how he set the broken thumb of a church organist, kicked by his buggy horse on the way to services and how the musician had gone on to play *Faith of Our Fathers, Holy, Holy, Holy*, and *Now the Day is Over* flawlessly. To Laura's giggling delight, he'd recount with relish the day he dug Number 8 buckshot out of an escaped convict's butt. And then proclaim the marvels of x-rays and penicillin.

"If only we'd had these things when I was a boy," he'd say, "think of the good we could have accomplished, the lives we could have saved."

And there, Grandie pretty much left it. If asked about his childhood, he'd go silent and start playing with the Broadhurst Clarkson.

In the rough times, folks always needed a diversion. For Doc Harrison, stargazing helped him shelve the troubles of the day during the lean years of The Great Depression and the concerns of World War II.

Just as it had his grief.

Laura thought the stars and planets and moon nice enough, but other things captured her fancy. Like sewing. Reading. Cooking.

Aunt Sadie kept her own counsel in most of this. She'd sip her sweet tea and echo a respective series of "yes, suhs" whenever Charlie opined on matters of personal health or local politics. But let the good doctor venture into child rearing or domestic duties and she abandoned all timidity.

A mutual respect prospered their arrangement. In rural Virginia's segregated society, Dr. Charles Harrison (white) and Mrs. Sadie Levels (colored)—as the decadal census recorded them—grew old together under the same roof as employer and domestic. When Aunt Sadie's health began to fail at the end of World War II, Charlie gave her the best of care, getting her seen in town when complications arose.

But diabetes creeps as an insidious, relentless foe and in Aunt Sadie's case, the scourge eventually claimed three toes on her left foot, two on her right, and the vision in her right eye.

As a teenager during the war, Laura yearned to be a teacher. After high school, she entered Madison College, a four-year, state teachers' school over the Blue Ridge in Harrisonburg. She applied herself and got good grades, dated a few fellows, but nobody serious, and always made it a priority to get back to Macon's Ordinary whenever she could.

On Thanksgiving of her junior year, she arrived home to learn that Aunt Sadie was back in the hospital.

Charlie minced no words. "Diabetic coma, Laura. Not much time left."

The old woman never regained consciousness. And with her passing, an era ended at Macon's Ordinary. Lots of folks, black and white, stopped by to offer their condolences, leaving cakes, pies, cookies and far too much fried chicken. Some were patients Charlie hadn't seen in years.

Going into Charlottesville now. Seeing specialists. Can't blame 'em. Those fellows are up on all the new things.

At night when he sought Mars in his viewfinder or marveled at Mizar and Alcor and talked to Nell, he pondered matters even more.

Sadie's up there now. I know you'll like her. Oh, me? Well, what do you think, Nell? Time to take down my shingle? Geez, I'm over 75. Why, I'm the last one in my class who isn't dead or retired.

And the double star would twinkle back clear and true.

Of course, Laura mourned for Aunt Sadie, but as Christmas approached, she worried about her grandfather. *What's he going to do now?*

That concerned others in Keswick, too. Folks in that part of Albemarle County still depended on Dr. Harrison. Lots of folks.

And they told him so. He'd doctored them all their lives. His almost-always-opened office in the village center helped them avoid half-day treks into town for impersonal appointments thronged in crowded waiting rooms.

Neighbors insisted he was a *young* 75. "Folks 'round here are pretty smart," he'd brag. "I AM a young 75!" And Laura would laugh, cheek-kiss him, and remind him he was really going to be 79 come May.

"Four years gone by? Well, young missus, you've grown up on me!"

And she'd smile and smooch him again, while Charlie, wise, wrinkled, and content, would drift his gaze to the backyard garden.

Sadie did do her job, Nell. Just like she promised.

That was when Laura told him about her summer job in Yellowstone.

Meeting Harney McGill, of course, broadened his granddaughter's life in an entirely different direction. Falling in love did such things. Marriage, motherhood, and little Ginny enriched it.

Charlie took three more summers to retire and as the years passed, he gloried in watching Laura's family blossom. Agile and fit for his age, he traveled more, visiting cousins and old friends in Saratoga Springs, Richmond, and Charleston. And on those evenings when he tested his eyes on Mizar and Alcor, catching the twinkling beams in his new binoculars, he talked to Nell and Amanda and thanked heaven for Laura's happiness. And his.

You'd both be real proud of her. And this fellow, Harney? Why he'd go to the ends of the earth for Laura. Course I don't know what to say about little Virginia. She's cute as a button. A real pistol! But I have to tell you... Ginny's just...well, it's hard to say Nell, but...she so reminds me of Mama.

The little girl's curiosity of course, had led Charlie to his mother's daguerreotype up in the attic. But it was Manassas that had stirred his deepest sentiments.

Nell, would you believe their re-fighting the Civil War? As a pageant? Papa would roll over in his grave! Can't believe I've lived so long.

And that's the question that really bugged Charlie Harrison.

Nell, Papa raged on and on about that war. Called it a terrible waste. Told me how he brought home his youngest brother Sam, wax-cold stiff in the back of a wagon. Gutted by typhoid. Never fired a shot. I can still see the tears down Papa's face. He joined up after that. Told me he had no choice.

Charlie would always remember the stabbing fix in his father's voice when he damned the war for stealing his dreams. But Payne Harrison also kept much to himself. Son figured father had gone off to war to avenge Sam's death.

But Charlie was wrong.

Chapter Nine

Keswick, Virginia, November 1963

N ice evening out, Laura. Good star night."

"Grandie? You'll catch a chill out there."

"Naaa. I'll bundle up, sweetie. It's only going into the 40s."

Charlie hadn't put out his telescope in years. The old Broadhurst Clarkson was more an antique curiosity than anything else. The fine coatings on the instrument's refracting lenses had deteriorated over time. The tedious eyepieces made his eyes water and leaning over the thing for more than ten minutes left his neck, back, and legs sore and stiff. Nowadays, Charlie preferred his tripod-mounted Bausch & Lomb binoculars.

"Glad you're down early for Thanksgiving, Laura."

"It's always good to come home." She paused, giving him one of her *happy-I-still-have-you* smiles.

"I think I do OK. By myself and all. I mean for an old guy. Lots of folks still stop in and say hi."

Laura waited, letting him find the right words.

"Course we both know I'm just passing time now." Charlie coughed, clearing his throat. "That's the way it is. Still love my stars though."

"I know. My earliest memories of you have that old telescope. I know that's how you...connect..."

"Still miss 'em, Laura."

He looked down, finger to nose. "Think I've lost my marbles?"

"Sir, I think you're the most loveable man I've ever known. And when Harney and Ginny get here for Thanksgiving..." She pulled him close, savoring his flannelled warmth. "Once, Grandie, you were all I had."

"Keep up this sentimental stuff, Laura, and my hair'll turn white!"

"A little late for that. But Grandie, tell me, how have you kept the flame burning all these years."

"Those you love, Laura, are never far away."

She looked with wonder into his eyes, then kissed him and opened the backdoor. "Here, take your cap and jacket. I'll be in the den reading."

"Join me."

"And freeze my tush?"

"Oh, come on. For old time's sake. Besides, there's something special out tonight."

"Talk about me being sentimental. Oh, OK. But for just a bit."

"You're in for a treat." He waved at the stars. "Gorgeous, huh?"

Before Laura could answer, a brilliant streak seared silent across the night sky.

"Wow! Look at that."

"Leonid meteor shower!"

"Look! There's another! And there! Goodness."

Over the next half hour, more than forty meteors bid for every turn of the head, every glance over the shoulder.

"Didn't the ancients attach great importance to celestial events?"

"Eclipses, meteors, sun spots. You name it. They worshipped the sky... and feared it."

"Ever make you wonder...what's up there?"

"Laura, the whole world's inter-related. And in marvelous, elegantly fashioned ways. We'll just never know it all."

"Harney says that."

"It'll be good to see him. They're coming Tuesday?"

"Right after school."

"Still expecting to be deployed?"

"Yeah. South Vietnam."

Charlie had read the papers. And heard the raw edge in Laura's voice.

"Back to train chopper pilots."

"Oh, look at that one!" A large fireball burned through the northern sky, breaking into three smaller fragments.

"Can't he retire in a few years?"

"Seven."

"Well, that's not so long."

"Grandie, I want him home. Ginny needs her dad."

"And a little brother?"

"Don't go there..."

Dammit. There I go again. When will I learn to keep my mouth shut?

"Ah...look at that one, Laura. How many's that? Thirty?"

"I guess."

"More in one night than I've ever seen." Charlie forced a smile. *I've upset her.* "Well, granddaughter, take this celestial event as a sign."

"Of what? You sound like one of the *ancients*."

"Could be. I am pushing ninety, you know."

FALLS CHURCH, VIRGINIA, THAT SAME EVENING

ll right, young lady. Ready for that geography test tomorrow?"

"Uh huh."

"I didn't hear you, Ginny. Got those oceans and continents down pat?"

"Yes, Daddy."

"Good. So what's the longest river in the world?"

"Mrs. Inkster isn't asking that stuff, Daddy."

"Well, don't you know the answer?"

"Amazon! No, no! The Nile!"

"Ahh! But can you spell it?"

"Yep. A-M-A... Oh, sorry. N-I-L-E. Nile!"

"Good! Got those teeth brushed?"

Ginny stretched her best smile.

"Let's take a closer peek." Harney McGill rubbed his third-grader's head and leaned down beside her, touching his nose to her chin. "Lots of pearlies in there, Virginia, but are they C-L-E-A-N?"

Giggles met his letters.

But her father stood up and pointed toward the bathroom. "March."

"Awwww, Daddy!"

"That's an order, girl."

Ginny McGill brushed her teeth as if shining a shoe from the inside out. Against a stopwatch.

"Ease up. Not so hard. And don't wait so long to spit."

The eight-year-old froze. Rolling her eyes like marble magnets, she slowly puffed her cheeks like a bulging bullfrog, then wiggled back and forth as if riding a lopsided rocking chair, eyes blinking, only to rush to the sink and splatter the pink porcelain white.

"Oh, Ginny, why do you...? Here, rinse out." She sipped and swished, then spit again.

"Nice and clean, Daddy." She jabbed her toothbrush into the Minnie Mouse holder beside the sink and grinned.

"Yeah, right. Nice and clean. OK, that's it for tonight's fireworks. Into bed with you."

"But I have a question."

"Ginny, you always have a question."

"How many more days before we go to Grandie's?"

"Like I told you. Thanksgiving's a week from today and you have school tomorrow and on Monday and Tuesday. I get five days leave starting Wednesday. With me so far, toothpaste girl?"

She nodded, eyes round.

"We go to Grandie's after school on Tuesday."

"I like his stories."

"So your mother warned me years ago."

"And I'm cooking the turkey. And putting out the cranberries and..."

"Whoa, all in good time, princess. Right now, sooner you get to bed, the sooner tomorrow comes. Let's see those clean teeth before I tuck you in."

Ginny broke her best, gum-friendly grin.

"Worth a million bucks!" Harney McGill proclaimed, walking to the bedroom door. "Don't forget your prayers."

"Nighty night, Daddy."

"Nail that test tomorrow, sweetheart."

"Uh huh."

Harney hit the light switch. "And the world's largest island is?"

F riday morning's Pentagon briefing confirmed more of Lt. Col. McGill's apprehensions. Since the overthrow and killing of South Vietnamese Premier Ngo Dinh Diem and his brother Ngo Dinh Nhu by a cadre of military generals three weeks earlier, the country continued to spiral into chaos.

We only had 800 advisors in country when JFK got elected.

At lunchtime, needing to run a few errands, Harney turned out of Pentagon Parking Lot DD-3 and steered his '61 Ford Falcon onto the George Washington Parkway.

We knew Diem and his brother were corrupt, but we supported them anyway. And what did that do? Peasants turned against us and vast sections of the countryside went to Charlie. Now three years later, we've got 16,000 advisors in country, our airpower props up ARVN, and Charlie owns the jungle. Dammit. To which we spray every living thing in there with this damned defoliant I keep hearing about.

Harney glanced across the Potomac, catching the Washington Monument. *Intel knew Diem was going down. And looked the other way.*

George Washington's 555-foot obelisk peeked and flickered through the Parkway's blur-by wall of trees. *And we wonder why Buddhist monks set fire to themselves in the streets. What would you do, General?*

He passed the exit ramp to Arlington National Cemetery.

Need to pay my respects there, sometime.

A solitary fisherman cast his line at Theodore Roosevelt Island.

Lucky you. Not a care in the world.

Key Bridge arched overhead.

Sure could use a good week up in the Bitterroots right about now.

Harney rolled down his window.

And some music.

He flicked the radio knob.

"...in Dallas, Texas this afternoon. We repeat. This is a Special Report from NBC News. Three shots were fired at President Kennedy's motorcade in downtown Dallas this afternoon. The first reports say the president is seriously wounded."

G randie, we'll have Thanksgiving at our house."
"Won't work, Laura. Not now."
"But it's still family time. Let's get through this together. That's what families do."

President John F. Kennedy's assassination in Dallas stunned the nation, America's first *where-were-you-day* since Pearl Harbor. Everything—except the NFL schedule, some would always point out—got cancelled by a tragedy that smothered Thanksgiving and derailed the travel plans of millions.

But it was worse than that.

People didn't know what to do.

And if they did, they didn't. Except watch television.

Ginny's school closed for the entire week. Harney's leave got cancelled. And Laura realized she'd have to return to Northern Virginia. *Come with me, Grandie.*

"No. No, my dear. Just won't do. But don't fret. I'll be fine here."

"Grandie, it's Thanksgiving. Families are supposed to be together."

Keswick's stooped, white-haired physician glanced toward his backyard. "I'll be fine."

D on't know what to tell you, Nell. World's gone crazy again. But it's not a war this time. Just...some crazy's shot the President.

He rubbed his right hand over the stone's inscribed letters. It was an absent-minded, detaching thing. A habit when depressed. Or when he just needed to clear his head. The coarse granite letters bulged with a visceral, tactile sensation. Rough. And real.

Freeing his mind to explore.

Freeing his mind for any avenue that beckoned.

Freeing his mind.

Not a financial panic, either. In fact folks are doing OK for the most part. But I'll tell you, Nell, the whole country's down. Everything changed after Friday. Never seen folks like this. At least they caught this guy.

Like most, Charlie found himself riveted to the live TV news coverage coming out of Dallas and Washington.

Nell, Harney's leave's been cancelled so Laura wanted me to go back with her to Northern Virginia for Thanksgiving. But you know I couldn't. Leave you and Amanda this time of year? Don't think so.

Laura had not been far off the mark: the ancients did believe the stars presaged momentous events. How else to make sense of a spectacular meteor shower when days later, the world mourns the tragic, traumatic death of the 35th President of the United States?

Charlie massaged the granite double Ls of his wife's first name. "Hell, stars can't predict the future."

Back inside, he plopped down in front of the TV in the den.

Thought I'd turned it off.

The National Broadcasting Company switched to Texas for more live coverage. Dallas police were about to transfer Lee Harvey Oswald, the accused assassin, from the jail in City Hall to the county jail in the Criminal Courts Building about thirteen blocks away.

So this is the guy.

Charlie had just leaned back when a dark form darted across the screen. A loud "pop" and a high-pitched squeal jerked the TV image into a blur of yells and swirling figures. A voice, flat and oddly mechanical, uttered, "He's been shot. He's been shot. Lee Oswald's been shot."

WHAT! Gunned down on live television! Broadcast right into my den! The guy that killed the President. My God! Is the country coming apart at the seams? Did I really see this?

Charlie left the TV on, but he couldn't watch.

The President's dead. Stone cold dead! His dreams of a man on the moon, of that torch being passed...gone.

The old country doctor stared to the small table beside his easy chair. His mother's image, captured on glass so long ago, smiled back.

How I owe you, Ginny!

Charlie picked up the daguerreotype.

How on earth did you keep going, Mama?

The fair young woman, full of song, serene and happy in eternity, presented a glowing picture of loving contentment.

Because you didn't know the horror that was coming.

The bright gilt frame, hidden those many years in the Saratoga trunk, retained a fresh patina.

But you had this taken when you got married...during the war.

The den TV droned on with updates and details about the late President's upcoming funeral. Burial would be in Arlington National Cemetery. Charlie stared at his mother's picture.

What happened in Dallas pales to the war that tore your life apart.

A television reporter revealed Jackie Kennedy's request to use the same catafalque that had supported the casket of Abraham Lincoln 98 years earlier.

So why the smile?

Dr. Charles Harrison had no answer.

Everyone lost someone. Remember what Papa use to say...how the war robbed him?

As a young man, he'd heard dozens of veterans speak of the carnage. And of the finality of Appomattox.

Your whole world was falling apart. Secession. Invasion. Everyone marching to war. Yet somehow, you and Papa fell in love.

Then it came to him.

But...you were young, vibrant. Saw only the good things. You had your whole life ahead. And believed your dreams could still come true.

Charlie stared out his den window as the TV droned its solemn litany of arriving dignitaries for the presidential funeral.

Now I'm nearing the end of mine. And my dreams...

He returned to his mother's smile. And slowly wrinkled one of his own.

Told you about Ginny, didn't I, Mama? Well, she smiles a lot, too.

U pwards*!*
   Not this damn nightmare again!

Every few months for as long as he could remember, Charlie Harrison confronted the same nightmare, something in the West Meadow, sudden and light-searing, rocking him to his core. Nothing stopped the suffocating darkness that roiled his rest. Not even his mother's reassurance and the cheers of those around him. It made no sense.

And here it comes again!

Charlie had no idea how many times this incubus had ambushed him, crept up and stolen his night's rest, catapulting him into the dawn, eyes bleary and fearful, curled in a drenching sweat.

Just this stupid West Meadow thing again.

He'd long ago given up trying to guess *what the hell brought it on. Sure as hell isn't going away.*

But could he ever understand it?

Because if I can, I can confront it. And one day end it.

But Charlie found no convenient insights into what, if anything, the dream portended. When everything exploded in searing incandescence and hurled him along an arcing shower of fireworks into an inky deep, he still found himself fighting to breathe beneath blanketing claustrophobia. *And here it comes again!*

Yet even as old fears mounted, familiarity discovered a warming corner.

I know this place...and...AND WHAT COMES NEXT!

It seemed so obvious, yet he hugged this revelation with great caution.

Dreamers never know they're dreaming until they awake. But here, for the first time, just as this crap is about to grab me, I can see it's not real. I'm not going to die! It's just a dream!

Charlie could finally stand back from his recurring nightmare, free of its grip, a mere observer to a spectral terror that had haunted him for as long as he could remember.

This West Meadow thing is just...a bit of phantasmagoria.

He smirked at that fifty dollar word. *Never will forget the day I won a spelling bee on that one!*

But grinning didn't calm him.

Something really did happen out there...

And Mama, if only you were here...

BOOK TWO

BOOK TWO

Honor your father and mother,
that your days may be long in the land
which the Lord your God gives you.

E X O D U S   20 : 12

Chapter Ten

White Sulphur Springs, Virginia
June 1860

Luke! Luke! Get up. We need to go!"

The hissed words snapped the boy awake as if his sister had thrown a snake in the bed. Luke Parker leered up wide-eyed, gripping quilts, then slumped back, growling to his mattress. Outside the mountain cottage, all was quiet. Dawn remained an approaching promise...interrupted by a finger in the ribs.

"Stop it, Alex!"

"Come on! You said you would!"

Alex Parker—Miss Alexandra Margaret Parker in proper Boston society—snatched the quilt off her brother's curled bottom and whomped him with a feather pillow. Nineteen and waiting on no one, she brooked her younger brother no patience when she set her mind to something.

"Thunderation, Alex! You're going to wake...!"

"Two minutes, brother!" A squeaky cabin door, then silence.

Luke sat up, rubbing the last of sleep from his eyes.

Dawn was meant to be spent in bed.

Pungent pine greeted Alex outside the family's cottage on Baltimore Row. She eyed the eastern ridge. The morning stars had already surrendered to the coming sunrise. A woodland path beckoned.

Perfect!

The blue-green mountains surrounding Virginia's White Sulphur Springs cast lurking hues of gray and black in the predawn.

But Luke knows the way. Said it's only a half mile or so.

The boy stepped outside, stuffing shirt behind belt. Alex teased him with a cold biscuit from the small basket on her arm.

"Apple butter?" she winked, pointing to an opened jar.

Her brother dunked bread and feasted, pawing another from the basket and jabbing the jar before his sister could stop him. Hunger pangs never mixed with exploration.

The day before, Luke had discovered a swift, emerald mountain stream plunging more than 40 feet.

"See them falls at dawn," said old Silas, the White's stable manager, when Luke asked him about it that afternoon. "And don't wait, boy. Only now when the days is longest, does it sparkle up all dem colors."

Rainbows? Alex loves rainbows!

Luke danced down the rocky path that snaked right and around a high wooded knob. His grins and nods said the rest. At three hundred yards, the trail forked. He pointed left where dense rhododendron splayed the trail. Ancient oaks and maples soared into lofty green canopies. Creeping mists cloaked the ground like a graveyard, chording a leaf-dripping patter.

And that's where brother and sister felt it, bedazzled like deaf folks vibrant to distant thunder. They raced ahead, trading switchbacks, leaning to the approaching roar, laughing and churning to see the falls first...to beat the other...to be free in this wild place...then halted breathless, awestruck before the hammering cascade drowning carriage-sized boulders, chilling in its billowing spray.

"Isn't it great?" Luke shouted into the din. Alex nodded but her gaze fixed on the ridge top. A searing, radiant fire burned through the trees crowning the heights.

Just a few moments more!

And then like a searing dagger stabbing into the gorge, sunlight streamed over the mountain, bursting color through the swirling fog. Diamonded petite rainbows sparkled from a thousand angles. Stepping into the stream swirled all color as the plunging water refracted the sun's rays into the infinite beauty of the visible spectrum. Downstream, a double rainbow arched across the mist.

"Bring your shovel for the treasure, little brother?"

Alex loved to tease. And thrilled to spectacles like this. *The magnificence. The beauty, the enchantment!*

Two hundred yards below the falls, a wooden bridge spanned the creek. A sign—Blue Knob Falls, with a whitewashed arrow—pointed upstream. In the other direction, visible through distant trees, a long, curving row of cottages dotted a spacious lawn.

"And you told me we were deep in the woods!"

Luke shrugged and pointed right.

Along each side of the stream, wild flowers blossomed to the water's edge. "Brother! Wild Sweet Williams! Oh, the lavender. And Jacks-in-the-Pulpit! Gosh, they're everywhere!"

The boy tilted his head and rolled his eyes as his sister plopped down on the creek bank. *What is it with girls and flowers, anyway?*

Alex sloshed for a closer peek at the hiding Jacks. Maidenhair ferns draped the moss-covered river stone, sprinkled here and there with the delicate white of Alleghany foamflowers.

She sure liked the waterfall. Guess these flowers are a bonus. But she's glopped up her shoes and caked her knees. High society girl? Hah!

Alex looked up, fishing her brother's smug silence. She wiped her brow, smearing her nose with a dab of clay.

"Putting on your rouge, sister?"

What? Alex tugged up a stone and hefted it his way, nailing Luke with a splashing bombshell.

"Hey!" Luke heaved a larger rock a foot to his sister's left.

Bonnet soaked and chin dripping, Alex glared back.

Brother! This means war!

G onna be a hot one, sir. What else for you, Master Payne?"
The old groom studied his first patron of the day, figuring the odds for a good tip at this hour. "Fill the flask 'fore you heads out?"

"No, Silas, none of your peach brandy," said Payne Harrison with a wave of his hand. "I need to get on the road."

Silas shrugged, still hopeful for a dash of silver.

Saddle Tiebreaker for me at dawn. That, Silas had done, promptly too, making sure Ernie, his stable boy, had fed and watered the horse.

Silas—he owned to no last name—epitomized the resort's high standards of service and gentility. With more than three decades as stable master, he was a beloved yet quixotic character around the luxurious mountain spa. White folks constantly nudged him for favors and quizzed him on everything from scenic trails and resort culinary favorites to local legends and the latest cabin gossip. He regarded it a matter of personal pride to meet their every request. Could he help it if he puffed up a bit when the ladies and gents marveled and thanked him?

"Nothin' else, sir?"

Payne Harrison mounted Tiebreaker and gathered the reins. He brushed his hand over his saddlebags, rubbing the hard leather bulge on the left, the stowed Colt revolver on his right.

"This Andrew Johnston..."

"You foolin' with him, Master Payne?"

"Tell me...about him."

"Well, sir, he's odd duck. Out beyond the Blue...Always..."

"How far beyond Blue Sulphur?"

Silas rolled his eyes. *Goin' way out yonder to see ole Johnston? That's some ride to wedge into this hot day.*

"Other side of Lewisburg. Up Kitchen Creek 'bout a mile after you pass the Blue. Big ole whitewashed stable in a green spread meadow all kept and rail-fenced. Nice stone house. That's Johnston's place."

Payne eyed the clear sky. "Silas, I regard you as the best judge of horseflesh in western Virginia. How good's this new speed horse of his?"

"You know 'bout him?"

"How fast, Silas?" Payne Harrison's gaze augured hard into the groom. The old Negro glanced left, then right like a sidewalk carnival barker.

"Twelve goes like the wind! Raced in April." Silas froze, his voice diving to a whisper. "Master Payne, I never saw such a horse!"

"And this Number Twelve, he's for sale?"

"Don't know 'bout that, sir. But I can tell you ole Johnston's always after the dollar. If you think you can just go up there and buy that horse, you got a hard road bump comin'."

"Thanks, Silas." Payne flipped a gleaming something to the groom.

The African snatched it like a frog on a fly. "Great Caesar's Ghost!" He brokered his best, toothy grin. "One dollar gold piece! Master Payne! My golly, I do thankee, sir!"

Silas' first patron of the morning tipped his hat. "Be back well after sundown. Wait up for me?"

"Always open, Master Payne! Glory be, thankee again!"

Payne nudged Tiebreaker into a canter as he left the stable. The stallion remained his favorite thoroughbred, a once dominant racer and still very fast over half a mile. He would never forget that spring afternoon—had it been six years?—when Jasper rode Tiebreaker to victory in the Dominion Derby. One thousand dollars in prize money! But Tiebreaker's victory in Norfolk the following summer over the legendary Red Eye was what marked Payne Harrison's arrival among Virginia horse breeders. His family's estate, Walnut Grove, ranked as one of Virginia's upcoming stables. Now, if his scouts were right, he could acquire a horse of almost mythic speed.

Despite the promise of a hot afternoon, Payne looked forward to a beautiful morning ride. Nearing the cottages along Virginia Row, he spotted a coterie of sweet, smiling matrons, friends of his mother's enjoying their early morning constitutionals.

"Good morning, Payne!" they chorused to Jane and Thomas Harrison's eldest son. Family acquaintances at the White stretched back decades.

Indeed, some of these ladies had known him as a toddler, recalling "little Paynie" and his long, curly blonde hair, rosy cheeks, and unforgettable sky-blue eyes. Older girls charged with watching him at afternoon rest, styled him *Master So Precious* or *Mister Gorgeously Cute,* making him all the more miserable when they dressed him as Cupid.

Yet his worst moments came at the hands of innocent strangers who mistook him for a little girl. Biting dolls and shouting *I'm a boy,*

"Little Paynie" battled the cheek pinchers and sweet talkers to which the big girls only cooed and giggled all the more.

Seven summers later, the apple-cheeked cherub sprouted into adolescence with unbounded energy, charging into nature and wilderness with a fascination for racing fast horses. Fishing in the Greenbrier ranked among his treasured pastimes and practice with Uncle Caleb's single shot pistol brought startling proficiency atypical of ten-year olds.

He became everyone's rapscallion. Summers conjured adventure. At age twelve, he and a cousin started down the James River on a makeshift raft. Four days later, they beached their unraveling vessel at ancient Jamestown. The local sheriff found them camping in the ruins of the old Church Tower filthy as street urchins, smoking grapevine, living off shad and catfish, and having the time of their lives. But back at Walnut Grove, Payne's voyage ended with a memorable trip to the woodshed.

Yet the oldest Harrison boy emerged unscathed from these wild emprises. Just shy of six feet, Payne had matured far beyond their expectations. Neighbors knew his word to be his bond.

Hailed across Tidewater as a superb horseman, he cut a dashing figure in the saddle, catching the eye of more than one fair admirer. Now as he approached his mother's friends, sunlight sheened his light brown hair. The notorious blonde curls of youth were long gone, but admirers relished his piercing blue eyes that so sparkled when he had a scheme afoot.

"Twenty-seven years old and not even engaged!" chortled one.

"Hush, Mattie. You shouldn't say such things," said another.

"Ladies! Do you want him to hear us?" hissed a third.

It was a common pastime, especially among the old gossips and hopeless hopefuls with their hearts all aflutter, to keep score on developing romances at the White. Sooner or later, they squawked, "Paynie" would meet his match. More than a few daughters from some of the finest families in the South had pined for his attentions.

Payne ignored these summer dalliances. He had no intention of settling down...not yet anyway. Oh, he had his share of delicious moments: the new minister's visiting younger sister from Savannah; a certain tavern keeper's daughter in Goochland County; and the young widow Turpin who kept a boardinghouse in Richmond. The first had been pure innocence, the second a most exquisite, ravishing surprise, and the third...well, no details there must ever reach his mother's ears.

Only once had danger loomed, and that the previous summer in the guise of Miss Anne Tayloe from North Carolina. For a while, her spell had worked the magic. But after two weeks, he realized her conversations finger-pointed too many references to hope chests, silverware, and child rearing.

He quelled the relationship on the Fourth of July. Never had fireworks above the White's spacious lawn proclaimed greater freedom. Miss Anne sulked for a day, regrouped the next, then recast her nets on the third, snaring a hapless Charleston banker's son at summer's end.

But that did not end the gossip.

Old biddies, meddlesome windbags. Love? A family? All in good time. No hurry for me to settle down. But if...well, if the right one comes along...

Payne mulled that possibility. Often. He just didn't feel ready for commitment. At least that's what he told himself.

All in due time...all in due time. But the right one? What does that mean? These cackling old hens...who are they to meddle in my business?

"And a good morning to you too, ladies." Payne offered a gallant sweep of his left hand, gritting out his best available smile. "Beautiful morning for a walk, is it not?" Then spurring Tiebreaker with the dash of an English cavalier, he galloped past the large oaks that lined the entrance to the White, disappearing into a swirl of dust.

ALUM ROCK HOLLOW
8 MILES WEST OF WHITE SULPHUR SPRINGS
THAT SAME MORNING

Nothin' but gold!

The tall, gaunt, bewhiskered man stared out the cabin window.

And then he had the damn gall to laugh me off and yell, 'What you'd expect Pegasus to cost?'

"Who the hell's Pegasus, anyway?" Lonnie Grinder wheeled from the window, slamming his fist onto the oak hewn table in the middle of the room.

Think ya can't be fooled with, huh Johnston? No paper, no trades? Only gold? And no goddamn Yankees?

A horse whinnied. Grinder stuck his head out the open front window and bellowed, "'Bout time, brother."

Amos Grinder, a short, stocky, barrel of a man, dismounted, tied up his horse and bumped open the front door.

"Looky here!" He stabbed a gleaming 14-inch Bowie knife into the table top with a cleaving thud. "Cuts meat like butter...bone like candle!" He slid his fingers down the handle. "Grips, too. And lots a' room fer notches."

"Give much?"

"Traded the coil's last drippin's. That short keg ya give me."

"And that other?"

"Got two gallons."

"Nah, I meant *the other*."

"Oh, that." Amos tugged a paper from his shirt pocket. "Here. Sketched 'er right up. Crept in a'fore sunrise. Twelve stalls. Plenty a' straw. Only two doors. And no locks! He's in the north one."

Lonnie snatched the paper, tucking a fresh chaw between cheek and gum. Leaning over, he slid his forefinger down his brother's new knife, meeting Amos' eager eyes with his own gaze of steel indifference. There he lingered, studying the sketch and working his cud, punctuating his silence with an occasional wad of black spittle into a gallon crock jar.

"Ain't no gold, brother," he said after some minutes, "so we go with the other. Somethin' simple."

"I'm listenin', Lonnie," said the fat man, jerking up his new knife.

"Well, we gonna rescue him."

"Don't buzz me now, Lon."

"Old Johnston be needing a new stable anyway. Ya got that ker'sene, didn't ya?"

"Ya mean...?"

"Horse like that needs to vamoose. If we just take him, then what? But if folks think old Johnston got careless and let his stable burn down, ya know...in the middle of the night, well, that's the end a' that."

"Oh, brother. I do like the way ya think."

"So...bring yer old nag?"

"Whatever for?"

"Use yer noggin, Amos! Swap before we spark. Gotta have the right number a' carcasses in the ash when folks crowd in the next morning."

"Golly, golly. Ya do figger down the details, don't ya?"

"Well, don't go carving yer first notch just yet, brother."

"Why's that?"

"Moon. Full in a few days. Gotta wait 'til it's down."

Sloe-eyed Amos Grinder nodded to his brother's wisdom, grinning eager and evil.

"So stick that ker'sene in the shed. Our speed horse ain't goin' no place just yet. 'Sides, no one's got that kind a' gold in these here mountains."

Chapter Eleven

B rother, you're in for it now!" Alex Parker gouged out a dripping glob of organic muck and with a deft fling of her right arm, slung the entire stinking mass at Luke, splattering him across the knees.

"You've ruined my pants, Alex!"

"Poor little boy, look at his britches!"

Charging his sister, Luke hit Alex at the waist, knocking her rump bottomed into the cold, ankle-deep water.

"Hellooooo there!" A man on horseback thundered across the bridge in full gallop, red bandana streaming from his neck.

Soaked, Alex scrambled to her feet. "Who was that? Do you think he saw me...like this?"

Luke pointed and smirked. His sister sloshed to the shadows beneath the bridge, peeking up through the planking as the rider reined in his horse with a loud, "Whoa, Breaker."

Some local, or a farmer.

But the elegant horse suggested otherwise. "Don't let him see me, Luke," she hissed.

"Morning, young fellow. Everything OK?"

"Ah...yes...sir." Luke's eyes danced between horseman and shivering sister. "Nice day...isn't...it?"

What's he looking at? Payne Harrison dismounted. Movement caught his eye. He stooped, leaned, and looked. The girl's shriek hit him square.

"Surely I'm not that ugly," he blurted. "Besides, trolls live under bridges. So come out of there. Let's have a look at you."

"Sir, please mind your own business. My brother and I are fishing here and we don't need your help!"

"Really? And what are we catching here this fine morning?"

"None of your concern, sir. Kindly let us be."

"Why yes, Ma'am. As you wish. But please forgive me if I ask what you're using for bait? I don't see many folks fishing mountain streams—they usually have better luck in the Greenbrier. But then what do I know? I might learn something, particularly from an enterprising angler like yourself."

Alex splashed into the daylight. "Sir, you talk too much. As for what bait we use...that's our secret. Right, Luke?"

The boy just shrugged, radiating his best what-do-I-know look.

Payne Harrison laughed out loud at the dreggy pair, but caught himself when he perceived the girl's genuine embarrassment.

"Here." He tossed down his red bandana. "Got a little bit of mountain on your face."

Alex glared, her cheeks burning in the stranger's lingering gaze. *You Southerners always grab "hospitality" to butt into other's affairs.*

"Thank you." She wiped her face in two curt, direct swipes. "I'll see you get this back...clean." *Busybody.*

"That's OK. Keep it. Use it the next time you..er..ah go fishing."

Alex gritted her teeth. *The nerve of this man...*

With a chuckle, Payne touched his hat, tipping Luke and Alex a mock salute. *Mountain kids chumming for crawfish. Oh well...*

On this June morning, Payne Harrison chased greater game. With no more thought to the two urchins splashing in the creek, he spurred his beloved Tiebreaker westward.

Robert Parker stepped from the porch of the third cottage astride Baltimore Row. *Clean air. And that sun sure feels good.*

His daughter sat on a small stool, pressing flowers into a scrapbook.

"Well Alex, what do you think?"

Alex surveyed the stretch of cabins to her right. "Quaint's the word. Nothing like Saratoga. Yet these mountains...the deep glens... the flowers...the wildness." Her face wreathed a smile. "Certainly magic here, Papa."

"Sounds like you've fallen in love with Virginia, my dear. And to think...this from such a fine Boston girl!"

Alex giggled and resumed pressing her flowers.

"Remind me to thank Henry," her father said.

T he Parkers' journey to White Sulphur Springs was a first for Alex and her family, thanks to her father's friend and business partner, Henry Latrobe of Baltimore. For years Latrobe had brought his family up to Saratoga Springs for the social season in August.

"You need to visit the White," he always insisted when they said their goodbyes. "But before the August crowds. It's glorious in those mountains."

Robert Parker always smiled, thanked Latrobe and mouthed something like, "Yes, Henry, we'll have to do that next year." But life and convenience always got in the way. Until this year.

As principal owner of the Parker Harness and Saddle Works, Robert Parker was a self-made man. The War Department's recent announcement that his company had won a large army contract for boots and accouterment boxes meant a huge boost in his business. To close the deal, Robert Parker needed to visit Washington, a perfect opportunity to piggyback a family vacation to the celebrated Virginia spa.

Emily, his devoted wife of 24 years, had sacrificed a promising career in music to marry him. She heralded from old New England stock traceable—according to her salty uncle Abner, a retired lighthouse keeper—to the *Mayflower*. If her husband's driving desire was success in industry, hers was a happy and prosperous home life for her family. For every risk Robert Parker calculated in business, she provided him with the emotional and domestic support that enhanced his prospects.

Three children blessed their marriage. Robert, Jr., the eldest, had just graduated from the United States Military Academy at West

Point. Rob had always longed to be a soldier, much as other boys dream of being a sea captain or President of the United States. Yet despite his father's best efforts to bring him into the family shoe and leather goods business, Rob had other ideas.

His sterling record at the Academy proved his point. A week earlier, his family had watched him march onto "the plains of West Point" to accept his diploma and a second lieutenancy in the artillery. With chiseled good looks and West Point polish, he carried a maturity far beyond his 22 years. Now with 30 days leave before reporting for duty at Governors Island in New York harbor, Rob welcomed the family free time in the Virginia mountains.

Alexandra was the apple of her father's eye. But she tolerated her christened name only on the most formal of occasions. Growing up, she sprouted into a thin, scrawny kid...a tomboy, friends said, who ran and scrambled with the toughest in the neighborhood. Because of her build, Rob called her "Sticks" or "Beanpole." They became the fiercest of rivals.

Rob dominated the feats of strength—the jumping, the footraces, the ball throwing. Alex excelled in riddles and word puzzles. But when Papa presented her a horse on her twelfth birthday, riding became the love of her life. Aunts and cousins exclaimed for all to hear that Alex bested Rob on horseback. Certainly by her uncles' measure, she was far more graceful.

Such words sweetened her triumphs, but in time, her rivalry with Rob only deepened her respect and admiration for her older brother. When he left for West Point, she assumed the mantle of eldest at home. And although missing Rob more than she dared admit, she devoted herself to her younger, different brother.

Luke Parker had not been expected to survive when he came into the world. The night of his birth, his father had searched in vain for a physician to attend his laboring wife. But the terrible blizzard of February 1847 blocked all roads.

Along the lane to their house, drifts measured nine feet high. Somehow, Robert Parker managed, it being a source of great pride to him that he had presided over the birth of his youngest son. When the doctor did finally make it through the wind-blown, crusted snow to check on mother and child, he congratulated the new father on his skill and common sense. But when he examined Emily, he gently informed her she could have no more children. No one was to blame he assured them both, it was just nature's way.

The baby remained weak, then sickened, lingering for days. Although only six, Alex never forgot the endless evenings her mother spent beside the crib, eyes wide at the doctors wringing their hands in the parlor, crying when she saw Papa break into tears as they told him little Luke was in God's hands now. On each of those fearful nights, she had knelt beside her bed—hearing the baby's hoarse hacks and pitiful cries downstairs—and prayed as hard as she could for God to save her little brother.

Little Luke.

She promised Heaven that if Little Luke lived, she would love her baby brother "specially hard" the rest of her life. Surely, that was quite a sacrifice, given her constant scraps with Rob. But for Little Luke, never would she make fun of him or call him silly names. And for good measure, she'd let him win every contest, be it a jump, a race, or a word puzzle.

Please God.

Alex never forgot her promise. Growing up, the two became inseparable, sharing trails and campfires, stories and puzzles. They chased novelty and adventure and while Alex was the better rider, Luke's soaring curiosity deemed him the explorer. When Papa announced the trip to the Virginia springs, both readied for a new frontier.

Until now, summer vacations meant going to Saratoga Springs in upstate New York. Arriving in late July or early August, the Parkers boarded at the upscale United States Hotel. Every day they rode, swam, and rambled about. In late afternoon, bands played waltzes, marches, and patriotic airs on the broad, sweeping lawn or serenaded passersby from one of several ornate gazebos. After dark, cotillions flourished as the elite mixing bowl for the crème of society.

Alex loved it all. The lights, the gaiety, the fun. Luke slinked off when he could, preferring the porch magicians working their tricks or spying on the spooners necking in the shadows of Lover's Lane.

The whole world it seemed came to Saratoga, whether for relaxation, business, politics, gambling, or just to take the waters. It was, so Papa said, the most famous resort in America. Now the family was at the White. It seemed adventure flourished here, too.

Yet this summer signaled change. A week before Rob's graduation, Alex had completed her own studies at the Cambridge School of Music. Demonstrating precocious talent as a child, she had started voice and piano lessons at age six, tutored first by her mother then by the best instructors in Lowell.

Absolute rebellion followed. Alex resented the two-hour indoor practice while Rob and Little Luke got to play outside. She eventually bucked all performances. That ended when Luke broke a finger and asked her for a happy song to cheer him up. Yet despite these rough, early goings, she found music came easily and when she sang, people got quiet and smiled.

By the age of twelve, Miss Alexandra Parker was a featured soloist at local weddings and soirees. For those special occasions, Emily Parker provided her daughter with a collection of fashionable dresses and exquisite evening gowns. Although hesitant at first, Alex found she liked the finery, that she felt wonderful and bright and special when she sang. And when her voice rose in song, friends and neighbors marveled not only at her music, but at the beautiful young woman she had become.

Home on summer leave after two years at West Point, Rob never forgot his first, new view of his sister. The kid he'd teased as "Sticks" was no more. By some miracle of nature, Alex had matured into a true beauty. Fresh-faced and blessed with a clear, porcelain complexion, she glowed in the emergence of young womanhood. Gone were the straight lines of the rigid "Beanpole," replaced instead with the graceful curves and full bosom of a young lady. Her luxurious, shoulder-length blond hair framed a face thoughtful and intelligent, yet still one of ready grins and delicious mischief. Her curious, deep amber eyes had always twinkled in happiness and mirrored her moods, but now her pleasures and desires reflected an awareness of her own femininity. No longer the tomboy, Alex Parker preferred holding teacups to frogs, throwing parties instead of rocks, and baking cherry tarts instead of mud pies. She still loved to explore and cherished adventures with Luke—the natural world remained a beautiful, enchanting place—but she also knew beauty, majesty, and happiness could come from within.

"She has a clear, remarkable, melodic voice," declared one teacher to her mother soon after Alex's sixteenth birthday. But to fully develop her talents—to excel—Alex needed professional training. The nearby Cambridge School of Music offered an extensive program perfectly suited to her talents, she suggested.

Alex spent the next two years at Cambridge honing her voice and stage presence, learning more piano and composition theory, and acquiring teaching techniques. In the winter months before graduation, she considered her options. Professor Willard Lancaster, headmaster of the Lancaster Female Academy in Baltimore and an old school chum of her father's, offered the best possibility. He had an opening for a voice and piano instructor commencing with the Fall term. "Write him," said Robert Parker, "and see what he has to say."

Alex hesitated only to get prodded by her father again. She wrote the next day. A favorable reply arrived a week later.

"Yes, Miss Parker, we do indeed have an open position in the music department," replied Lancaster, "and I invite you to Baltimore for an interview and audition. Kindly advise."

After Rob's graduation, the Parkers traveled to Philadelphia, then on to Baltimore. Professor Lancaster and his registrar and social director, Mrs. Eleanor O'Dell, interviewed and auditioned Alex. "You have such a marvelous voice, my dear," gushed Mrs. O'Dell in her rich Georgia accent after hearing Alex sing *The Grace to Which Thou Art*. Our young ladies will just love you!" Professor Lancaster concurred and tendered Alex a position.

Thrilled at the opportunity, but unsure about going so far from home, Alex deliberated a week before accepting. Her duties would commence the first day of September. In the meantime, she had the entire summer to relax, first in the Virginia mountains, then with her friends at Saratoga during the August high season.

A lex placed the last wild violets carefully onto the flat paper and pressed shut her flower book. *I wonder what Luke'll discover today.*

Her parents would never forget the sight of their muddy only daughter sauntering across the lawn of the White clutching wild flowers.

"Whatever in the world happened to you?" Emily Parker had asked as Alex marched up, kissed them both on the cheek and plopped down on the porch steps dripping mountain and stream.

"Oh Papa, you must see what Luke found!"

"And come back looking like you? I don't think so, daughter!"

"But there's nothing like it at Saratoga!"

"I'm sure...and I better not see anything like what sits before me when we're there in August."

Alex wiped the wet, blond tangles from her face and threw Robert Parker her broadest grin.

To which her father melted.

For that is what he and his wife lived for...the love and affection of their family. *The special moments.* With Rob set to begin his career in the Army, with Alex headed for a teaching post in Baltimore, and Luke full of life exploring everything, what more contentment could parents ask for?

Certainly the setting at the White was grand enough. Unlike Saratoga's hustle and bustle which twirled up and down the long porch of the United States Hotel and strutted across the lobby of old Gideon Putnam's Union Hall, spilling out along Broadway and into Congress Park, the meadows and lawns of the White projected a pastoral peace and quiet. *Latrobe was right; nature abounds in unbridled glory here.*

Yet like Saratoga, the White featured grand music on the lawn. Etiquette-minded matrons sponsored nightly cotillions in the Main Ball Room while eager young men sought the attentions of bare-shouldered belles...or failing in that...dicy games of chance among themselves in private rooms. Invalids came from all over seeking the promise of Hygiea with baths and promiscuous consumption of mineral-rich spring water. Gentlemen at the White, just like in New York, clustered in animated conversations under shade trees and along rock-lined paths, discussing everything from national politics and military affairs to handsome women and hot weather. And from every vantage, all could witness the fashion-conscious promenade of the rich and famous.

For Alex, this seemingly idyllic place had but one flaw: Southerners often traveled with extended family—uncles, aunts, cousins...and servants.

Slaves.

Servile Negroes were everywhere at the White. For the first time in her life, Alex Parker confronted the realities of the South's "peculiar institution."

Abolitionist sentiment flourished in the North. In Massachusetts, anti-slavery groups kept up a steady condemnation of the slaveholding South. Sentiments flared as activists described whippings for runaways, breakups of families, and the moral degradation rotting all touched by such depravity.

Who could possibly desire to own another human being?

Alex had posed that very question to Rob after hearing an abolitionist vent his rage on human bondage one evening at church. Neither had ever been this close to it. Yet while Alex could never condone the South's peculiar institution, she found herself accepting the status quo.

This is the way it is.

Each morning in the shade of the hotel veranda or along the front porches of cottage row, she encountered the mammies and black nurses tending the children of their masters.

"It's one giant baby show," she exclaimed to her mother the second morning they were there, after watching dozens of darkie women entertain, groom, console, scold, feed, or restrain the wild children entrusted to their care. Such scenes were an entrenched part of the ambience of the White. Such scenes unsettled Miss Alexandra Margaret Parker of Lowell, Massachusetts.

Chapter Twelve

Of all the resorts in the Virginia mountains, White Sulphur Springs enjoyed the highest acclaim. In summer, the well-to-do flocked to the spa, taking the waters, "the cure" as they called it. Doc Morrissett was not so quick to endorse such panacean attributes to the White's aquifer, admitting only that, "Well, Colonel, I reckon imbibing the stuff can't hurt."

Still, the Harrisons of Walnut Grove—always an extended entourage of cousins, aunts, uncles, friends, and servants—journeyed west from Richmond each August. Maybe this year, Jane Harrison prayed, the waters would alleviate her husband's gout.

Payne sympathized with his father's suffering, too. When the attacks raged, Colonel Harrison could not even stand a bed sheet covering his swollen, inflamed toes. Yet ten summers of drinking sulphur water laced with calcium, lithium or whatever, brought little relief. Could it be that most guests visited the White for reasons more social than medicinal?

Each season, prominent Southern families traveled the mountain roads to indulge the spa's ambiance. Planters, politicians, and even presidents vacationed here, not only to escape the summer swelter of the coastal plain, but to avoid the sudden outbreaks of cholera and yellow fever that could devastate such port cities as Norfolk, New Orleans, Savannah, and Charleston.

But this summer, business brought Payne Harrison to the White. Business that could not wait for the family's annual August sojourn.

Payne leaned forward and patted Tiebreaker. *You're still my champion, fella.*

Miles of road stretched ahead. Through the mountain gap and beyond the crossing of the Greenbrier River lay Lewisburg astride the great Greenbrier savannah, a fertile, sweeping grass valley cradled in the Appalachians.

Horse and rider entered Lewisburg at noon and took lunch at Buffalo Run Tavern. When Payne asked directions to Blue Sulphur, the tavern keeper—a bearded, burly fellow everyone called Buck—told him the spring was closed. When Payne mentioned Andrew Johnston, Buck's eyes narrowed on his dusty, road-worn customer. "What you want with that old son-of-a-bitch?"

Payne raised his mug and mumbled something about owing money.

Buck spit at the corner cuspidor, missing. He dabbed his chin, smearing the remnants of drooled tobacco gravy on a filthy rag. "Old bastard got you too, huh? Well, when you see him, tell him half this town lost 'gainst his goddamned nag last month. Never saw a horse run like that. Bustin' out last...then blazin' to first down the stretch. Somethin' wasn't right there!"

Buck's lunch patron offered only a weak smile, quietly taking another sip from his mug.

D rat this road dust. Payne wiped the sweat and grime from his brow. *So this is Blue Sulphur.*

Lush green meadows squared the abandoned resort on either side of the road. A tumbled-down, white-columned structure resembling a Grecian temple covered the most prominent spring. "Limestone," Payne murmured, eyeing the rocky outcrops edging the fields. *Perfect for blood horses.*

He looped Tiebreaker's reins over a locust post in the leaning fence skirting the road and pushed his canteen into the spring's flowing spillway. *Gawd! Tastes like gunmetal! Maybe I should have gotten Silas' peach brandy.*

A twenty minute ride brought him to an arching stone bridge. Beyond, across a rolling meadow dotted in dandelions, stood a whitewashed board and batten barn. Five horses grazed the shade of three towering oaks. A dapple-gray gelding caught Payne's eye. He guided Tiebreaker through the gate, then up a long lane into the yard of a Hessian stone manor house. A man—balding under hat, but mustachioed—emerged from an open door shed.

"Been on the road a while there, young fellow?"

"A ways." Payne dismounted. "Hot day. Nice shade here."

"Go right ahead. Make yourself comfortable. J. W., get our traveling friend here something cool from the house."

A tall, angular, younger man stepped from the shed, nodded to Payne and walked toward the rear of the house. In two minutes he was back with a glass of rye whiskey on ice.

"Still got a bit of January in there. Precious stuff now. But with folks coming off the road..." The old man took off his hat and scratched his bald head. The lily white pate contrasted with the wrinkled brown of his neck and face. "Reckon you be Harrison?"

"I see my note got through."

"Did." Andrew Johnston extended his hand in welcome. "This here's my boy, J. W. Hope you're partial on the "water." Comes from deep in the limestone out here. Good for the livestock. 'Specially horses."

"'Specially race horses." *He's sharp, all right.*

"Fact. Guess you wanna see?"

Johnston and J. W. led Payne through a gate, across the field, and into the stable. The friendly dapple-gray ambled over, curious.

Ahh. Here's a good riding horse. Probably a three-year old. Broad forehead. Alert eyes. Deep chest, short back, and look at those strong haunches. And energy to spare given his nervous, springy walk.

"Jeff Davis catches your eye? Fine colt, Eagle stock."

"Selling?"

"No, sir," said J. W., in a tone that settled the matter.

Andrew Johnston kept a dozen or so horses, half of them bloods, but Payne had ridden all this way to see only one. Months earlier, stable talk had reached him of a fast horse foaled somewhere in western Virginia. Such tales routinely buzzed betting lines and tack rooms, burnished by gamblers and speculators, and stoked with all manner of wild claims. But contacts in the Shenandoah Valley confirmed an unbeaten yearling out in the Alleghanies, undefeated in four races six to eight furlongs. The spring runnings—local events on rough grass—bore out the animal's raw speed. Known only as a number, the thoroughbred had outclassed all comers—and unsuspecting bettors—in every race. Word on his exploits was spreading east. Fast. Payne knew he must find this animal before the larger, richer stables went looking.

He had not a moment to lose. Rueben Taliaferro, Virginia's premier horse breeder over in Essex County, had arrived at the White the day before.

"I know 'ole Toliver's out here sniffin'," warned old Silas, "said he's gonna buy him no matter what, and get him in the Dominion Derby in August."

Payne enjoyed one advantage. His contacts in western Virginia—with a little money greased in the right palms—had pinpointed the owner.

The owner would sell, they said, but Johnston demanded payment in gold. And one other thing: no Yankees need come 'round!

Johnson unlatched the stable door. "You're not from 'round here."

"Chesterfield County, just outside Richmond."

"Tobacco country, ain't it?"

"Some, yes sir. But around Midlothian where I'm from, it's all about coal. Dangerous, dirty work...yet come Saturday in the spring, folks hit the track, especially those Welsh and Scottish miners."

"Course." Johnston studied his guest. "Folks in these parts 'preciate good horseflesh, too. Why, take this fellow. He's entertained quite a few 'round here recently."

Johnston paused in front of the stable's last stall. An oval wooden sign incised with the number "12" hung from the rafters. A deep chestnut stallion—muscled at 16 hands plus—stood in the corner tossing his mane in cautious regard of his visitors. A star burst of white painted his forehead.

"I hear he's emptied a few wallets. Covered the mile under one fifty."

"Yep. He'll go faster...if given some real competition." Johnston's smile faded. "Want him bad, don't you?"

Am I that transparent? Four different agents had clocked this colt, seeing him beat all challengers. His times over the mile defied reason: twice at 1:51, once at 1:48, and the last time out, a stunning 1:46.
Unbelievable for tracks out here. Few horses can run that anywhere.

With proper training and diet, especially in the Virginia tidewater, plus moderate winters and the prospect of more challenging races on better tracks, Number Twelve possessed enormous potential.

"If you mean to sell him...I'm interested."

"So you're from down Richmond way?"

"South side of the James."

"And you know how I want my money?" Johnston spoke in a sudden hush. He'd heard of this Payne Harrison and his lust for fast horses. That being so, he told himself, 'twas only a matter of time before young Mr. Harrison rode through his front gate. Others had already scrambled to buy. Two prospects had met his price, but neither had put gold on the table. This young fellow had the wherewithal to do just that. The Harrisons of Walnut Grove, he'd learned, had means.

"I heard the horse...names his own price. Twelve...twelve hundred."

"But in gold, boy."

Payne drew a deep breath, turned and walked to the edge of the stall. Jeff Davis ambled up to the rear of Number Twelve's stall. He whinnied and both animals nuzzled. *Odd for a gelding. Just not for sale.*

Yet the thoroughbred was. But twelve hundred in gold? Never had he paid half that for any horse.

Am I crazy?

"I want a week to work him at the White, on their track...in their stables. If I decide to bring him back, you keep a hundred."

He's got gold! The owner pawed for a curry comb.

"OK, but J. W. goes with you."

"Fair enough." Payne unlaced the heavy leather sack in his saddle bag and reached inside, counting out sixty $20 gold pieces, arranging them on a stable chair in twelve stacks of five each. "Bill of Sale?"

"Ah..yes...of course. Ah...J. W., tend to...the coins."

Seller and buyer stepped outside the stable and started toward the stone house. At his walnut plantation desk, Andrew Johnston scratched out a receipt for the finest thoroughbred he would ever own, signed it SOLD, and handed the paper to Payne Harrison.

"He's...everything...everything you could hope for."

"We shall see." Payne turned for the door, but stopped. "One question?"

The older man looked up, quizzical.

"Why gold?"

All the color left Andrew Johnston's cheeks. Facing Payne dead on, eyes narrowed, he nodded toward the north window.

"'Cause trouble's coming."

Chapter Thirteen

The horse showed extraordinary promise.

J. W.'s suggestions on Number Twelve's mannerisms, feeding habits, and saddle adjustments, even grooming likes and dislikes, proved invaluable. Using a local jockey Silas recommended, Payne timed the horse over five furlongs on three separate days. With sparing use of the whip, the rider pushed the colt to progressively better times on the White's small riding track, the best a stunning 62 seconds. Said Silas at week's end, "He don't belong back here in these hills."

Payne agreed. During the week's evaluation, he had resisted the urge to ride the horse himself. But now as J. W. prepared to depart, Payne decided to accompany him on Number Twelve—at least to the Greenbrier River crossing.

"Spare the spurs," said J. W., as they trotted out the White's stately entrance. "Just let him run."

Payne nodded. *OK, fella! Let's see what you can do!*

Hearing his new master's low whistle, Twelve broke into a gallop, quickly leaving Jeff Davis behind. Payne leaned over the horse's withers, his legs absorbing the surging, muscled rhythm of the animal beneath him, his torso angled as if pounding out a cavalry charge, his hair fingering in the wind. *Feel his acceleration!*

After three hundred yards, he tugged the reins. *No sense risking a stone bruise out here.* "Good boy. Now to get you home."

"Perhaps we shall meet again," said J. W. at the planked-over Greenbrier Bridge. "I'll be following Twelve's coming and goings. And bettin' on him if I've a hankering."

"A safe wager, friend. By the way, if you change your mind about..."

"Jeff Davis? Not likely. You got the speed horse, but Jeff commands a certain...presence." The two looked on as the dapple-gray nuzzled Number Twelve who nickered and tossed his mane.

"Take care of him. You'll never see another."

Payne rubbed the stallion's muscled right shoulder. "I know," he whispered, touching his cap as J. W. started across the bridge.

As a diversion on the way back, Payne turned aside from the main road. The morning seemed perfect for a ride along the scenic woodland trail that paralleled Howard's Creek. This roaring mountain stream channeled all the resort's spring waters into the Greenbrier. Silas had recommended this bridle path on a number of occasions, but Payne never seemed to find the time. Ahead, tall pines shadowed a forest floored in blooming wild flowers, ferns, and moss-covered rocks. *Ahhh...in the solitude of these mountain wilds... aboard this magnificent stallion...*

He smiled. Owning Twelve brought welcomed, happy challenges. The horse's acceleration at the bell, the way he carried his speed into the rail, and his extraordinary drive for the finish. The perfect horse?

Payne recalled his father's words the morning Tiebreaker won the Virginia Derby. *No matter win or lose, don't ever shame the family. This racing business is full of gamblers and low-toned rowdies. Yet if this be the path you choose, I expect nothing but honor brought to this house.*

Thomas Harrison had eyed his oldest son hard in the silence that followed...then leaned over and whispered, "I did put $400 on him today!"

But now his father was ill. His florid complexion, expansive girth, and swollen ankles bespoke more problems than gout. And Doc Morrissett knew it would take more than spring water to alleviate the Colonel's increasing shortness of breath and lack of stamina. Already Colonel Harrison had turned over the day-to-day management of Walnut Grove to his sons. Tobacco, wheat, and peanuts...

plus cattle, pigs, and sheep...added to half ownership in the Swift Creek Coal Mine far exceeded his slipping stamina.

None of these worries were new, but his father's health had become a growing concern. What would his mother do if something happened to her husband? Jane Harrison—at least outwardly—had other concerns.

"When will a fine young woman grace Walnut Grove?" she would ask, eyes twinkling. "You'll have your pick of the belles this season...again!"

He winced at that. Memories of the charming Miss Tayloe still loomed, closer, warmer than he wished. He would never forget her alluring smile from the other side of the White's Main Ballroom.

Was I in love?

He had no sure answer, but he welcomed the enormous relief once he'd disentangled from her fan-fluttering attentions.

Or was it intentions?! Better to let that Charleston banker's son have her. I don't need to be saddled with a horse...and a wife. Not yet anyway.

Payne guided Twelve along the winding trail high above the mountain stream. *What did old Johnston mean anyway? What troubles were coming?*

"Hey there, mister!"

A tall, thin, bewhiskered man stepped out of the brush and blocked the path, cradling a shotgun on his right arm.

"Goin' somewhere?"

Payne pointed up the path.

"Don't think so...this here's private prop'ty."

"This trail goes to the White. Everybody uses it."

"Hell they do! Now git off that horse!" He leveled his shotgun at Payne.

"Easy now. I don't think you understand..."

"What 'bout this here don't you understand?" The man cocked his weapon and took a step forward. "Now git down off that god-damned horse and start back that goddamned trail iffen ya know what's good for ya."

The one day I didn't bring my revolver!

"And my horse?"

"Forfeited! It's yer fine for trespassin'. Now ya best make tracks. This buckshot ain't gonna stay all neat and tidy in my gun barrel much longer." The tall man swept the shotgun up the path. "Git!"

Payne burned to challenge him, but the horse thief's firepower dictated otherwise. He backed away two steps.

"And don't try nothin' fancy down the trail," the man yelled, wiggling the barrel. "Touches off kinda easy, boy. I wouldn't..."

THUNK! The man pitched forward, sprawling motionless across the trail. His eyes bulged, socketed in surprise.

A face, not a day past fifteen, poked out from behind a large pine. "Didn't want to hurt him, mister. Honest. But he had that gun on you."

Payne ran to the downed man and grabbed the shotgun. "You're... you're that boy fishing in the creek! How'd you do that?"

"Just flat rocked him, sir." The youngster pulled another stone from his pants pocket and zipped it sidearm through the trees, clipping a branch. "See?" The lad sounded almost apologetic.

Payne exhaled in deep relief, trying to fathom this bizarre afternoon with a would-be horse thief thwarted by a boy who could fling a rock with the accuracy of a bullet, both materializing out of a silent forest.

"Lonnie! Lonnie!" The screeching came from the woods beyond the downed man. "Ya bastards, ya killed my brother! Both of ya sons a'bitches get yer hands up! And throw down that shotgun."

Payne darted his eyes into the thick brush bordering the trail.

"Didn't ya hear me? Drop that goddamned gun! 'Afore I drop you!"

I can't shoot what I can't see. Dammit. Where is he?

With no choice, Payne put down the shotgun. A short, fat, balding man, his face badly pocked with old acne, puffed up behind him brandishing a two-foot-long butcher knife.

"I should've cut ya clean just now, ya son-of-a-bitch, 'cept I wanted a better look at that blood horse. What the hell," he roared, "let's give Old Silver a little taste of the red anyway!"

He jabbed at Payne, slicing his left arm. Payne lurched backwards, losing his balance, and stumbled down the creek bank.

Grabbing the dropped shotgun by the barrel with his other hand, the fat man charged the boy. "As for you, ya little Yankee bastard..."

He slammed the boy full in the chest with the weapon, doubling him in pain. The youth reeled, gasping for air. The fat man swung again, but lost his one-handed grip on the shotgun and sent it sailing into the brush. Mad with rage, he slashed at the boy, forcing the frantic, struggling lad out on a large stone cliff twenty feet above the stream.

"Ya killed my brother. Now I'm gonna dice ya for the buzzards."

"Like hell you are," shouted Payne, blood running down his elbow. "Drop that knife! Now!" Having scrambled to get the shotgun from the brush, Payne leveled it at the fat man.

"Go 'head. Pull the trigger, ya bastard. And hit us both!" The fat man turned and swiped at the lad again, forcing the boy closer to the edge. The youth kicked back, nailing him on the left shin. The man bellowed, but kept swinging. Frantic to dodge the blade, the boy lost his footing and tumbled backwards, disappearing with a resounding splash into the deep, fast moving water!

"Ain't gonna be no witnesses, either!" He turned on Payne and threw the knife, his face gnarled in crimson.

Clutching the shotgun, Payne lurched to one side but lost his balance and smacked the ground.

BOOM!

The fat man vanished in the billowing smoke.

Payne ran to the rock's edge and pulled off his boots. The youth bobbed twenty yards out, limp on the surface.

Gotta go now!

The cold, deep mountain stream shocked, then seized his breath. Frantic, Payne side-stroked with his good arm.

Faster, faster! Dammit! Where is he?

He pulled up—treading—desperate to catch any glimpse of the boy. *If he gets pulled to the cascades... There! A glint of white!*

Kicking hard, he battled toward the face-down lad, grabbing him by the shirt, turning him face-up, then digging for shore. But the boy's dead weight tugged him deeper.

Then river rock bumped his feet. Gasping, heart pounding, Payne dragged the limp boy to a sandy spot and laid him level. An ugly bruise colored the lad's left cheek. *Come on, breathe! Get some air in those lungs!*

Although untended, Number Twelve had remained close. Payne retrieved a blanket and small flask from his saddle bag.

"Don't die on me!" he yelled.

On cue, the boy gasped, rolled his head to one side and spit up water. Trying to sit, he choked on more drool and fell back to the sand, coughing.

"You're going to be OK! Just relax. And breathe for me. Nobody's going to hurt you now."

The boy looked first to Payne, then darted his glance to the brush. He hacked again, clearing up more phlegm. Then tried to sit, leaning on Payne who clapped him on the back. "You gave me quite a scare there!"

He tried to speak, but Payne motioned for silence, glancing up the creek bank. "Get your breath. Dizzy?"

The lad shook his head.

"Can you sit like this for a minute?"

"Uh huh."

Payne opened his flask. *Surely, one swig won't hurt.* "Here."

"What is it, mister?"

"Some of grandma's home cough remedy. Good stuff, so you only need a taste. What's your name, kid?"

"Luke." The boy put the flask to his lips, made a face, and spit. "Gosh, mister, this is awful!"

"Well, don't tell grandma. Nice and easy now."

Luke forced it down, then hawked up the aftertaste.

"Ever ridden a real racehorse?"

"No, sir." The boy glanced at Number Twelve.

"Luke, we need to go. And please call me Payne. We met that day on the bridge...you and your sister..."

"Him and all the other Yankee trash that keeps comin' down here, messin' with us!"

As Payne turned, the fat man stepped out from behind a tree, dripping wet. A torn shirt sleeve hung from his left arm. Blood penciled down his forehead and dripped off his nose.

"Lousy shot, horse man. And the Yank there don't show much 'spect to his betters. Seems you both be needin' a little lesson in manners."

"Get behind me, Luke," Payne hissed.

"Old Shine here can carve up any smart-ass I find trespassin' 'long this creek. Then I just sling his guts to the buzzards." The fat man cackled and flashed another butcher knife. "Still got questions, pardner? Let's see who minds their manners now!"

"Sorry," yelled the boy, whipping his right arm into a blur, unleashing another stone that nailed the fat man square in the right jaw, dropping him like his brother.

"Good Lord, Luke! How'd you do that?"

The boy smiled sheepishly. "Skipping stones, I reckon. I can put 'em just about anywhere I want. Hard, too."

"That's incredible!"

"Well, I'm not as good as Alex."

"Whatever you say. Remind me never to get you mad at me. Still, we better get you to a doctor."

"But I didn't mean to kill him! I didn't..."

"Don't worry about that. This was self defense. Besides, I think they're just out cold. Feel like riding, Luke?"

"Yeah...now that I have my breath. But your arm?"

"Only a nasty scratch. Still, we best get the law down here."

Chapter Fourteen

They're gone?"

"Yup. No blood either." Sheriff John Pendergast dabbed the sweat from his brow and lifted his glass. "Join me, Harrison?"

"Look. That tall fellow—Grinder—I saw him nailed stone cold."

"Probably stone cold drunk. He and his brother Amos love samplin'. How 'bout you?"

"Sheriff, he meant to steal my horse. They tried to kill me and damned near succeeded with the boy!" Pendergast took another sip, avoiding Payne Harrison's icy stare.

"Look, there's nothing more I can do. Them Grinders...live up in Alum Hollow, make a little corn likker, probably steal a few hogs and chickens and whatever else's not tied down...but damned hard to catch. Even if I did bring them boys in, it'd be your word 'gainst theirs. And from what I hear, they got the worst of it."

Sheriff John Pendergast chomped brick-red cheeks and waddle-walked pants suspendered to a six-foot belt. He frequented the White's post office several times a week, the boisterous, friendly icon of local law and order to all guests. But staff knew him as a besotted incompetent who abused the spa's complimentary libation policy for officers of the law.

Payne pointed to Luke Parker sitting on a barrel in the front porch's shade, pressing a wet towel to his swollen cheek.

"That boy could be dead in the Greenbrier! I need to get him to a doctor. And you're telling me there's nothing you can do?"

"Let it go." Pendergast's pained, pudgy mug betrayed a man who wanted no part of the Grinders. In a week or so, Harrison and this bruised boy from up North would be gone, both on their way home... far from the vengeful Lonnie Grinder and his crazy fat brother Amos. *I don't want no trouble. Don't this fellow understand?*

"Let it go?" Payne whirled toward the door. "Fine! But know that next time I'll be better prepared!"

With his good arm, Payne mounted Number Twelve and pulled Luke up behind him. "Nice and slow, fella," he murmured, "almost home." His arm throbbed, but he needed to get the boy back to his parents. He guided Twelve up the tree-canopied roadway toward the cottages.

"Luke! There you are!" A young woman waved from a nearby gazebo, then broke into a run.

"Here comes trouble!" groaned Luke.

Payne dismounted, agony stabbing his injured arm as he let go of the pommel. "Here," he said, offering the boy his good hand and shoulder.

"Luke!" the woman gasped. "Your face! You're hurt! Let me see!"

"I'm fine...it's nothing." Luke nodded at Payne, "Thanks to him."

The woman turned, her eyes searching.

"Payne Harrison, Ma'am. An altercation on the trail with a few locals. Sheriff's on it." *Have I seen you before?*

Luke ditched all talk of flat-rocking the Grinders, saying only that Payne had pulled him from Howard's Creek during the scrap.

The silly girl under the bridge? No way. Must be her older sister.

But Alex recognized her brother's rescuer at once, tucking a strand of hair, then another behind her ear. *I'll die if he recognizes me! But his shirt's cut and all caked in blood.*

"We must have your wounds tended!"

"I'll be fine, Ma'am." *Poised, mature...unlike that Alex, I think her name was. This sister...I don't think she gave her name.*

"But, thank you just the same, ah..er..Miss...ah," said Payne. "It's only a cut. Wanted to get Luke back safe and sound."

"I'm Luke's sister. Luke, you know Papa will want a full accounting." *And he speaks in that Southern drawl...without sounding snooty.*

In Payne Harrison, Alex realized things were, well...she couldn't quite put her finger on it. He projected some...some intangible she didn't recognize...something clever yet concealed. He puzzled her. And troubled her. Yet marched with no swagger. And projected no allegiances. Might she corral this *something* in his intense blue eyes... and confident air? Perhaps. In time. But his appeal, she already knew, carried unknown challenges.

No matter! He hasn't recognized me. And he risked his life to save little Luke.

W e are deeply in your debt, Mr. Harrison," said Robert Parker after Luke's sanitized retelling of events along Howard's Creek. "Kindly have a seat here on the porch. Rob, my oldest son has gone for Dr. Myers."

"May we offer you something?" asked Emily Parker, putting down her embroidery.

Before Payne could reply, Alex appeared in the doorway. Three glasses topped a small tray; mint juleps for Payne and her father, lemonade for Luke.

"Thank you, Ma'am," his eyes locking to hers.

"These men...they've not been caught?"

"No, Mr. Parker. This Sheriff Pendergast wants me to drop the matter. Says nothing'll come of it...says it's their word on mine."

Robert Parker faced into the great oaks bordering the White, his hands pressed knuckle-white against the rail.

"In a few days Mr. Harrison, we'll be headed back to Massachusetts... to Yankeeland as you call it...and this all ends. Perhaps that's for the best."

"No! This can't..."

"Mr. Harrison don't you see there's really nothing to be gained here. You and I both recognize the regional tensions tearing the heart out of our country. I'm from up North; these Grinders are locals. Sheriff's right. How do you think a jury would decide?"

"With all due respect, sir, I believe justice would be served. The only reason it's failed you is this sheriff's...a coward and a drunk."

"Perhaps, but we're still at a disadvantage down here given the current political climate."

Payne knew what Robert Parker meant. He'd read the papers, heard the talk. A verbal war engulfed the nation. Northern abolitionists decried slavery and damned all masters. Southern firebrands shouted back that such meddlers best "mind their own business" or else, threatening secession. A divisive, regional rivalry—a cancer called sectionalism—threatened the American Union. John Brown's raid on Harper's Ferry the previous fall had splashed blood aplenty into the debate. Now a watershed Presidential election loomed.

"Dr. Myers's waiting in his cabin, Papa." Rob Parker jumped over the porch rail at Payne's feet. "Hell of a scrap, huh? Wish I'd been there."

"We're going to let it go, Rob. Mr. Harrison and I were just discussing the...ah...realities down here."

"Let it go? Papa, at the Academy..."

"We're not at the Academy, Rob."

The newly-minted second lieutenant pounded the rail. "Then these Southern scum better never cross my path!"

"Robert!" Emily Parker turned to her guest. "Mr. Harrison, my son means no offense."

"None taken, Ma'am. In fact, Rob, I'd join you anytime!"

"We wish you would." Emily Parker smiled and nodded to her husband.

"What my wife's really trying to say is we'd be honored if you'd join our table at the Grand Ball tonight?" Robert Parker winked and extended his hand. "Call it, 'in the name of good North-South relations.'"

"Certainly a workable diplomacy." Payne turned to Alex, "And my compliments for the mint julep, Ma'am." *What a contrast to her sister. Probably still picking wildflowers.*

"My pleasure, sir." *Hope he asks me to dance.*

"All right, Luke. Let's get our war wounds tended."

Alex stepped to the edge of the porch, watching this Virginian and her brother trudge down Baltimore Row toward Dr. Myers' cabin.

"Mother..."

"Yes, my dear," said Emily Parker, her eyes back to guiding stitches, "I noticed him, too."

P ayne winced more than once as Randolph Myers, MD, washed, then sewed up his knife-sliced arm. "Should be sore for a week or so...but keep it clean. Make sure the bandage and lint are changed every day. If you're lucky, you'll only get a handsome scar. By the way, still going to the ball tonight?"

"I have an invite." Payne winked at Luke.

"He wants to dance with Alex," grinned the boy.

"Oh, I see! Well, Mr. Harrison, Miss Alexandra makes a fine partner. Danced with her myself the other evening. I'll wager she has half a dozen jealous suitors by now. Am I not right, Luke?"

"How would I know?" Luke's swollen cheek had ripened into a mashed, oozing peach.

The notion of this balding, sixty-year-old physician partnered with the rag-a-muffin bridge girl challenged Payne's imagination. *And what's with Luke? No way I'm squiring his brat sister tonight with his older one waiting in the wings.*

"So you want to match me with Alex, huh, Luke?"

"Sure! She doesn't have a dance partner."

Why am I not surprised? "Well, no one's properly introduced us... so I can hardly...Perhaps your older sister?"

"You mean..." Luke stopped, realizing. "Ah, OK...OK. Just get to our table before the belles come in."

"Course if you think Miss Alex would rather be collecting flowers, I'll understand. Or is it lizards today?"

"Lizards? Miss Alexandra?" Dr. Myers rolled his eyes. "Really, Luke!"

The boy edged toward the cottage door. "AAhhhmmmm...really need to get going, Dr. Myers. Thanks."

"Tell your mother I said you're fine." He waved as Luke scampered across the green. "One intrepid shiner. Wish I had his energy."

"Indeed."

"As for you, Mr. Harrison, go easy this evening. Perhaps a waltz or two. Arm's going to talk to you. Probably show some laudable pus in a day or so."

"Could've been worse, Doc."

Randolph Myers extended his hand as his patient started for the door. "You know, Miss Alex and all, I envy you."

For decades, dashing young men had embraced the summertime social amenities of White Sulphur Springs. With a wink, Latrobe had mentioned this to Robert Parker, hinting that Miss Alex might well enjoy a reign during "the White's high season." The spa abounded with beaux, he said, from sons of plantation owners and industry captains down to penniless fortune hunters and dissipated wastrels. Alex could have her pick.

Robert Parker dismissed the notion. His daughter, he informed Latrobe, was focused on her career—teaching music in Baltimore. Alex had no interest in a serious romance. Besides, the social opportunities at the White could hardly match those Saratoga flaunted.

But Henry Latrobe wasn't finished. The White, he told his friend, hosted far more members of the military than Saratoga. Handsome men in uniform flourished at the Virginia spa, whether wagering about the bowling green, jawing politics on the Main Hotel's sedate veranda, or simply "taking the waters." For the Belles of the White, military etiquette packaged around silver-inlaid presentation swords and gold braid girded marvelous magic.

And military contracts are good business.

Robert Parker glared. Given his Puritan roots, he'd brook no party to that kind of talk. As for Alex, "Remember, Latrobe, West Point's already busied our household in brass buttons and spit-polished boots. My daughter can fend for herself."

Perhaps. Yet after three days, his only daughter remained to herself. Here in the Virginia mountains, Alex sensed differences. Southern girls returned her older brother's greeting with sweet smiles and soft words intoned in those regional accents. But all iced into silence when she passed. Uncertain, she withdrew, so much so that when a young man's tip of the hat or friendly "Good morning" came her way she managed but a weak, "And to you too, sir," followed by a wordless blush if the gentlemen lingered. That first week she went to dinner on the arm of her older brother. At least she had an escort. She was certain that as a Northern newcomer to the White—one matron had pointed in her direction and loudly branded her a "Yankee inter-loper"—few gentlemen callers would venture the void to make her acquaintance.

But surprises awaited. Alex was of age now, the magic ninteen, unmarried...and unattached. A belle! Such creatures thrived at the White. And if a belle was educated, polished...and endowed with love's smiling fortunes, she might—just might—be declared "a reigning belle."

As convention stood in such matters, a sweet girl but not nec-essarily a pretty one could find friends, partake of the waters, and perhaps *improve*. If Fate had been harder and left the damsel empty of personal charm and external beauty...well she needn't fling herself into the Greenbrier, but surely, the White was no place for her. Just ask the jury of knitting and gossipy mothers rump seated on the hotel shade porches. They saw all and judged accordingly.

Down among the cabins of Bachelor Row, rich planters' sons up from Charleston and Savannah and New Orleans had already spotted the stunning, unknown blonde on the arm of the Army officer. Heads turned. *Who's that? Where's she from? Where's she staying?*

All knew whom to ask...letting Silas exploit another silver mine.

"Mass'choosetts...name's Parker. Lodgin' down on Baltimore Row. Give me a day. I'll get more."

Every potential suitor knew the evening cotillion offered the best opportunity. These led dances with their dignified evolutions and square figures offered facilitated introductions. The second lieuten-ant, said Silas, was only a brother. And Alex loved the attention, accepted their invitations to dance, and by the second Saturday had the boys dangling.

What better way to spend a month of summer, a fanciful few weeks of fun and play...than to enjoy early morning explorations with

Luke, greet the welcomed attentions of more than a few gentlemen callers in the afternoon, and reciprocate the gracious introductions to Southern gentility in the evening? Belledom suited Alex Parker to a tee! What could possibly complicate this idyll?

Chapter Fifteen

D r. Myers' words still echoed when Payne entered the White's formal dining room that evening. Attired in a black velvet suit over a white ruffled silk shirt fixed with a handsomely tied cravat, he greeted old friends with a nod. His injured arm, although bandaged, dangled unslinged and despite the pain, he smiled in an engaging, confident air.

"Mr. Harrison!" Emily Parker motioned to a seat at Table Six. "It's so good of you to join us. I believe you know my older son."

Rob offered his hand in welcome. "Good to see you again, Mr. Harrison." Luke shrugged a friendly "Hi," his bruised cheek and black eye now puffed a cauliflowered purple.

"Your daughters have not yet joined us?"

"Daughters?" Emily Parker tossed back her head and clapped her hands. "Good heavens me, Mr. Harrison. Our Alex is daughter enough!"

"LADIES AND GENTLEMEN! It is my great pleasure...and distinct, high honor...to present to you this evening...the Summer's Belles of the White."

Showcasing feminine charms at the Grande Ball endured as the White's ultimate time-honored tradition. Payne had always refrained from "escorting," preferring to "sit back and regard the line" when the Grand Marshal announced the Formal Entrance. Any belle turning his head—"sweet young things" to the tobacco chewers and stick whittlers bedecking the Main Hotel's veranda—became a merited challenge for the evening.

"Miss Alexandra Margaret Parker of Lowell, Massachusetts ...escorted by her father, Mr. Robert Parker," boomed the Marshal, in a coupling of oratory and auctioneering zeal.

Daughter enough? Payne caught Emily Parker dabbing a tear as father and daughter approached Table Six.

The girl under the bridge? Could this lovely creature be...?

Payne rose and bowed. "My compliments, Miss...Parker."

Alex smiled and nodded. "Mr. Harrison, I am glad you could join us."

"My pleasure, I'm sure." He danced back to Alex's mud-streaked face wandering the wild flowers beside the mountain stream. *A girl of fascinating contrasts! Which are you, Miss Parker?*

She wore a low-cut, white muslin gown richly embroidered in rose petals. Around her neck gleamed an exquisite gold locket, accentuating the delicate lace bertha that graced her figure. With fine silk gloves, white satin slippers, and a blue silk ribbon tying her blonde hair, her elegance and beauty challenged every belle in the room.

"I see mountain trout on the menu this evening. Any chance you—and Luke—had a hand in the catch?"

Alex stabbed a stare at her younger brother.

"Not me!" shrugged the boy. "Everybody knows Alex digs the fattest worms...and loves to squish 'em on the hook!"

"Fascinating," said Payne. "I must see your technique sometime, Miss...ah...Parker. You are also quite knowledgeable on mountain flowers?"

"Oh, Alex loves botany," said Rob, puzzling on the turn in conversation.

The flower girl readied for war, firing visual salvos at both brothers. *But this Virginian's relentless smile and asking eyes...*

She replied with own smile, summoning a will that always served her in adversity, meeting Payne Harrison's blue eyes with her own sparkle of pure charm. *OK, enjoy your little victory. For now.*

She blushed in sweet, calculated surrender. "So...Payne?" Her words fluttered to the table like feathers.

"Yes, Ma'am. Perhaps we should leave fishing lessons for later... Alex?"

"Certainly, sir."

"At your service. Pleasure's all mine. But Luke, I must say Dr. Myers certainly knows what he's talking about."

Dinner at the White combined culinary elegance and traditional fare. Mountains of corn on the cob and large bowls of succotash and black-eyed peas complimented generous entrees of clam chowder Manhattan, egg stuffed with caviar, and roast prime beef *au jus* dipped in anchovy butter. Patrons savoring chicken patty *la Reine* and cold spring lamb could also enjoy grilled mountain trout followed by watermelon, apple cobbler, or wild huckleberry pie—the berries gathered from nearby mountainsides.

With good food, delightful company, and engaging conversation, Payne soon forgot his throbbing arm. Robert Parker, he learned, talked business all the time—shoes, boots, and military contracts. With some tact, he inquired of the Harrisons and their holdings outside Richmond, finding their coal mining venture particularly fascinating.

Rob spoke of military matters, expressing a strong desire to serve on the frontier, especially any posting in California. Emily Parker listened, nodding with her husband as he recounted the family's early struggle to make the factory profitable. She avoided Rob's glance when he spoke of going west.

Alex smiled and watched, eyes coy but darting, words soft yet engaging. When Payne Harrison spoke, his facial features reflected his feelings. Flared nostrils on emotion, a clenched jaw for intensity, raised eyebrows at questions, smiling eyes when he listened. Alex sensed ambition. This man knew what he wanted and exuded the confidence to get it.

"How many slaves do you work in your coal pits, Mr. Harrison?" Rob asked. Awkward looks silenced Table Six like a ton of dropped sand.

"Rob...Mr. Harrison is our guest!" Emily Parker looked aghast, clearly disturbed at her son's indiscretion.

Payne raised an open hand as he took a sip of water. Conversations swerving in this direction often plunged good people into regretted words...or worse. "I'm not sure, lieutenant." He set down the glass. "My brother Clay manages those affairs. I'm more interested in horses."

It was an evasive answer and he knew it. But as the Parker's dinner guest, he would not spoil their good graces—or digestion—with wranglings over Negro slavery.

"Thank you, Mr. Harrison. We both know of the economic differences that characterize our separate sections of the country. I apologize for my eldest son's lack of tact."

"I only meant to inquire whether...."

"That will do, Rob. Let's indulge more palatable topics tonight, given the circumstances. We owe Mr. Harrison a great deal."

Luke toyed with his fork.

"Of course. Mr. Harrison..."

"No offense taken."

Alex saw only her napkin, knife, and plate. These days, abolitionist talk intruded into nearly every conversation. She wanted to hear of Payne's family and visualize his description of Walnut Grove.

"Mr. Harrison, tell me about your horses."

"Well, I just acquired..."

Strains of a Viennese waltz drifted across the room as musicians began warming up for the dance.

"Looks to be an active evening," said Payne.

"Ahmmm, yes, I believe so," Alex mused. "Luke? The opening cotillion's being called. Got anybody picked out?"

"No way! But I bet you do!"

She glared back, white gloved hands pressing the table. *Luke's going to fuddle things up if he stays so stupid! Payne Harrison, please forget that day at the bridge.*

"I hope to see you and Mother on the dance floor before the evening is done, Papa," said Alex. "They're making up the first figures now."

"Fat chance I'll be out there this evening!" grumbled Robert Parker, ignoring his wife's dark glance.

"We'll see about that." Emily Parker would have her say.

"So Mr. Harrison, your horses? I must confess to some abiding interest in the sport."

PAPA! More business talk? The figures are forming!

As the evening's first cotillion opened with debutantes and escorts moving in patterned grace across the pine planked floor of the White's Grand Ballroom, Payne Harrison shared his passion of horses with Robert Parker of Massachusetts. He detailed the account of his first stakes win. Passions guided the future, he said, plus the lure of competition, the great races to be won, and yes, everyone's lust to own the swiftest horse.

Alex fretted, hearing about horse tracks but watching the dance floor fill. *If only he'd...*

"Been fascinated by horses all my life," Payne continued, "especially thoroughbreds. Dreamed as a boy I'd one day bring up a great racer and watch him vanquish all challengers!"

If he goes on like this all evening...

"Miss Parker, if I might have the honor..."

"Why, ah...yes, thank you!"

Payne glanced up from jawing horses. A fellow he'd seen in the bar—*from Louisville I think*—handed Alex a long-stemmed rose. She curtseyed, nodding to her mother and father while posting a too-sweet smile to Payne—*Kindly excuse me?*—and stepped to the dance floor.

Luke's good eye drilled Payne. *You better ask her.*

Well, OK, he did feel drawn to Alex. He admired her energy, her elegance, and now, the way she glided through the formations and patterns of the cotillion. As her father pressed him for more on thoroughbreds, Payne caught glimpses of her about the floor, seeing her change partners after two dances, then another after three, alive and glowing to the music and moment.

"I've acquired a horse of stunning potential," he confided to Robert Parker. But as he lifted his glass, his eyes met hers, demure and coquettish in three quarter time, waltzing the question, *still talking stables and saddle soap?*

"Walnut Grove sponsors the Dominion Derby?"

"We participate." Payne shifted his gaze. Over Parker's left shoulder, head back, Alex twirled, catching her partner's hands, laughing.

"Ever visit Saratoga Springs, Mr. Harrison?" Robert Parker spun the stem of his wine glass between forefinger and thumb.

"The resort spa in New York state? No sir, never had the pleasure."

"Well, I'd like you to join us at Saratoga this summer. August is the high season and we Parkers haven't missed in a dozen years. Call it our annual pilgrimage to the goddess Hygieia." He chuckled, setting the wine glass aside to wipe his mouth with a table napkin. Fingers intertwined, his hands settled to the table. "I'd also like your help, Mr. Harrison."

"Sir?" Payne asked, watching Alex chat with several young women on the far side of the room.

"Horse racing's growing. As you know, Virginia, Kentucky, and other southern states already profit from quality stakes races. We feel New York can do the same. Business acquaintances of mine, shall we say, are most interested in establishing a reputable, professionally run track. We believe Saratoga Springs is the ideal place."

Parker paused. *Am I going too far, too soon? Telling this young fellow...a Southerner, such closely held business plans?*

Puff-eyed Luke snaked his hand at a third slice of apple pie.

No, I can trust this man.

"I believe you could help us make such a track a reality."

Payne had never raced in the North. Yes, his subscription to the *American Turf Register* kept him abreast of racing news nationally but he paid little heed to *Spirit of the Times*, a smaller journal published in New York. He'd never given much thought to a Northern stakes race. *Makes sense though...especially a track at a resort as well known as Saratoga.*

"What do you say, Mr. Harrison?"

"Please, call me Payne." He liked Robert Parker, a man without pretense. "No offense sir, but 'Mr. Harrison' makes me sound old."

The manufacturer laughed. "Then I insist you call me 'Robert.'"

This Harrison came across as a congenial, enterprising fellow. One of the South's upcoming breeders. Racing in the North—operating for decades out of back-room gambling dens—could sorely use such men. And Robert Parker knew he could never repay Payne Harrison for saving his son's life. Yes, this man could be trusted. And he was someone who would not be bullied. Around Saratoga, that mattered.

"Well Payne, we'd love to have you and any of your family join us during the August season. And meet a few friends of mine. Who knows, next year this time, your new speed horse might even be pounding Yankee soil on his way to the victor's circle!"

Twelve racing up North? There's a thought!

Yes, Robert Parker talked sense. If Saratoga gained acceptance in Southern society, racing would surely prosper above the Mason-Dixon.

A fter eight dances, Alex returned to Table Six. *What does it take?* "Your father just invited Mr. Harrison to Saratoga."

What on earth? She took a very slow, deep breath.

"Goodness...well...you'll find Saratoga a bit different from the White," she began, grinding her heels into the dance floor.

"I'm sure. No watermelon, succotash, or black-eyed peas I'll wager on Saratoga's bill of fare."

"I expect you'll find our Northern tables adequate to your needs, Mr. Harrison." Emily Parker sputtered a nervous giggle. "If you find the food disagreeable, you can always take the waters."

"Yes, Ma'am," Payne grinned. "Yet permit me to offer a toast." He lifted his glass: "To good company and new friends, North and South."

"Here, here!" echoed Robert Parker, adding his own salute: "To thoroughbreds: may their speed, grace, and power always endure."

Payne emptied his glass

Not Alex. *He's had too much wine.*

Yet a moment later he turned to her, his glass refilled.

"To wildflowers...mountain streams...and astute anglers!"

To which Luke blurted, "Here! Here!"

And Alex blushed. *There is mocking in this man's words and deviltry in his eyes. Mr. Payne Harrison, you ARE drunk. And to think I...*

But he slurred not a word.

"Miss Parker, might I request the honor of the evening's Grande Waltz?"

His merry eyes landed warm and waiting, like an arriving holiday.

The waltz? Alex sensed the room brighter, the candle lanterns burnishing orange. *He's really asking me! Yes...yes, let's.*

In an odd, unpredictable way, he puzzled her, yet enticed her. For Alex Parker already knew Payne Harrison was like no other man in the room.

"Shall we?" He opened his hand.

And with gentle grace, she put hers into his.

D espite the pain and Dr. Myers' caution, Payne guided Alex flawlessly across the floor in three quarter time. Their fluid rhythm and smooth steps coupled their dance into elegance. And admiration.

Alex savored the caress of Payne's right hand to the small of her back. Never once did he tease her about fishing worms! *But who are you sir? And why do I only want to dance with you?*

Emily Parker finally uprooted her husband for a few twirls across the floor. She hadn't danced the night away, but at least she'd danced.

And Luke? Yes, he'd had a rough day and his black eye still throbbed, but his broad grin at evening's end confirmed his intuition. As his parents motioned him toward the exit, Luke wiggled his fingers in a mocking gesture at Alex. But she passed him by, her eyes on her partner.

Outside on the lawn, couples edged toward the shadows.

"So...Saratoga in August?"

"Yeah." Payne moistened his lips. A gravel path edged from the crowd.

"Saratoga's like the White...but also very different."

"You already said that."

"I did, didn't I?" Alex smoothed a corner of her gown and met his gaze.

Rising above the east ridge, the summer moon orbed like a giant balloon.

"Differences." *She's nearly a decade younger.* "Well, I'll count on you to keep me out of trouble."

"Goodness me. Such talk. I'm betting you'll love New York."

Alex toyed her fingers to Payne's. As they started up the gravel path to Baltimore Row, she realized she'd been smiling all evening.

"I need to tell you something." Her words caught him like a bat diving across the moon. "I thought you were quite drunk tonight."

Payne stopped, a statue in the shadows.

"I mean...after all those toasts...but, I guess after dancing with you, I was wrong. You are quite...accomplished. And I wanted you to know that."

Payne doubled, laughing. "Thought I couldn't handle a little wine, huh? Oh, my dear Miss Parker, you have a few things to learn about Southerners."

Face flushed, Alex painted to hurt, feeling his fingers wrap hers, pulling her close, very close, his breath sweet with wine, his touch urgent. *He is drunk!*

"And my schooling begins now?"

"No. No, you don't understand."

"I don't?"

How can I best say this? "Alex, I'm going to Saratoga on business. A lot's at stake. Your father knows this. I know this."

He paused, loath to continue. It was in her eyes. The way she'd followed him across the room...how she reddened when he'd learned her name. *For whatever reason, the smitten bug's stung Alex Parker. And if I raise her expectations, life's going to get complicated again. Besides, she's just a kid. And I don't need another round with hope chests.*

"You know so little about me, Alex."

"I see..." Her trailing voice squeezed her other words into hiding. She pulled her hand from his. Gravel crunched the silence before she spoke again.

"Payne?"

"Yes?"

"You didn't let me finish."

Payne stopped, puzzled.

"I wanted...to offer my own toast."

Slowly, deliberately, Alex cupped her hands to his face. For an instant, she doubted her purpose, but then she remembered Luke. And this man, this brave man who had come to his aid...*I need to do this. I want to do this!*

With care, her fingers caressed Payne's face, holding him with a soft, exquisite touch, bewitching in her boldness.

She's only nineteen...?

"My toast is to something that I do know about you." Alex hesitated, her amber eyes welling. It was all she could do to continue.

"For bravery, Payne Harrison...for saving my little Luke." A tear slid down her cheek. Then another.

With the warmth of her being, she kissed him, putting her moist lips to the left, then right of his face. Marvelously, sensuously, she thanked him.

"Alex...Alex." Payne formed her name slowly, sounding the syllable, not asking, nor demanding, simply marveling on a wonderful discovery.

Her misting eyes mirrored passion that roiled the depth of her being.

"I...I...didn't mean..." He'd not expected this warmth...this sentiment...or maturity. It was he who had misread.

He tugged her close, moving his hands to her waist, seeking the graceful curves of her hips. There, he held her, melting his lips to hers, savoring as she welcomed him.

It was just a moment, but one of enduring magic. Alex cupped her fingers over his, glowing. "Thank you for a wonderful evening, Payne Harrison."

"You...you are the Belle of the Ball."

"And you're sweet."

"Maybe another waltz then...at Saratoga?"

He pointed to a small lantern flickering on the porch. The Parkers had retired, leaving a candle burning.

"Yes," she whispered, putting her lips to his. "In Saratoga."

The place, storied in the nation's military annals, suddenly carried an exquisitely different promise.

Chapter Sixteen

Walnut Grove
Chesterfield County, Virginia
July 1860

B y Aunt Hattie's notions, the first three had been blessed. *Cheek-glowed babies,* she'd called them.

The old slave refilled her pea basket. *Good crop this summer.*

All the Harrisons Aunt Hattie had ever birthed showed it. *The good Lord's cheek-glow.*

"A blessed thing, color of life," she gushed to an exhausted Jane Harrison the morning "little Paynie" came into the world. Doc Morrissett's whack to the babe's wet bottom—always an anxious moment—had sparked the quiet, graying newborn into a lusty, pink squawker.

Cheek-glow, she declared to all who would listen, was the Lord's sign of long life. The births of the next two children—another boy, then a girl—presented this same good omen. All popped out "squirmin' and screaming," she'd say, eager to "make the Colonel and his Missus proud!"

Payne presented as apple red, a boy burnished by winter's cold blast and vigorous rides through the Chesterfield countryside. And

Auntie made no bones. He was her favorite. For her, Master Payne always had the extra moment, a kind word, that ready smile...even though he did like to tease.

But she still worried.

Why's he rushin' to ruin...throwin' his life 'way at that horse track?

In Clayton—two years younger than Payne—nature bequeathed hidden hues. A muscular man shorter but heavier than his older brother, Clay grew up serious, always studying on something and keeping it to himself. Clay Harrison had been born busy. His cheeks burned crimson only when roused to anger or flushed by embarrassment. But that was when he was a boy. Now that the Colonel had shouldered Walnut Grove's day-to-day on him, the flask in the plantation desk fueled most of his *glow*.

Sarah, the lone daughter, blossomed in radiant pink. Like Payne, winter's bluster, walks in the woods, and afternoons on horseback invigorated her to a vibrant, attractive hue. Yet in quiet moments, she projected serene beauty, a blue-eyed brunette fresh as a spring sunrise. She shared Payne's love of horses but shunned race day. No betting, drinking, and profane, tobacco-spitting types for her. "My little rose," the Colonel called her.

And then there was Samuel—quiet, alert, watchful. A late-life surprise for Jane Harrison.

Sam sported no *cheek-glow*, never exhibited the physical stamina that so marked his brothers. Thoughtful and intelligent, he showed little interest in agriculture or coal mining. A voracious reader and the best student of Thomas and Jane Harrison's four children, he planned to study law at Mr. Jefferson's University in Charlottesville come September. His mother prayed he would enter the ministry.

Yet Sam rarely missed race day. His bookish introspection vanished at the track. He'd rock on the balls of his feet before the crack of the gun, then scream with the wildest as the horses pounded into the final turn. Sam Harrison loved horses and envied his oldest brother.

As for Walnut Grove, Aunt Hattie called it home. Born and suckled right on the place. Warmth in winter, a roof against rain, food when hungry, a doctor in sickness...with three babies of her own. Yes Casper, her oldest, bunked at Mr. Gregory's carriage shop over on Gravel Hill and worked as the old man's smithy, but he usually got to see his mammy at Sunday meeting. Fortunately, her Molly and Jasper—who seemed as gone on horses as Master Payne—lived with her. But Obie, her man, lay under a stone in the periwinkle of the South Woods, dead these eight years from lockjaw.

The plantation itself—named by Payne's grandfather for the mature stands of black walnut bordering the drive and filling the woods—lay just beyond the mining village of Midlothian. The big house—two-stories of Flemish bond brick anchored on a raised basement of coursed granite—dated from 1791. It replaced a three-room log cabin built by Payne's great-great-grandfather in 1758. Only a ruined brick chimney marked that site.

Walnut Grove's front entrance mirrored the grace, hospitality, and prosperity of its occupants. Under a Federal style, elliptical fanlight of gauged bricks arching over the entrance doorway, visitors entered a center hall paneled in walnut cut off the place and floored in random-width heart pine. The front rooms—a parlor on the left, a sitting room to the right—opened off the center hall. The Colonel's study, library, and formal dining room—the Great Room—filled out the first floor plan. A curving Italianate staircase with turned walnut newel posts and balusters wound to five bedrooms on the second floor. More walnut supplied the trim, wainscoting, carved mantels, and recessed window seats. Oil portraits of Harrisons living and dead looked down from the walls of the library and main hall.

Aunt Hattie ran the house staff. In no nonsense mode. And applied the same to child rearing.

In her 53 years at Walnut Grove, she prized loyalty above all else...except praising the Lord at Sunday meeting. *How can Master Payne—you know I weaned him, Lord—continue habituatin' with those gamblers and racin' sinners on Your day?*

She prayed for his saving every Sabbath.

And what's this mess 'bout running off to Yankeeland when the Missus and the Colonel need him so?

The old woman put down her basket of peas. July's heat settled close. Seated in a rocker on the porch of the log cookhouse, she spotted two figures—Payne and young Sam—leaning against the fence north of the big house. Summer grass spread thick across the West Meadow where Payne's horses grazed on the "sweet greens" that flourished there. But as she watched, a brown cloud billowed through the fence and swept down the rails.

Jasper's ridin' again! I never...but who's on that other horse?

Aunt Hattie stepped off the porch, willing to sacrifice her seat in the shade for the Lord's work in the sun.

"That boy needs to hear from his mammy," she muttered, strutting toward the fence, "and now's as good a time as any, I reckon."

H eat don't faze him!"
Jasper dismounted, smoothing his hand down Twelve's flank. Payne thumbed his pocket watch. "Remember his time, Jasper?"

The black jockey flashed a toothy grin, track powder flecking his face like fine white flour. After this short workout, Number Twelve would race Tredegar over five furlongs.

"Fast!" said Jasper. "But he's got more. Bet on it."

"He ran a 1:02 three days ago. Think you can shave that?"

Jasper raised one hand to the broiling sun, rubbing the horse's neck. Number Twelve nickered and tossed his mane. "I can try, sir."

"Good! Ben? How's Tredegar? Well rested?"

Ben Baird chased easy money this day. Orphaned and with little means, the diminutive boy found work in the stables at Walnut Grove. He wanted no part of the coal mines that had crushed and buried his father. A clever, skilled rider, he'd earn at least ten dollars racing this day. Two week's wages in the mines, four weeks if Tredegar won.

"Warmed and ready, sir," said Ben, posting his game-face.

Payne spotted the approaching figure.

"My dear Aunt Hattie, how good of you to join us." For years, he'd suffered the old woman's condemnations. Today promised more raspings.

"I brought y'all some lemonade." She set down a crock pitcher and several mugs. "Mite bit hotter out here than in the kitchen."

"You're the best, Auntie!" Sam grabbed a mug. "Here, Ben. Jasper."

Payne just stood there. *No preaching about our devil's work?*

The thirst quencher kept pouring, her ebony face a monument of disdain weathering a stony silence.

"Everybody toasting?" All turned, seeing the Colonel wave, grinning, clutching his cane, advancing in baby steps. Amos, his house manservant, danced an umbrella above his tottering patriarch.

"This heat's rough without something cool to drink, sir."

"True, Auntie. But get me what I want." The Colonel puffed to a stop.

Aunt Hattie shook her head, but did as she was told, scooting toward the cellar door under the main house.

"So...going up against Tredegar, are we?" Sweat glistened the Colonel's forehead and slid down both cheeks, dripping from his jaw. He took out a handkerchief and smothered the top of his head and face in grimaced relief.

"Push day, Pap. Got to find out what he's made of."

"And you, Jasper? Payne tells me you're going to ride him 'round."

Aunt Hattie's boy touched his cap, flashing teeth. "All the way, sir."

"And Ben, don't let my son knock old Tredegar. You've seen him run."

Payne dug out his pocket watch. "OK. You two know the rules. Start on the first turn's lime. I'll hold you there 'til you're both set. Two laps. Finish right back here. Questions?"

Ben shook his head, all business. Jasper kept grinning.

The horses broke even, the early advantage in the Colonel's eye going to Tregedar. Indeed, coming out of the first turn, the older horse pounded close to the rail, keeping a steady half length ahead of Number Twelve down the backstretch.

Payne froze, fixed on his blood horses thundering head to head. Ben kept Tredegar tight on the inside. A smart money rider, he tapped his mount's strengths as needed. Jasper slipped another half length, but no more...neither gaining or losing...just there...like a ghost in Tredegar's wake.

Into lap two, the second horse remained the shadow of the first, a glorious match race down the backstretch as the riders began to blend, appearing as one. Coming out of the final turn, Ben switched Tredegar's flanks to preserve his tenuous lead. But there was no lead. And that's when Payne perceived Number Twelve—eyes wide, nostrils flared, and head rocking—far larger. And realized he was far closer!

"Hell of a horse, there!" The Colonel wrapped arms around his son. Aunt Hattie's whiskey, brought and gulped as the race began, usually colored his speech. "Heck of a katookus! Sakes a land, son! He runs like the wind!"

Payne hugged both jockeys. Ben burned disappointment but kept staring at Number Twelve. Jasper just grinned.

"Good race, Ben. But get him out of this heat. And easy on the water."

"Yes, sir. I pushed him...all I could get...but...your chestnut." Ben was still shaking his head when he entered the stable.

"And, Jasper, oh Jasper!" Payne rubbed Twelve's forehead. "You're not like the rest, are you fella?"

In all of this, Aunt Hattie had bided her time. She disapproved of gambling and horse racing, and the rowdies it attracted. But she too sensed something special here. The unexpected surge in that new horse, the Colonel's congratulations, the stunned, marveling look in her Jasper's eyes, the quiet sense of awe from Master Payne...perhaps this was more than about fast horses and loose money. Saying nothing, and not daring to spoil the moment, she trudged back to the log kitchen.

Lord, I need to sit down with You.

Jasper dismounted. "He's easy out...building...but no pounding, just all smooth and nothing forced. And he'll go faster."

"True, but he still needs pushing. Now go take care of him...then grab your fishing pole for the rest of the afternoon."

And the North dares to challenge us? What do Yankees know about racing?

That notion amused Payne, yet as he walked with Sam and his father to the welcomed cool of Walnut Grove's large shade trees, he wondered. Saratoga offered promising possibilities. Racing, horse breeding, sizeable purses. And bragging rights for the fastest, North or South! After what he had seen this day, this new horse matched any challenger on the track. *Those people up there will rue the day Twelve gallops across Northern turf!*

But something else tugged. Yes, he stabled a phenomenal contender. And soon would have the chance to prove it. He'd also heard of Saratoga's lavish entertainment and elegant facilities. High stakes and fine society beckoned. But were these the only enticements pulling him to New York?

Yes, he did think of her. *Every day.*

Alex Parker stirred his imagination. And traveling to Saratoga represented a sweet opportunity lost if ignored. It wasn't just about horses.

SARATOGA SPRINGS, NEW YORK, AUGUST 1860

A lex reined to a halt and tucked her white silk handkerchief—embroidered with a pink monogrammed French script "A"—into the pocket of her riding pants.

Sun's on broil today. She squinted toward town, sipped more water, and rehung her canteen on the pommel.

Oh, for a little breeze. Where's that boy?

"Luke? LUKE?"

Motionless, silhouetted on the ridge, she listened. Ahead, the trails split. *Pick, silly.*

Alex guided left. *Drat! He's always doing this...spurring off on some wild goose chase. Where are you brother?*

She'd never ventured this far into the rugged crags north of Saratoga. And although she hadn't told Luke, she'd not planned to spend the whole day up here. *He wouldn't understand.*

Again she stopped. No rustling leaves. Or neighing horse. *I'll wring his neck!*

She might have contented herself with a sensible morning stroll up Broadway, discovering the latest Saratoga fashions, greeting friends, and yes, she mused with a sly grin, garnering her own share

of smiling nods and turned glances...*all at a relaxed, refreshing pace...*
instead of wilting in this heat, parched, and grimed in all this road sweat!

The path narrowed and climbed through the trees. But fresh hoof prints signaled traffic.

"Up here, Alex!" Caution scored her brother's voice, his words coming like an ambush from a thicket ahead.

"Where are you?" She jerked her head, jaw firm.

"Over here!"

Luke stood on a rounded stone outcrop. "So where is your great find?"

"Shhhhh." Luke pointed into a narrow vale, a half mile across the glen. "Down there." A small cottage peeked from a grove of hemlocks. A sparkle of light flickered and danced nearby. "Know who lives there?"

"Should I?"

Luke goggled at his sister. "You really don't? That's old Tubby's place! People vanish down there!"

"Oh, shush! Surely you don't believe that poppycock. Angeline Tubbs? She's no witch! Just a harmless old biddy who stumbles around talking to rocks and telling fortunes."

"What about all those creepy cats and her coal-black eyes that crawl right through you? Not to mention her hook nose!"

"Luke, you actually sound scared."

Alex did feel an odd magnetism toward the sparkling light and the little old woman who lived in the quaint distant cottage. Down there, the forest seemed thicker, deeper; gnarled, aged oaks and hemlocks gave the woods a dark, primeval, ominous appearance.

"I'll go, if you go."

"No way, Alex!"

"Listen!" Alex turned toward Saratoga. The faint shrill of a steam whistle pierced the countryside calm.

"But not today. Told Papa I'd meet him at the station."

"Your loss, Alex."

There it is again! With no more thoughts of witches and spells, she abandoned Luke to his adventures.

"Got a train to meet, little brother."

Chapter Seventeen

Saratoga Springs heralded the arrival of each passenger train with the clanging of an ancient, cast bronze bell swinging high in the cupola of the brick railway depot, a tocsin pealing Saratoga's ritual meeting, greeting...and gawking.

Friends, business acquaintances, and relatives dashed for the barn-like station, scrambling a bedlam of eager, smiling faces into hearty handshakes and warm hugs. Porters and hucksters bumped and shouldered closest to the rail, touting and shouting the respective hospitalities of the hotels shilling them as the locomotive wheezed to a stop. And midst these greeters surged the gawkers...curious hopefuls angling for a glimpse of the famous, the beautiful, the notorious. Outside, drivers and chauffeurs blared fares and destinations in a noisy babble, offering conveyance to the best and finest on Broadway in everything from four-in-hand phaetons to mud-splattered dogcarts. In this "elegant chaos," co-mingled humanity engulfed the platform with one joyous, confused roar when the coach doors opened. Bewhiskered gentlemen elbowed through the crowd, hailing porters while their ladies waited patiently on the platform, angelically exhibiting the latest, lavish—and preferably French—fashions, from small bishop-sleeved muslin and cambric dresses, to exquisitely hand-stitched chemisettes...perhaps complimented by a white *peau de soie* hat trimmed in green ribbon and lilac branches or a *paille de riz* bonnet cloaking those much lauded ear-confining brims.

Payne had seen nothing like it. The noise and jostle of the passengers with their accent-animated speech and diced, frantic gesticulations, trampled new sentences into the previous with questions blurted rapid-fire, smothering any reasoned reply.

Is everyone up here always in such a hurry?

"Business or pleasure, me good man? Some of both I'll wager. Aye, ye look like a sporting gentleman."

The inquirer, a powerfully-built, well-dressed man twisted one end of his dark, handlebar mustache. Eye-sparkle bespoke a gregarious nature. Payne had ridden opposite him all the way from Albany without an exchanged word, the man buried in his newspaper. He'd gotten up a few times and disappeared down the aisle, but other than that, Payne had paid him no notice. Only now, with his paper folded, did he offer conversation. As the train slowed, the man stood, digging a gold watch from his vest pocket.

"Both, I reckon." Payne smiled, glad for journey's end. His two-day, bumping ride from Richmond north through Baltimore, Philadelphia, and New York, then on to Albany and Ballston, had him ready for a soak in one of Saratoga's famous hot pools.

"Here for the waters, sonny?" A tiny, bent woman grabbed the railing, her gray, wiry hair bouncing as she nudged toward the opened door. "Congress Spring's best for gout. So too the Columbian. But if it's kidneys that drains your goods, the Empire's curatives will flush everything!"

"Thank you...Ma'am," Payne said with sugared politeness. She reminded him of a long-dead great aunt. "That sounds...interesting."

"Have fun. But behave yourself!" Basking in the acknowledgement of her medicinal wisdom, she and her carpetbag darted from the car, vanishing in an amazing burst of ancient energy.

"Ah, me friend, there's Saratoga's hydropathic analysis for ye... and at no charge." The mustachioed man jabbed his thumb in the direction of the old woman's hasty departure. "Dare say she's dashing to the baths. Ye sir, on the other hand, look in need of Matilda Street."

"Matilda Street?"

"Gaming rooms. Don't ye know them?" The man waited, drawing his lips to a curious curve. "Not from 'round here, are ye?"

"Virginia." Payne extended his hand. "Harrison's the name."

"Aye, thought I heard a drawling in there! Welcome to the land of the Yankee! John Morrissey be mine." He met Payne's with a hearty, muscular grip.

"Who are you kidding!" Payne laughed. "That Irish brogue of yours is like music to my mares."

Morrissey busted into a full belly laugh. "I can tell ye are a good fellow! 'Course Saratoga be friend to every twang. That ye can wager on, friend Harrison! And we Irish playing our ponies!"

His eyes—intelligent eyes, thought Payne—beamed the delight of one entrusting a guarded secret. "Ye be a betting man?"

"When the chances are right," Payne answered. *If every Northerner I meet is as engaging as this fellow...*

"Aye! Now here's a man I can take to! Ye've come to the right place."

Morrissey stepped onto the platform and turned. "Make sure Saratoga shows ye her best. Sample her waters, her hospitality, her beauties...but by all means, visit Matilda Street."

"In that order?" Both laughed again, shaking hands.

"Just one more thing, Harrison." The Irishman leaned close, quiet. "Coming from down south...some will try to tweak ye charms."

Payne met him eye to eye. "I'll remember that."

Morrissey returned to the weathered smile, his Irishman's ruddy good looks chiseled with several scars. "Aye, then. See ye man."

Payne watched him step off the platform.

Interesting folks, these Yankees. A bounce of yellow caught his eye.

"Payne? Payne! Here he is, Papa. Over here!"

From the milling crowd, blurred and weaving in gathered tumult, people embraced friends and loved ones at every turn, backslapping and handshaking, yet taking care not to sprawl headlong over one of the dozen or more iron-strapped, curved-top hogsheads—yes, those famous Saratoga Trunks—that strong-backed attendants wheeled from the train's baggage compartment.

Payne glanced left. A set of waving arms brought bright eyes and a fresh, winning smile. He waved back. *Her hair's longer.*

"I see you found your way!" Energy bounced her words to him.

"Glad I didn't come by horse."

"We're not that far off the beaten track. But you sure brought the heat with you. This is the hottest it's been all summer!"

"Welcome to Saratoga!" Robert Parker shouldered his way forward, offering a hand and a cordial smile.

"Thank you, sir. Glad to finally get off that train."

"I can imagine," continued Parker, "but let me secure your luggage. I'll meet you two over at the far exit in a few."

Alex tilted her head. *He looks leaner, taller.* Yet it was Payne's blue eyes that fixed Alex's attention. *And that rich, soft call of his voice.*

"How have you been?" Payne took her hands, her touch soft like he remembered, her curving figure...exquisite. "Still after those wildflowers?"

She had wondered if he'd come all the way to New York. The regional tensions and everything. Few Southern families visited Saratoga any more. Now her hands were in his. *Powerful, intelligent...gentle hands.*

Alex looked up, fighting the rising blush. "I'm sure Luke will narrate his latest adventures." She knew how quick he was. *Do you always tease?*

"I'll expect a full report. But first...."

"I know exactly what you want!" Alex put a finger to his lips.

Payne arched his eyebrows, waiting.

"A nice hot bath in the spa, sir. There's nothing on earth like it!" She danced her eyes to his, her voice winnowing to a coquettish whisper. "I told you Saratoga has attractions the White doesn't!"

"Like?"

"Bryan's Hot Lithia Pool...right beside the Congress Hotel. It's deep, heavenly warm, and clear as glass. You'll have to go to the men's side of course! They don't allow..."

"Luggage belongs to this fellow." Robert Parker—a sweating porter in his wake—emerged from the crowd. "I hope the Congress will be to your liking, Payne. Ready, Alex?"

"Ah...yes. I was just telling Payne about the Congress Hotel."

The Virginian nodded, his wisp of a smile signaling to Alex a luxurious afternoon's soak might be just the thing.

Perhaps he should have brought Jasper. He'd toyed with the notion.

That boy...here, in Saratoga, gawking at Lord knows what...and Aunt Hattie...hoppin' and struttin' mad at me taking him to Yankeeland! Course gawkin's all I've been doing since I got off the train. As for this hot pool? Oh, for such luxury back home!

Bryan's soothing waters topped Payne's expectations. A dozen wonderful adjectives floated to mind, all true, relaxing and easing his tired body as he climbed out and grabbed a towel. Four other patrons bobbed on the simmering surface as primeval bubbles trickled up from the pool's warming depths. *This John Bryan, whoever he is, has quite an operation. Nothing like this at the White. Not in those cold mountain streams.*

But he missed Jasper. *Yet any trip up here with Negroes is out of the question.* The few darkies he'd seen in Saratoga worked as waiters, porters, hack drivers, or laborers. Only guests got access to the thermal pools...white guests. In the South, slaves had no rights. Race determined everything. And in the North, few persons of color could afford Saratoga's amenities; here, money kept things "tidy." So at the bedrock of society, it made no difference; everyone had...and knew their place. That's how things worked, North or South.

But something else gnawed at Payne. The free darkies here—the so-called freedman—how did they fit in? Servants at Walnut Grove received shelter, food, clothing, and medical care. The freedmen in the north were on their own. Few could read or write. *So who are these abolitionists to point fingers at the South?*

Many thought the name-calling and hate-mongering only brought out the fringe hot heads and firebrands on each side. But then John Brown attacked Harper's Ferry. And after they hanged him in December, it seemed everyone lost perspective. Now, just a chance contact might provoke...once they realized your origins. He'd seen it on the train...his Virginia accent turning heads, bringing smirks and cold looks after Philadelphia. *What was the country coming to?*

Beyond Bryan's, a tree-lined gravel path led up to Broadway. Union Hall, Congress Hall, and United States Hotel—long, low wooden buildings giving no inkling of the extravagant Victorian cornices, cupolas, balconies, and wreathed gingerbread fretwork to come—crowded the boulevard, fierce competitors for the patronage of the luxe and powerful. Rows of wine-glass elms shaded Broadway, easing the sun's glare. *Never this hot at the White.*

Payne ambled toward the center of town. On the corner below Bryan's, a cart vendor hawked flowers. As he pointed to a bouquet of carnations, garrulous noises burst from an open door fronting the street. "Bowling—Polished Lanes" stated a small sign above the sidewalk.

Looks more like a saloon.

Payne stepped across the marble threshold, finding a long bar stretched tight to the left wall, crowded with pre-supper patrons. Potted plants, brilliant beveled mirrors, carved hardwood furniture, and polished brass everywhere cramped four narrow, dented bowling alleys.

"Your pleasure, sir?"

"Scotch, please." Rolling balls and crashing pins bruised all conversations. He stuck his left hand at the bartender: "Two fingers'll do."

A blurred movement—hammered against a hard smacking sound—bumped him into a barstool.

"Well, I'd show 'em a thing or two!" A dark, oily-haired man, reeking and begrimed, pounded the rail. Two others—just as filthy and vulgar and nursing half-empty glasses—stood propped to one side, grousing no good.

"Yep, whip their butts, damn 'em, Jake. Everybody knows it's a cancer on the country. A lot of damn gall," said a wizened, shorter man bedecked in a gaudy, purple silk vest and top hat.

"Hell, Roy, if its trouble they want...it's shit they'll git! Goddamned Southerners!" answered a big, boisterous red-haired Irishman—his accented oaths challenging all in the room.

Payne edged back, but caught a finger in the ribs.

"You agree, mister?" The oily-haired man, his eyes watery and wiggling, glared close.

"On what, friend?" *Drunk...too much time spent finding bottle bottoms. Another loser.*

"On what? Hell, boy, ain't you paid no 'tention? Country's going to Lucifer in a hand basket and you ain't got no clue?"

"Awww, Jake, he don't know nothin'," grunted Roy.

"Heck, everybody's got an opinion. Lemme ask him." The Irishman slid up on the other side, inches from Payne's face, reeking of liquor and rotting teeth. "My friends and I think things are a bit uppity...like them no goods down in Virginia and Carolina and those hick Georgia crackers...loving their niggers too much to set 'em free."

"Yeah! And first one we find...we're gonna whip his ass!" leered Jake.

"Nothing like a little beer bravery," Payne mumbled.

"What's that, boy?" shot back the Irishman. "It's loud in here."

"Just up here on business. Don't really pay much mind to politics."

"To hell, you say! Hear that accent, Mick. This boy's one of 'em." The oily-haired man poked Payne again, this jab hard, painful, sinister. "Up here to oversee our 'fairs...are you? Massa?"

How in hell did I find these clowns?

"What kind of slow, weasel-speak you doin' there mister?"

"It's Harrison to you!" Nearby patrons quieted, backing away.

"I think your kind is liars!"

"Yeah! But Jake, they know'd better than to bring their coloreds up here!" growled Mick.

Payne recognized the bait.

"'Fraid you can't keep what's yours?" Mick sneered. He picked up Payne's untouched drink and emptied it into his glass. "Boy, you know you can't handle this good stuff."

Payne seized Mick's arms and spun him around. "Always so eager to steal what's not yours?"

"Get your goddamn hands off me!" Mick squealed.

The next instant crashed as a blur; from behind, Jake rabbit-punched Payne with a glancing blow to the head. More stunned than hurt, Payne shoved Mick face-down into a table, breaking his nose, then whipped toward Jake, only to catch a fist in the stomach.

Gut-doubled and gasping, Payne barely dodged a third blow as Mick, roaring and wild, missed with his own punch and slammed his fist into a chair. Howling and cursing, Mick grabbed a bottle.

Although knocked breathless, Payne swung at Jake, hitting him a glancing blow. Patrons fled, upsetting chairs and scraping tables across the floor. A solid uppercut spun Jake atop the bar. Mick raised his bottle...but never remembered what happened next. A hand—sudden, vise-like—seized his wrist and jerked him around, rending crashing sounds not heard in bowling alleys. Payne whirled to find Mick sprawled out cold, his face mashed and bloody, the full bottle of whiskey still clutched in his right hand!

"Enough of this!" Fury in his voice, a man pointed at Roy, cowering near the door. "You! Get your friends up and out of here. Now!"

"Lordy! It's Old Smoke!" Bug-eyed at the roaring man confronting him, Roy fled out the alley side door. Jake—bloody-nosed and limping—abandoned the unconscious Mick to the bar floor in favor of a hasty exit. The scrap ended as quickly as it had erupted.

"Aye, Harrison, a man who keeps his word. I'm glad to see ye didn't step aside. But ye did look like ye needed a hand there." The man squeezed Payne's shoulder.

Bleary eyed, Payne rubbed the back of his neck, gazing into the voice! *Morrissey?!*

"So, me friend, what's this all about?" John Morrissey broke into another of his belly laughs.

"No idea. I step off the train and two hours later I find myself in a one-sided bar brawl. Quite a town you have here."

"Well ye know, if ye're looking to tussle, ye really should go after one man at a time! Otto? Two fresh ones, please."

The white-aproned bartender who hadn't dared interfere up to now, reached for an unopened bottle of scotch and poured each man three fingers.

"Riff-raff! Thought I'd left their likes back in the city. Anyway, here's to ye Payne Harrison...and Old Virginia."

Payne lifted his glass, downing half before clinking it to the bar.

"Aye, we meet again, Harrison!"

"Rather suddenly...but thanks." Payne took Morrissey's open hand expecting another grip of steel, but this time found an engulfing glove of warm leather. This man carried an extraordinary build, yet Payne could see he was by no means muscle bound. Beneath the physical prowess, agility flashed...and Payne sensed in this jovial benefactor something far more powerful...perhaps a will or ambition intolerant of defeat. He'd never known anyone who could knock out a man with one punch, particularly a foe as large as that red-headed Irishman.

"I think I could have handled them," he murmured, but there was nothing convincing in his voice.

"All the better! But I'm not partial to me seeing a good man get hit from behind! Especially hazarding a full bottle of Irish rye." He slapped Payne on the back and laughed again.

"Guess I owe you one, huh? And please call me Payne." He lifted his scotch, but nowhere matching Morrissey's glass-emptying gulp.

"Naw! Ye and I who own the accents need to stick together! And Tom it is to ye! Dinner hour is nigh. But I think we'll cross paths soon again! I must depart, but here's to ye, Payne Harrison!"

John Morrissey paused at the door. "Aye! Nice uppercut by the way."

As he watched the big man depart, Payne realized he'd made his first friend in Saratoga. *Who said Yankeeland was so hostile?*

"Listen." Otto tapped his shoulder, his voice awe-hushed. "You're a lucky one. 'Old Smoke's' in your camp!"

"Old Smoke?"

"Yep," said Otto, eyes oval. "American champion prize fighter... the one and only. Did you know he once..."

146

Chapter Eighteen

Alex loved to daydream.

She spread her blanket on the edge of the bowling green. At this hour, it was all hers...and her companion's over there...this intriguing Virginian.

Handsome. But who really are you?

Here, she found her spices and pigments, her fabric and threads to mix and paint and cut and stitch, so she might savor the tastes, colors and textures of the day—the "little squiggles" she called them—that bobbed and soared across her imagination.

Just close my eyes and go anywhere.

Warm images curled close. Laughter...smiles...dinner with family. And this man...whose voice carried that slow, delightful drawl.

And food? Gumbo filet Bresilienne, saddle of mutton with currant jelly, roast spring chicken au jus, Russian turnips, tutti-frutti pudding and Kummel sauce. All followed by chocolate Africaines and coffee éclairs.

Then to music and dancing...swirled excitement! Just invite me outside for some fresh air—where we can steal kisses and taste sweet nothings.

But on the veranda, you speak of another passion...of racing horses...

You lust to find the fastest. And it is lust, for it...it sparkles in your eyes, moves your hands, and rings your words.

You tell me your dream...this passion. Yet I know that if a girl understands a man's passions...

But all this sweet...sweet clover...near a gurgling brook and happy children? I've splashed here a hundred times. And fled Father's clutches for "sugar kisses!" HA!

Yes, here in Saratoga's Great Meadow, Alex Parker's drifting daydreams rekindled the savored childhood memories of a five-year-old bundle of energy with blond ringlets full of bounce and squeals.

Yet why do I feel...confused one moment and giddy the next? This tugging and yearning...that so chases me frantic? I've always enjoyed the bowling green... the soft grass slope above the wading pool...taking the sun's warmth and...letting...go.

And the lingering memory of last night's dinner...Payne meeting Commodore Vanderbilt...the table conversation...the surprise carnation bouquet...and Payne's invitation to dance...! Ahhh...

Two schottisches, three polkas, and too many waltzes to count. Alex had done her best to follow his lead, panting...remembering no misstep. And someone had cooed for all to hear, "They make such a lovely couple!"

Why can't I put him out of my mind?

Handsome, strong, intelligent...that winning smile and yes, those heart-melting blue eyes. More and more though, she returned to his kiss at evening's end. A gentleman's touch, warm but firm, meeting her lips with grace but tasting of deeper passions. That was all...a single, wonderful kiss, but traced and touched with thrill and promise. And lest she deny it, yes, he'd left her...hanging...lingering...and wanting more.

I'll never let him know...But if I could....Mmmmm.

Yeah, kissing like this. Imagine him...just like this!

Like it's almost real! Feeling his breath close... Yes! So smooth...!

"Good! I knew you wouldn't forget."

Alex jerked back, blinking into blue eyes. Close. As was the voice.

"And so angelic, Alex. What's a guy to do?"

The looming face kissed her again!

"Payne Harrison! I ought to...."

"Just making sure you didn't spoil overnight. Or forget. Not to mention your morning charms were more than I could resist!"

"Forget? Spoil overnight? Charms! Sir! People can see us! How long have you been here?"

"Long enough, my dear Alex. But you were so...kissable?" Payne beamed like a successful candy thief.

"You advantaged me."

"Really now? And you had zero intentions of sitting out here on this fine summer morning daydreaming and looking so...!" Payne patched his finger to her lips, dipped his forehead, and narrowed his eyes. "Kissable!"

"Of all the nerve! Why I'll have you know that..."

"And I think you need more."

Alex froze wide-eyed as Payne cupped his hands to her face, tracing her lips with the tip of his tongue. No children pointed, no parents glared.

And this is pure pleasure.

Only swans graced the pond, gliding blissfully across the clear surface like down shadows on glass. Memories of summers past warmed like the rising sun. And the smooth, vibrant exhilaration of a dream-come-true with the dawn.

"So you followed me?" Alex pulled back, leery of gawkers, but felt only his gaze. She darted her own...to his eyes...to his lips, then back again.

"You said you loved this place, Alex. Especially at sunrise. Thought I'd find out for myself."

She bit her bottom lip. "And...?"

"A bit tidy for my taste. All this manicured grass and such. Course fishermen love to sample the waters. And by the looks of things...."

"Payne! You wouldn't!"

In a novel effort to beautify the grounds, city fathers had stocked the catchment ponds below the springs with spectacular schools of koi. Children of all ages flocked to admire the fish.

"Why Miss Parker, I'd never catch such beautiful fish with a hook!"

"What...?"

"Watch." Payne removed his shoes and socks, then touched the tips of his toes to the water. "Shhhhh. This is the delicate part."

You think you can bait fish with your toes?

Curious but wary, Alex eased beside him. Payne dangled his left foot into the water. Golden fish glided below.

Do they really think...?

"Get ready," he whispered. "See goldie, there...the big one with the black spot on the dorsal fin? Watch."

Alex leaned closer, her hand pressing Payne's right shoulder, her eyes gliding back and forth on the fish...and the slow dance of Payne's toes.

Will he really take the bait?

"Watch, Alex...easy now. See, he's..."

And that's when Payne's shoulder gave way, tipping her toward the pool. But instead of getting dunked, Alex jarred to a stop, dry and caught, cradled in surrounding arms, looking up from Payne's lap into his smile.

This time she did not linger, but met his lips with a zeal of her own.

You trickster! All right...I fell for it, literally, you clever fellow. But anybody who thinks he can catch fish on a toe...

Still, sir, two can play this game by the waters of Saratoga.

Indeed. The next time her mind wandered, Alex would meet the world with more than a smile on her face.

G entlemen, it's my distinct pleasure to introduce Mr. Payne Harrison of Virginia. Some of you know of his recent success in the Virginia Derby and I'm sure you have plenty of questions. But let me first say that in the short time I've known this man, I can attest that his knowledge of thoroughbred horseracing is matched only by the energy and enthusiasm you bring to turning a profit!"

Robert Parker's little joke garnered a few soft chuckles. "I believe you'll find his comments and suggestions engaging...and optimistic."

Of the men gathered in the small but posh Gentlemen's Club—a reservations-only, walnut-paneled meeting room behind the bar in the United States Hotel—Payne knew only Parker. Yet, William R. Travers, Leonard W. Jerome, and John R. Hunter ranked among the best connected businessmen in New York State. All had deep pockets and knew plenty of other men with even deeper ones. They brought to the table sponsorship, financing, prestige.

And expectations.

150

Payne offered know-how. As Robert Parker had outlined, these men knew little about horse racing. Even more so, they had no desire to sully their hands in the day-to-day business of assuring a fair contest, whether it be calculating payouts midst fluctuating odds or overseeing jockey weights and track maintenance.

What they had was money and the willingness to invest it...with the expectations of profit and a little fun along the way. What they wanted was an experienced hand to show them the way. But also someone they could trust.

This Virginian came recommended as one who could guide their plans for a Northern racing classic into reality. If reputable thoroughbred racing were introduced to New York, they believed all of New England would come. Employ a competent Southerner to make it happen and the whole nation would join them. Done right, ownership of a "national thoroughbred championship"—no, THE national thoroughbred championship—could be theirs.

Shares in the venture, they agreed, would be sold only by private invitation at $1000 each. With extensive planning and construction—a sizeable tract of land had already been optioned east of town—the region's first stakes race might be only a year away.

"What's the biggest pitfall we haven't considered, Mr. Harrison?" asked William Travers in the meeting's second hour.

"Everything must be free of reproach. Without that, we go nowhere."

"Certainly, Mr. Harrison," agreed John Hunter, "if we create a golden goose, we'd be foolish to pluck its feathers." Everyone laughed.

"You know," Payne continued, letting the mirth subside, "there is one concern we've not addressed." Heads turned.

"A number of Southern owners rely on black jockeys. Given this attack on Harper's Ferry last fall, few are going to risk their riders to the abolitionists up here." Payne stopped. He could see he'd said enough.

Amiable businessmen, their smiles wreathed in cigar smoke, holding glasses of sherry or the finest whiskey, expecting more dollars in yet another novel enterprise, chilled into a silent landscape of narrowed eyes and icy, expressionless faces. They'd not considered this, the fervor of the anti-slavery movement. Southerners hazarding valuable property near an abyss of the underground railroad? Then again, did they really want a plantation's slave jockey in their winner's circle?

Perhaps we should reconsider...

Awkwardness shackled the room, the gulf between North and South thrust front and center into the pitching dialogue.

The massive Gentlemen's Club door grated opened.

"Aye, sorry I'm a bit late lads but the Commodore sends his regrets from the station. Had to leave for the city—last minute thing, he said—but I bring ye all his greetings. He's passionate about this racing, ye know."

"I don't believe you've met Mr. Morrissey, have you Payne?" asked Robert Parker, trying to salvage matters.

"Me Lord, Robert Parker, Payne and I be mug mates from way back, don't ye think, Payne?" John Morrissey strode to the front of the room, wringing Payne's hand in friendship.

"This fellow's as good as they come, me friends. The Commodore likes him and so do I. He's what we need to make this go...and go it shall. Besides, I've seen his uppercut." Morrissey swung a fist and roared.

If there needed to be a testimonial, this did it.

"You didn't tell me you were involved in this, John Morrissey!"

"Ye didn't ask me, friend Payne. Besides, did ye tell these gentlemen of ye recent equine discovery in the mountains of western Virginia?"

"We're sure Mr. Harrison's grooming some admirable challengers," said Leonard Jerome. "The *Spirit of the Times* just profiled him. Certainly you'll enter your fastest in Saratoga's first stakes race?"

"When he does, you'll find no penny of "Old Smoke's" on anybody else," John Hunter declared. "I know you, Morrissey...you've got the inside scoop way before the rest of us."

"Come now, my dear Hunter, do ye think I would keep ye in the dark come race day? Surely ye know me better than that!"

"Well, Mr. Harrison," said William Travers, twisting his mustache with a practiced flair, "If he is as good as all that—as Mr. Morrissey says he is—we'll have to see what we can do to find him some real competition. And I might just take a gentleman's side wager on the matter...if you'll oblige me. So to initiate...and stimulate interest, let's wager a full share—$1000—my entry versus yours...say, next August? Is that a workable date, gentlemen?"

"It's your money, sir," said Payne. "A year should give us plenty of time to finance and build a track, to market and promote the event. I'll have my entry here the fourth weekend in August."

"Done!" William Travers rose and took Payne's outstretched hand, a wager between gentlemen sealed. "John, hold our bets until next summer? Let's see, we can call it...the North/South challenger stakes!"

Travers' clever ploy not only solidified the negotiations and a future date for the first stakes race, it glossed over the uncomfortable sectionalism that had moments before silenced the room. But there was more; Travers had gotten Payne to commit to the venture with an entry and investment of his own. The Virginian could hardly command credibility as a contributor to the project if he declined Travers' challenge.

So next August, it's North versus South; Number Twelve against...all of Yankeedom. This is going to get interesting.

E veryone picnicked at Saratoga. Unlike White Sulphur Spring's mountain setting, the upstate New York spa bubbled from rolling countryside. Giant tracts of sparsely settled wilderness stretched north and west of the town, craggy cliffs and dark, deep woods sporting picturesque meadow-rimmed ponds and deep glacial lakes.

Winsome, spectacular country for afternoon horseback rides.

Yes, patrons of the White indulged in picnics, but they were usually catered affairs spread on the expansive grassy green, summertime communal feeds where all one had to do was "meet, greet, eat, fete, and retreat." The same festive atmosphere pervaded Saratoga, but here humanity spilled out of the hotels and into the streets, parks, and countryside.

Payne reckoned on the differences. Saratoga, one popular writer had said, existed as "a caravanserai," swarming with dancers, drinkers, and rich people. Here, flirtatious belles bowled in muslin, perfectly styled and presented, dropping linen handkerchiefs for eager but naive young men who failing in favor or courtship, gambled, got drunk, and vomited pea green gruel after too much tobacco. At every major hotel, colored waiters scampered down corridors and through dining halls, hustling platters with white-toothed grins. Music seemed as much a part of the local weather as an afternoon's breeze, with German bands tooting brass and pounding drums from elevated bandstands in a never-ending party.

"Picnic? Sure, Alex, but let's make it an adventure!" Payne wanted no more of the basket-laden mayhem that crowded the greens and parks adjacent to Broadway and Congress Spring. After three days in town, he longed to escape the garish decor of hotel lobbies and slick, sidewalk dandies. "Let's get into the country, away from the crowds."

"Then take the trail north of Saratoga," said Luke. "You know Alex, the one we explored the day Payne got here? Ride out Hemlock Road several miles...near the climb to Mount Vista. Take the left trail along the ridge."

"Sounds scenic to me," said Payne. "Thanks, Luke."

By mid-morning, Alex had sandwiches, tarts, and several apples tucked inside a small haversack complemented with a canteen of lemonade. Payne visited the alley livery stable three blocks down Broadway and reserved two bay geldings for the day.

"Ye'll be needing better than them to win next year this time, good friend." It was Morrissey, dapper as usual, but in a hurry as he rounded the corner above the stable.

"Depends on the jockey. And the trainer!"

"Aye, good sir, 'tis true no doubt. But in the ring, when the chips are down, it is ye against the world...and that's all that matters."

"Like that nickname of yours? 'Old Smoke.' Is that it?"

John Morrissey's rugged face fleshed the scars of a bare-knuckled brawler. But it was his eyes—clear, bright, yet fired—that captivated Payne. *He looks straight through me, yet sees all.*

He recalled Otto, the bartender's wild tale...how Morrissey as a young gambler and a no-holds-barred fighter, bit, gouged, and maimed—as well as slugged—his opponents to win. Sure, others fought dirty and were just as savage. But John Morrissey always *won.*

Once when fighting over a prostitute, Morrissey had slipped and careened into a hot stove, upsetting the coals. To everyone's horror, his opponent pressed him into the glowing embers! Morrissey went berserk, wrenching up in ire and pain to soundly thrash the man. From then on "Old Smoke" instilled fear in most and caution in the rest. With little knowledge of so-called scientific boxing, he used his youth, strength, and clever manipulation of the rules to win. Promoted and managed with skill, he defeated Yankee Sullivan in 1853 for the American championship.

Morrissey then turned his fame into gold, buying several of New York's more successful gaming houses. Nurturing ties to Tammany Hall, the champ expanded his operations to Saratoga Springs.

"Don't believe everything ye hear, friend," Morrissey said, putting his arm around Payne as the two strode up the street. "But ye know, if it's worth fighting for, it's worth fighting dirty for!" he roared.

Payne hardly knew what to make of the man. Given his background and contacts, Morrissey might rocket this high-profile stakes race for all...or manipulate matters to his own private gain. *He will bear watching!*

"Let's saunter up Broadway," the boxer suggested with a knowing turn up the street, "a little excitement's come to town."

Band music beckoned in the distance, thumping a pulsed, martial air. People scurried curbside. A flag-draped carriage pulled by four white horses came into view. Cheers swelled and as the conveyance got closer, strains of *See the Conquering Hero Comes* thumped off the walls of the Congress and United States Hotel. Payne stretched for a better look, spotting a squat, robust man waving with a dignified air.

"Bully for the Little Giant," shouted a man to Payne's left.

"Absolutely!" yelled another. "Three cheers for Douglas. Hip, hip hooray! Hip, hip hooray! Hip, hip, hooray!"

In his campaign for the Democratic presidential nomination, Illinois Senator Stephen A. Douglas was canvassing the Empire State. All candidates for President courted New York.

The carriage slowed and the crowd edged closer. A large banner bearing the single word, WELCOME, draped above the entrance to the United States Hotel. Douglas poked his way through the mob, shaking hands as he climbed the podium. A practiced and honed orator, he adjusted his collar during the introduction, removed a few papers from his pocket and cleared his throat, letting the crowd quiet.

Saratoga, "this glorious place," is the property of the Union, he began, the whole Union, a place where citizens from every section, North and South, who love their country can come and enjoy the healthy benefits nature has provided. No one should feel alienation in any part of America for "we are all Americans."

Most cheered to this, but Payne spotted others who only watched... curious, studious types, intent to examine this man who sought to lead the nation through her current ills. *Hardly appears presidential, but sure knows how to whip up a crowd.*

With a national figure in town, Saratoga strutted with vigor. Douglas partisans finished the rally with more cheers and street noise. The candidate smiled and waved, but the excitement faded as soon as he disappeared inside the hotel. Politics seemed everywhere these days.

"So an outing...into the country?" Morrissey waved at the dispersing crowd. "Ye'll surely be more entertained than these just gathered."

"With Robert Parker's daughter."

"Oooooh...the sweet Miss Alex! Such an elegant lass, and a marvelous voice, too. Get her to lullaby ye Saratoga!"

Morrissey eyed Payne's empty face.

"Oh, get on with ye, old man. Ye really don't know what I'm talking 'bout? Here, let me verse ye in some local lore."

Clearing his throat, the former boxing champion broke into song, showcasing a rich baritone of his own. Gentlemen along the street as well as those shaded under hotel porches looked up with grins of recognition. And ladies who knew the words, hid their faces behind fans aflutter.

> Now they stroll in the beautiful walks,
> Or loll in the shade of the trees;
> Where many a whisper is heard
> That never is told by the breeze;
> And hands are commingled with hands,

Regardless of conjugal rings;
And they flirt, and they flirt, and they flirt—
And that's what they do at the Springs!

In short—as it goes in the world—
They eat, and they drink and they sleep;
They talk, and they walk, and they woo;
They sigh, and they laugh, and they weep;
They read, and they ride, and they dance'
(With other unspeakable things;)
They pray, and they play, and they *pay*—
And that's what they do at the Springs!

Chapter Nineteen

*T*he old oak near Luke's fishing spot! Perfect! We'll spread the quilt in the soft grass beneath it...right at the water's edge.

Alex loved the lake and its trailing, languid shoreline. Eyes closed, here she could savor the sounds of the day...the lapping water...the distant bark of a dog...children kicking gravels.

Listening not only summoned the music of life, for Alex Parker, it conjured the magic of music. Her earliest childhood songs had blossomed from nature's melodies. Tuning in the world, sensitive to the chords and rhythms of just *being*, she would hone and polish her harmonious talents on many, marvelous rhapsodic stones.

Her tactile senses were another matter. A man's touch, for example, could be anything from sensuous to revolting. The Boston girls at school giggled about boys "sending tingles up their spines" or "making their flesh crawl!" *Oh my! No screeching fingernails clawing a blackboard for me!*

But Alex at nineteen wanted to believe rough hands had more to do with a man's occupation than his intentions; calluses for a blacksmith, a carpenter, a farmer...soft pinkies and a clean manicure for the accountant, clerk, or schoolteacher. Yet even that could be deceptive; at the keyboard, nimble digits could mangle Mozart and butcher Bach.

So with hands, she looked for other things.

Like scars. Every cicatrix carried a story, especially those scoring hands, conjuring up an injury, carelessness, a bit of intrigue, or a failed feat of skill. Her curiosity soared on missing digits. Or nails mashed purple. Payne Harrison, she observed, had all his and no dark colors. Nor did he wear jewelry. That was for street dandies, or as Luke might say, pirates.

But finger rings...augured position, heritage, fraternity. Robert Parker's had once wax-sealed letters with the family crest. Now her father wore it as a golden heirloom, bequeathed to him from his father's father's estate. A man subscribing to such things, Alex believed, would love family, cherish home, and amount to something.

Some rings of course, signaled love. Alex glanced to her hands. *Pink and plain.* Yet unlike some she could name, she had no *naked* feeling, no burning desire to slip some man's proffered token onto her finger just yet.

"Gorgeous, clear day!" Payne dismounted, then assisted Alex. "Quite a pond," he said, wrapping the reins around the oak's low hanging limbs.

"For sure!" Alex untied her sunbonnet, leaning into the breeze with a quick-toss of her head. She savored days like this. Bright, warm, fresh...keyed to Nature's song.

"It's a long swim to the other side! But right over there's Luke's favorite fishing hole." Alex pointed to a low granite shelf knifing from the shore. "Once when he was six, a fish pulled *him* in!"

"And I bet you hooted, huh, big sister?"

"It was hilarious! He was so mad!"

Alex sat down on the quilt and opened the haversack. "Smuggled you one of these." Her voice beguiled pure temptation as she handed him a bottle of ginger beer. "Hope you don't think it's too Yankee!"

Payne smoothed a corner of the blanket and laid back in the shade, hands clasped behind his head, looking up through the limbs intertwined overhead. "You know, you're about all the Yankee I can handle today, but... well, I guess a gentleman's obliged to partake."

He worked the cork from the white and yellow earthenware and sipped, swishing cheek to cheek. "Not bad. 'Course it can't be as good as this Saratoga Water I keep hearing about."

"Oh, the invalids swear by the waters!"

"I'll take this." Payne swept his right arm at the lake, pointing to the distant shore. "Bet I could swim it."

His was a typical male boast and Alex knew it. She'd seen others go on like this, seeking to impress her. But Payne Harrison made the ritual fascinating. Not his bragging so much, but his hands talking... moving, yet unhurried. Yes, he projected a certain flair, a cute kind of assurance, but it all came mannered and packaged in a language beyond words.

She handed him an apple and sat down beside him. Thirty yards offshore, two men rowed a boat. Their wake diamonded in the afternoon sun like sparkling necklaces rippling to shore.

"You know, Indians revered these waters. According to legend, the lake reflected the heavens. A mirror on the sky."

Payne sank his incisors into the apple.

"And when the lake stretched perfectly flat...that's when the Great Spirit listened to the earth. A canoe might glide like an arrow across its glassy surface, but only in strict silence. No brave's voice must break the sacred quiet; to do so would doom the canoe to the deep!"

She waited for some nod, but got only fruit scrunches.

"There's another legend, you know."

"Really?" Payne looked up, wiping his lower lip.

"Yes, people 'round here say if you could ever skip a stone across the lake, your dream will come true."

Payne flipped his apple core at the water. "No way, Alex. Too far."

"No one says it's easy. Luke tries all the time."

"And you?"

"Sure. Everybody does."

"Yeah, but I bet you skip 'em like a girl."

Alex shoved him to the blanket. "I'll have you know I can whip Luke!"

"I'd like to see that. But don't break any of those sacred silences!"

"Oh, Payne! Stop! It's still a neat story."

The Virginian pointed at the distant rowers. "They believe all this stuff?" His finger missed Alex's nose by half an inch...on purpose.

So she bit him, growling playful little animal sounds.

He easily jerked free, but quickly wrapped her waist and pulled her over, eye to eye, inches apart, she atop, but fast in his arms. Both stilled...his fingers intertwined behind her...she tense and wary. But instead of struggling had it been another, she relaxed, captivated. *Nicely captivated.*

"We keep meeting like this," she whispered.

"So we do, but then last time, you could have gotten drenched!"

"But..." Her eyes twinkled.

Payne arched from the quilt, meeting her lips lightly. Alex pulled back letting him find her, relaxing at his touch, her hair falling like a delicate, golden canopy. Again he kissed her, as if discovering honey, moving from lips to cheek, buried in her beauty, savoring the brush of her tresses and drinking in her fragrance as she slipped her fingers through his hair.

Close. She desired him that way. His hands—such marvelous hands—moved slowly downward, ever so to her hips, finding and smoothing. Her fingers curled at the back of his neck, tugging his locks in a gentle twirl.

Emotions burned and blurred. Payne's touch, the moist warmth of lips tasting and sharing, grazing and breathing...*close, close. Yes, like that!*

As he nuzzled her, she leaned back, letting him move lower... finding that she loved him kissing her neck, again and again...softly, and oh so sweetly, thrilling to his touch. His gentle teasing, the seductive sound of his voice...all fueled her instincts. And with it, a growing, inner intensity. Like a candle hurried from a great distance, a point of light expanding, closing with an all consuming, exhilarating brilliance.

Images flashed. That day on the bridge at the White...the Grand Ball Waltz in Saratoga...his gorgeous blue eyes and that winning smile.

And this wanting to be near you...

Brighter still her candle grew, and with it Alex's desires climbed, powerful pulls yearning to be understood and daring her to experience. This man moved with her, but what was he saying? His words? She could hear him, but what was his music?

"Come to Virginia." His words cooed like lyrics. "Come for Christmas, Alex...to Walnut Grove...meet my folks."

Alex heard. But this...frolicking with a man...on a quilt...in front of the whole world... *What...what are you asking?*

"Come. Visit. Over Christmas. I know you need to get settled in Baltimore, but in December..."

She looked into him, searching.

"But Baltimore's...a long way. And I..."

"Alex...." Silence best weighted his words. "Just...come?"

She nodded, exhaling, having held her breath to his every word.

"Besides, Twelve misses you awful! You don't want to disappoint him!"

"Now there's a reason to visit Walnut Grove," she laughed, pushing him back to the quilt. "My real champion! But aren't you hungry." She reached into the haversack. "Any news from Virginia?"

"Sam's entering Twelve in a trial with Jasper aboard on Saturday at the Richmond Fairgrounds. I plan to see it."

"I thought you...were staying a bit longer?"

"Wish I could. Course the temptations up here are...you know, this ginger beer!" Payne grinned and emptied the bottle, setting it down with a satisfying, "Ahhhhh."

Just like a man.

But he'd given her a lot to ponder. Visit Virginia? What did she really know about this man?

Well, what is this I feel for him?

For Payne Harrison...

Whatever it is, it's real.

*S*he knows such things. And Luke knows the way. Luke always knows!

But Alex found sleep wouldn't come.

What am I afraid of? Well, what if...?

Her mind churned like a roiling stew. *Shouldn't dwell on it. What could that old biddy possibly know?*

She wanted to pull back the thought, glad at least she'd not given voice to her doubts.

But of course Saratoga's seer knew! Look at Angeline Tubbs' crooked nose! And those coal black eyes!

She could almost hear him laugh...teasing her. *Payne's far away. Home by now. Would think me silly, dreaming this stuff.*

Alex burrowed into the bed linens, savoring the soft, deep caress of her down pillow. *Far away...oh...that Southern man and his horses.*

Her lips creased to a smile. *Yeah, I'll go to Walnut Grove. I can handle that much. No matter what Angeline Tubbs says.*

O K. That's it."
   "You promised!"
"Don't even try, Alex. No way. You can see her cottage from here."

"Luke...!"

The boy shook his head again. "You wanted me to get you here. Well, here you are."

Any other time, Alex would have challenged her brother on such dereliction of duty, cajoling, manipulating, even shaming him into accompanying her to Angeline Tubbs's cottage. But Luke's demeanor...his stony silence on the ride out from Saratoga Springs... the resolute tone of his words now. No...this was it.

"Fine, I'll go this myself."

"And I'll wait here," he said.

Wait here? What good will that do?

Alex eyed the cabin in the clearing below. *He must not see me hesitate.*

"Got your quarter?"

"Yeah."

"Good, don't linger."

"I'll stay as long as I want, brother."

Luke watched from the brush as his sister guided her horse down the cabin's narrow trail. She dismounted, glancing back in his direction for a moment, but couldn't find him. Seeing no one about, she tied up to the porch post. *What am I doing?*

"A good afternoon to you, dearie."

A calico cat darted from under the porch, followed by three scampering kittens. Alex looked at the door from where the voice had come, seeing it drift ajar, but no one appeared.

"Don't get many callers...in the heat of the day." The words cackled, softly spitten. Yet Alex surmised they sounded a welcome of sorts. "Now, let's see you, dearie." A bedraggled, ordinary woman shuffled from the gloom of the cottage's interior.

At least she appears harmless.

Hardly five feet in height, Angeline Tubbs seemed as round as she was tall. She wore rumpled clothes—a tired, torn cotton dress, smudged with dirt here, a grease spot there—and covered her gray bun of hair with a plain, yellowed bonnet.

"A fair lassie you are." She put no question to her words. "Move not a mite, child."

Alex froze wide-eyed, as the woman circled. Halfway around, and without warning, Tubbs jabbed a finger into Alex's left shoulder, then stroked her hand down Alex's spine. After a firm squeeze to both wrists, she stepped back with a look of cautious satisfaction.

"You shall bring forth life to the world."

"Beg your pardon?"

"Dearie, I know you think I'm an old flub, a fake, a crank, reading palms out here in the woods...telling young girls what they want to hear."

You look like a dried peach...

The old woman spit to one side, a dark juice hitting just beyond the porch, clumping the dust into grey, fuzzy nodules.

"Judging me book by the rents in me cover?" Angeline Tubbs looked down, smoothing her left forefinger over the palm of her right hand.

She knows what I'm thinking!

"You know the torn and soiled are everybody's favorites, the books folks read the most."

Alex darted a glance up the lane.

"He's still there, dearie."

Luke? How does she know these things?

Unnerved, Alex rose. "I really shouldn't be bothering you." The future suddenly didn't matter that much. "Here's a..."

"Keep your treasure for the moment, dearie. I haven't earned it yet." She motioned for Alex to take a seat.

"I'm wondering why you came...instead of your brother." Tubbs darted another look at the crest line, her gaze lingering in the trees.

"He could tell me best, you know." Her words scooted flat and stale.

"But forget all those yarns you hear 'bout me, dearie. Stay a while, for I feel something with you...and that boy out there. But he's not why you rode out. I know that now. AH! Another steals you away! Hee, hee, hee!"

Alex felt warming reassurance in the old woman's words. She rubbed the quarter between her fingers and sat down.

"So you know...before I even ask?"

Tubbs tilted her head to one side, betraying a faint, wistful smile, but nothing more.

She's unfolding my secrets!

"Tell me about him."

"About Payne?"

"Ahhh, Payne. Peculiar name."

"He's different. Southern..." Alex smiled.

"And you love him..."

Alex looked into the old woman's eyes, seeing merriment and contentment...and realizing her words had not trailed to a question. Angeline Tubbs could be trusted.

"He wants me to..."

"Come for a visit. Then you must do it, dearie. This is the way of things for the two of you."

"Are you sure?"

"You tell me, dearie. Here, give me your hand."

Cautiously, Alex extended her right arm. The old woman took her hand and spread the fingers, tracing lines across Alex's palm. She hummed softly, but said nothing for some moments.

"You are virtuous yet possessed of great passion. I pray you will find the balance."

Alex listened, riveted on Tubbs' every motion.

"You love the sound of voices, the calling of hymns and great bursting into song. Such talent is from God, my child. But for you, I see sharing. The noblest of duties...teacher."

"I've been offered a position teaching music in Baltimore."

"A convenient destination to points farther south. Time will sing you more. Just be sure to listen." The woman's words waxed magic.

"Yes, but..."

"Hush child! I see more. Broken lines...shadows...a destiny delayed!"

The old woman dropped Alex's hand, squinting from deep furrows.

"Dear...Almighty...Providence! It is for him!"

Angeline Tubbs reached inside her apron, fingers rubbing. "I...I have worried on something...but know not what it means."

She hocked up more spittle and turned toward the ridge top. "But someday he will."

Chapter Twenty

Walnut Grove
Chesterfield County, Virginia
21 December 1860

And a Merry Christmas to you, Major Johnson. It's so good to see you and your brother again."

Edward and Philip Johnson nodded to Jane Harrison and stepped into Walnut Grove's front hall. Had her callers been anyone else on this winter's eve, one of the servants would have answered the knock at the door, but Mrs. Harrison was determined she personally welcome the Major and his brother to her annual Christmas party. Neighbors coveted her invitations. And with Midlothian's resident military hero home on leave, Ned Johnson captured the top of her list this year. Folks still talked of his heroics at Molino del Rey and Chapultepec.

Every Christmas, the Harrisons decorated Walnut Grove to embody the spirit and warmth of the season. Two robust holly wreaths greeted callers at the main gate, while a third, larger version garnished the front door. In the entrance hall, pine boughs bedecked the balusters to the upstairs landing, tied to every fifth banister with an elegant red ribbon. A larger red bow, smartly fixed to the newel post, offered candy canes in broad bunting to youngsters. The sweetness of vanilla-scented candles filled each room. Sprigs of mistletoe surprised every other doorway, and servants armed with piles of split oak tended the rooms' crackling fires. The bounty of the evening tendered Old Dominion culinary delights ranging from roast turkey, country cured ham, and fresh venison, to apple tarts, ginger cookies, and cherry pie, all downed on holiday punch, vintage wines, aged whiskey, and Aunt Hattie's storied eggnog.

"Major, it's been far too long." Colonel Harrison extended his hand.

"A fact, sir," said Ned Johnson, grasping the Colonel's welcome. "Leave sure is a touchy thing these days. First Christmas home in... well...I'm not sure. When's the last time, Phil?"

Ned's older brother shrugged.

"Certainly a lot of bees have buzzed the hive since last we met," said the Colonel. "But please, come in and meet everyone."

Heads turned when the Johnson brothers entered Walnut Grove's brightly decorated Great Room. A tall, fresh-cut cedar, its familiar scent rousing a festive pungency, dominated the chamber with three dozen burning candles, a host of glittering ornaments, and a crowning Star of Bethlehem.

"Payne, know who that is?" Clay nodded toward the rough-hewn man in uniform shaking hands with a circle of men including Doc Morrissett, Leland Hobbs, and Conner Goode.

Payne had never met Ned Johnson, just his brother Philip, a wizened old bachelor who lived at Salisbury. *Only horses over there pull plows.*

"Folks say he's either the bravest soldier to come out of Chesterfield... or a puffed up martinet." When Aunt Hattie's eggnog oiled him, Clay spoke his mind. "Or both," he added with a sloppy grin.

The Major's uniform readily set him apart from every other man in the room. But as a soldier, Ned Johnson hardly presented the stereotypical aloof bearing of a military man. Instead, he went about the room shaking hands with well-wishers, pausing for conversation and hearty laughs with old friends. And he had a clumsy streak, stumbling over a horsehair sofa as if he'd sprawled through a stable door.

Too early for sauce. He just got here.

Though not a tall man, Ned Johnson possessed a rugged, solid build. After a decade of hell-hole summers and ice box winters on the frontier, Johnson's rough, lined countenance reminded Payne of an old snapping turtle. His gargantuan, flapping ears framing thinning, sandy hair evidenced a man burnished by privation and outdoor living. Scraggly chin whiskers did him no favors. And his loud, booming voice warned all of a hard-bitten son-of-a-bitch who suffers no fools. Yet when Payne saw him, he wanted to laugh.

Lousy in the saddle, I bet.

"Took him five years to grind through West Point," said Clay, smug in his disclosure. "And the only reason he got by then was because no one had the balls to flunk out Thomas Jefferson's cousin."

"The President?"

"Yep. Grandpappy on his mama's side was Jefferson's first cousin. Nice connections, huh, brother?"

"Perhaps, but he looks like he could clean your clock."

Clay Harrison glared back, his face flushed by more than sharp words.

"What makes you so..."

"All right, you two." Alex poked a finger into Payne's backside as she came up behind him. She knew sibling rivalry when she saw it, yet she was finding her Virginia Christmas quite the festive affair.

So many friendly, happy people. And all these genteel accents!

"Alex, see that officer across the room? Clay thinks he's a buffoon."

"Not at all. Just a big-eared old bastard!"

"Such language, Clay!"

"Aww shush, dear Yankee lass."

Clay's had too much to drink.

"Remember Jimmy Meadows—George Cole's handyman—you know, the orphan boy the Coles raised? Well, that time when he went to Richmond to enlist a few years back...and came running home scared to death? Seems old Johnson ran the recruitment station in town. Jimmy swore he was the meanest, cussingest man he'd ever met."

"I'm not sure that's a fair measure of the man," said Alex, watching Johnson bow to Mrs. Henry Gregory, then salute old Ramsey Parsons, a veteran of the War of 1812. "I find him rather...*intriguing*."

"Then waltz on over Alex."

Payne had seen his brother like this before, bottled and boisterous.

"You don't approve, Paynie? I hear the man's a war hero. That in Mexico he carried off his wounded brigade commander under a barrage of bullets. Course, others swear he's skirt crazy!"

"And you'd best ease up on the eggnog, brother."

"He sure showed those greasers down there. And Alex, I happen to know he and his brother are both quite eligible bachelors."

"Shut up, Clay!"

"'Fraid the uniform'll steal your sweetie, Paynie?"

"That's enough, you two," said Alex.

Payne wiped his mouth, eyes glaring. *Johnson ogling Alex...? Hah! She's already caught the eye of every man in the room.*

But he too, found this Major Johnson interesting. He'd heard his father speak of the Johnsons' estate, Salisbury, a mile north of Midlothian.

"You're such a tease, Clay Harrison. Come on, Payne. Introduce me." Alex tugged Payne's hand and started across the room.

"Clay's drunk, Alex. Ignore him."

"Well, I'm with you, sir. Not him."

And you are stunning tonight.

"Oh, lookie here Ned, this here's Chesterfield's racin' man, Payne, the colonel's oldest boy." Philip Johnson slapped Payne on the back. "Meet my baby brother Ned."

"Mr. Harrison, please ignore my fossilized brother." Ned Johnson stuck out his hand—a thick, calloused ham—and wrung Payne's arm to the shoulder.

He IS rough. Loud, too. And look at those bags under his eyes, wrinkles on wrinkles on wrinkles, and his forehead goes on into next week...balding all the way back to...Gawd, are those ears?

"My...pleasure...sir," Payne mumbled, staring, then realizing Johnson's gaze had drifted to Alex. "And...permit me to introduce Miss Alexandra Parker from Massachusetts. She's an accomplished vocalist and music instructor."

Alex curtsied, smiled, and offered her hand.

Johnson bowed like a blizzard-blown fence post, pawing Alex's hand to his lips. "I'm ah, ah...it's my pleasure...to meet... You say... you sing?"

"Yes, sir. I teach at a girls' school in Baltimore. My father owns a business near Boston that supplies equipment to the Army."

"Well, I'm not very musical, ah...Miss...Miss...Baker?"

"Parker. My father owns the Parker Harness and Saddle Works in Lowell."

"Forgive me, Miss Barker. A bit hard of hearing here."

Payne noticed muscles spasm under Johnson's left eye.

"So...Barker's Furnace and Paddle Works? Don't recall it. Did several stints in the Commissary and Quartermaster's departments, but I never processed any requisitions on them."

Alex's eyes sparkled. "I'm sure you would know Papa's goods, sir. My father insists on the highest quality, particularly in saddles."

"Oh, cavalry? That explains it," said Johnson, gesturing with his glass. "You see Miss Barker, I serve in the infantry." He waved his whiskey with a flourish, spilling a third. Flustered, he fumbled for a handful of napkins from a nearby table and stooped to the floor.

"The servants will get that, Major," said Payne.

"No...no...my fault." Johnson coughed, trying to hide his embarrassment. Swabbing at the spill, he blinked even harder.

Payne leaned down to help. *What's with the eye?*

"Another mess in front of the ladies, Ned?" chirped Philip.

"Till your own field, brother! Just having a bit of seasonal conviviality, Miss Barker and I, are we not, Ma'am?"

"Well, if you'd paid attention," said Philip, "you'd know the lady's name is Parrrr...ker. Not Barrrr...ker. And you wouldn't slosh the Harrison's best liquor across the floor!"

Philip Johnson turned to Alex. "Kindly forgive my brother's social ineptitude. He's a lion before the foe, but a bleating lamb among the fair."

Ned Johnson stood up, his face red as the Harrison's hallway ribbon. Although ready to spit nails at his brother, he held his tongue, put down his glass, straightened his uniform, and then employing his greatest self-restraint, replied, "Pardon me, Miss...ah... Parker. Did I get your name right this time, my sweet?"

Alex laughed, charmed. "Perfect, sir!"

"Thank you, Ma'am. I'm at your service."

"My brother Rob is in the Army. Perhaps you know him?"

Johnson relaxed, more comfortable with a military question. "Parker?"

"Rob just graduated from West Point this spring."

"Ah, the Academy. I spent a hog's holiday in that place."

"Sir?"

"My brother's zeal for the Army," said Philip Johnson. "He knows nothing else!"

Both men leveled scowls at the other.

But Payne marveled at Ned Johnson's eye tic which now had settled into its own off-beat symphony. *And Alex doesn't even notice.*

"Miss Parker...bonds forged at the Academy are immutable. I consider your brother my brother...for those of us who get through West Point share a unique sense of belonging." Pride scored Ned Johnson's voice.

"Are you saying this makes Miss Parker...our sister?"

"Shut your trap, Phil!" The Major's cheeks burnished the brightest crimson of the Christmas season.

Payne got the distinct impression Johnson wanted to say more, but had taken his own counsel. "Well, sir, I'm glad to have made your acquaintance."

"And I'm wondering if the Major here, relishes the company of yet another Yankee!"

An intense, angular man brushed past Alex, offering his hand to Johnson. "Ashby Winters. We met in Puebla in the weeks before General Scott captured the City of Mexico."

"You have the advantage of me, sir."

"Commissary department. Come now, Major. We fed the army."

"I see. One of our supply contractors along the route from Vera Cruz?"

"Richmond Mercantile and Planters' Market, now. At your service, sir." Winters turned a cold gaze to Alex. "But given present circumstances, it looks like we'll be severing some of those brotherly...

and sisterly bonds with our Northern counterparts, would you not agree, Major?"

"Especially when South Carolina secedes." Leland Hobbs, a squat, rotund, balding man, nudged into the conversation. "And from what I hear, that could happen any day."

"When the Palmetto state breaks, should we look for the rest of the South to follow?" asked Conner Goode.

"Of course," said Hobbs. "With all this Yankee claptrap. If they know what's good for them, they'll let us go in peace."

"And if they don't?" Dr. Morrissett's challenge hushed the room.

"Then we'll just have to whup some ass," retorted Hobbs, a cocksure, crude knob of a man playing to the audience. "Everybody down here knows we can stomp Yankees like a line of ants."

"I'll remind you, Hobbs, you're in the presence of ladies."

"Colonel Harrison, I'd suggest our good neighbor Hobbs here is just giving voice to what every loyal Virginian is thinking." Ashby Winters turned and faced the wall of silent guests. "In fact, the decision's already come! It is my high honor to inform everyone here tonight that South Carolina has unanimously voted to leave the Union. Their state delegates signed an ordinance of secession in Charleston last night."

An audible gasp ended the room's hush.

"My God, then it's happened."

"Yes, Colonel. And more states are sure to follow. I'd advise our young men to heed Virginia's call when the time comes."

"Yessssir!" Hobbs' gleeful grin ground to a sneer. "And like I said, they come at us, we'll kick their ass."

"You're talking war here!" declared Dr. Morrissett.

"If they want it!" bellowed Hobbs. "Make no mistake, Lincoln and his lackeys can't stop us. But if they try, they'll rue the day in hell."

"You loud-mouthed braggart, you don't know a devil's whit about war. But keep this talk up and you and all your kind will get your own day in hell." Ned Johnson strode straight toward the short, balding man.

"I would expect you to go with Virginia, sir," Hobbs retorted.

"See this blue uniform? I serve the United States Army."

Hobbs stepped back. Perspiration glistened his brow.

Johnson loomed closer. "Ever heard the thunder of artillery, the ear-splitting screech of shot and shell...the screams of wounded, writhing men being bayoneted by murderers masquerading as soldiers? You talk war, mister, but you know nothing beyond newsprint."

Johnson turned slowly, studying every face.

"I guarantee you this. Persist on this path and unimaginable horrors lie ahead...for all of us."

He leaned his nose square in the short man's face. No nervous eye tic betrayed Ned Johnson now. Hobbs started to speak, but his lips only trembled.

Damn! Payne caught a glimpse of his mother near the Christmas tree, hand to bosom, fanning, aghast at the turn in her holiday party.

"And you, Winters." Johnson grabbed the Richmond businessman's arm. "Did OK in Mexico, did you? Need another war...to make another killing?"

"See here Johnson! Let me go. You've no call to accuse me."

"Nor you to insult this young lady."

Winters glanced to Hobbs who had edged back from the circle.

Johnson nodded to Alex. "Apologize, Winters."

Ashby Winters curled his lips in contempt. "I think not, Major. Events far beyond this gathering will soon speak for all of us in that regard."

"Winters, you don't hear very well."

"Go ahead, soldier. Start your fight. You'll be on our side soon enough and then what will you say? Angling for the best command, the choicest commission? Guess what? You'll have to come through men I know. So think about it, Major. Now get...get your hands off me!"

He paused, eyes narrowed, meeting Johnson's in open contempt. "Or perhaps you want to stay a blue-belly?"

Jerking hard, Ned Johnson spun Ashby Winters on his heels, wrenching the man's right arm behind him. "Winters, you need to learn some manners!"

"Damn you...Johnson!" he gasped.

"Direct your comments with a bit more civility to Miss Parker, if you please," growled Johnson, grinding Winter's arm into his spine.

"I ahhrggg...sorry." The words came sharp, guttural, and gasping.

Alex stared, stunned by the outburst from both men, until Johnson nodded to her and winked—a real wink thought Payne—signaling her to answer.

"Oh...apology accepted, sir," said Alex, unsure what to do next.

Johnson tightened his grip and shoved Winters toward the front door. "Sorry you have to leave so soon. But the night air might do you some good!"

Johnson spotted the short man. "You too, Hobbs!"

Hobbs scampered, grabbing both his and Winters' coats from a servant.

"Before you take your leave, I'm sure everyone joins me in wishing you gentlemen a very Merry Christmas. Right, Miss Parker?"

"From every state in our Union," replied Alex, as Johnson shoved Hobbs and Winters into the night and slammed the door.

In the pandemonium, the Major grabbed a cup of Aunt Hattie's eggnog.

"With so much holiday spirit spinning 'round tonight," he boomed above the din of voices, waving his hand, "I'd like to propose a toast."

All quieted as the Hero of Chapultepec raised his glass:

Virginia:
Where'er I go, whatever realms I see
My heart untrammeled, still returns to thee.

"Here, here!" chorused dozens.

The Major bowed, his shining forehead as bright as his craggy smile.

"And having offered this toast, I humbly request a favor. Miss Parker?" Johnson whispered, making sure he got her name right this time. Alex returned her own wink.

"I understand Miss Parker is an accomplished vocalist. I'm sure we would all be delighted if she would honor us with a seasonal rendition of one of her favorites. Would you do that for us, my sweet?"

Despite his giant ears, the eye tics, and coarse, awkward manner, Johnson's rugged charm hit home. Cheers and clapping filled the Great Room. All eyes went to Alex.

I've spoiled their party. And now they want me to sing?

But the applause swelled. People smiled and waved for her to come forward. *Nodding, happy people.*

Like Payne. *You can do this*, his smiling eyes seemed to say.

Oh, the charm of that man!

Alex closed her eyes, mustering to the mood.

But what can I possibly sing this night? God, help me.

And then she knew.

Smiling, Miss Alexandra Parker curtseyed and stepped forward. The room stilled.

And then the girl from the Bay State filled it with song:

> God bless our native land!
> Firm may she ever stand
> Thro' storm and night!
> When the wild tempests rave,
> Ruler of wind and wave
> Do Thou our country save
> By Thy great might.
> For her our prayer shall rise
> To God above the skies;
> On Him we wait.
> Thou who art ever nigh,
> Guarding with watchful eye,
> To Thee aloud we cry,
> God save the State!

S o, old boy, what shall I do?"

Payne Harrison had a lot to mesh on this cold winter's day.

"Good morning for a ride, don't you think?"

He offered Number Twelve a taste of sugar. "Yeah it's cold, but we've got the woods to ourselves. Course you don't have to say a thing. Just chomp the bit ... toss your mane."

Horse and rider cantered across Walnut Grove's West Meadow and turned toward the narrow path that angled into Chesterfield's Big Woods. Payne slowed the stallion to a walk. Snow threatened. Three icy inches already glazed the forest. He turned deeper into the woods under the leadened sky, the only sounds, Twelve's hooves crunching crust.

"She's special, fella. And crazy about you. Course, I may have something to say about that. But you read my mind, so you already know."

Look at me, talking to a horse. What does he really think?

Payne reined up. "Well, what DO you think, big boy? Is she the one?"

He listened, but in the Big Woods only stillness spoke. Paused on the trail, the thoroughbred's breathing gained Payne's attention, nostrils flaring as dual steam vents billowing into the January cold.

"What about you then? Are you really that fast?"

The horse didn't twitch a muscle.

"I know you can hear me. You always pick up my voice." He smoothed his hand down the horse's neck. "And I know you're smart..."

Payne eyed the winter sky. *More's coming.*

"..with a mind of your own."

He gathered the reins and tapped Twelve's left flank with his boot. In solitude, horse and rider resumed their journey down the path.

"Johnston told me you were aggressive, even as a foal. Said you were rougher than any horse he'd ever raised. That you'd just as soon bite and kick as run. But once you made up your mind, you could fly. Like the wind!"

I'm really dealing with two unknowns. Both of you are attractive, intelligent. And so independent. Agree?

The horse tossed his head.

"Me, too."

And nickered.

"Ahh..."

And nickered again.

"So you think she's the one?"

A soft breeze quickened through the forest, swirling the first snowflakes into sparkling, tiny funnels.

Chapter Twenty-One

Walnut Grove
Chesterfield County, Virginia
May 1861

J asper? What's that on your face?"

"What's you mean, Mammy?" The boy dabbed at his left cheek.

"You know my words. Baking bread in here for the Missus this fine mornin' and I see that long look you got. Spill it now, hear me?"

"Ain't nothin'." Jasper stepped off the kitchen porch.

"I reckon it is. 'Bout that horse, ain't it? Mammy knows."

"No, Ma'am."

"Don't sweet talk me!" She shot stares like bullets through butter. "Fess up, boy."

Jasper grabbed a broom.

"Done already swept it."

Jasper dropped the broom and plopped himself on a stool. "It's Master Payne. Full of temper 'fore he left yesterday."

"Figures. Been a bear in a beehive all week. Churned and spiced like witch's stew at a Sunday picnic. Him and Master Clay both!"

"Well, it ain't 'bout Number Twelve, Mammy."

"That little Yankee girl, then. You know he's goggle-eyed on her."

Aunt Hattie had seen the Christmas magic as plain as the December hoarfrost that crystallized her cabin window. *Just a matter of time. Master Payne's goin' down that church aisle for sure this time.*

"Ain't got no letter from 'er in three weeks, Mammy. Told me there's trouble up in Bal'mer where she's schoolmarming."

"What kind of trouble, boy?"

"Secesh stuff. Street fighting, Mammy. Yankee soldiers coming through. People got kilt."

"Secesh doin's is white folks doin's, Jasper. 'Member that. I reckon Miss Alex be just fine."

"Well, he ain't heard from her. So he went into Richmond...see what he could find out."

"Then let him be, boy."

Aunt Hattie glanced out the door. "Git on, now. Master Clay and Master Sam are lookin' for you."

As Jasper stood up, Sam waved from the stable.

"See? Mammy knows. Now here they both come."

"Got some bread, Auntie?"

"Yes, sir. With fresh butter if you've a pang to pamper, Master Clay."

"Jasper, didn't I tell you to muck out the stalls this morning?"

"Yes, sir. Just goin' to..."

"Then get your black ass hopping!"

"Master Clay, Jasper was just helping me sweep this old porch. It's my rhuematiz you know and..."

"Save it, Auntie. He's knows his chores around here."

"Fresh bread then." She held out a warm, soft loaf just from the oven...her eyes on the floor.

Clay Harrison grabbed the bread, turned, and stalked after her son.

"My boy didn't mean no harm, Master Sam. He'll scrub them stalls down."

"Don't fret it, Auntie." Sam watched Clay shout something at Jasper, then hurl a pitchfork into the larger of two mounds of fresh straw.

"It's all this war talk. Clay's burning to join up. Thinks he can get a commission. But Papa says he needs him 'round here." Sam clenched and unclenched his fist. "Papa can't do it anymore."

"He's been growlin' for weeks, spoutin' them rough words at his Mammy."

"I know Auntie. But Payne says the whole mess'll blow over in a few weeks." Sam tore off a bread hunk and buttered it. "Sure hope so. Derby's coming in June."

"Runnin' that new horse?"

"Yep! Fast, huh?"

"Land sakes, Master Sam. I don't know nothin' 'bout runnin' horses 'round no track."

"Jasper does."

"I've heard him go on 'bout that winner's circle. Why Master Sam, he's gobbled up by this racing business...just like Master Payne. Devil's gonna get 'em both if they ain't careful."

She stepped into the kitchen and started kneading another pan of dough. She worried about her boys, black and white. But this secesh squabblin' scared her.

"How about you, Master Sam?"

The Colonel's youngest turned and looked toward the stables. Inside, he knew Jasper was beaded in sweat in the breezeless May heat shoveling filthy straw and horse shit. Out back and out of sight, Clay was probably raising his flask, well on his way to another besotted afternoon.

"We're going to win!"

"Don't mean racin', sir."

"What then?"

"This soldier business."

"Payne says..."

"Didn't ask him. What do you say?" The old slave wanted straight talk now, a tactic that had always clicked with three of the Harrison children.

Sam munched the last of his bread. "Going to college. You knew that."

Aunt Hattie smiled, then pointed to a rider coming down Walnut Grove's dusty lane. "He's back! See if he's got good news."

Sam greeted his brother as he dismounted at the stable. "Anything?"

"Street riots closed her school."

"Where is she?"

"Don't know. Mail's disrupted. Lincoln's calling for 75,000 volunteers. Richmond's talking war!"

"WAR?"

"It's crazy, Sam! City's crawling with soldiers from all over the South. More regiments coming in every day. Never seen so many people."

"Think it'll last long?"

"Hell if I know. But the Derby's sure dead!"

"What?"

"Ain't happening! Everything's off. I could hardly get out of town without being yanked—there's a term for you!—into some half-baked cavalry company. They can have their stupid little war."

"No Derby?"

"Cancelled! Virginia wants her best riders and mounts in their precious cavalry. In these 'unsettled times,' as some stuffed-shirt major tried to tell me, 'betting on horse races is a frivolous pastime.'"

"What are you going to do?"

"Not putting on any uniform, I can tell you that."

NEAR UNDERWOOD'S MILL
SURRY COUNTY, VIRGINIA, 8 JUNE 1861

Another hot one, sir."

"Take 10 minutes at the bridge, lieutenant." Captain Joseph Mason pointed ahead to the stream crossing. "Top off canteens."

On the march all morning, Chesterfield's Yellow Jacket Artillery—soon to be Company C, 9th Virginia Infantry because the Southern Confederacy lacked enough cannon—staggered under a fierce sun. On Mason's orders, 93 men dropped off the dusty road and made for the nameless creek down the bank.

"About time we filled up," said Billy Ellett, grabbing his kepi. "I'm dry as a desert."

"Tell me about it," said Sam Harrison. "Mine lost its slosh hours ago."

"Well, I still got plenty," boasted Connie Snelling. "Need to get road tough, boys, if you wanna kill Yankees."

"Forget that. It's cool down time," said Billy, removing his boots.

Up and down the creek bank, men uncorked canteens and plunged them beneath the surface, water glug-gluging into the spouts. Others filled hats and kepis, pouring the stream over their heads to gleeful gasps of relief.

"All right men, don't stir it up," shouted Captain Mason. "No one likes drinking mud."

"Good and clear over here," said Sam, taking a long drink. "Cold, too," he gasped, wiping his grinning mug with his bandana.

In minutes, the dripping Chesterfield volunteers, a dozen days post muster, shouldered arms and reformed in the road. Ordered to march, they resumed their monotonous tramp, advancing across the stream on an ancient wooden bridge, knowing nothing of a farmer's cluttered barnyard and one-hole privy a quarter mile upstream.

And nothing of the pestilence that drained from both.

Chapter Twenty-Two

Walnut Grove
Chesterfield County, Virginia
August 1863

Payne knew they were coming. Only a matter of when. Five weeks after Gettysburg, the whole South still reeled from the shock of Lee's defeat in Pennsylvania. And this time government agents wouldn't be as solicitous.

Three times they'd paid him a visit, first "offering to buy" any surplus mules or horses. Eight months later they came bearing government quotas. "The Confederate States of America requires you to supply..." read the document handed him by a ramrod straight lieutenant. And back in April, when the butternut cavalry rode into Walnut Grove, they simply requisitioned half of everything, leaving him with vouchers printed on thin paper. Next time, Payne knew they'd steal whatever was left. So he had Jasper stash hay inside a shed near an abandoned coal mine deep in the Big Woods. There he'd hide Twelve, Tredegar, and Tiebreaker. And if the government found out... well, he had a second plan. Even with Sam dead these two years, he was ready for them.

ORANGE COUNTY, VIRGINIA, SEPTEMBER 1863

More goddamn paperwork?" Major General Ned Johnson pushed back the mountain of mail heaped on his camp table. "If all these pencil-pushing government clerks would start pulling triggers, why..."

"Sir, mostly brigade and regimental requisitions needing your signature." Sergeant George Rice handed Johnson a small envelope.

"Signatures I have. Saddles, sabers, and soap I don't. What's this?"

"A letter from your brother."

"Phil? What the hell's he want?"

Two and a half years after the Harrison's Christmas party, Ned Johnson commanded a division in General Robert E. Lee's Army of Northern Virginia, CSA. When Virginia left the Union, he did likewise, resigning after 23 years of service in the United States Army. As a major, Ned Johnson had once led 300 soldiers in blue. Now as a major general, he commanded 5,000 men in gray.

"I remember this fellow." Johnson pocketed his brother's note.

"Sir?" asked Sergeant Rice.

"Name's Harrison. Horse breeder. My brother recommended him. As you know, Gettysburg... has left us a bit short-handed."

"Bet the Quartermaster cleaned him out, sir."

"Maybe he saved one. Sure took his goddamn time signing up."

You're Harrison?"

Major Ed Moore folded the paper handed him and stood up from the oak stump he used as a stool. A cold, all day rain grayed the autumn afternoon, at times pattering out conversation inside the leaky, canvas walls of his tent. Order books and unfinished paperwork cluttered Moore's besmirched camp desk. As Johnson's acting assistant adjutant, he had tallies to reconcile, accounts to balance. And an impatient general to placate.

"Lieutenant Payne Harrison reporting for duty on General Johnson's staff." Payne stomped off mud and stepped inside the tent, expressionless and dripping wet.

"New, huh?"

"Joined up after Gettysburg, sir."

Ease up, lieutenant. I'm swamped here—as you can see—but, well dammit, I'll walk you over there." Moore picked up a dog-eared ledger and plopped it down on his stack of papers. "Need a break from this...this..."

He grabbed his kepi and stuck his hand, palm up, outside the tent. "Nothing like a promenade in a driving rainstorm."

"Looks like an all day special, sir."

"Payne? It is Payne?"

"Yes, sir."

"Well, drop the 'sir' stuff. Everybody reads the same page here."

"*Sir?*" Payne shrugged. "Sorry. I'll get the hang of it."

Moore slapped him on the back and laughed. "You're going to bear watching, Harrison. Now let's get you over to Old Clubby."

Ned Johnson located his headquarters in an abandoned clapboard house on the far side of a neglected, sprawling nine-acre corn field. Old stalks and stubble jutted up like a sea of broken, shaved pencils. Soldiers' tents, shanties, huts, and lean-tos crammed the woods on either side of the field, a sprawling, rural ghetto of split pine, torn canvas, and stack-barreled chimneys, smelling of rotting straw, damp wood smoke, and human waste.

"So, you're the new aide-de-camp?"

"Richmond promised me courier."

"Sure." Moore chuckled. "That always sounds better. But just so you're clued to things here, you do what Old Clubby tells you."

"You keep saying Old Clubby."

"Johnson's nickname. Plus Old Alleghany. Fence Rail. Brute. He'd rather smash your skull with a hunk of wood than spear you with etched steel. Prefers walking sticks, fire wood, and tree limbs to swords and sabers. Grabbed a fence rail in our first fight and never looked back. Some say he's crazy." Moore cleared his throat. "I know I don't want to tangle with him."

He dug a cigar stub from his coat pocket—"Sorry, only one left"—and glanced back at his tent. Number Twelve stood picketed with four other horses under a white pine.

"Yours?"

"Sentries said I had to report to you first."

"Splendid animal, lieutenant." Moore struck a wet match, tossed it and fingered another. This caught and he savored the draw, exhaling several puffs of blue smoke. "Sixteen hands?"

"Good eye, major."

"Well muscled, too. Fast?"

"Not around Yankee lead."

"Be mindful of that, Harrison." Moore eyed Ned Johnson's newest staff officer, then glanced back at his mount.

"Twelve can hold his own, given a fair start."

"That's just it, Harrison. Ain't nothing fair here."

"I mean to protect what's mine."

"Well don't die trying. Ever met the general?"

"I have. His place is near my family's farm outside Richmond."

"Then you know...he's...his own man?"

The major eyed the falling sky. "He's a rather different part of speech as some say around here."

"I've seen the eye twitch...if that's what you mean?" Payne laughed. "But my father says Johnson came back from Mexico a hero."

Moore worked his cigar, hawking and spitting as the two of them clumped across several soggy rows to a higher point in the field, flinging their muddy boots like swaggering sailors.

"Now with women," Moore continued, breaking the monotonous patter of the rain, "Old Clubby's clueless."

He pointed to a two story farmhouse overlooking the field. Men stood huddled around a smoky fire under cedars in the front yard. "Looks like he's in." The major sucked his cigar, but the rain had put it out. "Damn nasty day for a stroll."

M y best to your family, lieutenant. I can always use a man who knows horses." Infamous for his loud, gruff demeanor, Ned Johnson extended his hand in gentlemanly welcome. "Have a seat, lieutenant."

"Thank you, sir."

"Not you, major." Johnson threw his arm at the window. "Tromp back and get me those damned tallies. I know, I know. Shitty weather for arithmetic, but I need what I need, hear me?"

Payne had been warned of Johnson's mercurial temperament, of his odd mannerisms, and blue-throated profanity. Wherever the general went, the raucous cheers, jeers, and yes, fears of the men in the ranks followed. Cheers from his own men whom he had personally led into the thickest of the fight despite his high rank; jeers from outsiders for the odd-duck officer whose gargantuan ears—and dozens of soldiers had placed bets on this!—"flopped" when his horse trotted; and fears from the slackers...of the unforgiving disciplinarian who executed deserters and cowards.

"Back before supper, general," said Moore, as if nothing had happened.

"Good. Now get cracking. General Lee wants to know how many muskets we can level the next time General Meade comes calling. And as you know, major, Lee don't like guessing worth a gnat's ass."

Major Ed Moore saluted and stepped out the door just as another deluge dropped from the slate-misting sky. Sentries guarding Johnson's weathered headquarters didn't budge from their half-drowned camp fire as the general watched from the front window, chuckling as Moore broke into a run, slopping his way back across nine acres of mud and withered stalks.

"Good man there, Harrison. Do anything I ask."

"He seems very conscientious, sir."

"He is. But I need more like him." Johnson turned, ready and poised. "Think you'll measure up, soldier?"

"I mean to try, sir."

"Dammit! Trying won't cut it, Harrison. This army needs doers!" He slammed his open hand against the sill. "Understand me, lieutenant. We're fighting two enemies here."

Johnson motioned to the cedars. "Those lads around the fire? They'll do anything for home and country."

Jaw set, he stared into the slanting rain. "See, the Yankees we can deal with...most of the time. Even if Meade comes at us next spring with twice our numbers, Lee'll whip him."

Johnson slammed the sill again.

"Providence help us if we don't. But I assure you, lieutenant," his voice drifting to a whisper, "we cannot win if the *quiet* enemy prevails."

"The quiet enemy?"

"Traitors and spies, Harrison! The deserters and malingerers! The shirkers! The cowards! Our pickets eye the Yanks every day across the Rapidan but we hardly fight 'em once a month. Yet my battle with bootleggers and smugglers goes on night and day. Across my front. Around my rear. We've got miscreants hovering 'round this army who'd sell the Holy Mother down the river for another fifth of whiskey."

"Surely most..."

"Two and a half years ago, Harrison, I traded my blue uniform for this gray one. Richmond gave me command of the 12th Georgia Volunteers. Good men mostly, but green, summer soldiers if I ever saw the sun shine. To their credit, nearly all re-enlisted the next spring."

"Trouble found us pretty quick out there in the Virginia mountains. Measles, mumps, dysentery. A lot died. We were soon down to half strength."

"Those not sick, got homesick. And began to desert. But I couldn't let anybody go home. The blue sons-of-bitches on the opposite mountaintop outnumbered us four to one. So I cancelled all leave. Then our teamsters started smuggling rotgut into camp. Men got stool-hugging drunk, gambled on anything, and fought their best friends. When three soldiers got knifed to death one Saturday night in a scrap over liquor, I had to take measures."

"Got called every goddamned name in the book. Camp gossip had it that if the enemy didn't shoot me in the next fight, someone else would."

"What did you do, sir?"

"Caught the killers trying to desert. Had 'em shot at sunrise."

"You made examples of them?"

"Tried. You see, Harrison, it's about discipline! Without it this war's lost. As an officer on my staff, you must be hard, resolute, unforgiving."

What the hell have I gotten myself into?

"You're a courier. I hope you've brought a good horse. You're going to need him 'cause I'm going to send you into the thick of it. But if you happen on something not right, dammit, I want to know about it. Especially spies, smugglers, and moonshiners. Those quiet bastards. I mean to stop 'em." He hammered the window sill a third time. "God damn 'em. Got me, Harrison?"

Payne could only nod.

"Good." Johnson combed his fingers through his thinning hair, watching the rain beat against the panes.

Payne saluted and turned to leave.

"Ah, before you go..."

"Yes, sir?"

"I need your help on a matter. Something a bit more positive."

"Me, sir?"

"Yeah. Morale booster." Johnson winked. "You did bring a good horse?"

"My best thoroughbred, sir."

"Excellent." Johnson grinned. "That's a good thing, lieutenant."

"Then may I ask something?"

"Go ahead, Harrison."

"About that liquor smuggling. Ever catch the sellers?"

"Not in the mountains. But I found out who was behind it. Finally nailed one of 'em last month. Short, porky hick. Slippery fellow. He and his brother were knocking down some decent jack selling whiskey to my men up on Alleghany. Last summer they brought their operation closer to Lee's army. Wherever we went, they circled like vultures on a day-old carcass. Bastards sold 200 gallons of their shit before we caught 'em. That's what we know. Some of it wood alcohol. Pure poison! I had three men die and another two dozen go blind before we could confiscate the shit!"

"Blind?"

"Had to send 'em all home. I heard two more died later. Shot the fat son-of-a-bitch in front of the whole division. Buried him face down and had the teamsters run wagons over his sorry grave. No one'll ever find his rotten bones. But his damned brother got away."

"Remember his name?"

"Yeah, Grinder. But his fat brother's selling liquor to the devil now."

Chapter Twenty-Three

S how me again." The blue-uniformed officer pointed to a distant line of sycamores shrouding the south bank of the Rapidan River. "You damn Rebels sure seize the lay of the land."

"Now captain, sir. I done told you, I ain't no rebel." The scrawny, bewhiskered man spoke deliberately, his drawn out, mountain twang coloring his denial. "Just a business man. Nothing more."

"Business, my ass! Why did Johnny put a price on your head?"

"Captain, captain."

"Look, you're mine now. Remember that." Captain Hermann Boyle focused his binoculars on the far river bank. "Now where are they?"

"Lee's got his camps 'bout a mile to the rear," said the southerner. "Pickets dot the bluffs every hundred feet. Tight line. But they'll always barter. Just call out "double T" and that gets 'em coming."

"Double T?"

"Yeah, Trade Truce. You yanks got the whole store. Jams and jellies. Jars of pickles. Mustard, those smoked meats and all them newspapers. Course nothin' beats coffee and sugar. Southern boys crave that."

"And they bring tobacco?"

"Now captain." The tall man grinned what teeth he had.

"Oh yeah, how could I forget your spider juice."

"I always bring you the best elixirs, captain. That goat grog's for the flea-bitten gray backs."

"Don't give me that crap. We all know your Confederate scrip is worthless. And look what Old Johnson did to your brother."

"Son-of-a-bitch! I'll cut his balls off when I find him."

"Maybe you'll get your chance. Get us a decent place to cross."

"I told you Morton's Ford's your best prospect. The bluff slopes down to a long meadow. Lee keeps his guns far to the rear there." The tall man pointed to a low spot on the southern horizon. "Ford's right at that run of sycamores. Water's only hip-deep. Brush tangles'll hide you. Good place to lay down covering fire, too. Just zero in ahead of time."

"Already looked," said Boyle. "Dangerous as hell. And you know it. All open ground once you leave the river. And little chance for surprise."

"Oh, captain." Lonnie Grinder wrinkled to a sneer. "There's always a way."

G entlemen, let's give the men a gallop of our own." Surrounded by a half dozen mounted staff members, General Robert E. Lee spurred his faithful dapple-gray Traveller into a full sprint across a broad, open field three miles east of Orange Court House, Virginia. Cheers erupted from thousands of soldiers in gray, gathered in brigade formation before the rising slopes of Clark's Mountain.

"The boys are roused up today!" shouted an officer behind Lee.

"Just as I hoped, major," Lee replied, slowing to a trot after a quarter mile. "And on such a beautiful afternoon, too. Just look at that sky. Now there's a friendly shade of blue. So what do you think of my idea for a little diversion?"

"Well sir, General Ewell says..."

"I know, major. The horses are jaded...forage is scarce...we have to conserve. But I believe a good horse race is just what this army needs!"

"But all due respect, sir, he's not liking this one bit."

"I'm aware of General Ewell's sentiments. But General Johnson assures me otherwise. And I rather like the notion of a little spirited entertainment to keep this army on its toes. Besides, I want those people across the river to know we can still have a little fun over here."

Lee's party acknowledged the shouts and cheers of the men in the ranks with waves and tips of their hats. Ahead on a slight rise overlooking the field, a dismounted group of officers gathered around the bald, one-legged general ensconced in a carriage.

"Ah, General Ewell," said Lee, nearing the party, "I trust you are feeling dapper this afternoon."

"General Lee," groused Ewell, a beak-nosed, bearded man bulging eyes under a bare pate of porcelain white. "Fine afternoon to play war." He saluted his commander-in-chief without hiding his sour demeanor.

"My compliments to you sir, on this fine September day."

"Baldy Dick" Ewell as he was known, stomached no small talk. "I'm telling you, General Lee...this...this frivolous crap is all Ned Johnson's doings. Why, dammit, when I found out..."

"Now, now, general. I happen to think it's a great idea. Why, look around. Your men cover the hillsides. Cheering, upbeat, enjoying the afternoon. Putting the war on hold for a few hours. Nothing wrong with that. In fact, we need more days like this, my fine fellow. Can't fight those people over there all the time."

Lee spied a few men down the hill pointing at the riders and race horses, shaking their heads. Others came up, nodding and looking, each in his turn, handing something to a man writing in a book.

"Of course, I can't countenance wagering on final outcomes you understand," Lee continued, "but I anticipate a great race and a lot of fun. Don't you agree, general?"

Before Lee's Second Corps commander could mutter more disfavor, Ned Johnson cantered up in a cloud of dust with three staff officers. He whipped a salute to both Lee and Ewell and dismounted.

"Ahhhh. My good General Johnson. Please accept my thanks for organizing such a vigorous event." Lee, remaining in the saddle, extended his hand to his division commander. "Nothing like a spirited running of the equines."

"And damn the Yankees, sir. I hope this shindig'll fire up the men. I know I've been hearing a lot about the favorites."

"Favorites? Do tell."

A week earlier, Johnson had challenged the other two divisions in Ewell's corps to participate in a horse race. The issue at hand: Second

Corps bragging rights. When some of JEB Stuart's cavalry got wind of the contest, Johnson opened things up. Suspecting the mercurial Ewell would object, he quietly proposed the idea to Lee during a routine visit to army headquarters. Lee favored the notion and discounted Johnson's suspicions about Ewell. "Dick will come around. I'll talk with him."

"So who's your favorite, Ned?"

"Well, it's only campfire speculation, sir."

"Come now, general. I'd like to know," said Lee with a gleam in his eye. "Unofficially, of course. As you certainly know in this racing business, anything can—and does—happen."

"That it can, sir. But if you'll follow along with me, sir..." Johnson pointed to several features across the field. "We've marked off a three quarter mile arc. The start's across the way yonder, next to that lone oak. As you can see, the track runs straight for about a quarter mile, then round south into this long stretch right in front of us. Mostly all soft clover. The men cleared all the stones out weeks ago when they built fireplaces inside their huts. My headquarters flag down there marks the finish."

"And the entrants? Anyone I know?"

"There aren't any jockeys, if that's what you mean, sir. Each man owns and rides his own mount."

Six riders—two from each of Ewell's three divisions—had entered the race, but additions from the cavalry upped that to nine.

"So, Ned, you aren't going to tell me your favorites?"

"Ah, Stuart's boys are bragging the most, as you might expect. But I'm betting...er...ah backing the two entries from my own division."

"I would expect you to...back your own." Lee grinned at his division commander. He eyed the nine riders warming up their mounts in the flat just down the slope. *Such noble animals serve us. Yet they look so worn. Why must we sacrifice them on the altar of Mars?*

More soldiers crowded the sweeping high ground that bordered the makeshift track, dozens climbing into trees for a better look. Two regiments of Stuart's cavalry rode up, staking out prominent viewpoints near Lee. And to celebrate the afternoon, men from all branches of the service waved their ragged regimental banners. A bugler blew *Assembly* and a gray wall of cheers filled the valley. Nine horses and riders made their way to the start. Southern pride beamed in the Virginia sun.

Suddenly Traveller began to prance and nicker and toss his head. "Now good fellow, what's the problem?" asked his master. The commanding general gave a peculiar low whistle that usually calmed the horse. But Traveller continued his struts and kicks.

"I feel the same damned way, old boy," growled Ewell.

"Traveller's eager to see this race like the rest of us," said Lee.

Johnson waved a white handkerchief to the starter. One at a time, each rider moved his entry up to post, holding tight on the reins while an attendant stood in front. The usual prancing and high spiritedness delayed the alignment, but after a minute, all nine settled nervously into place. Two men pulled up a rope across the front.

Traveller stayed agitated, kicking and pulling, finally causing Lee to dismount so the animal could be tethered to a nearby tree. Only the starting crack of a nine-shot LeMat revolver brought the horse to quietude.

Three horses quickly surged to the fore, all sporting yellow piping.

"Looks like the cavalry'll be heard from today," shouted a sword-waving trooper down the ridge from Lee. The trio quickly opened a sizeable lead on the other six whose riders showed infantry blue. Going into the long turn at three furlongs, Third Place Cavalry had pulled ahead of Fourth Place Infantry by more than five lengths.

"This is done," boasted the cavalryman.

But Lee hadn't given up on his infantry.

Surely they'll be heard from?

And as he watched, motion near the rear caught his eye. *What's this? The very last horse is making a move!*

Lee thought it an illusion. A deep red chestnut had stumbled badly at the start, then fallen back to last. But now, going into the curve at three furlongs, the colt began to accelerate, passing the other blue entries.

"It's all cavalry today, boys! Hands down!" shouted a staff officer.

"You sound so sure, captain," replied Lee.

"Seems plain enough, sir. Look at the gap between three and four."

Indeed, as the riders swept toward the top of the long curve, the cavalry entries maintained a widening one-two-three lead over the trailing infantry mounts. Except for the red chestnut, which was now fifth. And about to pass again!

"Take a look at that one!" shouted another of Lee's staff officers, spotting the accelerating horse.

"Who?" yelled one of Ewell's men.

"Big red there, running in fourth. He's really going after it."

And that's when everyone saw him. The big chestnut with the three stocking feet and white star forehead.

"No way Three Sox'll catch us. Look at our lead."

"Oh, yeah. Look again!"

Indeed, as all stared, the fourth place horse—*Three Sox* they dubbed him—roared past Number Three Cavalry over the next furlong.

"He just found another gear!"

"No animal can maintain such... Look! He's passing on the outside."

Heading around the far curve, the three lead horses galloped past the wild cheers of a dozen infantry brigades—all shouting for the thoroughbred in third that wore their foot soldier's blue.

Lee also found himself mesmerized with this horse's come-from-nowhere run. Still accelerating, the chestnut thundered out of the turn for home, closing hard, Number Two Cavalry fading as Three Sox edged alongside. For one brief moment they matched stride for stride, then Three Sox nudged ahead!

With only a furlong to go, Number One Cavalry bore down on the finish line with a three length lead.

But Three Sox surged like a storm!

Thousands cheered as the lead shrank to two lengths. Then one!

Can this horse really come from last and win?

On two dozen fields in this war, Lee's men had fought against long odds and won. But the war just went on and on. And now the red chestnut underdog was matching strides with Number One Cavalry!

"He's going to do it! Three Sox is going to pass him!"

A nd at first, it seemed he had.
But Ned Johnson's racing judges ruled otherwise.
"Close, but Lieutenant Monroe kept the lead," declared Captain Willis Bluestone. "The red chestnut ran hard, but he still missed by a head."

Lee congratulated the winner, presenting the proud cavalry-man with a scarce bottle of French brandy and faithful Number One Cavalry with a bucket of fresh apples.

"The runner-up was from your division, General Johnson?"

"He was, sir."

"I would very much like to meet him," said Lee, looking at the disheveled second place rider before him.

"By all means, General Lee, let me introduce Lieutenant Payne Harrison, a member of my staff who just recently joined us."

Payne saluted. Lee extended his hand. "Fine animal you have there, lieutenant." He patted the horse's flank. "Magnificent, actually."

"Thank you, sir. Start was a little rough, but we stayed with it."

"You did indeed. A stirring effort you and...Three Sox here..."

"Number Twelve's his name, sir."

"Pardon me...You and Number Twelve thrilled the army today." Lee patted the horse again. "Three socks and a white star. I very much admire a horse of such powerful bloodlines. Where are you from, lieutenant?"

"Walnut Grove, sir, near Midlothian, just west of Richmond."

Again Traveller began a dust up, jerking on the reins, kicking in the dirt and nickering loudly.

"I apologize for my own mount, Lieutenant Harrison. Seems he's rather jealous of the attention your Number Twelve garners today." Lee whistled, but Traveller pawed at the dirt and tossed his mane, straining for freedom. Lee approached and whistled again, sternly this time, smacking the animal's flank. The Confederate commander then untied Traveller who gave a loud neigh and sauntered over to Number Twelve. Expecting trouble, Payne tugged Twelve's reins, but the horse nuzzled Traveller and to everyone's astonishment both animals quieted, nickering softly with only nudges and gentle bumps of camaraderie.

"Well, this is certainly a surprise, lieutenant."

196

"Indeed, sir. I..." *I know this horse!*

"They get along rather handsomely."

"How long have you owned Traveller, sir?" Payne asked.

Lee thought a moment. "I bought him right after Christmas, two years ago. His owner called him Greenbrier back then. First admired him when I was in western Virginia in the fall of 1861. Why do you ask, lieutenant?"

"I think I've seen him somewhere before, sir. Greenbrier, you say? Was he ever called any other name?"

"Not to my knowledge. I bought him from Major Thomas Broun who told me he had to pay gold for him."

Gold? Gold! Of course!

Payne walked up to Traveller and smoothed his fingers down the horse's forehead. "So, Jeff Davis," he whispered. "We meet again!"

Chapter Twenty-Four

The race did improve morale. At least in Ewell's Second Corps. The other half of the Army, General A. P. Hill's Third Corps, tried to organize a similar event, but Yankee intentions disrupted further runs on the clover. With General Longstreet's First Corps on detached service in Tennessee, the enemy meant to exploit Lee's weaker numbers.

And they did, in two fights out of three that fall. Confederate debacles at Bristow Station in mid-October and Rappahannock Station in early November foreshadowed an ominous future for the Southern war effort in Virginia. But three weeks later, Ned Johnson's division took on two Federal Corps in the woods and ravines funneling Mine Run and stopped the Yanks cold.

Was there something to this morale thing?

With colder weather, both armies settled into winter quarters. Payne spent his days carrying routine correspondence to Ewell's camp, to Lee's headquarters, to the cavalry, to any place Old Clubby ordered.

But not a single letter from you in two years. Where are you, Alex?

Packages and notes got smuggled through the lines all the time, but with no certainty. Payne had penned a dozen letters to Lowell, Massachusetts, since the start of the war, but had received not a single reply.

Then came Gettysburg. *And here I am, where I said I wouldn't be.*

Winter duty put him riding the division's frozen five mile picket line on the bluffs above the Rapidan. Often alone, his thoughts drifted to Alex. But along this front, Twelve got all the scrutiny.

"He'd have whopped that cavalry nag, given a fair start," growled one scout. "All Ole Twelve needed was another fifty feet," proclaimed another.

Payne came to regret the attention. *I joined up to protect you from the horrors of this war. Now you're at the center of it.*

"Get out there on that horse where the men can have at you," Johnson had said. "They need to see our best at the point of the sword, Harrison. But remember, you spot trouble, I want to know it!"

Where the men can have at you...

Our best at the point of the sword...

He understood what Old Clubby represented; a battle-hardened commander who'd personally lead his men straight at the enemy.

Some think he's crazy.

But others sensed growing desperation in a cause of fading hopes.

And they're going home...deserting...abandoning southern independence, while the rest of us, still willing to slug it out, fight now only to survive and preserve what's ours.

Like me...

*B*oom! *Booom! Boooom! BOOM! BOOOM! BOOOOM!*

Fiery spears arched across the Virginia gray dawn.

What the hell?

Six artillery shells shrieked over the Rapidan and exploded, walking mushrooms of dirty, deadly fire flowers across a stalkless cornfield. Then silence. Nothing more.

Ned Johnson stomped the hard ground fronting the frozen works of the 5th Virginia, rushed out on alert. Scouts soon reported the enemy had run up two guns under cover of darkness and opened fire. Only to hastily withdraw.

So Billy, what was this all about? Makes no damn sense. Old Clubby thudded his right fist into the palm of his left hand, then turned for camp.

But what does anymore?

With a jerk, he stopped and stared...north down the sloping field toward the ford. *Why would they shell an empty field?*

D espite Johnson's diligence, trade truces thrived along the picket lines. Payne saw it every day. Half-starved Confederates scraped for every creature comfort they could get, from delicacies like canned peaches, cinnamon, and decks of Caswell's French playing cards, to coffee and sugar, bartering with the only currency they had: tobacco. Yet when temperatures plummeted and snow whitened all, even Johnson looked the other way, especially when stuff came wrapped in newsprint.

"Scrounge every damned paper you see, Harrison," he said. "Richmond wants to read every scrap. Got me?"

Payne obliged. By January, he and Twelve had the picket line down to a dulling routine. Riding upstream, Johnson's sentries guarded four Rapidan crossings: Tobacco Stick Ford, Stringfellow's Ford, Morton's Ford, and Raccoon Ford. The winter war bogged into monotony.

That changed with a jar of pickles.

Or rather the wrappings around it. Payne found they weren't newspapers, just printed broadsides announcing a traveling troupe's evening entertainment in the camp of the Third Brigade, Third Division of the Union Second Corps. Listed on the program were Artemus: The English Acrobat, The Juggling Beamon Brothers, MagiCan the Illusionist, and a comedy routine by Fuzzy Funweather. *And Miss Alexandra Parker, vocalist.*

Alex? You're right over there?

Payne Harrison stared across the low ground that flattened north from the river, rolling the poster between his fingers.

"Any idea where their Second Corps is camped, Sergeant Gibbons?"

"Billy Yank's campfires cover the whole of creation." Ollie Gibbons waved north with his right arm.

Probably think I've forgotten you. I try to get through this war, but you're always there. And now I'm beside this frozen river close enough to...

"Lieutenant? You asked about Old Abe's Second Corps?" A sentry approached the small campfire to warm his hands.

"Yes, private."

"Well, sir, we just traded with a few fellows from the Second last night. Hancock's boys. They trade fair."

"How far's their camp?"

"Not sure, sir."

Johnson'll have my hide if he finds out, but dammit, I have to try.

"Any idea when they'll be back?"

The private pointed. "See that big sycamore out over the river?" Several figures moved in the brush, well back from the river bank. *On duty like the rest of us. And just as cold. But dressed in blue.*

"Gibbons? Any chance of a trade truce?"

"Kinda risky, sir, all the ice and such."

"Just want a parley. Won't take long."

"Make sure Old Clubby don't find out."

"Understood, sergeant."

Gibbons turned, cupped his hands, and bellowed, "Hey Billy? TT? TT?"

One of the men behind the sycamore waved back. "How's the weather, Johnny? We're all out of French bread and garlic powder."

"Smart ass," said Gibbons. "That's old MacCain. Nosy bastard, always sharp on a deal, though. Addicted to cigars, but he don't cheat."

Gibbons waved back. "Just a parley, Mac."

"No trading, Gibby?"

"I may have something of interest for you," shouted Payne.

"No tricks, Gibby!"

"He's good, Mac."

"OK, Gibby. But can't stay long."

"You heard him, sir. But don't worry. River's solid!"

Payne took out a pencil and a scrap of paper and wrote something, then folded it and put it in his pants pocket. Forty feet out on the ice, he stopped and faced the approaching man.

"Howdy, Reb. Sergeant Sean MacCain, 39th New York. Gotta make this quick. CO's due in twenty minutes."

"Lieutenant Payne Harrison, General Johnson's staff. I won't take long." Payne handed MacCain the broadside. "You see this?"

MacCain laughed. "Yeah, I was there. First part of the show wasn't much. Juggler set fire to his beard! But that lassie...could she sing!"

"Where are they now? The troupe? What camp?"

"Saw 'em last...last Thursday, I think. Probably through Second Corps by now. Third Corps would be next. What's all this to you, Reb?"

Payne pulled out his note. "I need you to get this to the girl."

"The singer?"

"Give her this, MacCain."

"Can't help you there, Johnny."

"I'll make it worth your while."

"With what?"

"Cigars. And the best plug tobacco out of Carolina."

"Gotta do better, Reb. This is risky. But say I can do this...all I gotta do is hand her this note?"

"No. I want you to bring her here. She'll come. Get her here safe and then back to camp again, and I'll..." Payne fingered a five dollar gold piece. "...give you this."

"You got gold?"

Payne turned to the south bank. "Gibbons? I can trust this guy?"

"He's a sharpie, but his word's ok," came a voice in the brush.

"Look, Reb. I can get into some major shit here."

"Yeah, and I've got four more of these for you when I see her."

MacCain ogled the gold. "OK. OK. But Reb, I can't force her." He darted a look back to shore. "How's she gonna know that note's real, anyway?"

"She'll know. Just get her here safe!"

The Yankee grabbed the coin and folded Payne's note around it, pushing everything into a small leather purse. "OK. Give me a few days, Reb. Need to pull some strings. But right now I gotta git."

W ho the hell was that, sergeant?" Captain Hermann Boyle jerked Sean MacCain up the Rapidan's frozen mud bank. "And let me see that paper."

"Come on, Captain. Just another rebel looking to trade."

"Don't shovel me that shit, MacCain. That was an officer."

"Captain said give him the goddamned paper."

"Enough, Grinder. Let's go, MacCain."

"It's in his purse, captain."

"What the hell..."

"He's holding back! And I know that officer."

"What about him, Grinder?" Boyle glanced back to the river.

"He owes me a little something. Just like MacCain here, owes us a little something."

"Let's have it, MacCain."

The sergeant bit his lip and dug out his pocket purse.

"I'll take that." Boyle opened the purse and took out a paper wrapped round and solid. "Care to explain this, sergeant?"

A nd that's how it's going to be." Captain Boyle flicked open his pocket knife and began sharpening his last usable length of desk pencil. "Find her and give her the note. Convince her to go with you. Whatever you have to do. But I want her at Morton's Ford on Saturday morning. Crack of dawn, sergeant."

MacCain could hardly believe his ears. He'd expected a court martial. Busted to private.

"Saturday. We'll have a wagon for you. Tell your rebel friend she'll meet him at the downstream curve on Morton's Ford."

"But..."

"No buts, MacCain. Your rebel friend gets his rendezvous on the sixth, first daylight. Let him know."

The sergeant nodded, marveling at his good fortune.

"And sergeant?" Boyle brushed the pencil shavings off his camp desk. "Anything that rebel gives you...ends up on this table. Understand me, soldier?"

Y ou the singer?" MacCain already knew, but he wanted the
girl's *yes*.

"Depends on who's asking." *Another fan. Well, remember to smile
and keep it brief.*

"Ma'am, you sang to our brigade one night last week up on
Hansborough's Ridge. Weren't a dry eye in camp when you finished
Home, Sweet Home.

"I'm glad you liked it."

"The boys, well, we couldn't stop talking 'bout you."

"Tell your men I thank them for their kind words. Now is there
anything else, sergeant? I'm very busy."

"This, ma'am." MacCain handed her Payne's note. Alex studied
him for a moment, then unfolded the paper:

> My lovely Alex:
>
> I don't know who will get this to you, but this note
> is genuine. I wrote but never heard from you. I'm in
> the ANV, 2nd Corps, Johnson's division. I must see you.
> All is safe and arranged. Please meet me. Despite the
> silence, the not knowing, and this war, please know I
> still love you! Believe me, Alex. Please meet me. Reply
> via this messenger. He can be trusted.
>
> I love you. Payne

"Were did you get this?" Her curiosity churned with a taste of
anger.

"A Confederate officer standing on a foot of ice in the middle of
the Rapidan handed it to me yesterday."

"How do I know it's real?"

"Well, Ma'am, he said you'd just know."

Alex reread the note, noticing small writing in the lower left
corner:

12 says hi.

"Oh, you dear man! You've seen him? You've seen Payne?" She
hugged the sergeant, then stepped back, wiping tears. "Tell me how
he is!"

"Course, lassie, I've seen him. Just five minutes worth mind you, but he looked hale and hearty." MacCain blinked, stunned at the girl's change of mood. "Ma'am, he really wants to see you. Rather insists actually."

A nything you do or try to do beyond the operational plan, Grinder, is at your own risk."

"Sure, Captain. Just want what's mine."

"Whatever, Grinder. Put out the word on a special TT. When the Johnnies hear you're trading good liquor for tobacco, we'll pull 'em out of the woods like ticks jumping a hound dog. Clear the whole picket line."

"Call it our winter special, captain." Lonnie Grinder pursed his lips and slapped Hermann Boyle on the back.

The captain ignored the mountaineer's classless breach of military etiquette. "Everyone'll be in place well before we get there. And tell MacCain nothing. Remember, the girl's only a diversion."

MORTON'S FORD, VIRGINIA, 6 FEBRUARY 1864

G entlemen, post your guns like last week and await my orders." Captain William Arnold, First Rhode Island Artillery, surveyed the pre-dawn river crossing. *Meade's pushing three brigades across at dawn. And my guns open this ball. Sure hope somebody knows what the hell they're doing.*

Arnold wrapped his arms about him in the chill and rocked back and forth. *And no damn campfires. Well, enjoy you slumbers, Johnny. We're calling on you come first light.*

Chapter Twenty-Five

Morton's Ford, Virginia
6 February 1864

D ead quiet from here on, Miss Parker." Sean MacCain whispered, fingers to his lips. "Crossing's a half mile ahead."

Alex shivered under blankets. Only crunching wagon wheels and mules' hooves announced MacCain's approach to Morton's Ford.

Has it been two years? Tell me you're fine. That everything's going to be all right. Tell me...you still love me.

"Hi there, missy." A thin, scrabble-looking rider leaned to the wagon. "Little something to warm your innards?" The man pawed a small flask to Alex. Even in the cold, he reeked of body odor.

"No. I'm fine."

"Don't worry none. Plenty to go 'round. Those graybacks have a real hankering for the good stuff."

Alex shook her head.

"Suit yourself, missy." Lonnie Grinder shrugged.

That man's disgusting. Been watching me since Sergeant MacCain came by last night. Like he knows me or something.

As Alex wrapped the blankets tighter about her shoulders and legs, a voice challenged the party. She heard MacCain give the countersign and two armed men stepped from behind a tree.

"The singer?" one of them whispered.

"In the wagon."

Alex watched the two approach. "I'm Captain Boyle, Ma'am. Come with us and do exactly as we say. There's not a lot of time."

From the start, Alex had thought this whole arrangement odd. Not to mention dangerous. *But if I can see Payne...*

"This is how it's going to be," continued Boyle. "Your reb's on the other shore with some others. They'll come over first. Then, he'll walk out to the middle alone. You go then. Don't worry. River's frozen solid. Grinder here, will escort you and make sure you're safe."

"But Captain, aren't you..."

"No, Ma'am. I'm...in charge...of the security here on shore."

"Don't worry, missy," Lonnie Grinder grinned and patted Alex on the shoulder. "I'll keep an eye on you."

"I'll be fine." *You make my skin crawl.*

"No, missy. Have my orders. You ain't going out there by yourself."

The February dawn revealed a frozen river bordered by dense tangles of briers, vines, and angled sycamores soaring from both banks. A small gap marked the ford's splash-ins. Across the river, an expansive, vacant meadow sloped up to a distant crest a half mile to the south. More than 40,000 Confederates encamped in the woods and fields beyond.

Alex spotted something white move along the far shore. *A small flag?*

"We see you, Johnny," yelled Boyle. "Start across single file. MacCain, go meet 'em."

"But..."

"You heard me, MacCain. That's an order."

As Alex watched, men popped up from behind trees and filed across the frozen ford, their uniforms nothing more than rags of soiled gray and butternut. Each man—Alex counted 29—carried a haversack or a burlap bag. All appeared unarmed.

"Hey, boys. Take in the cutie over there," yelled one. "'Bout time you Yanks paid up on all that Dixie weed you've been filching."

"Quiet down, Johnny. She's off limits. Remember, no guns."

"We hear ya, Billy. Coming over clean. Now where's the juice?"

"Right over there, reb. See those fellows by the wagons?"

Alex studied the long line. Beyond, she spotted a lone rider. He dismounted and tied his horse to a sapling.

"OK, you there, rider," Boyle called out, "approach half way."

The man stepped out onto the ice, a slouch hat hiding his face. He carried no burlap bag.

Can it be? Is that...?

"Payne?"

"Dammit, girl. Shut up!" hissed Grinder. "Now let's go." As Confederate infantrymen clustered around the trade wagons, Lonnie Grinder grabbed Alex by the wrist and pulled her down the river bank and onto the ice. She tried to wrench free, but the smuggler kept his iron grip.

Payne Harrison paid little attention to the tall bearded man leading Alex across the ice. He saw only the lithe blonde, baby-stepping towards him, trying not to slip. *She looks so frail!*

Alex jerked free of Grinder's grasp and wrapped her arms around Payne.

"I wrote you, Alex, again and again, but..."

"I know." She buried her head to his chest, smothering her rush of emotions into Payne's wool overcoat.

"When the academy closed, well, I couldn't stay in Baltimore. So I went back home. Did some tutoring. But the war went on and on. So, after Shiloh, I joined the troupe."

"Doesn't matter, Alex. I just want to hold you. You've no idea..."

They kissed, embracing for more than warmth. "Hold me, love. Hold me. Oh, how I missed you."

"You make my heart soar, girl."

She leaned back, smiling up at him.

Lonnie Grinder checked up river.

You bastard. Don't even recognize me.

Grinder jerked out a .44 Colt revolver and pointed it straight at Payne's head. "No more sweet talk you two! Get your hands in the air!" He beckoned over his shoulder with the handgun. "Start sliding toward Yankeeland and nobody gets hurt."

"Grinder!"

"See this barrel, Harrison? Get the hell to my side of the river before Miss Pretty here gets a bullet through her skull."

"He's crazy, Payne!"

"Still the horse, isn't it, Grinder? You'd do anything to steal him."

"He was meant for me, Harrison," Grinder sneered. "As you were meant for my friends in blue." He turned toward the north bank.

BOOM!

The first cannon shot of the Battle of Morton's Ford dropped dead tree limbs up and down the Rapidan valley. Alex whirled at the noise, slipping, catching herself, then going down hard. On the second blast, raced up by a third, Payne lunged at Grinder. The moonshiner fumbled his revolver and stretched to recover it, but Payne kicked the .44, spinning it across the ice. Clawing faces and grabbing hair, both men wrestled and dug into the other, skidding atop the frozen river.

"Run, Alex!" screamed Payne from under Grinder. "Get off the river!"

Alex scrambled up the river's southern bank. "Payne!" she screamed as the two wrestled out on the ice.

"Get on Twelve...and...get out of here!" yelled the Virginian.

Rounded stones protruded from the eroded river bank. Alex grabbed at several but found all frozen solid. Then she wrenched one free.

Upstream, around the river's bend to the west, two masked Union batteries opened on Southern positions with a concentrated salvo of explosive shell. Three infantry brigades, advanced during the night, prepared to storm across the ice. A week earlier, with the approval of his superiors, Captain Boyle had devised a trap, circulating rumors along the picket line that a large trading cache of liquor would soon be available for tobacco. Sergeant MacCain's scheme to bring Alex Parker to Morton's Ford for a rendezvous with her beau simply reinforced the ruse.

"I ought to have you cashiered, MacCain, but I'm going to approve this," Boyle had said, not informing the sergeant of the plan.

"Tell the Southerners they'll get safe passage to our side of the river to trade."

Duped Confederate pickets whispered the offer of Yankee liquor for Southern tobacco up and down the line. By Saturday's dawn, more than two dozen of Lee's men had snuck to the river's edge.

The opening of the artillery, positioned precisely where they had been sighted in against Morton's Ford the previous week, sprang the trap. Federals in the brush quickly surrounded all Confederates over to barter.

L ook at that, sir!"

Captain William Arnold spun toward his Number Two gunner.

"At the ford, sir! There!"

Arnold pulled up his binoculars and scanned the frozen Rapidan's lower crossing. Two figures wrestled atop the ice while a third hovered nearby, waving an arm. Two hundred yards to Arnold's right, General George Meade's first attack brigade approached the river.

My orders are to shell the wood line directly in my front and to my right, drive out the pickets on the bluffs and punch a hole in Lee's defenses so our infantry can get across. Now what the hell's this?

The fighting pair broke apart, one grabbing at the ice while the other scooted toward the south shore. Atop the south bank, the waving person suddenly spun in a blur. An instant later the far man dropped hard to the ice, jerking to still. The scrambler clawed his way up to the waver, and together the twosome mounted a horse— unseen until now—tethered in the brush.

"Trouble!" Arnold motioned for his gunners. "Number One and Two, wheel left and fix on the south bank of the east ford."

The Rhode Island commander thrust his sword at the empty, ascending cornfield stretching from the Rapidan's south side. "Lead on that horse. Fire on my order. Blast the brush to the left of that biggest sycamore."

Both crews swiveled their 4-inch Napoleons a half turn southeast, dropping their barrels two and three degrees respectively.

"Bear on those woods, men. COMMENCE FIRING!"

Lanyard jerks screamed two shells in a flattened arc toward the south bank's jungle of brush. Two seconds later, simultaneous explosions boiled fire and dirt and splintered wood sixty feet into the air, shredding the air with shrapnel.

But as Arnold stared through his glasses, a large chestnut horse and two riders burst through the haze, galloping hard for the rising plain.

"How in the...!"

"We'll get 'em, captain!"

"By all means, Lieutenant Bowers," roared Arnold. "Reload with case shot and don't forget to lead. Again, fire on my command."

Both gun crews labored while the captain followed the horse and riders through his binoculars. *Well, you're not gonna outrun case shot.*

"Gunners ready...FIRE!"

Another double salvo ripped over the river, exploding two and one half seconds later in the middle of the open field. As the cloud cleared, Arnold once more scanned the ground.

"Look! Higher up," pointed Bowers. "They're getting away, sir!"

Arnold raised his binoculars and spotted the two riders and stallion unharmed...in full bolt! *Damn!*

"Number One and Two! Sight to predetermined coordinates. Load to double charge! I REPEAT, LOAD TO DOUBLE CHARGE AT THE PREDETERMINED COORDINATES! WAIT FOR MY COMMAND."

In half a minute, both guns were reloaded and trained to the impact positions previously established to guard against a Southern counterattack.

Glad as hell we ran our guns up here last week. This ends now!

But as Arnold followed the two riders and sprinting horse, he did so with mixed emotions. *Sure carries his speed well. Even with two aboard. What a magnificent animal! Oh, this damn war. What a waste!*

Arnold pulled out his pocket watch. "On my signal, men!" *God knows I take no pleasure in this. We're three seconds out and they're eight... seven ...six...five...four...*

"FIRE!"

BO-BOOM! Again, the two Union cannon thundered red into the February chill, their double blast jarring both gun crews. Three seconds later, four 16-pound spherical case shot detonated, bursting fired brilliance across a neglected acre of last year's chopped down Virginia corn, searing the ground with a massive, crimson cauliflower of frozen dirt and flesh-ripping iron.

Probably blown to bits...

Arnold sighed and lowered his binoculars.

But his men still stared...south and pointing. "Sir! There!"

Arnold swept the field, searching for death.

But finding life.

Forty Christmases in the future, awe still in his voice, Captain William Arnold would relate to his grandchildren the story of the great horse who had outrun his cannon during the civil war.

But on this wretched winter morning, the artillery commander could only watch in disbelief as the stallion sprinted to the ridge top, three quarters of a mile from the Rapidan's south shore at Morton's Ford and vanished from view.

No horse is THAT fast! But...

Arnold lowered his binoculars.

My God, how can there be such a horse?

He faced into the Virginia dawn.

How...?

Chapter Twenty-Six

Headquarters, Johnson's Division
Orange County, Virginia
9 February 1864

N ed Johnson boiled with rage. "Holy mother of Christ! Here you go out, behind my back, and try to snake your Yankee girlfriend through enemy lines. Goddammit, lieutenant! What were you thinking?"

For twenty minutes, the general rained down the scourges of hell on Payne Harrison, excoriating his aide-de-camp for bad judgment, disobedience, stupidity, and anything else he could think of.

Yet Old Clubby knew his verbal rebuke was all the punishment he'd wreak on his newest staff officer. Gen. Ewell, who hadn't heard all the sorry details—*and didn't need to*—had given Harrison a battle-field promotion. *And I get to tell you the news, first lieutenant.*

In Dick Ewell's eyes, Lt. Harrison's timely warning had saved the army from a nasty surprise at Morton's Ford, enabling Lee's Southerners to smack Meade's three brigades back across the Rapidan with quite the bloody nose.

"Yeah. OK! You saved some butts out there, Harrison." *But how the hell did two dozen of my pickets get snagged on the enemy's side of the river?*

Old Clubby didn't need any campfire chat on that. "If it hadn't been for that speed horse of yours...well, that animal saved your ass, boy." *Mine too! Too bad we can't promote the damn horse!*

Ordered to congratulate but seething to castigate, Johnson could only blow smoke at his aide-de-camp.

"Anything you want to say, lieutenant?"

"Miss Parker..."

"A woman I admire," Johnson roared. "I heard how she nailed that miscreant Grinder out on the ice. Solid woman there, lieutenant!"

"She doesn't need to relive the details."

"Whatever, Harrison. Hell of a lass, though."

"Yes. But General, I can't send her back. And you and I both know she needs to get away from these camps as soon as possible."

"If you're smart, Harrison, you'll get her in *your* camp."

"Sir?"

"Marry her, boy. If you two are crazy enough to go courtin' 'tween the lines, you better damn well pop the question. 'Cause let me tell you something, *first* lieutenant, she's all primed to say 'yes.' Oh, she's Yankee blue but she's about the bravest woman I ever saw. Besides, if you don't ask her to marry you, I will!"

"What?"

"You heard me, first lieutenant!" Johnson tapped a paper on his desk.

"First lieutenant?"

"Yep. This note from General Ewell makes it official. With a week's leave. Thought you might want to know."

"Promotion! A week's leave?"

"You got lucky." Old Clubby mused, eyeing his aid. "Look Harrison. Ask her to marry you. Hug and kiss her when she says 'yes.' Then the both of you get the hell out of here and find a preacher."

"I...I...you mean...?"

"But know this. Scouts report lots of enemy activity to the east. Mostly cavalry. We don't know what they're up to, but it's not safe to go to Richmond unless you swing way west first. You're better off heading back toward the Blue Ridge. They marry folks up in the mountains too, you know." Johnson stuck out his hand, breaking to grin. "Congratulations."

Payne grabbed it with both of his. "I...I..."

"Just be back in a week, lieutenant. I never let my men go off and marry just any Yankee."

He watched his courier mount Number Twelve. *Enjoy while you can, 'cause when the weather turns, all hell's gonna break loose.*

*H*eavenly *Father, I confess my sin. I killed a man and I fear for my soul. Oh God, please forgive me. I meant only to save a life. Not take one.*

Seated on a log, Alex kept her head bowed, unaware of the soldier approaching her smoldering campfire.

I'm lost God. How much longer must I exist...in this place? Yet if this be my penance...I accept it. But please Lord, take me to a place of peace. Far from the fighting. Away from death and into life. Where love triumphs over hate... where...

"You OK, Alex?"

Payne! She jumped up, brushing woodchips and grit from her clothes.

"Been looking all over for you."

Alex spoke only hugs.

"Now, now." Payne brought her close. "I know sleeping in the supply tent isn't much. At least there's some privacy. Breakfast?"

Alex nodded, daubing her eyes. "Biscuits and gravy. One of your officers got me some coffee."

"Then smile for me. I've got good news."

News?

"A week's furlough! Effective now. We're going to Richmond!"

"What? I mean how?"

"Rail. We'll catch the Virginia Central. But we'll both have to ride Twelve. No horses to spare."

Alex buried herself into her soldier's coat. *Thank you, God...*

"Gotta ride south. Away...from all this. If the weather holds, we'll reach Louisa Court House late tonight. Twelve's all saddled."

Due south over Mountain Run. Through Old Verdiersville. South, across the Orange Turnpike. South, away from the Gray, away from the Blue. South, away from the war. Miles to go this winter's day.

For the most part, roads in central Virginia knifed through dense forest, rutted wagon trails connecting rolling farmland, sparsely populated in cabin and clapboard, windows shuttered, doors tight. Even behind Lee's lines, war marked the land.

The day had dawned raw, blustery. Even into early afternoon, the temperature still chilled. A leaden sky hovered. Few traveled the road. The pair pressed ahead, wordless, her arms around him, wrapping for warmth as well as stability.

Who are you, really, Payne Harrison? Has this war hardened you to the ways of the world? Has fighting scarred its changes on you...like so many others? Do you even know I'm in love with you?

They stopped for lunch in late afternoon at a roadside clearing. Alex rubbed her gloved hands. "Much...longer?"

"Brock Bridge crosses the North Anna in two miles." Payne eyed the gray sky, digging out some beef jerky, cold bread, and pickles from his saddlebag. "Not sure about Louisa before dark, though."

Ten minutes later they were back on the road, hearing only bending trees and leather saddle squeaks. Approaching dusk, the mercury plummeted. A brisk wind howled down the lonely, frozen byway. And the one-horse couple on it. Flakes swept against closed eyes, swirling in a soft, chilled white.

Still she clutched him, all she had. And the steed kept to his labors. Into darkness, she found words. "My hands...can we stop some place?"

"It's only..."

"I...can't go much farther."

"Ok. I see a light ahead."

Child, you must be frozen! Get in here by my fire and let Lucy Whistler get some hot stew in you. That'll warm your innards."

Lucretia Whistler's cabin stood hard by the Louisa Court House road, breaking a long, lonely stretch of overgrown fields and second-growth woods. At 59, she lived alone, her man dead these seven years from typhoid.

Her oldest son farmed over in Gordonsville; a second served in the artillery; her only daughter, a preacher's wife pregnant in Fluvanna County.

"And mercy me, sir, why take this girl out on such a night as this? Look at that stuff coming down! Must be three inches in the last hour."

"I'm Lieutenant Payne Harrison and this is Alex..."

"Glad to meet you both. You're at Lucy Whistler's now. Warm and safe. A haven with the Lord. I'm fortunate to have company on a night like this."

"We could sure use a place to spend the night. Just let me know what I owe you, Mrs. Whistler."

"Lucy. Make it Lucy. Everybody calls me Lucy."

"Thanks...Lucy. We've come a long way." Alex shook snow off her bonnet.

"I reckoned as much. That there twang in your talkin, girl," Lucy winked. "Not from 'round here, are you, dear?"

"No, Ma'am. I'm..."

"Not that it matters a pea's pod. And don't fret about owing me a thing. The Lord favors those of a generous heart. Here, both of you have some stew. And if you need a tug on that jug, by all means." She chortled and smacked her rear end with the palm of her hand, then giggled some more, pointing to a half-filled bottle on the table before the fireplace.

"Need to put up my horse, Ma'am."

"Straw and hay in the barn." She parted the curtain. "Ohh! A big one."

With the snow coming down, Payne led Number Twelve to Mrs. Whistler's ramshackle log barn. Two mules stood in stalls along with a dozen chickens roosting on the rafters. A tethered goat paced in one corner, eyed by several cats who scampered when Payne entered.

"Mrs. Whistler, bless you for taking us in."

"Told you it's Lucy, dear. Lucy. But I'm glad to help. Awful night to be out. But I must say, girl, you're taking a sizeable risk."

She put a full kettle on the stove.

"Your husband should know better. Why girl, if you're with child, you could injure yourself and that baby inside you. You can't just go running up and down these roads at all hours."

"But we're just..."

"Not that it's any of my doings. More stew?"

"Ahh...er...yes, yes Ma'am."

"I've got a nice room for you two. Let me fish out some more blankets and an extra pillow." She vanished upstairs and soon all Alex heard was bumping overhead, the wind outside, and the crackle of the roaring fire.

When Payne returned, Alex pointed upstairs and whispered, "She's getting our bedroom ready, Payne! She thinks we're married!"

Payne grinned and eyed the ceiling. And the bustling noises overhead. "You didn't tell her?"

"Look! You can see she doesn't let a person get a word in edgewise."

"Sure a talker, that's for sure."

"What are we going to do? She'll turn us out if she learns the truth."

"Pretend?"

"Uhhh! Men!"

"Shush. Here she comes, Alex."

"It's not much, but least it's warm up there. Heat from down here goes right up through the floor board cracks. Plus I put out three extra quilts." She rubbed her hands together and winked. "Hope you like my pillows. When I gather 'nuff feathers, I make 'em for folks around here. Tea?"

For the next half hour, Lucretia Whistler told stories and entertained, all the while watching the flames curl and leap around the logs. Only tea sipping stopped her words. "Got a son in the army. I see your uniform, and well, I see Warren. Like he's back home. Maybe somebody would do the same for him if he were out on such a night."

"I'm sure they would," said Alex. "It's nice to be here beside your fire, warm and safe."

They conversed for another hour, discussing weather, war, and Yankees. "Don't know how all this is going to turn out," concluded Lucy, "but General Lee'll see us through. That's what my Warren says."

Payne gazed into the embers while Alex, eyes closed, snuggled closer.

"Turn in when you want. I'm up early. But if you would, Payne, please put a few more logs on the fire before you go up. See you in the morning."

"Good night, Lucy, and thanks."

Outside, the snow continued to fall, drifting around the cabin. Alex touched Payne on the arm. "Twelve's in for the night?"

"Bedded down on clean straw. Snug log barn."

"Such a noble animal," she murmured, drifting toward sleep.

Minutes passed. Payne spun his fingers through Alex's hair and began to massage her neck. She smiled. The fire shrank into glowing embers. He got up and added more wood. The room brightened and shadows danced off the walls.

"Mmmmmm." Alex opened her eyes. "I'm so relaxed. Don't know if I could get off this sofa."

"Sounds like your bed's calling you."

"Mmmmmmm. You could be a real gentleman you know."

"How's that?"

"A girl needing her beauty sleep counts on her knight to see her safely to her boudoir."

"How about a quilted straw mattress in a log cabin attic? Been a long day. Here Alex, give me your arm."

Relaxed and dreamy-eyed, Alex raised her fingers. Glowing a fireside smile, Payne reached down, slipping one arm around the small of her back, the other under her legs. She draped an arm behind his shoulder and rested her head to his as he carried her upstairs.

You are so warm.

He laid her on the bed and started to tuck a pillow beneath her head. "A girl usually undresses before she goes to bed, Payne."

"Ah. Of course. I'll go outside."

"No, it's OK. Promise you won't peek?" She giggled, energized by his modesty.

He stood in the dark of the doorway, a lone candle burning on the night stand beside the double bed. She looked up and smiled through the shadows, removing her boots. Then her stockings.

I can feel his gaze.

Dropping boots and stockings at the foot of the bed, she leaned back and unfastened her collar, then unbuttoned her white shirt and waist. *He's staring. Wondering. But I trust him. I do. I really do.*

"Help me with this?" She turned and pointed to the laces tying the back of her corset. He loosened every stitch and she slipped free.

She unfastened and stepped out of her knife-pleated wool skirt, revealing a short, mid-thigh, yoked silk chemise.

She winked, pulled up the blankets, and snuggled in.

"Alex, you...you're stunning."

"Thank you, Payne Harrison. A girl likes to hear that, even if her boudoir is a log cabin attic."

"I'll get a quilt and keep the fire going."

"If you must..."

"I mean I..."

"Payne?"

"Yes?"

"Kiss me goodnight?"

In the solitary glow of their bedside candle, he leaned down and met her waiting lips. Instinctively, she put her arms around him. They kissed again, lingering this time, and he sat down beside her, letting his fingers comb gently through her hair. They edged closer, bunching the quilts. He lifted them and eased in beside her.

Warm. So hold me, Payne Harrison.

She traced her fingers across his shoulders, feeling him flex as he wrapped his arms around her waist. She clenched her fingers into the fabric of his shirt as if to remove it. When she did so again, he reached over his head and completed the task.

What am I doing?

But passions yearned. Side to side beneath the covers, they let their lips explore, he tracing his kisses to the nape of her neck, then downward. To his touch, she slowly flexed backwards, melting, her mouth agape with this delicious, tactile sensation. Again, he kissed her, this time his tongue tasting, exploring, tingling. Gently, effortlessly, he slid beneath her, bringing her atop him, his hands moving down her back, massaging deeply the day's many miles from her body.

Don't stop...oh Payne, it feels soooo good. Your touch is pure heaven ...your fingers...the tensions...oh, just don't stop.

And still the storm raged.

What am I doing? This isn't right. Alex! Think girl. Think! You can't!

But the lone candle in Lucretia Whistler's attic burned bright on this winter's night.

*P*ayne Harrison, do you know I love you? Do you?

Silence. The howling wind of the night had fled. The Virginia piedmont lay quiet under its pure blanket of white stillness. Only a smear of melted wax remained of the candle on Lucretia Whistler's nightstand. Peace. The late winter's storm was over.

Oh, that this war would be.

Alex kissed him. And Payne opened his eyes, finding hers. He still sensed the seductive heat and passion of her body...even as he awoke, but now with the coming dawn, something more—an intensity...a possessive yearning that harkened to no bounds—grabbed him, a protective devotion that knew nothing of geography or politics.

Alex snuggled close.

What now? Life and death swirl all around me. And I'm yours, Payne Harrison. Lucy Whistler already believes it.

Alex put her finger to her lips, then reached out and pressed it to his, warmed by his closeness.

Surely you know now. Surely you know I love you.

"Alex, I...ah.." He stirred. "I ah...I need to ask you something."

She kissed him again, softly on the chest.

"Everything's chaos. Men die around me every day. None of us... none of us knows when our time may come."

"Oh, Payne. Stop..."

"But Alex...no matter what. I want you to...I want you..."

"What, Payne?"

"I want you...Alex Parker...marry me. I love you and I want you to be my wife. Please?"

Payne? PAYNE!? You want me to marry you?

"For all time, Alex."

You...! You did know!
You really did know!
You always knew!

Chapter Twenty-Seven

Mule Shoe Salient
Spotsylvania Courthouse, Virginia
11 May 1864

N ed Johnson and several of his staff stared out into the dripping, black night. The all day drizzle had become a chilly, penetrating rain. Long lines of bedraggled soldiers hunkered down in boot-sucking mud, Johnson's entire division—or what was left of it—dug in behind massive earth and log works that angled though the soaked, mist-filled forest in a long, irregular arc the men likened to a giant mule's shoe. For three days, they'd battled snipers, sporadic artillery, and stabbing infantry testing their lines.

"Put a man on the works every ten paces," ordered Johnson. "Everyone sleeps with trigger fingers tonight." Apprehension stalked the hour.

Late that afternoon, Johnson had gotten orders to pull back his artillery. He stormed and cussed. Nothing indicated the enemy was withdrawing from his front and that evening in Neil McCoull's farmhouse a quarter mile behind the trenches, Johnson dashed off a protest warning.

"Harrison, rush this to Dick Ewell. I want my damn guns back!"

Payne had spurred Number Twelve to Second Corps headquarters in the rainy gloom of a dying day.

"Can't do a thing about it," snorted Ewell when he read the dispatch. "Tell Ned the order's from Lee himself. He thinks Grant's swinging 'round our right again toward Richmond."

P ayne Harrison paced atop the earthworks. Armed, anxious men crouched in the Mule Shoe, no lights permitted, desperate to keep their powder dry.

Ten o'clock and our guns still aren't back. Sure hope Johnson's wrong.

"Hear 'em, lieutenant?"

A mud-begrimed soldier nodded toward the front.

"Keep it down." Twelve stood hitched to an oak fifty yards to the rear.

"Voices, sir. People moving."

"Billy Yank's coming, sure 'nuff," said another. "Better get Old Clubby. Ain't nobody sleeping up here."

"Especially with our artillery gone!" growled a man behind Payne.

There is a nameless something out there.

"Listen! That's *Yankee Doodle.*" The rainy midnight serenade spread as more Federal bands and drum corps joined in.

But few, at first, heard the second sound. Masked behind the night's drums and brass instruments, it traveled as a low, vague grinding, rumbling minutes later into a guttural vibration.

Johnson better hear this.

Payne retraced his mud path to Number Twelve.

Boy, we need to go!

Old Clubby was snoring fitfully under a single blanket pitched on the floorboards of the McCoull house when Payne woke him.

"What the hell do you mean, Harrison?"

"In the works, sir. Everyone's convinced something's up."

"Dammit. Be specific."

"*Yankee Doodle.* We can hear 'em playing it. Far off at first, then... all across our front. You can catch bits of conversation, too."

Face frozen as if hearing bad news from home, Johnson betrayed no eye twitch or ear flop. "Anything else?"

"Just that grinding, the heavy vibrations."

"What the hell do you mean?"

"Like machinery being moved. And it's getting louder."

Johnson yanked open the front door of the farmhouse, his ear into the night. "Our guns back?"

"No, sir," replied a sentry.

"God dammit. I told Ewell we needed 'em back before dawn. Went up there myself after you saw him. Promised he'd go see Lee." Old Clubby stomped outside. *And they think they can lull us to sleep with band music...*

"Major Moore, go to Ewell. Wake his one-legged ass up and find out if our guns are coming back."

"Got it, general."

"Tell him I'm sending Harrison on the fastest damn horse in my command, straight to the artillery park to escort those guns back up here."

Johnson turned to Payne. "At least twenty of our guns should be parked in a field about two miles due south of here. The roads are shit in this weather, but lieutenant, the fate of this army may depend on your guiding them back up here in time. I need you moving now. Questions?"

"Who do I see, sir?"

"General Armistead Long. He's got Ewell's order, but he might have a case of the slows. Here's another note. I don't care if you have to jerk him out of bed! Understand me, lieutenant?"

Payne nodded and grabbed the sealed envelope.

"Now you and Twelve, git."

S peed meant nothing on the mired and rutted trail winding through the pitch black woods. Payne plodded past a half dozen intersections, relying on sentries for directions before spotting the first gun carriage.

"Reward time, boy." He dismounted, unfolded paper from his pocket, and let Twelve lick clean the last taste of brown sugar.

A portly man sporting a heavy black mustache tossed back a tent flap.

"I'm Lt. Harrison. Looking for Gen. Long."

"At your service, lieutenant. You from Johnson?"

"Yes, sir. He sent this."

"Figured Ned would be calling." Long opened Old Clubby's note, then looked at Payne. "Your horse?"

"In kind of a hurry, General."

"Thought I recognized Three Sox. But OK. Page's and Cutshaw's batteries. Kept 'em on alert." Long opened his hand to the drizzle. "Nasty night for such business. Take care of that horse."

Going back took three times as long. Mud-spattered teamsters struggled to guide their cannon and caissons through the hub-sucking mires that bottomed the wheel-rutted trail, sometimes demanding whole gun crews to dismount and pull the cannon free.

About 4:30 a. m. Payne and the first of Cutshaw's and Page's besmirched crews emerged from the woods south of McCoull's farmhouse. Payne spotted two wounded men pointing north.

"They're coming! Yankees! For God's sake, hurry!"

An indistinct mix of shouts and yells welled from the Mule Shoe a quarter mile distant.

"Where's Johnson?" yelled Payne.

Both soldiers kept pointing north.

"Advance these guns!" screamed a battery officer. And teamsters lashed their horses, driving the limbers down a ravine and into the oak forest backing the salient.

Payne raced ahead, spurring Twelve up one of the narrow paths that led to the very apex of the earthworks.

Johnson's in the middle of this. Should have known. Now to find him.

But armed Southerners clogged all the trails, wrenched from their soggy-blanket bivouacs, warned that the enemy was coming, scurrying to reach the protection of the mule shoe.

Courier and horse pushed through the armed mob. *There he is, raging up and down the works, swinging a tree limb!*

"My guns, Harrison! Where are my damn guns?"

"Coming now, sir! Page's and Cutshaw's..."

"Only got seconds, lieutenant. Look!"

Payne stood in his stirrups. A closing, dark moving monster filled the open fields beyond the salient, not regimented, sweeping lines, but men twenty ranks deep bunched in a vibrant mass, barreling out of the mist-filled darkness three hundred yards distant...hurling straight at the Mule Shoe!

"Over here, goddammit! Get those guns over here!" Johnson waved wood at two gun carriages emerging from the trees. An artillery shell screamed overhead and exploded, followed by another, drowning him out. The approaching thunder of an entire Union Corps, of twenty thousand tramping, running, storming soldiers, had already seized the attention of every man in gray.

A moment later they burst into range.

Confederates along the salient opened with weak, popping volleys, their fire power dampened by percussion caps sparking on wet powder.

"Harrison, get to Ewell," yelled Johnson. "Tell him I need every man he's got. We'll hold as long as we can."

Another shell exploded to Payne's left. Twelve reared and twisted, nearly dumping his rider into the mud.

"Easy, boy. I'll get you out of this."

But the thoroughbred, wild-eyed and verging on panic, thrashed and bucked. Payne wrenched the reins.

A chorus of cheers and yells catapulted from the Mule Shoe's west wall. Hundreds of Confederates fled across the rear of the salient, some stumbling into the deep traverses trenched back from the log works.

"Our lines! They've broken our front." Men yelled, falling back in disarray, pointing to the blue masses—bayonets fixed—scrambling over the breastworks. A man a dozen feet to Payne's right dropped to the ground, blood spurting in a crimson fountain above his right eye. A dumbstruck boy stumbled past, his left hand missing, his ulna and radius stabbing from the mangled stump of his wrist like the sharpened tines of a dinner fork.

"Get out of here, Harrison," Johnson hammered his oak branch against the morning rain. "Find Ewell!"

Payne smacked Number Twelve's right flank. The stallion reared furiously, dancing hooves into the mud, thrashing and tossing his head. The rider fought for control, tight on the reins, but to no avail.

"Git, Harrison, git! There's work to do!" Steeling his resolve, Old Clubby whipped his tree branch over his head and turned toward the enemy.

Number Twelve took off.

Payne jerked a last over-shoulder look. Hundreds of Yankees scrambled over the Mule Shoe in a dozen places, swarming the just-arrived guns of Page's Battalion, shooting the lead horses to keep them there. *Oh God, NO!*

Rider and horse raced down the forest path. In the lifting mist, splintered trees blocked the trails. Random minie balls whined from all angles, smacking into branches and trunks, showering the trail with sticks and leaves, ripping anything in their path.

A mile to Ewell's! Surely he's heard this by now.

An incoming shell exploded to Payne's right. Another screamed overhead, crashing into the creek behind McCoull's house. *Steady, boy!*

The red chestnut cleared a fallen tree and splashed across the creek. Payne felt the horse quiver. *Don't understand any of this either, fella. War's crazy. Sure didn't mean to put you into harm's way.*

Payne flashed back to that first afternoon. *You and Jeff Davis. Out there beyond the Blue Sulphur. Peace and quiet. And we know who rides old Jeff now.*

Three shells detonated in rapid succession to Payne's right—rearing the horse—followed by a shrieking, shattering fourth.

But old Andrew Johnston saw trouble coming. He knew! He...

Brilliance seared overhead...

Then nothingness...

Not a shred of sound.

Not a pinch of pain.

Not a scent of sulphur.

Nothingness...

BOOK THREE

FOUR THREE

For still the vision awaits its time;
It hastens to the end—it will not lie.
If it seem slow, wait for it;
It will surely come, it will not delay.

HABAKKUK 2:3

Chapter Twenty-Eight

C harlie Harrison had never been much good at predicting the future. Especially when he had little to go on.

Although the scenes of his lifetime nightmare remained vivid, they hadn't rushed him in months. Determined to confront his demons, he found to his cautious surprise that his dream had vanished like a ghost in the sun.

It haunted no more.

Charlie would have predicted anything but this and yet the dream's disappearance should have told him something. A recurring vision of such duration just didn't go away. This was a harbinger... some new chemistry toying with his perceptions. A passing fancy perhaps, reawakened. A comet in the sky...an idea whose time had come.

Yet after a year, he concluded just the opposite. Maybe the damned thing no longer mattered.

Maybe it never had. After all, who would have predicted this? But is there a simpler answer; like...what if old people simply quit dreaming, their minds too tired and cluttered?

But he knew that was nuts. Ginny and Laura often visited him in the Land of Nod, conjuring into silly, weird, or beautiful scenarios that bounced from butterfly picnics and talking tombstones to zebra hats and a swallowing man-in-the-moon. How he wished he could share the gaudy details with them...if only he could remember a coherent smidgen the next morning.

Yeah, we old folks still dream, just as we still laugh and cry.

But Charlie's ageless nightmare was indeed gone and after a second year had passed and then a third, he rarely thought of it. Fate had worked out the anguished details, he told himself.

And I'm just an old man who doesn't matter anymore. Waiting. With no more dreams left to come true.

Yet he prayed the world didn't work that way.

But what's a feeble, 95-year-old fellow to do?

He pondered that. A lot.

Well, I'm still breathing, so I'm pushing some purpose.

Yet down deep, things still gnawed. Charlie's gut fear of the West Meadow, of something out there IN the West Meadow, had never left.

Yeah, I'd go back if I could. Confront it once and for all. But that's not going to happen now.

Then again, Charlie Harrison had never been much good at predicting the future.

CHARLOTTESVILLE, VIRGINIA, 6 APRIL 1969

D r. Harrison! Good to see you again. Hope you're doing OK?" Charlie edged through the waiting room door and smiled at Harvey Winfree's receptionist. "How are you, Betty?"

"Fine. Please have a seat. I'll let him know you're here."

Betty Paxton Barnes, R.N., had grown up two miles outside Keswick. A year older than Laura—they'd essentially come up together—she'd gotten her nursing degree from UVA, married an insurance agent, and stayed in Charlottesville. She'd been with Dr. Winfree more than a dozen years.

"When's Laura coming down? Haven't seen that girl in ages."

"Actually, she'll be by in a bit. Down for Easter. Dropped me off so she could run an errand...or something."

"That girl's in town? Goodness me! Why when I catch up with her..."

The door behind Betty opened.

"Thought I recognized that voice. Get on back here, Charlie Harrison." Harvey Winfree stuck out his hand. "Let's have a look at you."

Charlie stood up, putting both his hands on Mrs. Barnes's desk for support. He paused, took a breath, and inched a step forward. "Moving a tad slower these days, Harv. Trucking a lot of miles, you know."

"It's not the miles, Charlie, it's the mileage. You taught me that. Remember? Always quote him on that one, don't I, Betty?"

"All the time. Did you know Laura's in town, Dr. Winfree? Can't wait to catch up with her. Been ages. How old's that girl of hers?"

"Ahh, Ginny's ah...thirteen. No, fourteen." Charlie blinked a smile. "Turned into quite my young lady the last year or so."

Harvey Winfree, M.D., ran a thriving family practice on Locust Avenue near Martha Jefferson Hospital. He'd been Charlie's doctor for 18 years. Keswick's retired physician was his second oldest patient.

"Doing OK?" he asked, showing his colleague to the examining room.

"Zip's all gone, Harv. Shortness of breath's about the same, but I'm getting more palpitations these days. And Miss Angina talks to me on the stairs. Not good." Charlie shook his head and stared at his shoes. "Headed out, aren't I. Just like Ike."

"President Eisenhower hung in there for quite a while, Charlie. News reports say he had his first MI back in '55. Fourteen years ago. Did you see his funeral train when it passed through here Sunday night?"

"Heard it. They took him right down the tracks east of Keswick."

Dr. Winfree opened Charlie's folder. "Still fending for yourself out there? Doesn't that place date back to the Revolution?"

"It's home. And you know me, Harv."

"Yeah, I know you. Stubborn old cuss. Now, let's get that shirt off and have a listen."

L aura McGill! Get in here and let me look at you! I want my hug!"

"Oh, Betty Paxton!"

"When your grandfather said you were down, I could hardly..."

"Mom?" Ginny peeked in the door.

"In here, Ginny. Betty Paxton, meet my 14-year-old. Last time you saw her, she was waist high. Ninth-grader now."

"Ginny! Ginny! Always loved that name. If I had a girl, I'd have named her Virginia, too. Course you know you got your mother's good looks. No doubt there! But that Irish head of hair! Oh, you gorgeous girl!"

Ginny blushed. "Mom said you'd say that, Mrs. Barnes!"

"Well, get her to tell you about the night we drove down to Richmond."

"Betty Paxton! Not another word!" Both women cackled. It helped that Dr. Winfree's waiting room was empty.

"And Harney, the hunk?"

"Still flying," said Laura. "Ginny gets her locks from him."

"Ginny, I still remember the glow your mother had when she came back from Yellowstone that summer. Smitten big time."

"Betty! Really!"

"Your mom was one head-turner 'round here. Why I remember one night on campus, these three guys..."

"Hush, girl. You haven't changed a bit."

"Well, you can't deny your daughter's got that same eye twinkle you sported 'round here back then! I could tell Ginny all kinds of things!"

"Oh, Mrs. Barnes, do!" Ginny gushed.

Puberty had indeed begun its wonders. The little girl Grandie had so loved to tease approached womanhood. At five feet six inches, Ginny McGill already cut a lithe, athletic figure. With her flaming red hair tied in a pony tail and freckles bridging her nose, Ginny would garner her share of "turned heads." Yet a quiet purpose reflected the green of her eyes, and her voice, while often playful, could spell melodies when she spoke of matters closest to her.

"And where is that hubby these days?"

"Nam."

Betty Paxton geared into neutral. "You must really miss him."

"Visiting Grandie...helps us get by," Laura braved on.

"He loves having us down," added Ginny, "so we can spoil him."

"Your grandfather's a wonderful man. I've known him all my life as your mother will tell you. Ginny, believe me, he's worth spoiling!"

"Betty, level with me. Do you see any changes in him? I mean, from the last time he was in here at Christmas?"

"Well, he's slower. And more stooped. Course, he's always been soft spoken. Gosh Laura, he's well into his nineties."

"I don't get down as much as I'd like and I..."

"They should be out soon. Dr. Winfree will want to speak to you. So tell me, Ginny, what do you like to do? Write poetry? Play the piano?"

"No, Ma'am. I'm more into sports! Especially softball."

"Goodness, girl. That's me. Second base in the church league."

"Ginny's in girl's fast pitch in Fairfax," replied Laura.

"Oh, way out of my league, dear! Don't know how you see that ball, much less hit it. What position do you play, Ginny?"

"I pitch."

"No way!" The secretary rolled back her eyes, feigning fear. "I'm not standing in any batter's box against you."

"That's the problem. The league banned her as too dangerous."

"What! Well, laugh at 'em and move up to the older girls."

"Rules won't let me," said Ginny. "I have to be 15. No exceptions. I don't know what to do. I just want to play."

"Who taught you to pitch?"

"Daddy. He always catches me when he's home. Says I have lots of room to improve, though."

"How many games did you win last year?"

"Ah...all of 'em."

"Girl!" Betty Paxton Barnes smacked her ballpoint to the desk. "Your dad must be very proud. I bet you miss him."

Ginny nodded, her smile weak.

L ungs clear. Both kidneys fine. Liver's still under your rib cage. You eating OK?"

"I get by. So far, so good, huh Harv?"

"You know your issues, Charlie. Angina. Pedal edema. Early CHF. Plus an enlarged prostate and old man arthritis."

"Yeah. A few loose bolts."

"You're still shrinking, too, Charlie."

"I know. Osteo."

"Well, you insist on living out there alone. Charlie, if you fall down the steps in that old place..."

"I'll break every bone in my body."

"Not to mention your neck. And no one will find you for two days."

"That's not true. My mailman stops by every morning to chat."

"Charlie! Listen to me, pardner. You know it's not prudent anymore."

"I'm not going to any old folks home, Harv."

"Yeah, yeah. We've been down that road, too."

Charlie pointed at Winfree's medical school diploma hanging behind his desk. "Never got mine framed."

"Charlie, I'm telling you what I think's best. How about Laura?"

"Talk to her. I'm not leaving Nell."

Dr. Harvey Winfree sighed and shook his head. Picking up a pen, he began filling out the forms for Charlie's lab work. "We'll talk again when I get your blood work back."

D r. Winfree says you shouldn't be living alone anymore."

"So what's new, Laura?"

"Yeah, but if something should happen..."

"Like what? Fall down the steps? I'll crawl and call. Simple enough."

"Grandie. Listen to you. At least get a live-in maid. Aunt Sadie worked wonders around here when I was growing up."

"I had a little girl to raise back then."

"OK. Fine. So let me try Plan B. Ginny and I have a problem and I think you can help us."

"Problem? What problem, granddaughter?"

"Softball, Grandie."

And what Laura proposed, Grandie loved. A couple of phone calls and a bit of paperwork over the next month soon settled matters. Simply put, when school ended in late May, Laura and Ginny moved down to Macon's Ordinary. With Harney serving in Vietnam, Ginny banned from softball, and Laura tied only to a month-to-month apartment lease in Falls Church, it all made sense.

She soon landed a job as a summer school reading teacher and Ginny made the Charlottesville senior girls' softball league after a single tryout, impressing the coaches with her above average fielding skills, agility with the bat, and keen sense of game strategy. But it was her pitching that left them stunned. A rising high school sophomore with this kind of speed?

And for Charlie, it was like old times.

With Harney overseas, Laura focused on caring for her grandfather who savored the attention. *Outlived my day, but by golly, my family's with me.*

Laura harbored hopes, too. *Grandie has to realize he can't continue in this house alone.*

And Ginny? She won her first start, striking out eight and walking two.

Grandie attended every game, even when she wasn't pitching. The evening air invigorated him. The action on the field entertained him. And folks in the stands came by and said hi. But best of all was the night sky. Feeble as he was, Charlie returned to the backyard that summer, venturing with his binoculars for a glimpse of Mizar. No way he'd pass the Arab eye test anymore. In fact he couldn't really image much of anything except the moon. But he knew where to look in the night and that was enough.

Yet there was another reason to return to the stars. In this summer of 1969, Charlie Harrison, 95 years young, eagerly awaited a coming miracle.

KESWICK, VIRGINIA, 20 JULY 1969

I can't believe this, Grandie! They're really up there."
"I know."
"Take your afternoon nap?"
"With all this going on?"
"It's incredible. Never seen TV coverage like this."
"Yeah, you have, Ginny. Remember when President Kennedy was shot?"
"Oh. That."

"He pledged to put a man on the moon and now, by golly, it's happened."

Laura walked in from the kitchen. "Still watching this NASA stuff?"

"Mom! It's right on television."

"Set yourself down, Laura. Neil Armstrong's actually going to do it. First man on the cheese."

"If he doesn't disappear in all that moon dust. Look, you two, supper's ready. Whenever you want it. Hot or cold. Your choice. I need to clean up the kitchen. Call me when he's ready to step out."

Ginny watched her mother leave. "What's with her?"

Charlie coughed, shook his head. "Lot on her mind, I guess. Your dad."

"She always goes weird when he's away."

"Weird? So now I'm weird?" Laura stuck her head back into the den. "Look, Virginia, while you're making new friends and burning a softball past every girl in Charlottesville and having an otherwise marvelous, carefree little summer down here, your father's on the other side of the world putting himself in harm's way doing God-knows-what."

"Mom, we hear from him every week. I read his letters, too."

"Ginny, you don't know what you're talking about! Your father's not telling me what's going on. Nothing. He's holding something back. His letters are empty. No emotion in 'em. Writes about the weather, wishes us all well, and asks about you and your softball."

"Probably too busy, Mom."

"NO! Something's wrong. I can feel it!"

"Mom...Get a grip."

"Don't talk to me that way, young lady. You know your father always writes two letters a week. I've only gotten three in the last month."

"Maybe they got lost. Maybe he's been reassigned!"

"Stop it, Ginny! Read 'em again. Something's wrong, I'm telling you. Your Dad's not in them. 'Hi, how are you doing? How's Ginny? What's the latest from downtown Keswick? Miss you guys. Gotta go. Blah. Blah. Blah.'"

"Mom..."

"Ginny. Your father's a helicopter pilot. Look at the letters. No mention of any of that. Look at the envelopes. None of his letters have ever been smeared with mud before."

Charlie slept through Neil Armstrong's first steps on the moon. Missing his afternoon nap combined with NASA's repeated delays to green light Apollo 11's first extra-vehicular activity pushed man's first ever moon walk into the early hours of the next morning for viewers in the eastern United States.

But Ginny caught it all. The stark white and gray of the moon's surface. The black eternity of space swallowing the lunar horizon. The awkward, bouncing gait of Armstrong stepping off the ladder at one-sixth G.

That's one small step for a man, one giant leap for mankind.

Around midnight, with Grandie snoring, Ginny had eased back his recliner and covered him with a blanket. Several times, especially when Armstrong opened the hatch, she was tempted to wake him, but the sight of her great-grandfather so at peace in his easy chair...

"So I missed the fireworks," Charlie said the next morning.

"Grandie, you were so zonked. I couldn't wake you."

"I'll catch the replays, Ginny. Won't miss a thing."

But Charlie knew better. *Blew it. But it's Ginny's future. Not mine. I'm just wallpaper now. No more big moments for me.*

"You know, Grandie, NASA's planning another moon landing before Christmas. Least that's what they're saying on TV."

"Ah, I'll have another shot." He laughed at his pun. "If I'm around."

"Hush that talk, Grandie," said Laura. "Glad to see you're up, by the way. And the TV finally off. Of course you'll be here. Stop this nonsense."

"I wonder what Mama and Papa would say to all this." His voice trailed to a whisper. "It's so beyond...what they knew."

"Where did that come from? You never talk about your parents."

"On days like this, Laura, memory-making days, they edge close."

Ginny glanced at the daguerreotype of her great-great grandmother on the side table. "She looks so happy."

Charlie cradled the glass image. "That's the way I remember her." His face wrinkled in recollection. "You know...you remind me of her..."

"Awww, Grandie."

"I'd agree," said Laura, "especially your smile, Ginny. But you've definitely got your daddy's freckles and head of hair."

Ginny brushed red strands behind her right ear. "Mom, I didn't mean those things last night."

"I know, dear." Laura sagged against the door. "But the...never knowing." She gazed out the window. "And it's...different this time."

Ginny hugged her mom, eyes welling. Neither spoke.

Charlie's words, soft and unexpected, broke the silence. "Mama once said the same thing."

Laura looked up. Her grandfather still stared at his mother's image. A wistful smile wreathed his face.

"You told Papa how you'd often despair of every seeing him again. I was little, but Mama, I remember your tears. You from Massachusetts. Papa from Virginia. Falling in love with the country into war. Not knowing if any of it would last. But you told Papa something I've never forgotten."

"What, Grandie?"

"That an incredible wish she'd once made had actually come true." Charlie's face softened. "I've always wondered what Mama meant by that."

Laura reached to the old man. "Grandie...I...I just want Harney home."

"May I hold her?"

Charlie gently handed Ginny the daguerreotype.

I feel I know you.

She pressed the picture to her heart, looking at her mother. "She loved Grandie's daddy just like you love mine, Mom."

"Oh, Ginny." Laura touched her daughter's cheek.

"And her dream came true. Really, Mom. You can see it in her face."

KESWICK, VIRGINIA, A WEEK LATER

U ncertainty. If any one factor loomed above all the rest in her misery index, *not knowing* topped Laura's list.

Fueled by an empty mailbox.

You never said it would be this bad. Yeah, you told me there'd be times when you'd be away. When I'd not be able to call you. When I'd have to love you from a distance. But darn it, Harney, I didn't sign up for this.

Lieutenant Colonel Harney McGill had just two weeks to go on his second tour in Vietnam when Neil Armstrong stepped onto the moon. Slated to come home the second week in August, Harney knew what might happen. Decorated combat pilots, especially chopper pilots, came at a premium. And three month extensions in a combat zone, while not automatic, were a fact of life. And they did burnish careers.

At 36, Harney didn't want to give it up. He'd promised Laura this tour would be his last. But he still "had the itch" and, well... when opportunity knocked...Harney McGill always opened the door.

Orders arrived on the Fourth of July. He and four other senior pilots would establish a forward air rescue post in Thailand. Cooperating officials in the Royal Thai Air Force had finally given their tacit approval, but insisted everything be low key. *Below the radar.*

That included mail home.

Won't be back in August, Laura, but for sure by Thanksgiving. I know you'll understand.

Not this time.

And mister, you're missing softball, too. Ginny's seven and one...with a gazillion strikeouts. You should see how she heats that ball past those older girls. Just like you taught her.

Laura stepped into the backyard of Macon's Ordinary. *Need some fresh air. But nothing again today. Why don't you write me?*

In the garden, Laura didn't dote on the markers like her grandfather, but she adored the daisies and black-eyed Susans and rose bushes that nestled them. She'd tended Grandie's flowers all her life.

Like cooking and knitting, she owed her love of gardening to Aunt Sadie.

But you can't help me now. Ginny's whipping softballs, thank goodness, having a great summer. And Grandie's doing OK, considering.

So it's me. Everything's wrong. Nobody cares. And all I want is you home. Safe. And soon. Is that so much to ask?

But on this July day with Apollo 11 and Chappaquiddick dominating the headlines beside the war in Vietnam, Laura wept.

At least there's peace here.

For the most part, she hid her depression, only letting her emotions go when no one was around.

Like after Ginny caught a ride to softball practice.

Or while Grandie took his afternoon nap.

Or when she walked among the flowers.

This is my Tranquility Base.

But Charlie knew. Despite his years, his fragility, he recognized depression when he saw it. He knew melancholia fueled cynicism, stoked listlessness, and smothered spirit.

No matter how young.

He'd been down that road himself a half century before and he hurt for his granddaughter now.

"You've tended a marvelous garden this summer, Laura." He nudged open the screen door and stepped into the backyard, jabbing the ground with his cane. "Your grandma would be mighty proud."

"Still miss her don't you? After all these years?" She turned to him, wiping back tears.

"The love of my life, Laura. And your mother, I..." Charlie coughed and shook his head. "It's always good...to visit." He turned and tapped Nell's stone with his cane. "Don't you think so, dear?"

"You two...only had 15 years. Like Harney and me now."

"He'll be home soon." Charlie smoothed his hand to Laura's shoulder. "My folks had it a little rougher, you know."

Laura looked up, eyes moist, red. "Wasn't he at Gettysburg?"

"No. Joined up a month later. His youngest brother was dead from disease by then. Anyway, Papa got a staff position with one of the generals and served into the following spring."

"And got married during the war?"

"Yeah. When it started, Mama was teaching music at some girl's finishing school up in Baltimore. Papa planned to visit. But Ft. Sumter fixed that. He wanted no part of the fighting, but the Confederate government kept coming for his horses. Finally took 'em all. Or the Yankees did. All except one, his fastest, which he saved by riding it into the army."

"But how did they get back together?"

"Took three years. Said he bribed the Yanks. Crazy story. Met Mama in the middle of a battle. They fled on his horse. And did he go!"

Charlie stared past Ginny...into the past, speaking now in a whisper. "Papa called him Pegasus. Said that horse outran all the enemy's guns!"

"That's incredible!"

They got married in Richmond, but with the war going on, he paid a family friend—a man named Latrobe—to get Mama safely back North."

"They had just days together?"

"They lived in desperate times...loved in desperate times."

Chapter Twenty-Nine

Six Miles North Of
Saratoga Springs, New York, June 1864

A h, come in, dearie. What a pleasant surprise to see you again."

Alex forced a nervous smile and stepped inside Angeline Tubbs' cottage. "I hope...I'm not intruding?" *She looks...ordinary.*

"Heavens no, dearie. Always have time for those in love. We can always use more love in this troubled world." Tubbs shuffled to a table, sweeping aside two cats with a broom. "Get on, Notty and Pickeral. We have company."

She settled onto a broad back bench that fronted the table and motioned for Alex to take a seat opposite. Despite the bright June morning, the cabin seemed cloaked in shadows. Candle stubs littered corners, shelves, and the table top, melted wax trailing down like stalactites, a curious drapery of sorts that pooled peaked, little mountains atop the cabin's planked floor.

It's a wonder this place hasn't burned down.

"How is your brother? Luke, I believe?"

"Father has him learning accounts this summer. My parents are afraid he'll enlist. With Rob in the army, they think one son's enough to save the Union."

"So many are fighting." The Sage of Saratoga sighed. "And with you, my dear, I sense strain. A loved one is..."

"Oh, Miss Tubbs. Why do you say that? I mean...how do you know?"

The old woman patted the girl with reassurance. "You told me just now, dearie...in the slowness of your step as you walked to my front porch. In your sorrowful knock on my door, my child. With those red and teary eyes, when I first saw you. In the soft, sad tenor of your voice."

She reached out and touched Alex on the hand.

"And with that love ring on your finger."

"There's no one else to hear me," Alex said, wiping tears. "All the way from Virginia. So many are dying down there. I hardly got through the lines. Miss Tubbs, you helped me once, but...but this time, I just don't... Payne's been missing four weeks. I'm trying to find him. But no one knows anything!"

"Ah...the passion of a loving wife. I've seen much of it in this war. Passion, at least, is a good thing." The seeress reached for a candle.

"Here, dearie. Let us find our way. Really does work, you know." A surprising bit of glee launched her words.

"Ma'am?"

"Candles, dearie. They not only show us the way when our world goes dark, they guide us to our hopes and dreams."

"But the whole world's gone wrong," Alex sobbed. "Payne's... No one knows if he's dead or alive. And it's all my fault!"

"Hush child. How can you, a beautiful new bride, so full of life, be to blame for anything in this terrible war?"

"Oh, Miss Tubbs. If only you knew. If only you knew!"

"Whatever do you mean, dearie?"

"I never thought things would come...to this."

"What things, child?"

Alex shook her head. But the candle's flame softened the woman's aged, wrinkled face, bequeathing her a measure of trust and benevolence.

"I...I...I killed a man."

"And why do you say that?"

The candle flickered.

Alex related the details of her serendipitous winter meeting with Payne Harrison at Morton's Ford. Tubbs dabbled in the candle's melting wax but said nothing until she had finished.

"And this man who escorted you out on the ice?"

"He was revolting, foul-mouthed, and reeked of filth."

"And after he pointed the gun, and when Payne told you to run...?"

"I fled. But when I reached the riverbank, I turned back. He meant to kill Payne and steal Number Twelve."

"The horse?"

"Twelve is his fastest thoroughbred. The one he hoped to race here."

"That was very brave of you. Virtuous. What did you do next?"

Alex stared into the candle's flame.

"What did you do, dearie?"

"I...I...killed him." Her words clanked distant, mechanical.

"The foul-mouthed man?"

Alex only nodded, mesmerized by the burning wick.

"But you said he was going to shoot Payne?"

Alex closed her eyes as if to erase the memory.

"So you shot him?"

"I had no gun..." She faced Tubbs, suddenly energized by the memory.

"Then how did you come to kill this man?"

"I...I flat rocked him! He had that pistol pointed straight at Payne."

"Flat rocked?"

"Hit him with a stone."

"A stone?"

"I freed one from the river bank. Luke and I grew up skipping stones."

"You...you skip stones, dearie?"

"All my life."

"Ahhhh. I saw your brother Luke..."

"Luke tries. He keeps saying he's going to beat me, but he doesn't know how to wrap his finger 'round a good stone. Luke's just a flinger!

He's still stuck on throwing sidearm. Underhand's the only way to skip rocks."

"Underhand? Dearie, you mean like this?" Angeline Tubbs rolled a stiff, awkward motion with her arm, wincing.

"Not exactly. It's more...well I'd need a stone to really show you."

"Then we must go outside, child. You need to show me."

"What?"

"It's important, dearie. You must show me."

In front of the cabin, Alex dug up a worn, flat stone. "I hold it with my forefinger curled 'round like so. Then I just underhand it with this sweeping motion. Start over my head and end up in front of my waist."

"Do it, lass. Show me!"

"Well. OK. See that bucket there, over by your shed?"

"Yes, show me."

Fingering the stone around its curvature, Alex brought her hand over her head and then in a blur, swept down in an underhand motion, releasing the rock in a clockwise spin. A half second later, it smacked the wooden bucket three inches right of center.

The old woman froze. *You're...the one! It wasn't your brother that day by the lake. How could I have been so blind?*

"God marked me after I killed that man, and for my sin, poor Payne..."

"Peace my child. Come with me back to the table." Awe rarely hit Angeline Tubbs. But when it did, she moved quickly to wring its meaning. *So if you are the one by the lake...oh, what great revelations await!*

Inside the cabin, she brought out a small wooden box and set it beside the burning candle.

"You did something, but you know not what you did."

"I killed a man."

"No! You were brave and God saw that. You fought evil and won. God will not punish you for that. Besides, I speak of something else."

"I love my husband..."

"And you know how to skip a stone."

"Whatever are you...?"

"Alexandra...Alexandra, I saw you that autumn morning by the lake. Before the war. You skipped more than 40 stones into the mist. Remember?"

"I...I've skipped lots of stones. Everyone knows the legend. But no one's ever gotten one across. At least I've never heard of anyone. It's just for fun. But everybody likes to try."

"Precisely." Both women looked at the other across the candle's solitary flame. "And the legend, my dear?"

"Skip a stone across and your dream will come true. What about it?"

"That autumn day. That last one you skipped. You didn't wait."

"I don't remember. That was a long time ago."

"I never forgot. I saw it all and until now, I thought it was Luke. But no, only you skip underhanded. And you were alone."

Alex listened, trying to recall the raw morning by the lake.

"The fog fell before you knew. But I was walking the opposite shore. And I saw."

"Saw what?"

"This."

Angeline Tubbs opened the box, revealing a folded piece of paper and a polished, palm-sized stone.

"You mean...you mean...?"

"Yes, dearie. You got this one across. I saw it spin in the gravel that day. And penned these words that night. You skipped...the perfect stone."

"But...?"

"And now your dream can come true."

"But Payne..."

"Your dream?"

"You mean...?"

"Wish into the candle's flame with all your heart."

The glow burned bright, pushing back shadows where moments before hopelessness and fear had lurked.

"Take it, dearie. And these words I wrote." The old woman lowered her words to a hush. "Preserve both. They speak to the future. And our dreams. Never forget that. It is a great gift. If you believe."

Alex pressed a quarter dollar to the table.

"Fret not the silver, dearie. Go home and welcome your husband."

"How can you say that? How can you be so sure?"

"There's no magic involved, dearie. And no one's going to the devil."

"But...but..."

"Child, you've heard the stories about me. How I divine the future from chimney smoke. Tell fortunes by reading palms."

"Uh, huh."

"All poppycock. Common sense mixed with some good observation, a smidgen of intelligence, and a healthy dose of showmanship."

"Showmanship?"

"I entertain. I predict the obvious, the most likely. Anybody can do it, but I package it by dressing odd, acting peculiar, and speaking in antiquated tongue." Tubbs threw her arms in a wild wave and laughed, "Living alone up here with all these cats doesn't hurt either!"

Why did I come here? She's a fake, a fraud.

"Take back your coin, dearie. I didn't earn it today."

"But why, why are you telling me these things?"

"Ahhh. You still don't get it, dearie?"

"There's nothing to get. You're just a weird old woman who tells people what they want to hear."

"Not this spring morning, Mrs. Payne Harrison."

"What? Why...?"

"Did I call you by your married name? Because that's your reality. Just like that smooth stone in your hand. It's real. And the legend's real. And you getting it across the lake is real. I saw you do it!"

"You believe that stuff?"

"Do not hundreds try? Didn't you believe, dearie, every time you sent a stone skipping? Didn't you want to believe...?"

"Maybe. At the time." A tear slid down her cheek, then another. "I should go. I've intruded upon your day."

"Alexandra, remember what I tell you now...as one who has lived long."

Tubbs held out her hand and tipped the candle, spilling hot wax into the center of her palm. Without flinching, she squeezed the molten mass, leveling her gaze at Alex, eyes burning passion and sincerity, fervor and hope, pain and love. "Never ignore the real magic, the unseen, improbable, interwoven destinies that connect us all."

"The real magic?"

"Adventure, happiness, security, and love, dearie. If you believe."

"But Payne?"

"Does not the world still turn though never we see it?"

S he waved goodbye from her cabin porch as Alex started up the trail.

"God in Heaven, one of your faithful departs. Protect her, shield her. And guide me in what is to come. Though I am aged now, yet still I am able to serve. I pray you grant me the time."

Angeline Tubbs unbowed her head and glanced at the sun.

Not yet noon. Think I'll hike into town and see what Old Smoke's up to this fine day.

Chapter Thirty

Fort Delaware
Pea Patch Island, Delaware
June 1864

N *othingness.*
         Then pain.

For at least a week—could have been longer—he had had no idea where he was. Or who he was. In fact, not knowing didn't matter. There had only been light followed by dark.

And always the pain.

But now that he could sit...and see and hear those around him—like this smiling man standing beside his bed with a group of four younger men—he began to grasp things.

"This fellow suffered a deep laceration and severe concussion in mid-May. While on the path to recovery now, he still exhibits some memory and cognitive issues. Not surprising, of course, for someone who's been in and out of consciousness for nearly three weeks."

What's this...all about?

"Yet despite being with us for more than a month, and healing nicely I might add, he remains unable to tell us his name."

"Harrison. My name's Payne Harrison."

"Well! What a pleasant surprise!" The man turned. "Coming around, are you...Lieutenant Harrison?"

"How do you know...?"

"The insignia on your uniform, sir. Of course, we got rid of your rebel rags more than a month ago."

"What...what are you talking about?"

"You're in our care now. Took quite a whack on the head. Shrapnel I suspect. By the time we got a look at you, you were a real mess."

The man bent over and pried up a bandage behind Payne's right ear. "But look now, gentlemen. On the mend."

Fighting a spinning room, Payne sat up. "You're...doctors?"

"John Fromberger, MD, at your service." He paused, surveying the makeshift hospital ward of eighty beds walled in stone. "Let me amend that, Harrison. Here, we try."

"Here?"

"Pea Patch Island, Delaware, lieutenant. Fort Delaware. No more war for you. That's the good news."

"Good news?"

"Yep. No more fighting for you. See, you're a prisoner of war."

But how did I get here? I don't remember a thing. And where's Twelve!?

"You'll recall, gentlemen, every time we examined this patient, he'd converse with us, but was unable to state his name or anything about his past. Classic amnesia. I wonder, sir, now that you recall your name, can you tell us where you're from and with what unit you served?"

"Is this some kind of interrogation?"

"You've suffered a serious head injury and I'm simply trying to gauge your recovery."

"Chesterfield County, Virginia. Walnut Grove Farm. I serve on General Ed Johnson's staff...but where's my horse?"

"Observe, gentlemen. It seems his fog is lifting."

"Why didn't you quiz me on this before?"

"We did. And you gave us a dozen answers...or a blank look. You had no recall. And as you now realize, no short-term memory." The doctor patted Payne's shoulder. "Sorry, can't help you on your horse."

Dr. Fromberger discharged Payne that afternoon. Minutes later, prison guards escorted him to a bunk in Casemate 7, deep inside the fort.

"New bivouac, reb." The guard flung open the door. "Get use to it. Don't give us no trouble and things'll go just fine."

Pea Patch Island sat in the middle of the Delaware River about forty miles downstream from Philadelphia. Fort Delaware, an immense, pentagonal brick and granite fortress, dominated the lower end of the seventy acre island. Upon the outbreak of war, Federal authorities had quickly converted the bastion into a prisoner of war camp, putting enlisted men in hastily constructed board and batten buildings outside the fort while locking the officers in the stone casemates within. With walls towering thirty-two feet, ranging from seven to thirty feet thick and bordered by a deep moat thirty feet wide, the bastion proved a formidable, despairing challenge to anyone thinking escape.

"Ahh, Harrison. Glad to see you made it." Capt. Willis Bluestone stuck out his hand. "Your bunk's under mine. Get clobbered in the Mule Shoe?"

"I don't...remember."

"Count yourself lucky, then." Bluestone turned to his dozen fellow inmates. "Hey, fellas, remember this guy?"

"Nah, Willie." A rail-thin major, his left forearm wrapped in yellowed, pus-oozing linen, shook his head.

"Should we?" asked another, eyeing Payne with suspicion. "Somebody in here owe you money?"

"Think horses, gentlemen," said Bluestone. "Horses!"

"I've seemed to have lost mine and, well, if you fellows..."

"Wait!" said the bandaged arm man. "You rode ole Three Sox!"

"Twelve. Yes. I'm trying to find..."

"Remember that race? Early last spring. Hell of a come-from-behind!"

"Another fifty feet and his horse would have caught that front yellow-leg," said Bluestone. "Meet Lieutenant Harrison, fellows."

Everyone gathered close, words in welcome, hands extended. "On Old Clubby's staff, aren't you?" asked the suspicious man, now bustling grins.

Payne nodded slowly, so the room didn't swirl.

"Then you were at the Mule Shoe?"

"My horse..."

"Hell of a fight, that one," said the thin man, flailing his hurt arm. "And Ellis here got captured there. You too, Henry."

"Not if we'd gotten the goddamned guns back in time," said Ellis. "Been a different dance then. A real butcher's ball!"

"It was anyway," said Henry. "We fought Billy twenty hours. All in the rain. Gore and guts and mud. Everything and everybody got killed, captured, or mud-stomped out of sight. Never saw so many dead horses."

Payne reeled into a dead faint, but Bluestone and two others caught and carted him to his bunk. Like them, Three Sox's owner was a prisoner of war, wounded and captured in the fight at Spotsylvania, known thereafter as the Bloody Angle. They'd aid and nurse him as best they could. But each fretted his own world of worries, sensing Southern independence slipping away, concerns far grimmer than the fate of one junior staff officer's missing mount.

SARATOGA SPRINGS, NEW YORK
LATE JULY 1864

T hen we understand each another?"

"Aye, I need this to succeed more than ye, savvy?"

"Ahh, sonny. Even if it takes greasing a few palms?"

"Exceptional times, me dear woman...call for exceptional talents."

"He, he, he! Talents! Straight from the Biblical texts, good man. Couldn't have writ it better myself."

"Maybe, but there be at least one small detail needing ye counsel."

"Pray tell?"

"He won't know anybody. He'll need someone he can trust."

"Ahh...yes."

"This will put us square? Level the table?"

"My dear fellow, you've reaped handsomely over the years given the wisdom of my counsel on such profitable concerns."

"Aye, Aye. But no credit to that pinch of steel and ounce of sweat on me own part? Plus invested personal treasure?"

"The cost of doing business. Nothing more. But back to his friends."

"A necessity I fear. Someone he will know, trust. Have ye a name?"

"I do. Go with the lad. You've seen him about. A clever, wonderful boy. Courageous, too, I hear.

FORT DELAWARE, PEA PATCH ISLAND, DELAWARE
AUGUST 1864

D on't complain too much, Payne, old boy. It's worse out in the sheds." Willie Bluestone ladled his cup of thin gruel and brought out two, inch-long, wiggling white maggots. "Think of 'em as augmentin' your meat ration."

The newest prisoner looked away, stomach swirling.

"Now outside, the rank and file chase tails. Whatever darts under the plank walks. Lovely critters, too...a few, I hear, as big as cats."

The captain jiggled his spoon, watching the worms writhe.

"As for me? These'll do!" And with a wink, he opened his mouth and tongued the metal clean.

Payne Harrison gagged.

Across Pea Patch Island, Confederate prisoners gobbled rats. All they could trap and kill. As well as maggots in their soup, downing mosquito larvae with their drinking water, using whiskey or brandy, readily available for those with funds, to still the "wiggles" and mask the brackish taste.

Two days a week, all prisoners got crackers instead of bread, commissary corruption lining someone's pocket while Fort Delaware's long-termers courted scurvy. Head lice populated every inmate from scalp to shoes, while filth, be it dirt, sweat, garbage, or excrement, endangered the entire garrison. Measles, mumps, smallpox, and typhoid wreaked their havoc, but ordinary diarrhea and dysentery killed the most, skyrocketing when cholera gutted its take. And all knew, "those who go to the hospital seldom return."

But Lieutenant Harrison had already bucked those odds.

M ajor General Albin Schoepf, Polish-born, former Austrian army captain, commanded Fort Delaware. Mild-mannered and of genial disposition, Schoepf tended toward civility with the prisoners in his charge. He always knocked on the casemate door before entering. He welcomed free expression, tolerating the boast of some that the South would never be conquered. "Gentlemen," he would reply, "I think you are mistaken and underrate the determination and resources of the North."

Captain George W. Ahl, Fort Delaware's adjutant-general, proved Schoepf's opposite, a man with no scruples respecting the prisoners sent him. Inmates knew Ahl dominated General Schoepf to the point of intimidation, especially after a Confederate officer was murdered. Despite Schoepf's investigation, the offending sentinel went unpunished through Ahl's manipulations. Prisoners regarded Ahl as cowardly, cold-blooded, and cruel.

In late June, rumors circulated that Confederate authorities in Charleston, South Carolina, had placed fifty prisoners—Union officers of various rank—in parts of the city at risk to incoming fire from Federal batteries, all to thwart the continued shelling of innocent civilians. The talk persisted and the Union press urged retaliation, ranting that fifty Confederate officers of matching grade should be similarly exposed to Confederate fire. Now the order lay on Schoepf's desk.

"All I know is the little son-of-a-bitch bellowed out fifty names," said Willie Bluestone. "Only majors and above."

"And they're all leaving?" Payne looked out the barred casemate window.

"Yep. Five generals and fifteen colonels. Including your Johnson. All going to Charleston under the guns."

"Old Clubby'll love that! Anything to get out of here." Payne had nodded to Ned Johnson a few times across the fort's interior yard during daily exercise. "Ahl thinks he's sending them to hell, but Old Clubby's just itching for the party to begin."

Payne took in the Delaware's wide sweep. "Really think they'll go?"

"All left by steamer before dawn."

"What! I'd take my chances under shell fire any day rather than spend another hour in this hole with that ass Ahl."

A key turned in the casemate's massive lock.

"Is that so, Harrison?"

George Ahl shoved open the casemate door with a heavy wooden stick and stepped inside ahead of six armed guards. "It's fascinating what we hear if we just listen. Real clever, ain't you, Harrison."

Where did this weasel come from?

"And how fortuitous for you, lieutenant. For-tu-it-ous? Get it?"

No prisoner moved. Or spoke.

"Well, what the hell. One fort's as good as the next, huh, Harrison? But if you don't like it here," Ahl waved his stick, "we can always find you suitable accommodations elsewhere."

"Not without General Schoepf's permission!"

"Shut up, Bluestone! Guess what? You're out, too. Get your crap. Both of you. You've got two minutes."

*G*od, *damn this war.*

> *I had no quarrel with these people. But I had no choice. Did I?*

Payne stared across the sweeping marsh of Pea Patch Island.

Freedom...and Alex are over there!

Getting out consumed him. Every day. *That...and finding...*

He eyed the colored troops guarding the Dead Line, eying him.

They'd love to drop a hammer on one of us today. I hear they actually bet on who will kill the next reb.

Payne clenched both hands.

But I can get through this. Have to. Yet Twelve...I thought I could prevent...I thought I could keep you out of harm's way.

Sea gulls circled and dipped overhead, free.

You were the best Jasper I ever saw. Maybe the best anyone ever saw. You just never got your chance. Goddamn this war.

The August sun broiled on prisoner and sentry alike.

And now you're gone. Just like Sam. You trusted me. With everything. And now you can never be. And I... Well, all I can be is sorry, dammit. And that's not good enough.

Deep furrows plowed Payne's filthy face.

I just don't know...anymore.

How to...pick up the pieces...

If there are pieces...

God...please damn this war.

Chapter Thirty-One

A ll prisoners anticipated the Tuesday mail call. A squad of eight privates headed by a sergeant inspected every arriving letter and package, stashing them in crates until Mail Day. About a third of the inmates got something. Letters from home, mostly. Or packages containing anything from Bibles, combs, and soap, to shirts, socks, and cakes. A few received notices of fort-deposited funds, money they could spend with the post sutler.

Payne Harrison received no letters or packages. Missing in action, no one knew where he was. Or even *if he was.*

Then he regained his memory.

General Schoepf's official and private mail always reached his desk before 11 a.m., mostly routine traffic from the War Department about commissary supplies, security, logistics, and new arrivals. Schoepf acknowledged each by wire or in writing, aided by a secretary and file clerk. Orders for prisoner transfers were hardly routine.

"Elmira? General, who's the lucky bastard?"

"Harrison. Old Johnson's staff officer." Albin Schoepf initialed the War Department document and put it on his 'to file' stack. "This man's no troublemaker, but he's sure pissed somebody off."

"He's a rebel smart ass! Busted him to the barracks two weeks ago."

"Don't gloat, captain. Just get him ready. Pickup's tomorrow."

The next morning, an officer and two non-coms stepped off the daily steam transport servicing Pea Patch Island. After showing identification and official papers, sentries escorted them to Schoepf's office.

"Major Nathaniel Meagher, general." He tapped a silver-tipped walking cane to the floor. "This is Sergeant Haskill and Corporal Vincent. I believe you know why we're here. We'd like to be on our way as soon as possible."

"We shall do what we can, gentlemen. Staff's getting the prisoner now. If I might ask..."

"Excellent, general. We're operating under certain time constraints. I'm sure you understand."

"Ahh...yes...ahh, certainly. But if I..."

"A bit of an accent you have there, general. Where're you from?"

"Er...ah, Poland."

"I see. Well, you can understand we have quite a ways to go ourselves."

"Of course. But...tell me, what has this prisoner done?"

"That, sir, is still under investigation. Kindly show me where I can sign for receipt of him...?"

"Certainly, major. Just this standard release document. You've seen them before. Yes. There." Schoepf nudged a quill and ink well toward Meagher.

Bootsteps echoed beyond the doorway.

"Greet your new pals, Harrison." Ahl stood outside Schoepf's office. He prodded Payne across the threshold with his wooden stick.

"First Lieutenant Payne Harrison," barked Meagher, "late of Major General Edward Johnson's staff, Second Corps, Army of Northern Virginia?"

Despite a scrawny beard, ragged clothes, no shower in two weeks, and eight pounds lost to diarrhea, Payne stood erect. "Who's asking?"

"Shut up, Harrison. Corporal, manacle and hood the prisoner. You know protocol. I want this man bound and covered while in our custody."

"What the hell's this all about? Who gives you the authority...?"

Before Payne could protest another word, Sergeant Haskill belted him across the face, then spun him head first into the wall, grinding his arm into his back. "Not another damn word, reb. You don't want to play our game!"

Payne struggled but quickly realized resistance was futile. *Pray I never get a chance at you, friend...*

"Really, gentlemen? A head bag?"

"We should be on our way, general" said Meagher, ignoring the dust up. "Transport leaves in 20 minutes. Looks like you're running an efficient post here, though. Disciplined. No nonsense. I'll put in a good word for you."

Schoepf beamed and returned Meagher's salute, then watched from the window as they escorted the handcuffed, hooded prisoner to the dock. With no more fuss this day, he returned to his mail, calling in his clerk to tidy up the stack of signed 'to file' documents.

*T**hey've mistaken me for someone else!* But Payne's every protest nailed the business end of Meagher's cane to his ribs. "Prisoner, step down."

Hands on either side guided Payne along a sloping walkway. Despite the close attention, he still stubbed his boot against a plank board and sprawled forward. Rough grips gathered him up and pushed him on.

Guess we're off the steamer. Now what?

"Prisoner, walk."

He could only obey. Manacles chaffed his hands. His head hood had but a single slit, his every breath in the August heat a battle for air against sweat, disorientation, and creeping claustrophobia.

They walked at least ten minutes, footsteps sounding a series of buildings and alleys. Payne noted two left turns, a right, a final jog left.

Cobblestones...streets...now six steps up.

"Prisoner, wait here."

Three knocks followed by two more brought the creak of an opening door.

"Package?" asked a strange voice inside.

"Prisoner, state your name."

Payne couldn't even swallow, his mouth pasted in cotton.

262

"Prisoner! State your name!"

"Harrison," he gasped.

"Package delivered," said Meagher. "All yours. Here."

Hands pulled him inside, into a chair. A door locked.

"Keys! Give me the handcuff keys."

I know that voice!

"And get his hood off! Now!"

"Who...are you? WHO ARE YOU!" demanded Payne, blinking.

"It's Luke, Payne. Luke Parker. God, I'm glad we got you!"

"LUKE? LUKE!" Payne bear-hugged his brother-in-law.

"Listen, I'll explain later. Right now, you need to get out of those rags. We don't have much time. Here are some clean clothes and boots, everything you need's on that table. We've got a coach in the alley."

Within minutes, Payne, Luke and two accomplices were on their way to catch the train at New Castle.

"I...I...don't know what to say!"

"Freedom's sweet, huh? Thank Pat and Unger, here.

"Meagher?"

"No, they're long gone!"

Payne darted glances between the pair. "But how? Who...?"

"Guess!"

"No idea. Since mid-May, I...well, life's been a blur. One big fog. And this makes no sense. Sorry. Just numb I guess. But who...who did this?"

"Come on, fellow. You married her."

"Alex! ALEX? But how? My god, how?"

"She's a force to reckon with, brother-in-law. You should know that by now!" Luke had grown half a foot and added more than thirty pounds in the four summers since Saratoga. At eighteen, he carried the build of a wrestler. "When she hears about today, she'll be fine."

Payne closed his eyes, savoring freedom. "But how did she know? How'd she do it? I just don't understand."

"That's what he said you say."

"He?"

Luke laughed. "Bet me, actually. Said you'd have no clue, given the war and all. Called it a sure bet."

"Who, Luke?"
"Alex's helper."
"WHO, LUKE?"
"Old Smoke! Who else?"

In the privacy of their train compartment, Luke dished Payne all the details. At least those he knew.

"I've seen him around Saratoga lots of times," he said. "Everybody knows John Morrissey."

"And he came to you?"

"Yeah, said he needed someone you'd trust. And recognize." Luke poked out his adventure grin. "No way I'd miss this!" He punched Payne on the arm and pointed to his face. "And no shiners this time!"

"You're a good man in a scrape, Luke Parker!" Payne looked at the two men seated opposite. "And you work for Morrissey?"

"When Old Smoke needs things done," said Unger.

"And Meagher and his boys?"

Pat gawked straight ahead. "Don't know who you mean."

"But what about..."

"Old Smoke's damn good at nailin' down details," said Unger. "Let's leave it at that."

"But I'm supposed to go to Elmira. Orders..."

"You mean these?" Unger held up a bulging envelope.

"My prison record and transfer papers? Off General Schoepf's desk?"

"As I told you, Harrison...all the details." Unger stared stonefaced.

"But how in the...?"

Unger never blinked. "Got any idea what prison clerks make, Harrison?"

Erin go bragh! Here comes a good man!" John Morrissey opened his arms as Payne stepped into his office. "Payne Harrison! Off vacation now are ye?"

"Snatching me from that hellhole, John Morrissey, probably gets me in your debtor's prison for life, good friend. But still, I'll hug you."

"Careful what ye declare, there, dear Payne, or I be a calling in me chips on ye, should the times so dictate."

"I'll hazard the chance. You simply amaze me."

"Couldn't let ye just rot in there, now could I?" Both men embraced.

For all practical purposes, John Morrissey controlled Saratoga Springs. While Lincoln had fought to restore the Union of states, John Morrissey had dreamed and planned, bribed and invested, and plotted and schemed, expanding his gambling operations and influence not only around Saratoga Springs, but across the Empire State and into New England. He ran everything out of a back room in the Congress Hotel and curried favor with hundreds of officials across a score of jurisdictions.

"I hope ye appreciate the change in scenery. Given that dying's become so fashionable of late. I thought ye'd appreciate a 'livelier' option."

"What's the catch, John? I know you."

"No hooks. Only Yankee common sense, old boy. War's going to be over soon. Ye know it and I know it. Just a matter of time."

"I don't care about the war."

"Whatever ye say. But there's the future to contemplate. And I think yours is right here." Morrissey paused for emphasis, splaying his hands to Payne. "The racing offer still stands. Life can be good to ye here."

"I'd planned...to do just that."

"Now 'tis I who hear a catch..."

"Virginia..." Payne shook his head. "It's home...and this war..."

Morrissey pursed his lips, waiting.

"John, when this ends, Virginia will need all her sons and daughters...those left anyway...to build her back."

"Spoken like a knight of old, Payne Harrison." The boxer walked over to his window overlooking Broadway. "But what of the woman in ye life?"

"She loves me."

"Aye! But ye've not seen her in months."

"Alex arrives in Saratoga tomorrow. Luke's gone for her."

Old Smoke pulled a cigar from his top desk drawer. "And while the war still rages what will ye do?"

"I admit my options...are limited." Payne stared at the floor.

"Then let me advance a notion." Old Smoke clipped the butt of his cigar and rolled it between thumb and forefinger. "Stay 'til the war ends. There's work for ye here. Purpose, too. I'll put ye both up in a cozy place on the edge of town." He lit his cigar and made it glow.

Makes sense. Alex...here. And I can work with horses...

"So, good friend? Throw in with me?"

...and hang on 'til the fighting stops.

Payne wrenched up his burning stare, leveling his gaze—and a grin—at Old Smoke. "Aye, John Morrissey, aye!"

Chapter Thirty-Two

75 Miles North Of
Nakhon Phanom Royal Thai Air Force Base,
Thailand
August 1969

T wo Sandys over site!"
        "Others enroute, Frank?"
"Standing by for confirmation, sir."
Lieutenant Colonel Harney McGill eyed his fuel gauge. *Ample.*
But if Charlie starts scrappin', this BUFF's gonna chow down some fuel.
McGill's Sikorsky HH-53B, the Air Force's largest airlift rescue
helicopter, flew into the gray evening rain. Her crews nicknamed
these choppers Big Ugly Fat Fellows. BUFFs for short.
"Nine down?"
"Affirmative, sir."
McGill gritted his teeth. *Third chopper this week.*
"Coordinates and visuals grid the crash site to a spot a dozen miles
northeast of Keo Neua Pass," continued Lieutenant Frank DeLiotta,
"on the gooks' side of the Laotian border, about four clicks north of the
villages of Kim Cuong and Ha Tan. But no place to land. All jungle."

"And in Charlie's backyard. Damn!"

"Intel says so. Route 8 crosses into the North at the Pass. Funnels east, straight to the Ho Chi Minh Trail. Gooks keep it busy."

"Then the clock's ticking on those guys down there."

McGill kept an ear to radio traffic. Two other choppers—another BUFF and a Jolly Green Giant, the Air Force's HH-3E—filled the sky behind him. Two Douglas A-1H Skyraiders—nicknamed Sandys— had scrambled on first alert to cover and protect the crash site. When the rescue choppers arrived, the Sandys would maintain suppression fire during the extractions.

"Beepers?"

"Not sure, colonel. I hear 'em, but can't pick 'em out. All this noise..."

"Well, we need to nail down each of those beepers. Let's get those radios working. If we're forced to insert, we've gotta have those confirmations."

The steady, all day rain blanketed the mountain border between Laos and North Vietnam. Flying at 200 MPH—"full blow" crew members called it—the choppers pounded on, less than 500 feet above the jungle canopy. Flying low and fast best avoided the enemy's lurking 37-MM and 57-MM radar-controlled antiaircraft guns.

"Two Sandys are it, sir. Nakhon and Udorn just got more trouble. A Phantom's down west of Thanh Hoa and one of the Navy's LTV F-8 Crusaders vanished over Hanoi about an hour ago."

Down there, somewhere, our guys are counting on us. Someone's husband, son, lover. Someone's father. Probably busted up and hurting, too. If alive. Thank God the Thais let us operate close in.

Laura's and Ginny's taped photos peeked from a corner of the left instrument console. *Hard time, today, girls. Transports keep getting shot up. Outgoing mail's even down. Hold those smiles for me 'til I get back?*

"We've got reports the wreckage is hard to spot, sir."

"No fire?"

"Not even smoke. Sandys report no one's popped a thing."

"OK. Tell 'em we're 3 minutes out. Ground fire?"

"None so far."

"You PJs ready?" On an ideal rescue, two para jumpers dropped a pointed metal "spear" with foldable paddle seats down through the trees. Attached to an onboard hoist with 250 feet of 3/16 inch steel cable, this penetrator as the crew termed it, could bring a downed airman straight up through dense jungle. For the injured, the PJs usually tossed a coin on who would go down and assist.

"Get us in close, sir, closer the better in this weather." Airman Floyd Rector motioned toward the ground. In the distance, a swath of splintered trees marked the downed chopper's plow to impact, the wreck itself broken and buried in the undergrowth. Both Skyraiders circled overhead. Radio contact confirmed five men uninjured, another with a possible broken leg, and three missing. Signals came from three locations west of the wreckage.

"Don't like this cloud cover," said McGill. "Hope those flyboys keep an eye on things. Any more from the ground?"

"Two positive beepers and some broken radio traffic."

"OK. Tell 'em to pop smoke anytime!" McGill banked counter-clockwise above the crash site, honing on beeper signals emanating from the survival vests of the downed crew.

"Color at 4 o'clock!" yelled Rector.

A curling red cloud snaked up through the jungle canopy.

"Fifty meters too far south, High Angel," crackled a radio voice. "Muddy Bottom, here."

McGill banked left, coming to a hover fifty feet above the trees. "Let's get 'em!"

The penetrator plummeted with a zinging whine.

"More smoke, sir. Three hundred meters right."

"OK. Patience. How's our help?"

What! Three hundred meters? What the...?

One of the Sandys streaked to the left, zipping a burst of red straight into the jungle.

"Charlie at 9 o'clock!" broke the radio. Harney McGill caught the rapid, biting staccato of ground fire.

Hot LZ, dammit! Here we go again!

"OK. Muddy Bottom, cover your ass. Flyboys dusting gooks."

"Copy that, Angel."

The second Sandy screamed overhead, banking hard. Two concussions rocked the ridge above the crash site, erupting dual fire balls skyward.

Gotta hold her steady. Nice and smooth. Don't need any tree snags.
The radio crackled again. "OK! Got it! Good! Muddy Bottom
here. Haul!"

The up-whine of the loaded electric winch screamed into a higher
pitch. *Steady now. Gotta keep Buffy balanced.*

A punching sound spit through the cockpit tailing a streak of
blue dust.

Then another. And another.

Bits of wire and metal sprayed in all directions. An instant later,
a dozen more thuds tore apart the BUFF's underbelly.

NO! NOT NOW!

Harney McGill's chopper shivered as more enemy ground fire
ripped through the fuselage and chewed up the BUFF's rotor blades.
With a sickening tilt, the helicopter spiraled left and plunged into
the dense, dripping jungle.

MACON'S ORDINARY, KESWICK, VIRGINIA
FOUR DAYS LATER

An article on the Irish!" Ginny scampered up the tavern's
stone front steps, her fingers wrapped around the September
National Geographic, eyes locked on the red-dressed blonde adorning
the cover. *She's cute.* Then thumbed through the rest of the day's mail.
Nothing again.

Her mother was slicing pie apples when Ginny entered the
kitchen. She darted her daughter a look, waiting.

But Ginny could only shake her head.

Laura McGill dropped her cutting knife into the bowl. "I...I don't
know anymore, Ginny. Your father's never..." She blinked back, trying to see.

"Mom...watch. There'll be something tomorrow."

Laura set aside the apples, wiping her eyes. "Maybe...maybe."

"Oh, who's Mildred Blake?"

"Mildred? Oh, a cousin of Grandie's. Lives up in New York State.
Why?"

"He got a letter from her."

Mildred Parker Blake, the widowed daughter of Charlie's first cousin William Parker, lived in Saratoga Springs, New York.

"Didn't Grandie visit her up there."

"It's been a few years."

"Somebody say I've got mail?" Grandie shuffled into the kitchen.

"From your cousin Mildred."

"Anybody else?"

Laura shook her head, but braved a grin. "Nice *Geographic* story on the Irish though." She nudged the yellow-bordered magazine across the table.

"Haven't heard from Millie in ages. Card last Christmas. But always something going on. That woman. Into everything." He sat down and opened the envelope. "Hope she's OK."

"My game's at seven, Mom. And we're picking up Elizabeth and Nanci."

"OK. OK. So supper at six, everybody." Laura waved as if brushing words away. *How can you not write me? Do you have any idea how much I dread the mailman? I can't even go out to the box anymore.*

"Millie wants to visit." Charlie turned over the letter. "Says she's been going through some of her dad's things."

"Uncle Billy's been dead more than ten years, Grandie."

"Longer, Laura. Passed away the summer after Ginny was born. He was my first cousin. His father, Uncle Luke, was my mother's brother. Confusing?"

"Did you know him?"

"Oh my, yes, Ginny! Talk about a character! Why I recall one time Uncle Luke decided he was going to..."

"Is that all you two can talk about?" Laura pushed back the bowl. "I need a walk."

Charlie phoned New York that evening.

"Are you sure Tuesday suits, Charles? I certainly don't want to put you out, but Father wanted you to have these things. As I was saying, I was cleaning out the basement and ran across this box. Haven't looked, but it had your name on it. I remember Father telling me before he died. I just forgot."

Charlie replied he'd be thrilled to have Mildred come and visit. It had been way too long. But at 95, he really didn't travel much anymore. Yes, Laura and her daughter were staying the summer while her husband was in Vietnam. But please, please come. The tavern always had room for family.

"It'll only be two nights. But with Laura there, seeing her and Ginny will be a real treat. Even then, I couldn't stay more than three nights."

Mildred Blake could go on and on, especially on another's dime. "I need to spend a few days in Wilmington and Harrisburg, too. Cousins on Mother's side. And then there's the DAR reception the last of the month. Same weekend as the first big stakes race. And you know I never miss..."

"Stay as long as you can, Millie."

"Wonderful, Charles! Let me finalize a few things and I will call you tomorrow evening. Arrive Tuesday?"

"That's fine, Millie."

"By the way, Charles, you doing OK?"

"Usual stuff, Millie. Cane all the time. But the girls are here and that means a lot."

"Still stargazing?"

"A little. Can't use the lenses worth a hoot. But Millie, just going out there under those stars...has its own rewards."

"You're timeless, cousin. You know that?"

"Sure don't feel it these days, Millie. But if I've got you fooled... You know, I think I'll take a peek tonight."

But on this third Friday evening in August of 1969, clouds obscured the skies over much of the southern and eastern United States. On the diamond, Ginny struck out nine and led her team to victory, but hers was the only star shining. In the Gulf of Mexico, a thousand miles to the south, meteorologists with the National Hurricane Center had just upgraded a tropical depression off the coast of Cuba to a small but potent hurricane with wind speeds reaching 115 mph. Four hundred miles to Charlie's north, on Max Yasgur's 600 acre dairy farm in Sullivan County, New York, singer and song writer Richie Havens concluded his opening performance at a weekend rock festival with an improvised rendition of *Freedom*. And in a windowless office deep in the Pentagon eighty miles up Rt. 29, an anonymous officer with the United States Air Force prepared to redial the busy telephone number of a retired physician living a half dozen miles east of Thomas Jefferson's Monticello.

Charlie was in the den reading John Scofield's article, "The Friendly Irish" in the new *Geographic* when the phone rang.

"NO! NO! OH NO, GOD! TELL ME IT'S NOT SO!"

Laura? My God, that's Laura!

"YOU MUST HAVE THE WRONG NUMBER! PLEASE SAY IT'S NOT SO! PLEASE!"

"Laura? Laura? What's wrong, Laura?"

Charlie fumbled for his cane and tried to stand up, but had to grasp the edge of the table to keep from falling. He could hear Laura wailing into the parlor phone. Fear knotted his gut.

Ginny ran in from the kitchen. "Mom! Mom! What's wrong?"

Charlie tried to grasp the girl's hand, a feeble effort at best, but a true one from a man who had comforted and aided people all his life.

"Front parlor, Ginny."

"NO! NO! NO! PLEASE GOD! NO!!"

Ginny pushed past her great-grandfather, her face pale as paper, anxious, round eyes searching, lips aquiver. "DADDY! IT'S ABOUT DADDY!"

By the time Charlie inched into the parlor, Ginny was around her mother, hugging, tears streaming, with Laura vacant, clutching the phone.

I don't remember it ringing. After I talked with Millie, I settled in the den with the Geographic.

Laura stared straight out the front door, coursing her fingers through Ginny's hair.

"What in heaven's name, Laura? What...?"

"They...called."

"Who?"

"Harney's down." Her words landed flat, wooden, zoned. She stood more as mannequin than person, invisible strings tugging her focus to something far away. Only Ginny's hug kept her standing.

"Is he OK?"

"In the jungle. Weather's bad."

"What do you mean, Mom?"

"No fire, though. That's what the man said. I hope he can stay warm."

"MOM? WHERE'S DADDY?"

"Down, Ginny. In the jungle."

Charlie took the phone from Laura's grasp.

"Hello? This is Dr. Charles Harrison. You were speaking with Mrs. Harney McGill, my granddaughter."

The voice on the other end, sincere and soothing, yet formal and direct, introduced himself as an Air Force family support officer. He repeated that Lt. Col. Harney McGill's Sikorsky HH-53B had been shot down four days earlier over North Vietnam. There had been no observed explosion.

No fire. That was the good news.

Despite intense rescue efforts in deteriorating weather, only one crew member—dead in the wreckage—had been recovered. The others, including McGill, were missing in action.

B y Saturday morning, Camille, the season's third hurricane, was bearing down on the Gulf Coast with forecasters issuing a hurricane warning for all points between Biloxi, Mississippi, and St. Marks, Florida. That evening, reconnaissance aircraft measured winds around the eye at 150 mph. Virginia's weekend weather forecast indicated rain, possibly heavy at times.

Up in New York, the Woodstock Music and Art Festival on Max Yasgur's 600 acre dairy farm had exploded into an around-the-clock orgy of popular rock bands performing before an estimated audience of nearly half a million people. Traffic jams locked roads in all directions for miles. Rain mired the campgrounds and shortages of everything from clean water and food to toilets and first-aid tents turned the site into an enormous morass of mud, trash, and filth. Drug use flourished, including LSD, heroin, marijuana, and a hallucinogen-laced Kool-Aid which sickened hundreds. But *Santana, CCR,* and *The Grateful Dead* played on.

Charlie phoned Mildred after supper.

"Oh, no! Charles. I cannot imagine...You're sure?"

"An Air Force officer came by this afternoon. All he could say was that Harney was shot down last Monday. He assured us every effort's underway to locate him and his crew."

"And my dear Laura?"

"Up all night. Ginny, too. We're all coping the best we can. Betty Paxton, one of Laura's friends, was over today. A huge help."

"Oh, Charles, this just makes me sick. This war and all. Tearing the country apart. Why, just look at this deplorable free-love mess going on down state. Depravity! Hippies and dope and all that wild music at this Woodstock thing. Flower children! Dear, cousin, what's this country coming to?"

Mildred Blake was on a roll.

"And now we've got the hurricane of the century bearing down on Florida. Category Five. I tell you Charles, nothing's been right since those fellows walked on the moon last month. They messed up something up there. Only God knows how we're going to make it right again."

T his was not the time to visit. Yes, it felt akin to mourning, but it was really worse because Harney McGill's fate ached with heart-wrenching uncertainty. So Mildred Blake stayed home.

The weather didn't help. Rain. Nothing but rain.

Folks around Keswick would soon learn of the downed pilot, the red-headed fellow from Montana who had married Doc Harrison's granddaughter. And they'd stop by Macon's Ordinary to express their concern and hopes and love.

But on this night it was pouring outside. Hard. And folks stayed home.

Still, no one was much concerned. This Class 5 hurricane had certainly wreaked havoc in Florida, Alabama, Mississippi, and Louisiana, with record storm surges, severe flooding, and property loss. Early estimates tallied 150 lives lost across the deep South. But now it was breaking up.

Yet as Camille's remnants moved into Tennessee and Kentucky, and then barreled eastward, the storm regained power, colliding with large masses of moisture-laden air in the Ohio Valley. By the time it got to Virginia, the rain had become a thundering, torrential downpour that continued unabated all night.

Flash floods and landslides devastated the James River basin, washing out roads and downing power lines, uprooting large trees, and with rocks and mud, smashing through houses and wrecking automobiles. When authorities missed the updated forecast and issued few warnings, people perished, including more than one percent of the population of nearby Nelson County south of Charlottesville, either drowned, crushed, or buried as they slept, poor people mostly, living up in the hollows of the Blue Ridge mountains.

Many Virginia locales recorded more than a foot of rain that night.

The state eventually counted 153 people dead or missing and 313 homes destroyed. Wrecked bridges numbered 133 with 25 miles of primary roads and 175 secondary miles obliterated. Total damages exceeded $19 million. Camille was the worst natural disaster in Virginia's history.

By Monday when the music stopped, Max Yasgur's dairy farm was trashed. A mostly word-of-mouth, free rock festival where 500,000 individuals had gathered to advocate and celebrate love and peace, Woodstock could not escape some harsh realities. Petty crime, mainly theft and vandalism, plus drug selling sullied the festival's ideals. Acres of garbage littered the Yasgur farm and adjoining properties, from abandoned blankets and muddy clothes, to mountains of beer cans, broken glass, rotting food, and human excrement. Two babies were born and at least three women miscarried. Three people died, one from a drug overdose, another from a fall, and a third killed when run over by a tractor while sleeping in a field.

In Virginia, restoration began immediately. The National Guard and state highway department erected temporary bridges. The Salvation Army and Red Cross, along with church groups and charities rushed in clothing, food, utensils, and drinking water. People took in their homeless neighbors and hundreds walked the mountain hollows, fields, and river bottoms, looking for the lost. In time, the Old Dominion healed.

So did Max Yasgur's farm. People removed the trash and put back the fences. They cleaned up the cans and bottles and broken glass. The muddy fields greened under the next summer's sun. And memory of the music and idealism and social harmony merged into legend.

But fortune had something else in mind for Macon's Ordinary.

C harlie?"

Huh?

"Charlie."

Somebody calling me?

"I am, Charlie."

Ah...well, I...

"Yes?"

Well, ah...what can I do for you?

"Oh, you don't have to do anything for me, Charlie."

But you called me, didn't you?

"I did."

Well...why?

"Because we're buddies. You and I go back a long ways, Charlie."

I know you?

"Always."

But I don't recognize your voice.

"Sometimes you don't listen very well."

I treated you the best I could. Prescribed the best medicines available...

"I never came to you for treatment, Charlie."

Not a patient of mine?

"I knew you years before you became a doctor."

You did? When?

"In the beginning, Charlie."

The beginning? That's curious.

"Curiosity is a good thing, Charlie. You always had plenty. And I'm glad to see Miss Ginny's got her share, too."

You know Ginny?

"Oh, yes. Marvelous girl!"

Look. You say you knew me before I was a doctor. And you claim to know my great-granddaughter?

"Yes, Charlie."

Well...well, how can that be?

"You are so full of questions today."

And you're playing games.

"Not a bit."

Then what's this all about?

"Just an old friend saying hi."

Charlie didn't realize he'd been dreaming. Not at first, anyway. Everything just...seemed too real. The conversation. The voice. The warmth.

In fact nothing hinted that it was a dream at all. He'd awoken with every detail still keen.

No dream left him like that.

Even after lunch, the exchange remained sharp. It was, he marveled, rejuvenating to enjoy such clear recall.

But with whom?

That was the perplexing part. He had no idea.

Of course, he had other dreams. Especially about Harney. Lurid, dark stuff. But with those, thankfully, daylight washed away the details.

The Department of Defense had nothing new to report. And Laura's daily vigil for any news quietly slipped into a dulling routine of letter writing and phone calls, which left her numbed between tempered stoicism and abject despair.

At least his West Meadow nightmare was gone.

But I'd wrestle that in a heartbeat if it would bring Harney home.

Laura's husband had been missing in action for nearly a year. The Pentagon had several stale reports of POW sightings in North Vietnam but nothing could be substantiated, much less confirmed.

And the war just went on and on. It crushed him to think of Laura as a war widow and his beautiful Ginny, fatherless.

Can nothing be done?

Chapter Thirty-Three

Cumberland Church, Virginia
7 April 1865

The glow of a solitary lantern pushed the dark beyond the corners of his dilapidated camp desk. Here, in the quiet of the tent, he had his thoughts to himself.

Outmanned...outgunned...outmaneuvered. How can we prevail when Grant holds such advantages?

General Robert E. Lee parted the tent flap and stepped outside. Dare he confront what he pondered, surrender of the Army?

The concept goes against my very being.

But nothing this night offered hope. Again and again, everything pointed to disaster—the decimation of the army via desertions, captures, and casualties; the paucity of rations and supplies; the wholesale exhaustion of men and animals; the relentless, gathering encirclement by Grant's forces.

Am I left with but one choice? Surrender?

The word came hard.

Must I do such a thing? Can I do such a thing?

B ut Lee did do such a thing, exchanging with Grant over the next thirty hours a series of confidential letters seeking an end to hostilities. About half past eight on Sunday morning, 9 April, Lee summoned Sergeant George W. Tucker to bring Traveller. With Tucker holding the reins, Lee patted his faithful dapple-gray and reassured the horse with a soft, low whistle, a soothing, special tone between master and mount. The animal brought him great comfort.

Is Grant trying to force my hand? Our lines are barely holding. No matter, his letter requires a response.

He'd spent the night sprawled on the ground wrapped in a single blanket. The morning's events had already left him drained, wearied.

"I would like to sit down. Is there any place where I can sit near here?" Lee directed his words to no one in particular, but spying a shady spot under one of several apple trees close by the road, he planted himself on a makeshift seat of fence rails assembled by some of his staff. An aide posted Traveller under a nearby tree. *Now, we wait.*

Sometime after 2 p.m., a Union horseman appeared under a white flag, riding from the direction of Grant's last known location. A lone Confederate officer accompanied him. Even from this distance, Lee could see the Southern officer's mount mirrored no comparison to the magnificent red stallion of the Federal. When the pair neared the apple orchard and prepared to dismount, Lee got a closer look.

I know this man.

The officer dismounted and approached with his Confederate escort who saluted. "General Lee, allow me to introduce Colonel Orville Babcock."

Babcock, a stiff, precise officer in his mid-twenties sporting a manicured Vandyke beard, saluted and handed Lee a small envelope.

Lee opened and read Grant's letter.

Your note of this date is but this moment (11:50 A.M.) received. In consequence of my having passed from the Richmond and Lynchburg road to the Farmville and Lynchburg road I am at this writing about four miles west of Walker's church, and will push forward to the front for the purpose of meeting you. Notice sent on this road where you wish the interview to take place will meet me.

As Lee reread the words, Traveller whinnied, pawed at the dirt, and whinnied again. Over his reading glasses, Lee reassured his horse with the low whistle. But Traveller nickered and pranced about, bringing a similar response from Babcock's horse.

Lee eyed the red chestnut. "A fine animal you have there, sir."

"Ah...yes...General. I'm quite satisfied with him."

Lee had no heart for prolonged small talk but Babcock aroused his curiosity. "I must ask you, Colonel, have we met before?"

"I do not believe so, General. I attended the Academy long after your term as Superintendent."

Traveller reared and yanked at his reins, twisting towards Babcock's mount. The larger, red horse whinnied and shook his mane, not in confrontation, but as if to acknowledge some caballine bond of yore.

"Well, our horses certainly have something to say."

"I am sure I would have remembered such a meeting, General Lee. But I only acquired Rubric last spring." Babcock masked his awe of the Southern general in the formal tone of one brooking no interest in light conversation.

Again, Lee whistled to Traveller. The horse quieted but kept facing Rubric, alert, with ears pricked. Babcock's mount calmed in the same instant, but pawed at the dapple-gray with a fancied preference.

"Sir, General Grant desires me to assist you in any arrangements you find necessary to facilitate this conference. The meeting may be within your or our lines at your preference."

This Babcock is all business. Yet, this is as it should be.

"That is most welcome, Colonel. Can you insure this present truce will extend through the interview?"

Babcock wrote a short note in Grant's name, notifying General Meade to continue the cease-fire until further notice. That done, there remained but one thing to do. Lee mounted Traveller and motioned for Colonel Charles Marshall of his staff and Sergeant Tucker to join him. Then, with Babcock aboard Rubric, the four horsemen started toward Appomattox Court House.

How I long to escape this. Must surrender really befall my men? Almighty God, I have failed them. Can I not do one thing good this day?

Sight of the magnificent Rubric lifted Lee's spirits. Thoroughbreds had always stirred him, even as a boy. *Ah, Traveller, you are also impressed.*

Babcock's horse tossed his head, revealing an angry white scar under his tousled mane. *Looks like shrapnel. Why must war wreak its havoc on such a splendid animal?*

Col. Marshall led them into the yard of a comfortable house for the meeting, the home of one Wilmer McLean who had fled the war's approach four years earlier at First Manassas. Lee dismounted and handed the reins to Tucker. "See that he gets some of this grass, Sergeant."

Now we wait.

I met you once before, General Lee," Grant began, "while we were serving in Mexico, when you came over from General Scott's headquarters to visit Garland's brigade, to which I then belonged. I have always remembered your appearance, and I think I should have recognized you anywhere."

"Yes," replied Lee, "I know I met you on that occasion, and I have often thought of it and tried to recollect how you looked, but I have never been able to recall a single feature."

Can we not address the matters at hand?

"I presume, General Grant, we have both carefully considered the proper steps to be taken, and I would suggest that you commit to writing the terms you have proposed, so that they may be formally acted upon."

The Union commander nodded. "Very well, I will write them out."

Lee drifted his gaze out the window, to the beautiful Palm Sunday afternoon. Outside, all was coming green, another spring bringing new life.

But so much of Virginia lies ruined. How will we ever restore her?

Grant opened his order-book, lit his pipe, and began writing.

His words will decide our fate for generations to come.

Lee returned to the window. *Traveller looks content. He's got good green grass today. How he has comforted me these many months...a loyal friend in camp and field.*

Only the studied scratching of Grant's pencil broke the silence in Wilmer McLean's parlor. When he had finished, the Union commander rose, approached Lee with the order book, and asked him to read the document. The Confederate commander put on his spectacles

Several more minutes passed before Lee put down the order book and nodded. "This will have a very happy effect on my army."

Said Grant, "Unless you have some suggestions to make in regard to the form in which I have stated the terms, I will have a copy of the letter made in ink and sign it."

"There is one thing I would like to mention."

Lee approached this matter with care. "The cavalrymen and artillerists own their own horses in our army. Its organization in this respect differs from that of the United States. I would like to understand whether these men will be permitted to retain their horses."

"You will find," Grant began, "that the terms as written do not allow this. Only the officers are allowed to take their private property."

An awkward quiet hushed the McLean parlor. Lee reread the terms; Grant rethought them.

"No, I see the terms do not allow it; that is clear." Lee put down his glasses and said nothing more. He would not beg.

The Union commander inclined his head, started to speak, then paused and brought both his hands together to rest against his pursed lips.

"Well, the subject is quite new to me," he began after a moment. "Of course, I did not know that any private solders owned their animals, but I think this will be the last battle of the war—I sincerely hope so—and that the surrender of this army will be followed soon by that of all the others, and I take it that most of the men in the ranks are small farmers..."

These are the words of a man gracious in his victory.

"...but I will instruct the officers I shall appoint to receive the paroles to let all the men who claim to own a horse or mule take the animals home with them to work their little farms."

Lee exhaled, relaxing for the first time since entering the McLean house. As for the hundreds of Yankee prisoners still held by his army, "We have no means of feeding these men. We don't even have rations for ourselves."

"Suppose I send over 25,000 rations," said Grant. "Do you think that will be a sufficient supply?"

"It will be a great relief, I assure you."

Yet even with the men fed, how do I tell them they are surrendered? That they must go home and remain there, to bear arms no longer?

Lee gazed again into the April afternoon. Tucker had Traveller loosely tied, permitting the dapple-gray to graze at will under a massive pecan tree. Rubric munched nearby. Each horse sought the other's company.

A fine animal. I'm not sure when I've seen a more magnificent horse. Admirable deep red coat. Muscled, full of power. Three stockings, too.

And now the war was over.

Lee stood and shook hands again with Grant, bowed once to the others in the room and stepped outside. Federal officers on the porch bolted to attention, hands in salute.

How do I do this? My God, grant me the strength.

Lee paused to put on his hat. He saluted slowly, acknowledging the men around him, then walked a few feet and stopped at the top of the porch steps to pull on his gauntlets. He fisted one hand into the other, turning his gaze to the yard and beyond.

Out there, my boys are waiting. Wondering. What shall I tell them?

He had no answer.

Oh, that I could bring them good tidings this Palm Sabbath. With peace restored, God, grant me thy peace. And let me do one good thing this day.

Lee sought Traveller. But instead of his faithful mount of so many campaigns, he spied two horses in the yard. Not a blurred, double image seen through filling eyes, but a clear vision of Traveller and that other horse...Babcock's splendid thoroughbred.

Of course! Three stockings! How could I forget? And with that star on the forehead! Three Socks!

"Orderly! Orderly!" He slapped his gauntlets.

Motioning to Sergeant Tucker, Robert E. Lee started down the steps of Wilmer McLean's Appomattox home. Although defeated in war, the Southern commander mounted Traveller with a new confidence and purpose, on a new mission now to accomplish at least one good thing this day.

Chapter Thirty-Four

Walnut Grove
Chesterfield County, Virginia
15 April 1865

A unt Hattie loved the coming of spring.

When the Lord brings back His world. Sunnin' the flowers and singin' the birds. Stokin' warm days and spreadin' clover. And oh yes, growin' corn.

"In this pack house, Jasper. I 'member some shuckin's up in the loft. Fetch the ladder out of the barn and get up there 'fore Master Clay wakes up. That seed corn's 'bout all we got left."

The old woman unlatched the door and stepped inside. This was where she'd found the colonel on that last day of January.

Heart quit. Right over there. Eyes opened, but stone stiff in the winter chill.

She couldn't scratch the image out of her head.

Guess you had to take him, Lord.

The colonel's passing marked a sad start to 1865. Aunt Hattie knew things looked dark.

Oh Lord, Miss Jane's still down and so sad. All those lines and tears 'cross her face. And Miss Sara's dumpin' 'long there, too.
Why, Lord? Not that I question You. Thy will be done.
But You already took Master Sam. And now the colonel. Maybe even Master Payne's up there with You. We just don't know 'bout him. He and that wonderful horse of his. Gone! It's all so hard, Lord. Callin' 'em home in this terrible time when we need 'em so.
But hear my prayer, oh Lord.
And this war. Please end it. So much sufferin'. Please, Lord, hear my prayer.

With the Southern army's collapse and flight from the siege lines around Petersburg on April 2, the Confederate government abandoned Richmond. Agents torched warehouses full of cotton, tobacco, and military supplies. Looters spread their own chaos. Government records vanished from the city or were consigned to the flames. Artillery shells in the Tredegar arsenal exploded in the conflagration and more than 20 blocks of Richmond's vital business and financial center were destroyed. From Capitol Square down to the James River, mountains of broken masonry and twisted metal lay heaped amid the tottering walls and blackened ruins of factories, shops, warehouses, government buildings, banks, businesses, and private dwellings.

And as Federal forces swept south across the James, Yankees tore through Walnut Grove, breaking Jane Harrison's good china, stealing her silver, and slashing the colonel's portrait in the Great Room. They seized the remaining mules, wrecked the brick ice house, and stole the last four hams from the smokehouse.

At least those bad soldiers didn't burn down Miss Jane's house.

Aunt Hattie turned and looked out the pack house door.

God always ends His winter with the promise of spring. It's His renewal of the world. Maybe rain this afternoon.

But this spring promised more. Peace quieted the war-torn land.

Peace. And this galloping notion called freedom.

"You know Mammy, those Yankee soldiers told us we could go."

"Mind me, Jasper. You can't believe 'em. They're stealers. You saw what they did to Miss Jane's things. Broke up all her dinner plates, stole her silver. Poured that good wine in the piano. Even cut the poor colonel's picture with that long knife. Decent white folks don't do such things."

"I know, Mammy. But the blue soldiers still say I's free. Soon's the war ends. That I can be my own man. A free man, Mammy! Free! You, too!"

"Hush that talk! Your place is here with your Mammy, boy. Don't forget that. Hear me?"

Jasper framed a scowl, but said nothing more as he leaned the ladder against the loft side of the pack house.

"Don't shun your Mammy like that, boy. Now get up there and fetch me that seed corn. It's bagged in a wooden box up on the high shelf."

Sullen, Jasper climbed to the loft and crawled inside. He was back in a minute, clutching a small burlap sack by the top and bottom.

"What now, boy?"

"Mice." He poked his finger through a hole in the sack. "Still got five or six pounds, I reckon."

"Come on down." Aunt Hattie waved her hand. "And don't spill none."

But Jasper pointed at the road. "Soldiers, Mammy. Three riders."

"What? More Yankees?"

Jasper shielded his eyes and surveyed the horsemen coming up the long lane. Recent rains had spun road dust into mud. An extra mount trailed the trio.

"Can't tell yet."

The riders approached the turn to the main house.

"Jasper?

But her boy could only stare.

"What? What is it?"

"Mammy! OH, MAMMY! GLORY BE!"

"What? What?"

Jasper clambered down the ladder, spilling corn from his sack, and grabbed his mother by the shoulders.

"It's him, Mammy! He's back!" he yelled, bolting for the front yard.

"Come back here, Jasper. What you talkin' 'bout?"

"It's a miracle, Mammy! A real miracle!"

"Get back here and clean up this seed corn! What's got in you?"

That boy! I'm gonna make him pick up every kernel! So help me, Hannah!
She eyed the gathering clouds.

More rain. Well, I best see what all this ruckus is about. Can't be nothin'
good. Yankees showing up like this. Stealing all over. I better hide this corn.
When they goin' to leave us be?

Aunt Hattie joined her boy against the white-washed five paling fence, riveted by the riders dismounting in the shade of Walnut
Grove's front yard.

Why, they're us! And Great Jehovah, that's... Oh, praise be to God!
This is a blessed day!

A bearded, white-haired man uniformed in mud-spattered gray
nodded toward the house. "I am looking for the Harrisons." He
smoothed his hand up the neck of a tired, muddied dapple-gray, pat-
ting the horse with a loving rub. "I do hope we are at the right place."

Aunt Hattie nodded, eyes aglow.

Oh Lord, how marvelous are Your works, how mysterious Your ways!

A season of peace...and a harbinger of promise had returned to
Walnut Grove.

I understand, General. God be with you and your family."
Robert E. Lee tipped his hat to Jane Harrison. "I regret I can
give you no further news on your son."

"When did you see him last?"

"Spring, a year ago, I believe. Just before..." Lee slapped his
gauntlets to his leg. "I want you to know I regarded him highly...
Ma'am, he was one of General Johnson's best couriers."

Jane Harrison choked back tears.

"I can tell you this, too," Lee continued. "That was a brave thing
he did at Morton's Ford. Extraordinary..."

"This...means a lot to a mother, sir." She beckoned for Aunt
Hattie. "A glass of cold spring water before you go? I would offer you
more, but..."

"Thank you, Ma'am, but it's threatening more rain and..." Lee
turned to his two companions. "We still have some distance before us."

"Then accept my thank you, general. Your visit...lifts my hopes."

"I thank you, Mrs. Harrison. It gratifies me that I could return some property... I saw him run once, you know."

"I will give this to Payne, if..." Jane Harrison held up a small envelope, forcing a smile. "Thank you."

"I pray Providence will deliver your son soon...and safe. Meanwhile, we must all reunite as good citizens."

Aunt Hattie waited, eyes still dancing. Jasper hovered nearby, gawking.

Lee mounted Traveller, but caught the black woman's sparkle. "That's right. You heard me correctly. All...must strive to be good citizens now."

"You mean...?" The old slave took a step forward.

"I do."

Lee faced Jasper. "You, too."

The jockey brightened as the ex-general leaned over and patted the unsaddled stallion.

"Take good care of him."

BOOK FOUR

Call to Me, and I will answer you,
and show you great and mighty things,
which you do not know.

JEREMIAH 33:3

Chapter Thirty-Five

H i, Charlie."
      Ah...oh. Hi.
"How is your today?"
You here again?
"I hope that's OK?"
Well, yeah. I'm just...sorry I...well, I still can't quite place you.
"I understand. It has been a while."
You did say you were an old friend?
"I did."
Well...ah...
"Everything OK, Charlie?"
That depends.
"On something else?"
You can say that. So why is it...this is going to sound crazy, but...
"Why is it you fear me?"
Look! How do you know these things?
"I know you."
But you can't. You're not real.
"Oh, but I am. Charlie, I've known you all your life."
How can you say that?
"How can I say what? The truth?"
*Don't spout double talk. You're trying to confuse me. You're just another
dream. I know now. You're...*

"A good friend."

OK! Fine! Then tell me who you are, good friend.

"All in good time, Charlie. You have to trust me on that."

Why?

"Because of Laura and Ginny. Soon, Charlie, very soon, they will need you. More than you know."

Look. I'm just a tired, old man. I'm no use to them.

"How wrong you are, old friend."

Old friend. You keep saying that. What's the deal here?

"Because I am...your old friend."

I don't know you.

"That's what you think. Charlie, I was with you from the start. I watched you dig in The Ruins, rooting out those buried old bricks in summer's heat, sweating your grandma's black beads. And I loved when you ran free across the East Meadow and splashed into the Water Cress Spring, when you sniffed the spearmint and jerked cattails out of the marsh. When you played hide and seek with your imaginary playmates in the thicket."

And you knew about...?

"I was there, too, Charlie."

You were?

"In the West Meadow, Charlie."

H e'll be 98 in May, Laura."

"And he's my grandfather, Dr. Winfree. Better off at home with his family than in some...some old folks nursing barn."

"Laura, I'm sure you mean well, but your grandfather needs daily care now. Close attention. And with you out of the house... you teach?"

"Reading specialist...here in Albemarle. Ginny and I've been with him almost three years."

"Well, who watches him during the day when you two are out?"

"I worry about that, Dr. Winfree, but Grandie told me years ago he'd prefer to die at home when his time came."

"Look..."

"I'm not ignoring what you're telling me, doctor. And I don't mean to be flip. I know there're risks. So does my grandfather. He took care of a whole community for more than fifty years."

"Laura, he can hardly walk up steps anymore. The effort leaves him gasping. You've seen how swollen his ankles get. Not to mention the arthritis. And those two cancerous moles I took off last winter. He's frail. Father Time's talking now."

"OK. So when's he going to die?"

"Come on, Laura, you know I don't know that. He could live three more days or three more years."

"Precisely. And as long as Grandie can walk out into his backyard and look up into the night sky, I'm going to make sure he gets to do just that."

"I admire your pluck, girl."

"I can do no less." Laura paused, spotting Dr. Winfree's framed med school diploma on the wall behind his desk. "Gosh, Grandie graduated in 1903."

"Always been there for you, hasn't he?"

"The only person I've known all my life."

Harvey Winfree laid Charles Harrison's medical file aside. "So, how are you doing? Any news?"

"We...get by. It's hard on Ginny, not having her Dad around."

"But you?"

She bit her lower lip. "They think Harney's near Hanoi. I have to believe that, Dr. Winfree."

"You hail from hearty stock, Laura."

"Grandie's my tower of strength. Yeah, he's frail, but in his own way, he keeps me going. I know he needs us and that gives me focus. Keeps me from dwelling on Harney all the time. In a way, it's like he's still doctoring."

"I remember a story I heard about him in med school, Laura. Back during the Spanish Flu. World War I had just ended and all the doughboys were coming home. Within weeks, dozens started getting sick. Then they began to die. Everywhere. The state quarantined Keswick and most of eastern Albemarle. Charlie Harrison was the only physician folks had out there. But he doctored everybody. Braved it out. And never got sick. A miracle, some called it. Charlie went into homes no one else dared visit. And he stayed at it, even when the flu killed your grandmother."

"Grandie never said much about that..."

"Would you expect him to? God! What he did that winter..."

Laura spotted a deliveryman across the street getting out of his truck with a bouquet of flowers.

"You know, he still talks to Grandma...out there in the garden. Even mumbles in his dreams. Just goes on and on. Vivid stuff. Like he's actually living them. And then he wakes up so refreshed... changed. Dr. Winfree, putting him in a home..."

"You make your point, Laura."

"That old tavern is his home, doctor."

"And you are one true granddaughter, Laura McGill. So what's this about a trip to New York State?"

"Grandie's pondering a trip to Saratoga Springs this summer. Used to visit the place years ago. Has a cousin up there. I promised to drive him, but Ginny and I need to come back. We'll return for him before school starts."

"And you want my blessing? You already know what I think."

"I just need you to get us a referral. Call it...professional courtesy." Laura smiled.

The doctor shook his head. "Betty Paxton warned me about your charms, Laura McGill."

U pwards!

No! It can't be back!

Wrapped in gut-wrenching fear, Charlie felt himself rocketing.

But it is! After all these years!

Yet he knew better.

The dream had ambushed him this time. Out of nowhere, without warning. Come straight at him. Hard.

And yet it had changed.

As always, he soared upwards, drifting down in the next instant, hands guiding him to some place, some destiny. Friendly voices, encouraging, cheering. His mother calling his name, urging him to something he knew not what. Yet her soothing voice reassured and quieted his fears.

So he listened and smiled. *Mama.*

Until exploding incandescence—a great, searing brilliance—roiled existence and pitched him headlong into emptiness.

Letting him fall.

Down and deep.

Crashing into pain.

As everyone watched.

And that's the way it always was...awakening wide-eyed and gasping.

And alive.

But not this time. Darkness ended the dream.

Darkness!

Yes, IT was back. Without warning.

And now for the last time...

"You think so?"

Huh?

"That I'm here for the last time?"

That YOU'RE here for the last time? What are you talking about? Coming at me like this, haunting me. Who are you?

"Patience, Charlie."

Then tell me why you're here.

"I'm here for Millie. And you, Charlie. Millie wants you to visit. And you should."

Millie? How on earth..? Look here, how do you know Mildred Blake?

"She's your Saratoga cousin."

Yeah.

"Visit her, Charlie."

She was coming to Virginia a few years ago, but that hurricane...

"Go see her, Charlie. With Laura and Ginny. They need to visit, too."

Look. I can't get around anymore.

"Says who? You're fine in here with me. Lucid. Animated. With it. You can be the same when you're awake. If you believe. Besides, Laura and Ginny are counting on you. Charlie, you can do this."

Believe? Laura and Ginny? Look, I'm almost a hundred years old. I don't travel well. I get tired easily and I need to pee every hour.

"Excuses. Come on. I'll meet you there."

You're crazy!

"Want to know who I am? Find out in New York. I'll be there, old friend. Bring out the best in you, too, Charlie."

You're a dream. Nothing more!

"Oh, but Charlie. I'm YOUR dream."

Stop it! Why do you torment me?

"Meet me there. In August. In the high season. Did you know your mother loved Saratoga in August?"

Mama?

"She really misses you, Charlie. Remember her bacon and buttermilk pancakes? And how she'd sing to you in thunderstorms?"

You...you know about...?

"I was there, Charlie."

And so...Saratoga?

"Yes."

And I will know you?

"As an old friend, Charlie."

An old friend?

"It will be fun, Charlie."

Chapter Thirty-Six

State Route 80
North Of Cooperstown, New York
8 August 1972

Yogi's your favorite? Come on, daughter!"

"He's cool, Mom." Ginny pounded the $6.95 genuine Hall of Fame souvenir baseball into her Wilson softball glove.

"But he's a catcher and you're a pitcher." Laura checked the rear view mirror. "Awake back there, Grandie?"

"Resting my eyes. But listening to you and the ace here."

"Ever been to Cooperstown before?" asked Ginny.

"No, sweetie." Charlie blinked awake. "Baseball's Hall of Fame didn't exist first time I came to New York."

"How many times have you been to Saratoga?" Laura kept her eyes on the road. The glistening blue hues of a large lake sparkled through trees off to her right.

"First time was back in '04, I think. Just married your grandma." Charlie rubbed his face. "Remind me to take you to Congress Park."

"Saratoga's ball field?"

"Not exactly." Charlie laughed. "So Yogi's your guy?"

"Yeppers."

"And I thought you'd stay with a pitcher and go Koufax."

"No way, Grandie! He played for those awful Dodgers."

"But he's a great pitcher."

Ginny gloved her baseball again. "No better than Lefty Gomez."

"How do you know all this, girl?"

"She reads everything she gets her hands on, Grandie."

"I know. We head to Saratoga right as Cooperstown has their induction ceremony!" Charlie tapped his great-granddaughter on the arm. "No wonder you were 'cool' on going to New York with ole Grandie."

Ginny poked back. "I hope Saratoga has softball. All I hear is horses."

"Millie will know." Grandie shut his eyes.

They drove on in silence, taking in the roadside beauty. "Otsego Lake," said Ginny, reading a small road sign at a pull off overlooking the lake. "Says James Fenimore Cooper cited this lake in some of his works. *The Last of the Mohicans. The Deerslayer. The Pioneers.* But he called it Glimmerglass."

"I didn't know that, Ginny. Did you, Grandie?"

"Don't know many Mohicans, Laura, but I could sure use a pit stop."

E xcepting her butler Jamison and maid Leah, Mildred Blake lived alone in a grand, lime-green Victorian on Saratoga's Phila Street, a house dating to the 1870s and boasting tan shutters and intricate gingerbread cornices around the eaves, all bordered by a wrought iron fence worthy of a graveyard.

"Oh, my dear Charles. I'm just thrilled to have you and yours up for a visit! To think...all the way from Virginia." Mildred leaned over and pecked the old doctor's cheek. "Been far too long."

"It's so kind of you to have us. Grandie's been talking about visiting for weeks."

"Pleasure's all mine, Laura. And Ginny. Let me look at you. Give your old Yankee cousin a hug, honey."

Mildred Blake was usually quite the priss with her proper manners and high society airs, but with kinfolk in town, she dropped most of the pretense. To her Virginia cousins, she exuded nothing but charm and hospitality, a matronly bent to be sure, but genuine from the heart.

Charlie tapped his cane to the sidewalk. "I told Ginny you were a veritable font on what comes and goes in society circles here."

"Ginny, your great-grandfather exaggerates. Course, if I can help..."

"How about softball? I need to keep my edge."

"Edge?"

"She pitches, Millie. Her team's tied for first."

"Oh. Practice. Well, Ginny, I don't know about softball. August is racehorses around here. I'm sure Charles..."

"I've heard all about that. But whatever..."

"You don't sound very excited, dear."

The girl shrugged.

"Well, I...I do hope you'll see the Sanford next week."

"Oh, Millie. Ginny and I need to be back home by the 12th. I've got two pre-school conferences that week and Ginny begins playoffs."

"But I thought you were all staying through August..."

"We'll be back for Grandie before Labor Day."

"I see." Mildred geared down her disappointment. "Well, doctor. Looks like you're stuck with me and all my Empire State girl friends."

"I'll try to stay in trouble, Millie."

"Charles! You've not changed a bit."

"Would you have me any other way?"

"I shan't answer that, sir. But I will tell you, all of you, that tomorrow I've planned a marvelous picnic down by the lake. Remember the last one we had, Charles?"

"That was a while ago."

"You'll love it. Now everybody, come on in. Jamison will get your things. Leah's got her wonderful spaghetti marinara waiting."

W ow! Take that in!" Ginny waved at the far shore. "This lake's a lot bigger than I thought."

"Bet it's deep, too," added her mother. "Gorgeous day for a picnic, Millie. Grandie—let me get the door—pick out a spot."

Charlie swung his legs out of Mildred's maroon 1971 Pontiac station wagon. With a jab of his cane, he stood, looking up and down the beach.

"There." In a measured, deliberate pace, he started toward a grassy patch near the shore, a single, magnificent oak towering shade overhead.

"Fishing's pretty good, too," said Mildred. "My grandfather always cast his line off that ledge of rocks."

Laura spread two blankets while Ginny grabbed the lunch basket.

"Get Grandie's lounge chair, will you Ginny?" Laura nudged her grandfather. "Bring tackle?"

"As if..."

"Doesn't matter, Charles. This is one of the prettiest spots on the lake. Our fried chicken and potato salad will have to wait. Walk, anyone?"

"Count me in," said Ginny.

"Good, you two. I'll stay here with Grandie."

"I'm fine, Laura." Charlie wrinkled his nose. "Don't think you have to worry about the tide coming in."

"I'm not leaving you alone."

"Worry I'll get into mischief, granddaughter?"

"No, silly. I don't want you getting too much sun."

"My dear, I'm 98 years old."

"But..."

"But what? The old Grandie needs watching?"

"You don't understand..."

"You gals go for your walk. I'll ogle the water."

"OK, OK. You win." Laura spun toward Ginny and Mildred. *What's eating him?*

"We'll be back in half an hour, cousin."

Charlie watched the three women move down the beach, Ginny running ahead, stopping to skip stones while Mildred paused to point out a significant feature here, a scenic view there. In five minutes they were around a bend, out of sight.

So...Saratoga one more time.

Charlie took in the lake like a rerun movie, in this case trying to squint out a jogger on the opposite shore. *One last time.*

In the middle, a rowboat. Two fishermen patient in their quest.

Maybe I should 'take the waters.' Hah! Me, old country doctor nearing the century mark seeking some panacea from storied old Saratoga.

A warm breeze stirred, lapping lake against shore.

OK, you said you'd meet me here.

A car horn sounded from the other side of the lake.

So here I am, all the way from Virginia.

August's lazy afternoon settled on the lake.

Can't wait all day, you know. The girls'll be back soon.

Charlie eased off his tennis shoes, squiggling his pale toes into the sand. *Course, I've no idea who you are. Or how I'd know you.*

The lake calmed as if to mirror the sky.

But you seemed so sure.

"Hey, Pop. How ya doing?"

Charlie opened his eyes to find a tall, strapping youth looking down. With the sun in his face, he could see little of the young man.

"Just wondering about on a Wednesday. How 'bout yourself?"

"Wondering, huh? That's funny. Hey, I'm Henry. But I go by Hank."

"Glad to meet you, young man."

"You too, Pop. Nice day to try, don't ya think?"

"Well, I didn't bring any tackle."

"Didn't mean fishing, Pop. Never been much on that." Hank reached down and picked up a small stone, flicked it aside and reached for a second. "Ahhh. Lake's almost as smooth as glass."

"Hey, Grandie! We're back," Ginny waved from down the beach, breaking into a run.

"Sure weren't gone long."

"Just around the bend there," she said, catching her breath. "Mom...OH, hi!...was concerned...for you."

Grandie nodded toward the young man. "Ginny...Henry, er.. Hank. Hank, my great-granddaughter, Ginny."

"Hey. Nice to meet you. Walking the shore?"

"Just a bit. This is my Grandie. And that's my Mom and our cousin Millie coming up the beach."

"Oh, I know Mrs. Blake. Everybody in Saratoga Springs knows her!"

"Hank Forsythe! Imagine this!" Mildred hugged the young man. "How's your mother? I've been meaning to call her."

"Hi, Mrs. Blake. Mom's fine." Hank turned and spun his stone across the water. "My afternoon off from the track, so I thought I'd take a try or two."

"You working there?"

"Just like last summer. But I better get going."

"Well Hank, enjoy your day. And good luck."

"Thanks, Mrs. Blake. Nice meeting everyone."

"He mows grass at the Saratoga Race Track," said Mildred, watching Hank jog down the beach. "Bright kid. Mother's in my DAR."

"Ice tea or lemonade?" asked Laura. "You, Grandie?"

Charlie nodded toward the lemonade, watching as Hank stopped by the water's edge. Again, the lad bent over and picked up several stones. With each, he faced the lake and sent one skipping.

"Ginny," said Mildred, "I just realized we've got plenty of chicken and potato salad. Run down there and invite that young man to join us."

"Ahmmmm." Ginny looked at Mildred, who returned a tantalizing wink.

"Sure!" She waved at Hank, who waved back.

"Always at it, aren't you, Millie?" Charlie watched Ginny run to the water's edge. "You ole matchmaker!"

H ey, Hank. We've got extra chicken if you want to join us. Mom made brownies, too."

"Yeah?" Hank sent another stone spinning, watching it smack the surface five times before sinking.

"You're good."

"I work at it."

"What do you mean? They're just rocks."

"Not to everyone. We make a wish before we skip 'em."

"Make a wish? I can do that. And skip a rock? Anybody can skip rocks."

"Yeah? Try getting one across the lake."

"What? That's impossible. Besides, I'd rather throw softballs."

"You play softball?"

"I pitch."

"Cool. I'm more into baseball, but then guys usually are."

"What position?"

"Outfield. Sometimes backup catcher." Hank reached down and dug another stone from the mud. "Wanna try?"

"Sure."

"Here. But make a wish first."

"A wish?"

"Sure. Anything. Don't be bashful."

Ginny glanced back up the beach at her mother. *OK, I know you're watching me!* She fingered the stone, positioning it just so, seeking balance between forefinger and thumb.

"OK. Wishing!"

"Good. Go for it!"

Raising her right arm high, Ginny brought the stone downward in a powerful underhand motion, releasing it in a blur.

"Holy cow! That sailed at least 50 yards before it skipped! You sure don't throw like any girl I know."

"You say you catch?"

Hank bent down and dug out another stone. "Second string."

"Ginny nodded toward the picnic area. "We better get up there before my Grandie wolfs down *all* the fried chicken!"

Chapter Thirty-Seven

I'm glad to see you, Charlie."

So...you are here?

"Yes. I've actually been waiting for you, Charlie."

Could have fooled me. Say, listen. How is it I keep dreaming you up anyway? Whoever you are.

"Isn't that why you've come to Saratoga? To find out? Charlie, you know I've been with you all along. You just haven't...well, noticed. Until now."

Come on! That's silly. You're just some weird concoction spinning my dreams of late.

"I know you've been busy taking care of Laura and little Ginny..."

Now that's another thing. How do you know what I do?

"And you're going to the track next Wednesday?"

Yeah. Millie and I. Good seats. How do you know that?

"Look for me there, Charlie."

At the race track? What will I tell Millie?

I won't need a seat, Charlie.

Well, how will I know you?

"You'll know."

Even though I've got no clue what you look like?

"You'll know it when I get there."

You're not making much sense.

"Patience, Charlie. In time."

In time?
"Yes, Charlie. Our time is coming."

*S**he's having a wonderful visit. And Hank, you seem like such a nice
young man.*

Laura watched her daughter power into her wind up. *I do love the
evenings up here.*

Crush-stretched leather cracked across Mildred Blake's backyard.

"Pretty good arm there, Ginny." Hank dug the softball out of his
more than warm catcher's mitt and tossed it back.

"My split curve, Hank. Hums but I can't always hit the corners.
Let me try this."

WHACK! "Real smoke there, girl. You've got some
underhand!"

Laura forced a smile. *Nice picnic down by the lake, too. And Ginny
getting some pitching in. But we just got here...and tomorrow we go home.*

"Let me know when that fastball's coming, Ginny. That last one
was a downright *screamer!*"

*Grandie sure loves it here. Getting caught up with Millie. Telling his
stories. And this spring he was so withdrawn. But now he's back. Color's
good. Even stayed up last night to take in the stars.*

SMACK! "Major league heat on that one, Ginny!"

Harney, you'd love Saratoga. Peaceful. A kind of magic here.

THWACK! "Ouch! Darn! Caught that wrong!"

But Harney! Ginny's growing up on us.

"A few more, Hank?" Ginny ground the softball into her glove.

*And you're not here...to see any of it. I don't even know where you are.
The Air Force tells me nothing! NOTHING! All we get on TV is that.....*

CRACK! "OWWWWW! Ginny! Where'd you learn to pitch
like that?"

*...despicable Jane Fonda cavorting about Hanoi saying we're all a bunch
of war criminals and urging our boys to desert and mutiny. And now this
Ramsey Clark, condemning America while assuring us North Vietnam's
treatment of their POWs "could not be better."*

"My Dad. Always played catch with me...far back as I can
remember."

*You've been gone more than three years... Three years, Harney! I'm deal-
ing with Grandie, but Ginny's all the future I have without you. I can't...I
can't keep on like this...*

Laura fought tears as Ginny ran up to the back porch.

Oh, dear God, just tell me he's alive.

"Hey, Mom?"

Laura turned, grabbing at a tissue from her purse.

"Something wrong?"

"Nothing, Ginny. The sun's just bright. Good workout?"

"Ah...yeah, Hank doesn't let much get by. Not even my wild
stuff."

"Her game's ON, Mrs. McGill."

"Well, Hank, my Ginny does love her softball."

B een more than 50 years, Millie, but the place still looks the
same."

"Heavens, Charles. Has it been that long?"

"Well, I have been back a few times. But when Nell and I first
came up, you were just a toddler. Such a cutie." Charlie eased himself
out of his cousin's Pontiac. Cane in hand, he crunched gravel and
stood up.

"Hush, Charles! Mother said Amanda babysat me that time." She
pointed left. "Take that path over there."

The retired physician shuffled across the parking lot toward the
stately oaks guarding the path to Saratoga Race Track. Flower beds
along the walk popped begonias in pink, red, and white. But Charlie
kept his gaze fixed to the stands.

"I know Amanda loved seeing the horses run. Just like Papa.
Took her here once...after Nell..."

"Charles..."

"It's OK, Millie. I..."

"Cousin, I still remember Mother telling me. It had just snowed.
But all I kept thinking was...*Mommies can't die...Mommies can't die.*"

Charlie stopped to catch his breath. A roar broke from the
grandstand.

"The big race is seventh?"

"Yes, plenty of time." Two gray squirrels scurried through the begonias and scratched up a nearby oak.

"I remember there was this spectacular horse. Amanda followed his every race. Nobody could beat him and she said he was the greatest race horse of all time. Well, we had to go see him."

"Summer of 1919? Gosh, I was only six."

"Yeah." Charlie scratched his head. "Can't recall his name. But your folks had already invited us up. I told Amanda we came all the way up here just to see her horse run."

"In the Sanford?"

"I believe so. He went in the overwhelming favorite. But he lost."

"Oh, you mean Man O'War!"

"Yeah. That's the name." Charlie stepped off the path, letting others pass. He raised his cane toward the track. "Man O'War losing over there—the only race he ever lost I think—crushed Amanda. Some horse named Upset beat him. Imagine that!"

"I remember Father going on about Upset. But Man O'War's still considered the greatest racing thoroughbred of all times. We won't see his likes again. Poor Amanda."

"I know. She never mentioned much about Saratoga after that."

"That's sad."

"Same thing happened to Papa, you know. Had this great contender. But then the war came and the Confederate army took every animal he had. Only way he saved this horse was to ride him into the army himself."

Mildred nodded toward a side door off from the main gate, flashing two tickets to an attendant who waved them through. "Doing OK?"

Charlie paused again to get his breath. "Getting...there."

"Only two landings, cousin."

"K."

"Grandfather told me your father helped establish this track."

"He and Mama were up here when the war ended. Papa'd been a POW but got out somehow and came here."

"They stayed in Saratoga?"

"I think so. The organizers needed someone to standardize the betting. So Papa did it. But he wanted to go home. When the war ended, he and Mama left for Virginia."

"Oh, Frankie!" Mildred Blake waved at an usher four rows over. "Grandfather told me about this horse-loving rebel his sister married." "And Mama had me nine years later." Charlie grinned.

"Frankie, kindly show my Virginia cousin to his box seat," said Millie, slipping the boy a dollar.

"Cheap date, huh Millie?"

"You really know how to charm a girl, Dr. Harrison!"

"Afternoon's young, my dear."

M idst a mob of 18,000 thoroughbred racing fans, Charlie wanted no part of the betting lines.

"I'll go to the window for you," Mildred offered.

"Don't bother, Millie. I can pick 'em as they go by."

And in the next race Charlie did just that. He studied the racing form, eyed the horses as they made their way to the starting gate, and jotted down his win-finish-show picks along the margin.

"Charles! I don't believe it!" Mildred danced in the aisle as his selections stormed across the finish line in precisely that order. "Why didn't you let me place your bet?"

"And jinx 'em, Millie?"

Seizing the moment, she introduced Charlie to a bevy of her friends in nearby boxes, waving them over to admire her cousin's "wining card." As one of Saratoga's best known social hens, she chatted away, boasting of her 98-year-old Virginia cousin who had just nailed the second race. Fragile, but gracious and yet perhaps a smidgen perturbed at all the fuss, Charlie stayed seated as he smiled and shook every well-wisher's hand.

Shucks, they only want to know who I like in the next race.

But Charlie's penciled-in prognostications failed in the third and fourth races and his new found friends soon drifted back to their seats. Mildred excused herself to "say Hi" to her dentist, seated four boxes to the left, then as the fifth race got underway, she made her way up into the grandstand to visit with her hair dresser. With each run to the tape, spectators roared and screamed their enthusiasm or angst, cheering the winner or lambasting the losers, all reflecting their wagers' successes or failures.

Millie must know everybody. Darn if I do.

Charlie craned his neck to glimpse the entrants to the next race.

"Miss me, Charles?"

He turned quickly, but found only his grinning cousin.

"Just admiring the horses, Millie."

"I didn't mean to leave you for so long. But everyone loves to gab. Hope you didn't mind?"

Charlie shrugged a smile.

Millie spotted Frankie in the aisle. "Time yet?"

"After this one, Mrs. Blake." The boy turned toward the track as the bell sounded, watching the field break from the gate. "Off to a good start," he yelled over the roar of the crowd. "Pick any winners today?"

"My cousin here, but he won't bet!"

"Bet on the Sanford, sir. I got twenty bucks on Linda's Chief."

"Why that horse, Frankie?" Mildred Blake leaned closer.

"Undefeated in five races, Mrs. Blake! Stable talk has it he's the best two-year-old out here."

"I heard Northstar Dancer's pretty fast. Angel Cordero's aboard."

Frankie shook his head. "Might place. Then again today's race has two scratches. So with only five entries, the track's not taking any show bets."

The lead horse in Saratoga's sixth race edged ahead a full length going into the final turn. Thousands in the grandstand clambered to their feet, cheering on their favorites.

"Thanks, Frankie." Mildred patted Charlie on the shoulder. "There's your hot tip, cousin." Everyone faced the finish line watching the lead horse barrel down the dirt track tight to the rail and win by two lengths.

"Frankie says the next race is the one to bet on."

"And I shall. Who do you like, cousin?"

"No idea. Only five horses?"

"Yes. Two scratched. Something to drink, Charles?"

"Lemonade would be nice."

Mildred returned with refreshment as the five horses and their jockeys passed the grandstand, acknowledging the cheers and applause of the fans. Saratoga's 59th running of the Sanford Stakes Race loomed minutes away.

"OK. My money's down. I can still get yours in."

"I'm enjoying just being here, Millie." How long's this race?"

"Six furlongs. Half a mile. The track's a mile and an eighth oval. That puts the Sanford's post position on the backstretch."

Millie pulled up her binoculars. "Seems Frankie was right. The morning line on Linda's Chief hasn't changed. Still 3 to 5."

A dark, high-spirited colt edged into the first starting gate. "Just put a hundred bucks on you, Number Four!"

Charlie watched each thoroughbred enter the gate.

Such noble creatures.

"He looks fast, cousin. Sure seems on the bit today."

The starters closed the rear gate on Linda's Chief as others quickly guided Number Five, a large, dark red chestnut, into the second stall.

Wonder if Papa had any idea Saratoga would prosper like this?

Eager patrons began to stand.

Of course he did. Racing was his passion! And these were the moments he lived for. These last seconds before the start...

...and those first seconds after his horse finished first!

A ND THEY'RE OFF!

The five broke in a blur. Powered, muscular motion interweaving on a living tapestry of glistening browns, reds, and grays thundered down Saratoga's long dirt backstretch.

"Linda's on the rail, third," shouted Frankie, who had stopped by to watch. "Northstar Dancer's just ahead, right behind the leader."

"Who's that?" asked Millie.

"Trevose," yelled Frankie. "Don't worry about him."

But half way into the race, Trevose still led.

"Watch Northstar and Linda's Chief. Trevose'll fade."

"You sure, Frankie? What about those last two horses?"

"Sailor Go Home? No way. And that chestnut running fourth? Big Red? Oh, what's his name? Too far back. Not today."

Around the long turn, all five horses pounded toward the head of the stretch, Linda's Chief edging into the lead, the race two thirds done.

"Come on Linda, come on!" shouted Millie.

But the race was not over.

"Golly! Look at Big Red!" shouted Frankie.

In fourth and seemingly blocked by Trevose and Northstar Dancer, the red chestnut had found another gear. Accelerating quickly with a tremendous looping stride, he broke to the inside and rushed past the pair on the rail. With only a furlong to go, he bolted ahead of Linda's Chief.

Increased his one length lead to two.

And won by three.

"My God!" exclaimed Millie. "There went a hundred bucks. Where on earth did that horse come from? And who is he?"

Charlie fumbled with his racing form.

Electrified by the dramatic finish, clamoring patrons of the 59th running of the Sanford Stakes thundered their surprise.

And approval.

Charlie looked up. "Secretariat, Millie. His name's Secretariat."

Chapter Thirty-Eight

L et him sleep, Leah. And get started on the laundry. We had one
rousing day at the track yesterday."

Mildred Blake went back to her morning paper.

This Vietnam mess.

Her mug of Maxwell House in one hand, she turned to page two.
Uggh! How could I forget sugar?

"SO WHERE WERE YOU?"

The four words barked from the first floor guest bedroom. *Charles?*

"BUT HOW?"

Mildred jumped from her kitchen table and darted down the hall.
"Charles? Charles? You OK?"

"YOU'RE SURE?"

"Charles? Who are you talking to?"

"YOU PROMISE...?"

Mildred pushed open the bedroom door. "Leah! Leah! I need
you!" The old man lay gasping in the antique walnut canopy bed,
curled under his blanket like a twisted, buried log.

"Cousin?" Mildred shook Charlie's arm. "Are you OK?"

Leah peeked into the darkened bedroom. "Yes, Mrs. Blake?"

"Help me here, please." Mildred turned on the table lamp.
"Charles! It's Millie."

The old man squirreled to one side, burrowing his face into a
feather pillow, shunning the sudden, bedside brilliance.

316

"You gave us a start, cousin." She smoothed her fingers across his forehead. "I didn't know you talked in your sleep."

Charlie gargled a few consonants, clearing his throat.

"Hog...wash." He yawned, throating more sounds. "Didn't... sleep well."

Mildred straightened out the covers and turned off the lamp. "We had a grand day yesterday. So go back to sleep. It's early yet."

Again he coughed and turned slightly, his body relaxing as if melting under the blankets. A minute more and only his slow, quiet rasp broke the room's quiet.

H e awoke a few minutes before noon. Leah brought orange juice which he sipped but the old doctor showed little appetite for anything else.

"Feel like getting up, cousin?" Mildred asked about three.

He shook his head.

"You've got me a little worried. Feeling OK?" *He looks so exhausted.*

Charlie smiled. "If I had a nickel...for every time...I've asked that."

"I'm asking it now, sir."

He sighed and closed his eyes. "Yeah, you are."

"Charles?"

But he'd drifted off again.

Something's wrong. Laura's under awful stress, but she needs to know.

D r. Myron Crawford closed the bedroom door. "He watched the Sanford?"

"Had a wonderful time. Charles charmed all my friends after he called that second race."

"I was there, too," said the general practitioner. "Nice crowd. Great day for racing."

"Charles was his old self yesterday. Loved watching the horses. But last night he got so lethargic. And this morning, when we couldn't get him out of bed..."

"He's resting comfortably now. I got him to talk. He's lucid, but very weak. Hypertensive. Ankles a little swollen. But he's breathing

OK and his lungs seem clear. Glad his granddaughter thought to bring his records. His heart isn't pumping like it should but that's seems an ongoing issue. I don't think he's in any immediate danger."

"You're sure?"

"He's frail, Mildred. And I'll be frank with you. Pneumonia's my biggest concern. I want him up as soon as he's able. Keep him eating. Get him moving around. Sunshine. Time in the backyard. He knows what he needs."

"His granddaughter's coming at the end of the month."

"OK. That should work. Just don't let him overdo it. Remember, he's 98. Any pain or shortness of breath and I want to see him right away."

Mildred Blake gazed out her front door onto Phila Street. "Doctor, I had hoped he'd have a wonderful visit."

"He still can, Mildred. Keep his granddaughter up to date. But assure her there's no reason to rush up here. I'll check on him in the morning."

The doctor picked up his black bag. "By the way, you nailed it. He's one wild sleep talker."

"I told you. But until now I had no idea."

"It's nothing to be concerned about. More a curiosity than anything else. Some kind of motor breakdown on dream speech. Carries no known psychological or psychiatric significance."

Mildred opened the front door. "But some of the things he says. It's like he's having an actual conversation."

"You noticed that, too? I must admit I had a good laugh in there a while ago before I woke him. He was really going to town."

"What on earth about?"

"It was all a bit jumbled. Something about a west meadow and twelve people coming home, some buried bricks, and him finally getting a chance. He was definitely fired up. Not an argument, mind you, but he'd get out a phrase, then go silent for 20 seconds as if he were listening. Then come right back with a sharp rejoinder. Sure wish I could have heard the other side of that conversation."

"He's always been his own guy, doctor."

Myron Crawford laughed. "Let me know if he predicts any more races."

Y ou're looking chipper, sir."
"Nothing but an old bag of stiff bones here today." Charlie
eased himself into a seat at the kitchen table. "I feel like your old
grandfather's clock. Unwound and all run down."

"Oh, Charles, you're timeless. Now listen, Leah's got the day off,
so I'm making buttermilk pancakes. With maple syrup!"

"Millie! Your Yankeeness is really showing."

"Shush! Who else could I cook for?" She retied her apron. "Paper's
there if you're interested."

Charlie opened the daily only to have the Business and
Advertisement sections—which Mildred always ignored—parachute
across the tile floor. "Old klutz here. Sorry 'bout that, Millie."

"I'll get it. OJ?"

"A taste, thank you."

She poured him half a glass, then stooped and picked up the
paper, matching it back into sections. "Laura called. She and Ginny
will get in late tomorrow night. They're up for the races on Saturday."

"Really?"

"Yes. The Hopeful. Another of Saratoga's long running traditions."
Charlie logged her words. "Maybe there, then," he said, nodding.

"What?"

"Oh, nothing." He smoothed the front page, drawn to a below-
the-fold headline. "You see this? Our last combat troops in Nam are
headed home?"

"I've heard that a dozen times."

Charlie sipped juice.

"And you know we'll hear it again," continued Mildred. "Mark
my words."

"Poor Laura." Charlie followed the article to page six. "Maybe
this'll speed Harney coming home."

"She sees that headline, her hopes will soar. Like those Paris talks."

"Now...Millie."

"I give 'em a week, a month at the latest before this newest 'light
at the end of the tunnel' winks out. Your cakes, doctor."

"Thank you, my sweet."

Milldred passed him a stack of three buttermilk pancakes on her
best Blue Willow. "How long has he been missing? Here's syrup."

Charlie lifted each flapjack with his fork as he poured, letting a patty of butter cascade yellow across, then down the side of the stack.

"Three years. No news since February. Pentagon thought he was in that Hanoi Hilton."

"Then he is alive?"

Her words cast a sharp, unexpected hook, demanding he address a fear he thought he'd cornered months ago. Charlie carefully folded the paper and stared out Mildred's kitchen window into downtown Saratoga.

My roots run deep here. Mama, you spent the summers of your girlhood in Saratoga. And Papa, your passion for horses and racing brought you to this place. I never realized what being here meant to you 'til now. Yet you both decided to live in Virginia.

"So he...is alive?"

"Washington can't confirm a thing." He munched in silence, holding up an index finger as he swallowed. "But I have to believe he is."

The wrinkles in Doc Harrison's ancient face smiled hope. Whatever was back there in those shadows, whatever had stormed into his sleep all these years...well, whatever it had become—or been replaced by—challenged everything he remembered about his boyhood...even his entire life.

And in an oddly positive way.

Yes, it pried at his past, prodded his memory, and dared details of events long forgotten. The old nightmare had morphed into something very real...because it talked at him...challenged him...cared for him.

Yet thwarted destinies loomed. Might they be redeemed?

"I guess, Charles, believing is all we can do."

"True, Millie. But I'm nearing my last page."

"Stop that talk."

"You know it's so. But I'll tell you something... For the first time in a long time, I feel some real purpose. Here in Saratoga."

"What do you mean?"

"Mama and Papa were here when the war ended. For some reason, I don't know why, I feel like I've come home. Fate maybe. But when Papa was reported missing, Mama endured and believed he was alive. Somewhere. Yet he wasn't on any POW list and everybody thought him dead. Still Mama believed he was out there...and that he would come back."

"They loved each other, Charlie."

"It was more than that, Millie. Mama came here believing in a miracle."

"A miracle?"

"Yeah. Getting her husband back from the dead."

"Grandpa Luke never mentioned that."

"I guess we'll never know what really happened."

"True, but I know he always held Payne Harrison in great awe."

"As did my father for Luke Parker."

"But do you believe in miracles?"

Charlie glared. "Where was Nell's miracle? And Amanda's?"

"Oh...God, I didn't mean...please forgive me, cousin."

"I'm too old to believe in such things."

"But..."

"Millie, for half a century, I told my patients I believed in miracles. I had to. I was a doctor. My business was healing and hope."

"But do you...really believe?"

"We all die, Millie."

"That's no answer."

"But it's the truth."

"Yes, but there're things out there we can never know."

Charlie shut his eyes, wrestling to grasp something just out of sight. "Miracles," he said, curling soft the word from his lips.

"I believe in them, Charles."

"Good." Contentment cornered his eyes in crow's feet, his lips burnished in the smile of one looking into another time.

"And you?"

The hall grandfather's clock ticked away the silence.

"Sometimes. They are far rarer than most people realize."

"I would imagine..."

The old man opened his eyes. "Millie, it's one thing to believe. But getting others to join you is what makes them real."

SUMMER 1865, SARATOGA SPRINGS, NEW YORK

I 've got me confidence in ye, Payne Harrison. Ye'll have a stable of champions in three Christmases."

Payne shook his head. "The South's ravaged. I don't know what I'll find at Walnut Grove."

"Did I say it would be easy? Ye lost a great steed, that Number Twelve as ye called him. Great potential, I gather."

"Never had a horse run six furlongs in 1:11..."

"Aye, as ye said."

"Did it twice. And clocks don't lie."

"Then there'll be another great one. And ye know how I know? Because ye heart's in it, Payne Harrison. Every day."

"Another? Not in a hundred years, but I thank you all the same."

John Morrissey extended his boxing hand. "Aye, take it, good friend. I regret I'll never knock ye to the canvas with it."

Payne laughed. "Then I'll not make this a goodbye, John Morrissey."

"Ere ye do, that would be the day I take back me word and let ye sample a bit of this here." He shook his fist in feigned might. "But ye seemed bent on dear Virginia. I don't envy ye there."

"It's home."

"Aye, good friend. Home is where ye heart is."

"You know...there's no way I can ever repay you." He looked the ex-champion boxer in the eye. "Getting me out of Fort Delaware..."

"Bureaucratic bungling, I'm told, dear Payne. Scrambled records. Besides, Old Abe didn't miss ye."

Payne clasped Morrissey's hand. "You'll always have a welcome in the Old Dominion. You know that."

"Mind ye, keep an eye peeled for me left hook, good friend."

L ast time, we put the blanket under the old oak. There on the grass."

"I remember. And that's Luke's favorite fishing spot." Payne pointed toward the granite shelf jutting into the water.

Sunlight splashed the fall afternoon. A gentle breeze swept the lake, pushing little ebbs against the shore. A good day for a picnic. But on this Wednesday, few people were about.

"Still think you can swim it?"

"Swim it?"

"You were angling your best to impress me. Have you forgotten?"

"Did it work?" Payne wrapped his arm around his wife's waist.

"What do you think, soldier?"

"Maybe I'll find out today?"

"Confident fellow, are you?"

"When I have to be."

"Enough to swim across?"

Payne eyed the open expanse. "I swam the James once." He turned to Alex, bold in the aura of his Harrison ruddy cheek-glow.

"But it's nothing compared to this." He pecked her on the lips, paused, and returned in a delicate, longing kiss.

"Course, if you wanted, I'd make it a round trip!" He eased back. But she tugged him closer, pulling him to the blanket.

"Warm me. I never want to lose you again," she whispered.

Fire...and that promise in her waiting eyes.

"So...so you're OK with going to Virginia?"

"I married you in war, Payne Harrison. I married you for better or worse. And I married you in Virginia.

"Alex..."

"I married you for your dreams, no matter where they take us."

Payne breathed in the air...and the freedom. "My folks don't know if I'm dead or alive. Morrissey created a paper trail, Alex. Fake documents, orders. Then destroyed it. Couldn't chance a message through the lines."

"But the war's over, mister."

He kissed her forehead, cradling her, savoring her softness. "And we're here in the tranquility and peace of this place."

"Shhhhh," Alex whispered, "Remember the legend? No brave's voice shall break the silence." She snuggled closer.

"Unless they're dying of hunger!"

"Oh, Payne Harrison. Honestly!"

"Did we not come here to eat?"

Alex stood and removed her bonnet, tossing her head and letting down her hair. "What would you feast on, sir?" Her eyes dared an answer.

"For starters, a few ham biscuits and one of those ginger beers." He swept her up and pitched her lightly, catching her breathless. "Then it'll be dessert time!" Laughing, he clutched her and rushed toward the lake.

"Payne! PAYNE! You wouldn't DARE!!"

He scooted to the water's edge, arms entwined and frantic, lips seeking hers, the mud-spattered girl under the bridge. The afternoon breeze settled and the lake stilled.

"Listen!" Alex cooed between kisses. "Hear it?"

"What?"

"The silence. The lake...it's ours." She studied the far shore. *It was here. And quiet like this. But darker...and misty.*

On the far shore, a teamster unhitched his horses and led them to the water's edge.

"That fellow," Alex pointed.

"Yeah, seems to be the only other soul out here today."

"Watch him."

"What?"

"He's taking a try. See?"

"At what?"

"Skipping stones."

"Fat chance he'll land one over here."

"Well, he's trying. At least he believes!"

"In what?"

"Remember? Skip a stone across and your dream will come true."

"Come on, Alex! Have you ever heard of anyone skipping a stone across?"

She turned toward the water, wordless. *He would never believe me.*

In silence, husband and wife watched the teamster throw stones, one after the other, while his horses drank. Not one approached a third the way.

"It's too far. Anybody can see that."

"Yeah...sure."

"Look, even if some fellow did manage a miracle, you'd have to believe in magic to think some wish would come true."

"Maybe it was destiny."

"Huh?"

"There's nothing wrong with magic or strength. But then there's also purpose. And fate. And belief."

Payne reached down and picked up a small, rounded stone.

"OK, watch." He slung the rock across the water, watching it bounce five times before sinking. "Guess practice makes perfect, my love. Here, I'll try again."

This time, he sped a flatter stone more than sixty yards, but it too died after a dozen skips.

"It's the trying, Payne."

"Or having a perfect stone, huh?"

Alex stared at her husband, pale filling her face. She slid her hand to the small leather pouch in her waist pocket. *This must stay with Luke. It means nothing anywhere else. Luke'll understand and keep it safe.*

"Guess you just have to believe."

"I did once, Alex. In Number Twelve. But that dream vanished at Spotsylvania."

"So did mine," she said, holding him close, "but I believed."

He looked into his wife's eyes, puzzling, then at the teamster, watching him fail yet again.

"I mean, Alex, you'd need a perfect stone." He leaned down and kissed her neck. "Perfect day for a picnic, though."

"Yes," she said, loving his touch, but savoring her fingers' caress of the leather-pocketed slice of granite from Angeline Tubbs.

All polished.

And perfect.

Grandie! Ginny and I would have been up here two weeks ago, but Millie said to stay home." Laura hugged her grandfather. "How are you? I'm so glad to be out of that car!"

"Fine, dear. But don't fret on me."

"Tell her, Charles. Dr. Crawford came by here three straight mornings on his way to the hospital."

"Well, you tell me, Millie?" Charlie opened his arms for Ginny. "Where's my kiss, sweetie? Did you guys win?"

"Barely. Swept the first three games then squeaked by in the final, 8-7." She *muaaahed* her great-grandfather on the left cheek.

"I'm sure Hank will want to know," said Mildred.

"Have you seen him?"

"Last weekend, girl. Wanted to know when you were headed up."

"He'll be at the track on Saturday, Ginny," added Grandie with a wink.

"Another race?"

"The 68th running of the Hopeful Stakes." Mildred smiled. "It'll be a fun afternoon. I told Hank to bring his catcher's mitt."

Ginny blushed.

"Don't be so hard on her, Millie. I'm going to show Ginny how to bet."

"Grandie, don't tell me you've gotten corrupted while we've been away?"

"He's behaved admirably, Laura. Even got all three finishers right on the money the first time he tried it."

"How much did you win, Grandie?"

"He wouldn't let me place any bets for him, Ginny."

"I told Millie she'd jinx me." Charlie thumped the table.

"That's rubbish, Charles, and you know it."

"Think so? I'll get Ginny to do my wagering for me."

"Forget it, Grandie. You know she's only 17."

"Fair enough, Laura. But somebody better place my money at the window."

"You sound rather sure, Charles."

"Let's just say I'm a believer now."

"A believer, Grandie?" asked Laura. "In what?"

Charlie just smiled.

Chapter Thirty-Nine

Andnd to round out our tour of the downtown, that monument on our left honors Ellen Hardin Walworth."

Mildred Blake reveled in pointing out Saratoga's many scenic and historic sites, expecting perfection should she pop a quiz.

"Walworth...?"

"One of the four founders of the DAR, Laura. Prominent family. But can you believe it? Her son shot and killed her husband down in New York City. Let me see. Back in 1873, I think."

"Before my day," said Charlie, hands clasped behind his back.

Mildred arched her eyebrows in her best what-will-the-old-codger-say-next scowl. "Anyway boys and girls, welcome to Congress Park. That Grecian temple over there covers Congress Spring, a prominent Saratoga watering hole since 1792."

"People up here sure make a big deal about drinking water."

"Not as much as they used to, Ginny," Mildred laughed. "But I'll tell you something. I think we should take Grandie back to High Rock Spring after our picnic here in the park."

"Whatever for, Millie?" Charlie shuffled along behind, head bobbing.

"So he can tell Ginny about Alexander Bryan."

"Who?"

"You know. Saratoga's own hero. Bryan's bravery helped us beat the British in 1777."

"If you say so." Charlie scratched a line across the gravel path with his cane and winked at Ginny. "Old Bryan must have first fortified himself with a few snorts of that mineral water."

"Charles, you're hopeless."

"What's so special about High Rock Spring?"

"Laura, that's where Saratoga's youth elixir flows out of the ground. The Mohawks believed this to be the Medicine Spring of the Great Spirit."

"That's weird."

"Local lore, Ginny."

"Yeah. Well, I read old Bryan skipped a stone across the lake before the Battle of Saratoga."

"Ginny, a lot of people believe that really happened."

"Well, let me start a legend, Millie."

"OK, Charles, what might that be?" Impatience toned her words.

"I'll sip that Mohawk youth juice if you guarantee I'll hit a hundred."

"Cousin, you've imbibed Saratoga water for years."

"Right you are, Millie. Straight from the spigot in your house."

Even Millie laughed at this. She eyed her watch.

"OK, we eat when Laura and I get back from the art and antique show up on Broadway. In the meantime Charles, find us another great picnic spot."

Mildred faced the park's landscaped grounds. Pea gravel paths crisscrossed acres of manicured green, weaving a trail by historic springs and reflecting pools. Ornate benches under shade trees overlooked well-tended flower gardens, sculptured fountains, and signs everywhere pleading "Please Do Not Feed the Ducks."

"You ladies go do your thing."

"Now, Charles. I've been planning this for a month."

"Don't mind us, Millie. Ginny and I won't run far."

The nonagenarian and his 17-year-old great-granddaughter watched the two women disappear into the mix of art patrons, racing aficionados, and summer tourists clogging Broadway's sidewalks.

"Gee, Grandie, this is like a giant landscape garden with fountains and temples and everything."

"Been like this as long as I've been coming here."

"Have you had a good visit?"

Two joggers sped past, feet crunching gravel in a matched cadence. Charlie watched them without a word then turned his attention to two boys tossing a Frisbee.

"Millie said you had a little spell. You had us worried."

"Don't fret on me."

"But when she called..."

"You know how my cousin overcooks things." Charlie waved his hand as if flicking a fly, eyes following the Frisbee.

"Grandie. Mom really needs you. With Daddy still missing, she's...she's barely holding it together...she cries herself to sleep at night. She doesn't know...that I know...but I can hear her. Why if something happened to you..."

"You know Ginny, those boys are pretty good with that thing."

"Grandie! Mom and I are very concerned about you."

"See how they snatch it from the air. That taller fellow actually lets it spin on his forefinger!"

"Don't you even...?"

"Virginia." Her given name came in a deliberate whisper, trailing into four syllables. "Things'll be fine. You need to believe that, sweetie."

"Grandie, what...what does that have to do with anything? Millie told Mom that...that you were talking in your sleep."

"And who...who do you believe, my dear?" His eyes met hers, tired but intent, soft but certain.

"I know Grandie, but..."

"It was just a bad dream. The rest of me is...well...a little weathered by age. But everything, my dear...is all taken care of."

Ginny's eyes began to fill. *You're just trying to reassure me, but...*

"You know, Mama really loved it here. Did I ever tell you what she told me about Saratoga?"

Ginny shook her head.

"Remember how you helped me find her?"

"Yeah...yeah. That old glass photograph up in the attic."

"I really ought to see what else is up there."

He put his arm around his great-granddaughter but it was like squeezing bronze.

"Ah, well, Mama fell in love with Papa here. In Congress Park."

"How do you know that?"

"She told me when I was about six. Said it was a lazy summer afternoon, like this one. She was watching the clouds go by, daydreaming...admiring the ducks along the creek, when she dozed off and began dreaming of Papa kissing her. It became so real that she awoke to find him actually doing it!" Charlie chuckled in the retelling. "Papa said he knew she was smitten all along."

"Smitten?"

"Yeah. Googie eyes. Dreamland stuff."

"Huh?"

"My dear. Smitten: 'to fall head over heels in love with.' Mama denied it, of course."

"I learn a new word almost every day with you, Grandie." Ginny snatched off her sunglasses. "And what did your dad think of her?"

"Mama always said Papa was more interested in race horses."

"I've heard you say that. But was he?"

"I think he was the smitten one. Adored her. Still loved his horses though. He had this one..."

"You never shared your father's passion for horses."

"Guess I don't have many horse memories growing up. Mostly just Papa's stories from before the war. Look at those fellows toss that Frisbee?"

"I see 'em, Grandie. But what about your father and his horses?"

"He came up here a few times before I was born so Mama could visit her brother Luke, Millie's grandfather, but he never got back into racing. Money was too tight. I mean after the war..."

"What did he do?"

"Farmed. Wheat, corn, tobacco. Some hogs and cattle. We got by."

"Horses?"

"Tell you the truth, they scared me. But your mom's mom, my little Amanda, was crazy about 'em. Rode every chance she got. Always going to shows and local races. We even came up here special one time to see a stakes race. Same one Millie and I saw a few weeks ago." Charlie took off his hat and wiped his brow. "Sweetie, I guess this horse business skips generations."

A couple with a baby carriage strolled past, mother and father glancing smiles and nods to Ginny and Charlie.

"Did I ever tell you Mama used to sing me lullabies when I got scared?"

"You? Scared?"

"Oh yeah! Used to have this dream...well, never mind that." He stopped and scratched another line in the gravel. "Have a seat under this maple?"

"Sure."

"You know, Mama would come into my room, sit on my bed, and sing to me. When she sensed I needed soothing."

"She was your mother."

"Look out!" The Frisbee spun into the gravel at Ginny's feet. "Sorry 'bout that," yelled the taller of the two boys.

Ginny rifled the Frisbee back with a snap of her wrist.

"Wow, Harry! She throws better than you," shouted the shorter boy.

Ginny smiled and waved.

"You just turned some heads."

"Shush, Grandie."

"I just love this place." Charlie grinned across the green. "Sometimes, I can still hear the sound of Mama's voice."

"You're the original romantic, Grandie."

"We call it bedside manner in the doctor business. See, Mama had this...intensity about her."

"You said she was a very talented singer."

"No, I meant other things."

"Well, you said intensity."

"Yeah. Well, remember that nonsense Millie was talking about? That fellow skipping a stone across the lake during the Revolution?"

"What about it?"

Charlie lowered his voice. "Listen, I've never told anyone, but..."

"What, Grandie?"

The old man looked left, then right.

"What? Grandie?"

"Promise me you'll keep this to yourself!"

"OK, already. I promise. What?"

"Mama told me she did it."

"Did what?"

"Got a stone across!"

"She skipped a stone across the lake? That's nuts."

"Said she made a wish and did it. Just like the legend, so she told me. And Papa got out of that prisoner of war fort."

"Everybody can see the lake's too wide. You believe it?"

"Naaa!" Charlie laughed. "But it makes a great story."

"I wonder if Millie or Hank ever heard of anyone doing that?"

"Mama never told Papa. Only me."

Sounds like his old self. Memory's back. Funny. "Want to walk a bit?"

"Sure, sweetie. Great day for a stroll."

They ambled down the gravel path toward the Spit and Spat Fountain, enjoying the lush beauty of Congress Park for several quiet minutes.

"What you said back there? I'm with you. Nobody could get a stone across the lake, but I do have something you can bet on."

"What now, Grandie?" Ginny shook her head with smile.

"I know who's going to win the Hopeful tomorrow."

"Get real! You and thousands of other bettors!" *And here I thought he was back to normal!*

The old man stopped. "This is the real deal. A certainty, Ginny."

"How can you be so sure, Grandie."

"Wait 'til tomorrow," he said, stabbing the grass with his cane.

B ut Charlie Harrison had little to say through the first five races at Saratoga Race Track the next afternoon. And Mildred noticed.

"You're rather quiet today, Charles. Last time here, I could hardly rein you in!"

"Just taking in the world. The Hopeful's after this?"

"Seventh race, cousin."

"Well, in that case, how about something to drink, everyone?" Laura pointed at her grandfather. "Another lucky lemonade?"

Charlie nodded. "That worked last time."

"Ginny, would you and Hank run up and get five lemonades for us?" Laura opened her purse.

"Now listen." Mildred handed Hank a ten dollar bill. "This is on me. I'm the one feeling lucky today."

"I hope you bet on the right one, Millie."

"I'll bet mine, cousin. You bet yours."

The Hopeful Stakes was a Saratoga classic. At 6 and 1/2 furlongs and boasting a purse of more than $75,000, it was the first Grade 1 stakes race of the season for two-year olds. Its very name summarized the aspirations of each owner and trainer who placed an entry in the race.

"Sorry you missed our picnic yesterday, Hank."

"Couldn't get away, Ginny. Boss didn't let us go 'til after five."

"Well, you did a great job." Ginny waved at the track.

"Awww. Anybody can cut grass."

"Sure, but you're the one who did it and it looks great."

"Whatever you say," Hank laughed and took another step forward in the refreshment line. "Hi, Mrs. Billups. Five lemonades, please."

"Well, Henry! Who's your friend?"

"Meet Ginny McGill. Up from Virginia. Ginny, Mrs. Billips. She lives over on Grand Avenue."

"Welcome to Saratoga, Ginny. Got a favorite in the Hopeful?"

"I don't really know much about racing, Mrs. Billips. But my Grandie said he knows who's going to win."

"And who does he like?"

"Golly, he hasn't told me yet."

"Go with Secretariat, girl. But hurry. That race is due off around five. Enjoy your lemonade. Sure is warm today."

"Well, Charles, going to bet?"

"Who do you like, Millie?"

"Trevose. He's got the rail. And he ran well in the Sanford."

"But didn't win."

"True, but I think Trevose has heart. Ah, here's Ginny and Hank. You two have any favorites?"

"Grandie said he had it all locked up, so I'm going with his choice."

"And you, Hank?"

"Well Mrs. Billups, the lady at the lemonade stand, likes Secretariat."

"Why is that, son?" Charlie leaned toward the youth.

"He won the Sanford, the betting odds are way in his favor—3 to 10, I think—and I read he's run the fastest six furlongs of the season."

"Hank, you either know your horses, or you spend too much time cutting grass down here." Mildred smiled.

"How about you, Grandie?" asked Ginny.

Charlie looked across the track. On the far side, nine two-year olds neared their respective gates. He raised his binoculars.

"Number Seven wins," he said softly.

"Seven?" Millie checked her racing form. "That's Secretariat. Like Hank said, he's the odds on favorite. You can't win much there."

"True, but he can't lose."

"Ohhh...the expert speaks!" Mildred brought up her binoculars while Laura and Ginny shared a peek through Hank's. "Certainly looks good. See those flanks. But he's no big secret, not after winning the Sanford."

"What were you going to tell me about him, Grandie?"

Charlie Harrison edged himself up, out of his chair. The last two horses approached the back of the starting gate.

"Seven was foaled in Virginia, Virginia."

"I can see the headline now: Virginia's Stallion Wins The Hopeful." Mildred cackled. "Come on, cousin. You can do better than that. If you're so certain, tell us how much he'll win by."

Jaw set, Charlie narrowed his gaze at the big red chestnut entering the starting gate. The grandstand buzzed in growing anticipation.

"Charlie? How much?"

The retired physician held up all five fingers of his left hand.

The bell for the 68th running of the Hopeful Stakes sounded at two minutes to five on the 26th day of August 1972. Answering the roar of the crowd, the gate burst open with Sunny South and Branford Court fighting for the early lead. Down the Saratoga backstretch, Stop the Music pressed the leaders, everyone else fighting for position, with Secretariat last.

"He's already in trouble, Charles." Mildred sounded glee in her voice.

But Charlie Harrison kept his eyes on the trailing horse.

And that's all it took.

The Virginia stallion suddenly accelerated, looping around the entire field in the long, sweeping turn and taking over the race. He emerged at the top of the stretch with a four length lead. The crowd of more than 20,000, already on their feet, jumped and whooped and yelled. Few had ever seen anything like this.

"Look at him go!" shouted Laura.

And Ginny screamed, "Grandie, he's going to win! He's going to win!" And spilled half her lemonade.

Charlie's pick finished just 3/5 of a second off the track record. And five lengths ahead of the next horse.

"Grandie, this horse is way too cool!" Ginny said, hugging her great-grandfather.

But Dr. Charles Harrison looked as though he'd seen a ghost.

Chapter Forty

S o you're still not sure?"
It's more than that.
"Then talk to me, Charlie."
It's...it's hard to explain, don't you see?
"Try me."
Try you? Didn't I just do that at Saratoga? But OK. Look at me. Here, with you, I can think clearly, reason with purpose, grasp what you say. It's like...I'm young again.
"And when you awake, the world spins when you sit up, your fingers ache when you pick up a spoon, and your knees wobble with every step. You forget what you had for breakfast, stagger around with a cane, and find simple subtraction impossible."
No secrets from you, I see.
"Charlie, I know you struggle with your every breath."
And I think you're just a dream.
"I am your friend."
And the horse?
"Patience, Charlie."
You keep telling me that.
"Then stoke a little faith on it, Charlie. Believe."
Faith you say? How can I believe in anything when my granddaughter doesn't know whether her husband's dead or in some hell hole on the other

side of the world? Every day I see the pain in Laura's eyes, the fear, the not knowing. And my God, what's to become of my Ginny?

"I'm here, Charlie."

You're here? Pray tell me the 'why' of all this.

"OH, Charlie. Why did you go into medicine?"

Oh, come on!

"Let me tell you. Curiosity. At least you started out that way."

You make it sound so simple.

"Think about it. Haven't you always wanted to explore what's around you? Trek into the Big Woods? Dig treasure out of the dirt? Imagine your own playmates?"

You know more about me than I do.

"Curiosity added to problem solving. That's what got you interested in medicine. You used your brain to battle pestilence. You curbed pain and nursed life. You battled disease and postponed death. You took innate curiosity and made a career of helping others. You gained confidence and believed in yourself. And at the end of the day, Charlie, you did what we all hope to do...you made a difference."

Postponed death?

"Everyone dies, eh, Charlie?"

Yeah, well...

"And don't forget the stars. Starting with the closest one. How many evenings have you watched it set beyond the Blue Ridge? And remember the first time you saw the ghostly glow of the Northern Lights, or mapped the path of Venus and Mars across the night sky, or stood in the snow, awed as white-hot iron streaked the sky two hours before dawn?"

OK, you make your point.

"Perhaps, but you know it is more than that. Why did you commune with Mizar and Alcor for half a century?"

How can you know this?

"Because you know there is no death, Charlie."

You tell me these things yet you stay in the shadows. You said you'd meet me at Saratoga and all I saw were the outcomes of a few horse races before they happened. Wrapped in a surreal sense of déjà vu, I might add.

"Charlie, do you have any idea how many people lust to do just that?"

OK, OK. Funny. Score one for you. But answer me the 'why' to all this.
"Ginny."
Ginny?
"Curiosity, remember?"
Yes, but...
"She hails from hearty stock, Doctor Harrison. She just needs to believe."
Look, she knows I love her.
"All the way to the stars in heaven, Charlie. That's why you have to show her."
Show her what?
"What's in the Meadow."
What?
"I will help you, Charlie, but our time grows short."

O h drat! Disqualified!"
"Who, Ginny? What are you talking about?"
"Grandie's horse, Mom. Remember the winner of the Hopeful?"
"At Saratoga. Secret something or other."
"Secretariat. Won the Futurity Stakes a few weeks later."
"Futurity Stakes?"
"I told you. The race at Belmont Park."
"In New York. All right, Ginny. All right. I know you find it all fascinating, but what gives with you and this racing stuff?"
"Mom, there's something about this horse. Hank sends me updates on him. Got the latest *Daily Racing Form* in the mail this afternoon."
Laura sagged against the kitchen counter. "Ginny, I just don't... oh, never mind. I told you twenty minutes ago to clear your books off the dining room table. And wake Grandie from his nap. I've got supper ready."
"I was taking a break, Mom. Heard the mail come and..."
"Enough. I need you in the kitchen. Not reading racing forms."

"But Secretariat beat Stop The Music again, the same horse he beat in the Futurity. Only this time he was disqualified. I can't believe it."

"Ginny, go wake Grandie."

"Already up, Laura." The old man's voice carried from the den. "Nothing like two females going at it in the kitchen to spike a hearty appetite."

"Listen to you. At least I hope you had a good nap."

"Peace and quiet, Laura. But what's this about our horse, Ginny?"

"He got disqualified at Belmont. The 101st running of the Champagne. Ran by the entire field, but bumped the runner-up."

"How many did he beat?"

"Eleven, Grandie."

"Ahhh, eleven. Plus one. Twelve." The old man mouthed the word. "When does he race again?"

"Hank says he'll be in the Laurel Futurity in two weeks. In Maryland."

"Maryland? Mama taught music there. Girls' finishing school in Baltimore. Right before the war."

"I see that look in your eye, Grandie. What are you saying?"

"I think we need a road trip, Laura. What do you think, Ginny?"

"YESSS!"

One of the dangling light bulbs below the attic rafters was out. Other than that, nothing had been disturbed. In the top lid of the Saratoga trunk, Ginny found everything precisely as Charlie had left it on that marvelous day of discovery a dozen years before. A jumble of loose papers, two ribbon-tied bundles of old letters, an inkwell, several bulging manila envelopes, and those hunks of broken white chalk.

Only Alexandra Parker Harrison's stunning daguerreotype had been removed, displayed in a protective case atop a small table beside Charlie's easy chair in the den. *Guess it's these papers Grandie wants.*

Ginny picked up the ribbon-tied bundles. *Don't forget the loose papers.*

She put everything into a large grocery bag, including the manila envelopes. *These, too.*

She closed the lid and walked over to the door leading to the rickety stairway, flipping the switch to the solitary shining 100 watt light bulb.

It's freezing up here.

G randie's conking out early these days, Mom."
"I know."

"Well, I got the old papers out of his father's traveling trunk like he wanted. But it's a real mess around that chimney up there."

"Good. At least now he won't try it. There's no way he'd get up those narrow steps anymore. I don't even like going up there."

"Well, I'll leave this bag in the den beside his easy chair."

"That's fine."

Ginny turned to go, but paused. "What is it, Mom?"

She warmed her daughter with her softest smile. "Oh, Ginny. I see you, I see your father. Always have. You have his hair, his nose, his freckles."

"Mom...Mom...."

"It's just that...honey, your father asked me to marry him nineteen years ago tonight!"

Mother and daughter embraced, sharing life and tears in the parlor of Macon's Ordinary.

"But...but..."

"What Mom?"

"Sweetie, I heard from the Pentagon today. Haven't told Grandie yet, but they think...Washington believes your father's alive. ALIVE, GINNY!"

"WHERE? HOW do they know? WHAT did they tell you?"

"Two independent sources think they spotted your dad in a prison in the mountains north of Hanoi. Some place called Mountain Camp."

"DO YOU BELIEVE THEM?"

"I want to, Ginny. Kissinger says the Paris peace talks are progressing. I read what he had to say. 'We believe that peace is at hand. We believe that an agreement is in sight.'"

"But Mom, we've heard that before."

"I know, but we have to believe. Especially now. Oh honey, I can almost feel your father out there."

"You'll tell Grandie in the morning?"

"Yes. Don't want to wake him. He gets so exhausted these days. Sleeps half the afternoon you know."

"And this prison's called Mountain Camp?"

"Name like that would give your father an edge, I'd think."

Laura threaded her fingers through her daughter's red hair. "So a horse race on Saturday?"

"We need to go, Mom."

"Need to?"

"It's important to Grandie."

"I know it's all you've talked about for two weeks, young lady."

"Well, yeah, I want to go, too."

"Why, Ginny? I just don't get this racing thing."

"Like I told you Mom, there's something about this horse."

What is this fascination with you and racing, child? My own mother—your grandmother—was this way. Bewitched by horses. Grandie's father, too. Every other generation. My mother had her Man O'War. Now you're spellbound by this new horse. Why?

Ginny kissed her mother on the forehead. *Perhaps I'll find out in Maryland.*

Y ou're up early, Grandie." Laura stepped into the den.
"Must be my afternoon naps."

"Well, let me get breakfast going. Warm enough?"

"Fire's fine. Put on a few logs when I got up."

"Fine?" Laura eyed the dying embers. "It's practically out. How long have you been up?"

"Not sure. Found these old papers, and well, I started reading."

"Ginny dug 'em out of that trunk in the attic last evening like you asked. But you were already asleep."

"Girl's the apple of my eye, Laura."

"Best daughter I have, too, sir." She put on another log and stoked the fire with the poker. "I just don't get her sudden take with horses." Charlie coughed.

"And this new one...the one we're going to see this weekend in that Maryland race. What's cooking, Grandie?"

"You mean Secretariat." Charlie hawked up more phlegm. "Well...your mother was enthralled with Man O'War. Guess girls go batty over horses."

"I'm thinking boys, Grandie."

"Are we talking Hank now?" His words carried a certain sparkle.

"You tell me. Look, he's a fine young man, but Ginny's only seventeen."

"I'll keep my eyes open. Now what was that about breakfast?"

"Let me get Ginny off to school. I have a nine o'clock today. Should be home by three. We'll get on the road right after that."

Laura looked at the unbundled documents on the table. "Find anything?"

"Mostly receipts, an old day book, ledgers from Walnut Grove."

"No love letters?"

"A lot of things were lost in the Christmas fire, you know. What's here is mostly about the farm, Papa's stable, expenses, a few breeding contracts. Still got another bundle to go through."

"Why bring 'em out now?"

Charlie gazed at the flames waltzing the new log in the fireplace. "Curiosity, I guess."

B y 9:30 that Friday morning, the doctor had the house to himself. He put another log on the fire and slipped into his easy chair.
One last bundle. More old receipts, probably.
Charlie untied the faded blue ribbon.
Yep. More tobacco sales. Grazing rentals. Nothing here.
But a single word scribbled on the outside of a small envelope near the bottom of the pack caught his attention.

Save.

Inside lay a folded letter, ink fading. Charlie removed it and began to read.

April 15, 1865

Madam:

It is my pleasure to return to you property of your son. I admired Number Twelve the first time I saw him and cheered for him during the "Orange Races." I subsequently feared he had been lost when your son was reported missing in action at Spotsylvania last spring.

In the events of the last few days, however, I recognized Number Twelve as the mount of a federal officer who had found him in the custody of the U. S. Quartermaster's Department after Spotsylvania. Through a bit of barter, I am pleased to repatriate Number Twelve back to his Virginia home.

Please accept this noble veteran with my compliments. I wish you and your family the blessings of Providence in these difficult times. And I shall continue to pray for the safe return of your son.

Your most obt. servant,
R. E. Lee

Mrs. Jane Harrison
Midlothian, Virginia

Goodness! Papa did get him back. And from Lee, himself. But why don't I remember? Surely, Papa would have told me about this.
But Number Twelve. That rings a bell.

L aura met her daughter at the front door. "How was it today?"
"We had a nasty pop quiz in math, but I think I did OK."
"Good."
"I can be ready to go in a flash!"
"Well Ginny, that's just it."
"What, Mom?"
"Grandie's upstairs in bed. Not feeling very well."
"You mean...?"
"'Fraid so. This came on sometime after I left this morning. Our weekend plans are out the window."
"Darn. I was really counting on seeing Secretariat run again."
"I know. Grandie, too."
"What's wrong with him, Mom?"
"Fever, headache, nausea. Definitely too sick to travel. If he's not better by morning, I'm calling Dr. Winfree."
"Does he know about Daddy?"
"I didn't have time this morning. He was so into reading those old papers, you know. Now this..."
"Tell him. Maybe he'll perk up."
"That can wait. We'll alternate keeping an eye on him tonight."
"Oh, Mom!"
"Ginny, don't 'Oh, Mom' me!"
"I was really looking forward to this trip!"
"Well, if it's any consolation, they're calling for rain up and down the eastern seaboard, starting tonight. That track's going to be a mess tomorrow."

L ocated mid-way between Washington and Baltimore, Laurel Race Course was indeed a mess the next day. By the time of the featured seventh race, the track was a morass of mud and slop. Yet the Laurel Futurity carried a purse of more than $133,000 and at a mile and one sixteenth, this speed run would highlight only the most promising two-year olds. Just six horses entered the starting gate. But bettors would enjoy no big pay day with race favorite Secretariat going off at 1-10.

344

At the bell, Rocket Pocket lived up to his name by sprinting to the early lead, increasing it on the back stretch. Whatabreeze and Angle Light trailed while Stop The Music seemed unhurried. The Lark Twist, in fifth, would never be a factor. And running unconcerned on the outside, Secretariat again brought up the rear.

But this time the crowd knew what to expect. And at the top of the turn for home, Secretariat throttled around the rest of the field, wide to the outside curve, going from fifth to first in just two furlongs. The move still stunned everyone, and down the home stretch, he led Stop The Music by eight lengths despite rain and a muddy track. With no bumping, no disqualification. And crossed in an astounding time just one fifth second off the track record.

The news didn't reach Macon's Ordinary until the next day when Laura bought a Sunday copy of the *Richmond Times-Dispatch*. Ginny read every word. Charlie had spent all of Saturday in bed, but when Laura returned with the paper the next morning after church, he was up and about in his slippers and housecoat, feeling much better, thank you. After lunch, when they sat down in the den and she told him about the optimistic news from the Pentagon, a decided blush of color—the old Harrison cheek-glow perhaps—warmed his countenance.

Good, promising news, he declared. All around.

Then Laura left her grandfather to his wood fire...to the broad view of the Virginia countryside from his den window where the retired doctor reflected on other things.

Like that letter in his father's papers.

And the horse he had long forgotten.

On Ginny's sudden love of equines. And in particular, this stunning thoroughbred, Secretariat.

And on dreams recent...and long ago.

Chapter Forty-One

L aura! Laura! Let me help you."
"Oh, Betty Paxton. Grandie and I were just wondering how long we had 'til the polls closed. Can you help me with him?"

"Don't worry. They're open 'til seven."

Charlie swung open the car door. "Yeah, but my dear, you don't know how hard it is for us old people to get moving on these cold days."

"Nice and easy then, Dr. Harrison. Laura and I'll make sure you get to that ballot box."

"Haven't missed an election since William Howard Taft. Couldn't leave a lady in labor that day as I recall."

"Well, Grandie, let's get you inside so you can ink your X. Betty Paxton, can you grab his left arm as he stands? I've got your cane, Grandie."

With great care, the two women helped Charlie walk some 60 feet to the entrance of Stony Point Elementary School. Signs touting RE-ELECT THE PRESIDENT and McGOVERN '72 staked the grass along the school's sidewalk. "Dr. Harrison," said a man at the first table in the gymnasium, checking names. "Good to see you out today."

"Thanks, Howard. Civic duty, you know."

"Who do you like, doc?" asked a woman behind Betty Paxton.

"Oh, I'm sure I'll find a good man on the ballot somewhere, Amy."

Country doctors often doubled as polished diplomats. Yet in this election it didn't matter whom Charlie Harrison voted for. Richard Nixon won a second term handily, carrying the Old Dominion by more than half a million votes and securing every electoral vote in the Union save those of Massachusetts and the District of Columbia. National Security Advisor Henry Kissinger's "peace is at hand" statement two weeks earlier had carried the day. America wanted out of Vietnam, a graceful exit for sure, but out nevertheless. Nixon promised the nation "peace with honor." Dr. Kissinger's words brought hope. But nagging questions pursued the president and his Committee To Re-elect the President...persistent inquiries about a bungled burglary of Democratic National Committee headquarters in an office-hotel-apartment complex down in Washington's Foggy Bottom.

Nixon moved quickly to cement his war intentions, warning that the United States would "take swift and severe retaliatory action" if North Vietnam violated the proposed peace treaty.

Two days later, Secretariat raced for the last time as a two-year-old, winning the Garden State Stakes. Once again last out of the gate, the chestnut stallion trailed half the race, then at the top of the stretch burst past the rest of the field and won by three and a half lengths. Thanksgiving at Macon's Ordinary garnered no such excitement. But Charlie always had dinner guests over for the holiday. So Laura invited Betty Paxton Barnes and her husband as well as Dr. Winfree and his wife to join them for Thanksgiving dinner. Ginny got out of school early on Wednesday and helped her mother prepare the turkey and trimmings, complemented with sweet potatoes, cranberry sauce, succotash, corn bread, and of course, cherry pie.

But Charlie didn't have a slice. "Too much turkey, my dear."

Laura knew better. He'd hardly touched the white meat, much less the cranberry sauce and his sweet potatoes. As for pie, he'd "get a piece later."

No one said much. All knew. Bent and hammered by age, Charlie could hardly get around with his cane. Hard of hearing, short of breath, and possessing little stamina to climb the stairs, he seemed to have "gone back" since summer. Yes, all knew, but only Dr. Winfree dared broach the subject in the den during the Dallas/San Francisco game that afternoon.

"Looks like a long day for the Cowboys."

"Cowboys? Oh, yeah."

"So how ya been, Charlie?"

"What?"

"I asked how have you been."

"You can see for yourself, Harv. Pretty much all used up, I guess."

"Any new aches or pains?"

"At my age everything aches. How would I know what's new?"

Dr. Winfree nodded with a grim smile. "Why don't you come in over Christmas and we'll check things out."

"I'm not going into any home, Harv."

"Did I say anything about that?"

"You know where I stand. Long as I can get out of bed, pick up a spoon, brush my teeth, and wipe my rear, I'm staying put."

Still got fire. And his thinking's clear. "You go guy."

"What? Oh yeah. Well...got my girls to take care of, too."

"I know. Just being pragmatic, Charlie. But come see me. That's all I'm asking. You know Laura and Ginny'll be in favor of that."

"You like to twist my words, don't you?"

"You know I'm on your side, pardner."

A roar blared from the TV as San Francisco scored another touchdown to take a commanding lead.

"Come see me, Charlie?"

"Sure, Harvey. If I'm not too busy. Couple of things to do."

November's optimism on the war ended on the second Monday in December when North Vietnam's Le Duc Tho abandoned the Paris Peace talks. An irate Nixon immediately began plans to hammer the North Vietnamese back to the table. Both sides braced.

Five days later, 129 B-52 Stratofortresses took off from Anderson Air Force Base in Guam. Besides search and rescue, support included F-4 fighter escorts, F-105 Wild Weasels to attack surface-to-air sites, and F-4 chaff planes, Navy EA-6s, and EB-66s to scramble enemy radar.

They attacked in three waves hitting storage depots, rail yards, and power plants with more than 90% of the bombs being released over target. The second day's bombers took off just as the last of the first day's B-52s returned to base. American casualties tallied six B-52s to heavy SAM and antiaircraft fire on day three.

Dubbed Operation Linebacker II, the Christmas bombing as it came to be called, halted for 36 hours over the Yule holiday. The North Vietnamese seized full advantage to restock their SAM sites. When the Americans resumed bombing, these and the airfields became the new targets. Before it ended, more than 20,000 tons of bombs hit Hanoi and Haiphong, destroying bridges, factories, trains, weapons, airfields, and command infrastructure. By the eighth day, Hanoi had had enough and signaled a desire to return to the Paris Peace Talks.

But Nixon, determined to hold the enemy to their word, continued the bombing for two more days. With virtually free rein over the skies, American pilots confronted but one dilemma: a lack of targets.

G randie? Asleep?"
The old man stirred, letting the newspaper on his lap slide to the floor of the den.

"Got a minute?"

"Oh. Ginny." Charlie blinked, sitting up in his easy chair. "Sure. Just daydreaming a little."

"Sure nice and warm in here." She took a seat on the couch.

"Always been the tavern's coziest room," Charlie said. "You know, the original bar ran right across the floor there. Along that line at your feet. Same floor though. In the old days around Christmas time, I heard old Macon would bring out the grog at a penny a glass. Had every farmer and field hand in Keswick Station tipsy."

"Oh...Grandie..." Ginny blinked back tears.

"Now, now. Why's my girl crying?"

"Mom's..."

"Come tell me, sweetie. This old doctor's always in when his Ginny comes calling."

She cleared her throat. Took a deep breath. "Mom's...just not herself. She told Betty Paxton she wasn't going to the Christmas party. And Mom's been to every one since we moved down here."

"That Betty Paxton spikes some pretty wild punch as I recall."

"I know you just want to cheer me up, but Mom's more down than I've ever seen her."

"She masks it around me, I guess."

"That's because Mom's worried for you, too. About what might happen..."

"Didn't I tell you everything's going to be fine? Taken care of."

"You know what I mean, Grandie."

"I've led my full life, sweetie. Don't worry on me."

Ginny wiped her eyes. "It's all about this bombing and stuff. But now she's worse. Just has this look. You've seen her."

"I know, Ginny. Depression's an awful thing."

"Well, what can I do? What can we do?"

"Just love her, Ginny."

"But I do."

"I know. She needs all you can give her right now."

"Oh, Grandie...you say these things..."

"Love's the most powerful force in the world."

"I've heard you say that before."

"Yep. And when your mother was your age, I told her the same thing."

Unable to see her Grandie, she reached out with both arms.

"Now, now. Here's my hanky, sweetie."

I n her spare moments over the Christmas holiday, Ginny concentrated on completing her college applications. Superb SATs, solid high school grades, and several glowing recommendations would serve her well.

"Where did you say you were applying, Ginny?" asked Betty Paxton.

"Syracuse, Virginia Tech. Those are my first choices. I'll probably try JMU, where Mom went. And maybe VCU."

"Not the University?"

Ginny made a little face. "Charlottesville's too close."

"Well, my cousin's boy goes to Tech. Loves Blacksburg, but says the winters turn the place into *Bleaksburg*." Both laughed. "Dr. Winfree did his undergrad work at Syracuse, you know."

Betty Paxton glanced at her watch. "They should just about be done in there. Must be giving your Grandie the once over today."

"I'm just glad he's here. Still tries to diagnose himself, you know."

"Is your Mom coming by?"

"She...wasn't feeling too well. Cold and all."

"Tell her...Oh, here he is now."

Dr. Winfree walked Charlie into the waiting room with a hand on his arm and helped him to a seat.

"Hi, Ginny. This old horse doctor's in pretty decent shape for someone nearing the century mark." He patted Charlie on the shoulder.

"And that's all you need to tell her, Harv. Enough said."

"Of course if he had his way, Charlie would tell me I've said enough."

"Smart man." Charlie rolled his eyes. "Did you go to med school?"

"Rumor says so, Dr. Harrison. As for you, Ginny, here are his updated prescriptions. Charlie and I've talked some more about a way to assist his walking. I've suggested a wheelchair to help him around. Hand rails around the house. Move his bedroom down to the first floor. That kind of thing. Here's a note for your mother. How's she doing by the way?"

"Mom lives for the news, Dr. Winfree. The bombing...really gets her. As far as Daddy, we've heard nothing since October. They think he's in some camp in the mountains."

"Well, if there's anything I can do..."

"This girl could use a glowing reference to Syracuse, Dr. Winfree." Betty Paxton winked at Ginny.

"Great! Go Orange! You want to apply?"

"I'm sending them an application."

"What are you interested in?"

"Well, the closest I can get to softball is physical education. I'm thinking sports medicine. But then I've thought about maybe being a vet."

"How about if I write you something by the end of the week?"

"Thank you, Dr. Winfree. That would be great."

"Just don't bill her for it, Harv," said Charlie.

"Wouldn't hear of it, my good man. I'll send that to you!"

G inny missed the headline. Busy with her college applications, she folded Wednesday's *Daily Progress* atop sections of two previous day's editions.

A day passed. Then two. With Laura in Charlottesville at the grocery store, Charlie settled down for some quiet reading time. Only then, in Friday's edition of the sports section did he spot the follow-up.

"Well, well! How did I miss this?"

He inched his way to the kitchen, set aside his cane, and started into the stack of newspapers atop the butcher block. When he opened the sports pages for December 27, the first page headline grabbed his imagination.

"Ginny, did you see this?" he called, knowing full well she had not.

"What, Grandie?" Ginny stopped folding towels.

"Here...in the paper."

"About the war?"

"No. About animals, sweetie."

"Huh? What are you talking about?"

"Look!" He held up the newspaper:
SECRETARIAT HORSE OF YEAR 1972

C harlie could still hear his great-granddaughter going on and on about Secretariat. *Sure gets fired up 'bout that horse.*

The next day, Saturday, the *Daily Racing Form* arrived in the mail, courtesy of Hank. The Hightstown, New Jersey, publication touted Secretariat's news in a banner headline. A nice photo of the winner accompanied the front page story.

Wish I'd gotten a closer look at you in Saratoga.

The retired physician turned to page four for the rest of the article.

Hope Ginny sees you run again. Know I won't. Motorola will have to do.

Charlie focused on the horse's image. *I'll keep you right here, fellow.*

He slid the *Daily Racing Form* into the table drawer beneath his mother's daguerreotype.

So what else this winter's day? New Year's Eve's tomorrow.

Another year passes.

Chapter Forty-Two

*H**arney! Harney! Oh, please God, tell me this is true!*
"Laura, my dear, it's happened!"
"Can you believe it, Grandie? The war's actually over?"
"Sure sounds like it. When did Nixon say the treaty gets signed?"
"In four days. January 27. Right in Paris."
"And our POWs?"
"Freed within 60 days! Grandie, our prayers are answered!"
"And I can sleep tonight. Sorry Ginny missed the President's address. Light's on the front stoop."
"Sue Tompkins said they only needed her to baby sit till eight. Guess they ran a bit over."
"Well, the sandman's calling me, Laura. I'm dragging."
Charlie kissed his granddaughter as the front door opened.
"GINNY? That you, dear?"
"Yeah, Mom. Mr. Tompkins just dropped me off."
"Did you hear? Did you hear the President tonight?"
"Nixon? No."
"The war's over! They're signing a peace treaty in Paris on Saturday."
"MOM! FOR REAL?"
"YES, SWEETIE, AND YOUR DADDY'S COMING HOME!"

353

The first of the freed arrived at Clark Air Base, Philippines, on 12 February aboard three C-141As and a C-9A, all painted white and marked with a distinctive red cross on the tail. Each arrival was telecast live via satellite, giving an anxious, waiting American viewing public a dramatic, real time window on history. Indeed, reporting at this scale garnered a global broadcasting first. As a news story, the images of daughters running to fathers they hadn't seen in five years and of overwrought wives wrapping their arms around husbands too long in harm's way, moved millions.

Operation Homecoming had begun.

The same scenario played out with each new plane that landed on the Clark tarmac; forty more men safely home to wives, children, families, and friends, free from the bars and beatings of the Hanoi Hilton, free from the shackles and shame of Dogpatch, free from the humiliation and hunger of Rockpile, free from the isolation and insults of Mountain Camp. Free from these enemy hellholes and a dozen more just like them.

Free!

Military intelligence had identified nearly 1,200 Americans alive and imprisoned by the North Vietnamese and Viet Cong. As the days passed, the tally of those repatriated to the United States inched upwards.

At Macon's Ordinary, Laura McGill lived by the phone, waiting for the good news, waiting for the summons to catch that flight across the Pacific, waiting for the call that would confirm her husband "on the next plane out."

But no call came.

Into mid-March the POWs continued to arrive at Clark. At Keswick, Laura listened for the phone to ring. On St. Patrick's Day she placed her own call.

From the Pentagon operator, she endured four transfers to three men and a woman, finally conversing with a male voice who sounded official, sterile, and very much like he was reading a script.

Lt. Col. Harney McGill's status remains unchanged. MIA. The dual sightings of the previous year are unproven rumors. His name is on no Hanoi-supplied list of individuals incarcerated in North Vietnamese prisoner of war camps. The enemy claims no knowledge of Air Force Lt. Col. McGill.

Laura staggered from the telephone, spending the rest of the day in bed, alternately numb, distraught, or angry, trying to grasp any thread of hope in a situation seemingly, suddenly beyond hope. Bewildered and fearing, Ginny went off to school those first spring mornings not knowing whether to worry more for her mother...or her father.

On the first day of April, the last POWs arrived in the Philippines. Only 591 Americans had come home: 325 airmen, 138 sailors, 77 soldiers, 26 marines, and 25 civilians.

Harney McGill remained among the missing.

Other than console his granddaughter, Charlie did the only thing that came to mind. He went into his backyard, beside Nell's and Amanda's stones, set up his tripod, and put his binoculars to the heavens. Feeble and suffering a head cold, he managed a fleeting glimpse of Mars, Venus, and the three dagger stars below Orion's Belt, trying his best to resolve the second "star," the Orion nebula. After twenty minutes of frustration and ignoring the evening chill that had dropped into the thirties, he turned his binoculars toward the Big Dipper. To Mizar and Alcor. It had been years since he'd separated the renowned double star with his own eyes, splitting the light as the Arabs of old had done to test their eyesight.

It was a lot easier when FDR was President. Not now.

What he sought...what he needed...was to speak his fears, his faith, and his heart. Out here, Nell would listen. Amanda would comfort. And Charlie Harrison would find the will to continue.

When he thought back on it later, perhaps it happened then. But perhaps not. He never would know exactly when the urge came.

That short term memory thing.

But it really didn't matter. Maybe out in the backyard, beside the stones, looking into Mizar and Alcor. Or when he watched Ginny come through the front door after school, eyes red, bravely trying to mask the grief that hit her when she stepped off the bus and started up the stone sidewalk.

Still, something was out there. Something. He was sure of that.

Because it didn't fade from his memory like the name of Keswick's new postman, what's-his-name from Gordonsville. Or what he'd had for breakfast that morning.

But what to do?

He pondered everything before the fire in the quiet of his den that evening. Something remained in all this. Tugging. Important. Something that was coming.

Charlie glanced at his mother's image on the table.

I've never forgotten the sound of your voice, Mama. You always sang my fears away.

Alex Parker Harrison smiled warmth and beauty and love.

How glad I am Ginny asked about you.

And that was when Charlie Harrison realized what he had to do.

*E*ight inches at a time. That's enough.

Charlie grasped the handrail and lifted his right foot, smacking it on the first step. He dragged his left foot up beside it.

One. That wasn't so bad.

He did it again.

Two.

Inhaling, he paused, sweating out six more deep breaths.

Nice and easy. Four more to the first landing, then six to the top.

Slowly, with purpose, the old doctor climbed up the stairs to the second floor of Macon's Ordinary. He stopped on each riser, clutching the handrail, gasping. At the top he dared a peek at his watch.

Four minutes.

Bowing his head, he closed his eyes to slow his spinning world.

Bet Roger Bannister didn't feel like this.

He plopped down on Nell's horsehair love seat beside the door to her old sewing room and put his forefinger to his wrist.

Already over a hundred.

Charlie stared past the tavern's six bedrooms to the door at the end of the hallway.

I don't know...

His chest ached for four minutes.

What the hell am I looking for anyway? Am I crazy?

Again, he fingered his wrist.

Eighty, I reckon. But still thready.

He stood up and faced the hall.

Haven't been up there in a dozen years.

He slid his right hand against the wall, shuffling his feet toward the distant door.

Two minutes.

He bent over at the threshold, the world swirling again.

What do I hope to find? Even Laura doesn't go up here anymore.

Hand on the doorknob, he pulled, and forced his eyes up the dark attic stairway. The narrow, one handrail, single-boarded, steep ascent stared back.

No damn way.

But he meant to find one.

Guess I can sit and go up backwards.

So he started. One butt-riser at a time.

Got to use my legs. And arms.

Second step. Then the third.

Pump's pounding again. Easy, fellow. You got all day.

Facing out from the steps he sat, Charlie grabbed the handrail with his left hand, pressed down with his feet and began to stand, but only enough to seat his rump on the next step.

"Crap," he gasped. "Must...be...out of shape."

Fourth step. Fifth.

No wonder Aunt Sadie never came up here.

Sixth step.

Cardio's back over a hundred. Try to breathe.

On the seventh step, he slumped for two minutes, beading sweat.

Leg's...going to cramp...if I'm not careful.

Eighth step.

How did...I ever get...that trunk...up here?

Ninth step.

Well...then I was 30.

Charlie glanced over his shoulder, the stairs swirling like a pinwheel.

Three more to go.

He pressed down and backslid up another eight inches.

Once...I get up here...how am I...going to get DOWN?

Dripping sweat like candle wax, he tried to breathe, but spots danced before his eyes.

Least...it's all...down hill!
Eleven.
But...I...can do this.
One last time, he pushed, feeling his back inch toward the landing.
Having...a baby...can't...be...this...bad.
Twelve.
Now what?
Charlie sagged against the attic door only to have it swing open into the gloomy cold, mothbally air.
Going to be sore...for a month. If I live...that...long.
He strained for the light switch.
Only one bulb burning?
He tried to stand, but floundered like a beached bass.
"Still winded." He gulped, and again pressed his finger to his wrist. *Can't count. Too fast.*
He scooted toward the old chimney, a few inches at a time, grinding the seat of his pants across the rough pine and hand-forged nails, wiping up dust and crushing the dead flies that littered the attic floor.
Glad Ginny...didn't cover it back up.
Charlie sat on a box of old *National Geographics* and raised the top of his father's Saratoga trunk.
She said everything...lay in the top tray. Yet...there's nothing here but an inkwell...and this chalk.
He lifted the tray.
Gloves and a riding crop. But...no more papers.
He groped beneath. *Horse blankets? Why would Papa save these?*
Charlie pushed aside the top blanket, exposing a small wooden box. He picked it up and unfastened a small catch.
More pictures. Post war stuff.
The images returned him to familiar scenes.
Ah. Walnut Grove. Taken up near the Turnpike. There's Papa's carriage. Wonder who that is inside? Must be a picnic or something. Bunch of folks.
Charlie craned his head under the single working bulb.
And a horse. Can't see who's on him.

Better box these up. Look later. If I can get my bones downstairs.

I f there was any good news coming to Macon's Ordinary, it arrived from the two schools Ginny wanted to attend. In the third week of April, both Syracuse and Virginia Tech sent their congratulations of acceptance.

But where to go? At least she had until June to decide.

The new mailman for whom Charlie always managed a wave despite forgetting the fellow's name, delivered another envelope addressed to Ginny the same day the Syracuse acceptance arrived.

It was from Hank, enclosing several recent copies of the *Daily Racing Form*. After a quiet winter, Secretariat had won his first two races as a three-year old, both contests run at Aqueduct Race Track in Queens, New York.

"But check out the Gotham," Hank wrote. "The race he won on April 7. He tied the course record for a mile!"

Hank spilled his exuberance for the big red stallion all across the page. He'd now seen the horse run—and win!—three times at Saratoga.

Of course, Hank Forsythe had seen lots of horses win at Saratoga. Yet only one had captivated the imagination of a cute, red-headed, fast-pitch softballer from Virginia. His correspondence with Ginny blossomed and Charlie cherished the glow on his great-granddaughter's face whenever mail arrived postmarked Saratoga Springs, NY.

Then came Operation Homecoming.

Was Harney really not coming back? Laura had never known her mother. Was she to lose her husband, too? And must Ginny go into young womanhood without a father? Just as her mother had?

H ow's our horse doing, Ginny?"
      "Don't know."
"You don't know? Didn't Hank write this week?"
"Yeah."
"Well?"
"He lost, Grandie."

"Lost?"

"Last Saturday at Aqueduct. The Wood Memorial."

"Big race?"

"It's the lead up to the Kentucky Derby."

"Goodness...what happened?"

"Something wasn't right. He was a different horse. No drive. Ended up third. He just didn't have it."

"I knew we should have gone to Maryland last fall."

"Grandie, you were too sick."

"Then you and your mother should have gone. If I'd known how much this meant to you. Sweetie, I was up walking two days later."

"He's just a horse, Grandie."

Her words hit like a thunderbolt.

Child, how can you say this?

"Grandie, this was his longest race yet. He faltered."

"And?"

"Some say he's got bad knees. That he's moody, doesn't have enough stamina for the longer distances. And that he hasn't had any real competition."

"Ginny, I know you love this horse. How many has he won?"

"Ten straight. Now this."

"And you know all about him. What do you think?"

"Some say he's too good looking to be this fast."

"And that's bad?"

Ginny forced a grin. "I don't know, Grandie. Ever since Daddy..."

She met her great-grandfather's waiting look. Slowly, she reached out and touched his hand, her eyes seeking, questioning.

"What do YOU think?" she asked.

Charlie didn't blink. "I can't wait for the Derby."

*Y**ou here?*

"Charlie! We are good?"

Yeah! In here, you're close. Just around the corner. But I'll tell you, this Kentucky thing? That's got me curious.

"Ahh. Curiosity."

Of course, you know none of this makes much sense.

"But you believe it will? And soon?"
Well, you keep telling me that.
"And Laura?"
Life's hard. In disbelief. Numb. Reflective. Angry. Trying to pick up the pieces. But eaten up by a world of doubt.
"You are great comfort to her, Charlie."
I'm a burden. Just another worry.
"You are wrong, Charlie. But tell me...about Ginny."
She's got too much heaped on her plate, too.
"Get her to join you, then."
Join me?
"Sure. Get *her* curious."
I tried.
"I know. And you are close. So keep at it."
Whatever good it does.
"Curiosity is a good thing if you believe, Charlie."
Believe? In what?
"Me. I know you do."
Yeah. Well...
"So, Charlie, just take the girl's hand."

Chapter Forty-Three

*B*elieve? *OK. I'm turning on the TV, aren't I?*
Charlie stretched back in his easy chair.
Doesn't even start 'til 5:30.

But WTVR-Channel 6, the CBS affiliate out of Richmond, already had Jack Whitaker, Haywood Hale Broun, and Frank Wright on the air, interviewing owners, trainers, and fans, getting the inside scoop from retired jockeys, breeders, gamblers, and hype artists. Comparisons with past champions, especially Triple Crown winners, fueled the excitement for this 99th running of the Kentucky Derby. CBS Sports cameras explored every corner of Churchill Downs, capturing thoroughbreds in the stables, fashion-conscious celebrities in private boxes, and a landscape of "ladies in hats." The infield seemed a sea of lounge chairs, beer, blankets, blondes and brunettes, with hundreds, in fine Derby tradition, sipping mint juleps from souvenir glasses. The good times always rolled beneath Churchill Downs' twin spires on Derby Day.

"Got it on?" Ginny danced into the den during a commercial and plopped down on the sofa.

"The usual hoopla, sweetie. Still twenty minutes to post."

When coverage returned, TV cameras captured the 13 Derby hopefuls parading past the clamoring crowd. Once in the paddock behind the green-trimmed, white-painted grandstand, each jockey, smartened in distinctive stable racing silks, saddled up on the bugler's traditional call to post.

"Heard from Hank?"

"Yes! Sent me the latest on Secretariat. After that mess in New York, a lot of people doubt he'll win this."

"You?"

The moving strains of *My Old Kentucky Home* played from the television as each horse and rider emerged from the paddock tunnel.

"Get your Mom. She'll love this."

"I asked her, Grandie. She said she'd rather read."

Her mother wouldn't have missed this for the world.

Over the galloping expectations of the crowd, announcer Chic Anderson introduced each horse and jockey, each trainer, owner and stable they represented.

"Well, Ginny, what do you think?"

The number one horse, Restless Jet, approached the starting gate.

"It's one huge party, Grandie. I mean...all the people. And the fancy clothes. You'd think somebody was throwing a fashion show."

"And a bunch of horses showed up?"

"Yeah. I mean...all those flowers!"

Starters guided Sham, horse number four, into his gate.

"Still haven't answered my question, sweetie."

"Secretariat?"

Charlie nodded.

The number six horse, Twice A Prince, reared and fell backwards, dumping his jockey. Attendants scrambled to help.

"I think...if it's meant to be..."

The loading resumed. Our Native filled gate seven.

"...it's meant to be."

Destined?

"See, Grandie, if he's that good, he can't lose."

"My dear, if you put it like that..."

Secretariat entered gate ten, speed horse Shecky Greene took eleven.

"What I'm saying is if he's really that good, how can he not win?"

Charlie fixed on the TV screen. Last horse Gold Bag entered his gate.

She believes!

At seven minutes past the five-thirty start, thirteen thorough-breds burst from the gate to "run for the roses."

I wish Papa could have seen this...

G randie, he's..."

"Patience, sweetie."

Thundering past the stands for the first time, Shecky Greene took the early lead with Sham, Gold Bag, and a half dozen other horses bunched close behind. Secretariat trailed dead last.

"Grandie!"

"Patience."

As if on cue, the red chestnut moved along the inside and passed two horses going into the Clubhouse Turn.

"Faster, Red!"

"It's a mile and a quarter, girl."

Shecky Greene widened his lead on Gold Bag, with Sham third and challenging. The field swept around the long curve as the stands roared, cheering their champions. But this race was about more than bets and bourbon and bragging rights. This was The Derby. The Run of the fastest and the strongest. An interweaving blur of horses and riders, animal carrying man. People came to this track on Derby Day to see more than high-priced blood horses flashing silks and racing numbers. This was the time and place where equine speed and beauty ruled. And the fastest and strongest prevailed.

But Derby fans came for more than that. Here reigned tradition. History. And elegance. And out on that track, on this one day of the year, if they were lucky—fated some might say—they might glimpse *magic.*

"He's rolling to the outside, Grandie!"

Secretariat edged right and accelerated. Around Navajo, then by the well-regarded Forego, he surged past My Gallant, Restless Jet, and Angle Light. Yet five more horses pounded ahead.

"Look at that Shecky Greene! He's pulling away."

"We're not half done, Ginny."

Down the long back stretch, these five bunched toward the front, Sham narrowing on the leader.

Cheering in the stands turned to screams as Sham and Shecky Green went into the far turn still battling for the lead, Royal And Regal pounding a half-length behind. But these screams were not for the leaders, for nearly all eyes were on the big red horse now, out of nowhere and running fifth, almost vaunting in his rush to pass Gold Bag.

Ginny jumped from the sofa. "Look Grandie, look! He's flying!" But Charlie could only stare at the screen. *Who are you!*

At the top of the stretch, Secretariat swept into third, running wide but free...and in the clear.

MY GOD! WHO ARE YOU?

Coming out of the turn for home, Secretariat exploded from the center of the racetrack, driving hard, neck and neck with Sham.

"Come on Big Red, come on!"

And joining Ginny, a hundred and thirty thousand other fans, every soul standing, waved and stomped and cheered and cursed as the two thoroughbreds thundered toward the wire, widening their lead over the rest of the field to nearly ten lengths.

Then the chestnut found one last gear.

"Never in all my born days!" shouted Charlie, as Secretariat stormed across the finish two and a half lengths ahead. "Oh, Ginny! He did it!"

And indeed Secretariat had, not only breaking the track record, but running the first sub-two minute Derby in history. Yet more impressive than this, pointed out one official, in fact unheard of in a race of this distance, said another, this "three sox chestnut" had run each quarter of the race faster than the one before!

Magic!

But who said three sox? "Did you hear that fellow, Ginny?"

"About him running faster and faster? Yes! It's fantastic!"

"Yeah, but what did that guy call him? Three sox?"

"Oh that's Secretariat's three white feet. Plus the white star on his forehead. It's his trademark."

Three...white...feet... Charlie reached to his left but felt a quick pain in his elbow. *Three sox?*

"Sweetie, can you pull out the drawer there and get me the magazine with Secretariat's picture on the cover?"

"Sure, Grandie. Here you go."

The old man studied the front cover, then fixed on the rose-blanketed horse on TV. Then back to the picture.

What...is...this?

"He sure knows he's the Champ, Grandie. Look at him!"

Charlie grappled to get himself out of the easy chair. Stiff, he limped over to his walnut roll top desk. *Why didn't I look at these when I brought'em down yesterday?*

"Need help, Grandie?"

He dug into the second drawer. Inside lay the small wooden box from his father's trunk in the attic.

Near the top, I think.

Charlie stepped to the window. Into the bright May sunshine. He fumbled up the small catch and lifted the lid. One at a time, he examined the photos. Walnut Grove, the image of his father's carriage, the picnic crowd.

Then the fourth picture.

A fine albumen print of a horse. With a jockey aboard.

Who...are...you?

Charlie tilted the image, taking advantage of the sunlight.

"Oh, God!" he said in a whisper.

"What, Grandie?"

At least sixteen hands, too. And from the toning, surely a chestnut.

"Grandie?"

With a star on the forehead and THREE...WHITE...FEET!

"Grandie, something wrong?"

It's you! IT's YOU!

"What is it, Grandie?"

Tears blurred his world as the old man looked up. "Sorry, Ginny. Just a picture," he said, "just a picture of an old friend."

Chapter Forty-Four

G randie, you heard Dr. Winfree!" Laura shoved open the front door of Macon's Ordinary.

"Sorry dear, but it's the same ole mush...every time I go in there."

"I don't want to argue, Grandie."

"Nor I, Laura, but..."

"Then stop!"

"Fine. But this other thing...it's a...big deal." He halted, blocking the threshold. "For you...Ginny...all of us."

"A horse race? Come on!"

Charlie grabbed the door knob to steady himself, hacking a cough, then fumbled a step inside.

"Sorry." He shook his head, grunting to clear his throat. "Look Laura...if...if you'd...just listen..."

"Grandie. Think! All the way to Baltimore for a silly horse race?" She bore down on her grandfather, jerking shut the door behind her. "I mean, how could you, given what's happened?"

He stared at the floor. "This isn't about...a silly horse race."

"Then what is it?" Laura stalked past.

Eyes closed, Charlie wiped his forehead. "Remember Manassas?"

"That was a dozen years ago. What about it?"

"I wasn't keen on going. Wanted to see Grissom go up. See history made."

"But you decided the re-enactment was more important."

"I was thinking about Ginny."

He's not budging on this.

"Look...last fall...when...I got a little under the weather...and we didn't go to Maryland?"

"Yeah?"

"No problem...with...a silly horse race then."

"That was different, Grandie. And you know it!"

"But Ginny...needs to see...this horse...run again."

"And why is that, sir? Harney's in some hell hole and you..."

I need to sit down. Charlie clutched the edge of the parlor table. "Laura, I...I know...you think..."

"That's just it! You don't know what I think! How can you go to a horse track when Harney's..."

"This isn't...about racing...dear granddaughter."

"Then what is it about? I've seen the glow on Ginny's face when she goes on about that horse."

"It's not...what you think."

"Then, what is it? Listen, Grandie. We need some normalcy around here."

Normalcy? Charlie tried to focus on the floor. *I used to know what that was. Sprains, cuts, and colds. Every day. With an occasional kidney stone or broken arm thrown in.*

"You can forget Baltimore."

But now? Everything's...a big blur. Can't get my breath. Dizzy after five steps. Pain in my hips and ankles...and places I forgot I had.

"OK, Grandie, work your old silent treatment but the Preakness is out."

Why am I so...so drained? When I dream...it's not...

"What's so special about this horse, anyway?"

Tell her, Charlie.

"What did you say?"

"This horse. What's so special about him, Grandie?"

Go ahead, Charlie. Tell her.

The old man jerked his head toward the front door, then looked up the staircase, searching, eyes wide and darting, mouth agape, lips twisting.

"Grandie? You OK?"

"HOW DID...YOU...GET IN HERE?" he shouted.

"I came with you, Grandie." Laura leaned down and cupped her hands to Charlie's face. "I'm right here, Grandie. What's wrong?"

"Went there...to see history..."

"That's right." Laura hugged her grandfather. "Talk to me, Grandie."

"But now...you tell me no..."

"Tell you what, Grandie?" Argument forgotten, Laura smoothed her fingers across her grandfather's scalp, warm, solicitous, scared. "It's Laura. I'm right here. Tell me what's wrong."

"Ginny...needs to go. Ginny needs...to go!"

"Go where, Grandie?"

"To see him. She needs to believe."

"To believe? Believe what?"

"Twelve."

"What? Twelve what?"

"History, Laura. History."

"What about history, Grandie? History made? You're confusing me."

Charlie shook his head and slumped to one side, breathing in short, rapid jerks. "Not made...not made" He gasped midst guttural sounds. "Changed."

Drool spilled from the left corner of his mouth.

Laura struggled to keep her balance, sliding beneath her grandfather so he wouldn't smack his face on the floor. "Who, Grandie? Who?" she pleaded, frantic, crying, cradling Charlie's head in her lap.

But the old physician just stared at the ceiling, face fixed, bubbles foaming from his lips.

C an't we see him, Dr. Winfree?"

"Busy night, Laura. Bad wreck down on 29."

"But...but he needs us..."

Harvey Winfree looked at his watch, then down the hall.

"We're all he has..."

The physician took a deep breath. "I'll go in there with you."

Laura nodded her thanks through tears. Seconds later, she and Ginny stood at her grandfather's bedside in the Cardiac Intensive Care Unit of Charlottesville's Martha Jefferson Hospital.

"He's sleeping right now, Dr. Winfree," said nurse Hannah Wilson. "BP's one sixty over ninety-six."

"Need it lower, Hannah. I'll let you know if we up his meds."

"Yes, doctor."

Laura could hardly look at her grandfather. "He just collapsed, right as we got home from your office. I didn't know what to do."

"You did the right thing getting him back here. Looks like a stroke, Laura. Speech impairment and his left side shows paralysis. That's about all we know right now. Tomorrow should give us a clearer picture."

Laura smoothed her grandfather's arm, listening to the steady beep of the heart monitor and the quiet rasps of his breathing.

"He was really upset. Then this. I..."

"That's not unusual. Stroke is often heralded by sharp, sudden pain. Confusion. Even agitation."

"But we were arguing and..."

"Laura...you didn't cause this."

"But if you only saw how angry he was. He insisted..."

"He's 99 years old, Laura." Harvey Winfree patted Charlie on the knee and smiled. "And stubborn as a mule."

Ginny stood silent, doe-eyed at the sight of her Grandie lying in the ICU's gadget-clamped, stainless steel railed bed.

"Doing OK, sweetie?"

"What were you two arguing about, Mom?"

"Not now, Ginny."

"It was about the race, wasn't it? You didn't want to go."

"Not here, please."

Ginny looked at the bed. "He wants me to see Big Red race again."

Charlie stirred.

"Hey, old boy." Dr. Winfree stepped to the bedside. "Harvey here. Now just try to relax."

But the patient shook his head and raised his right hand.

"Grandie, please listen to Dr. Winfree," said Laura.

Charlie would have none of it. He tried to sit up, but slumped back. "Ginny?" he gasped through the oxygen mask.

"Easy, pardner," said the doctor.

But again the patient called the girl's name.

Harvey Winfree nodded. "Soothe him," he whispered.

Ginny looked on her great-grandfather, small, drawn, and hurting, an ancient man three generations removed from her future. He had always been in her life. Now, beside his hospital bed, she feared the coming goodbye.

"Ginny...Ginny." He whispered her name clearly, but with effort.

"Right here, Grandie." She beamed him her bravest smile.

"Laura?"

"Mom's here, too."

He sighed and eased back into the pillows, but kept his eyes on the girl. "You need...need..."

"Yes, Grandie?"

"Twelve."

Ginny leaned closer. "I need twelve what?"

"You must," he whispered.

"Must what, Grandie?"

"This...noble steed."

"This noble steed?"

"Papa's..."

"I don't...I don't understand."

Charlie reached for her hand, frustrated, fumbling to form the words. "Promise...me," he said finally, exhausted.

Tears welling, Ginny nodded slowly, wrestling to read meaning in the old man's tired eyes. "Dr. Winfree says...everything's going to be OK."

Charlie brightened. "Oh child...believe...it will."

*H*aven't felt this good in years!
    "I'm glad for you, Charlie. For both of us, actually."
Why's that?
"Cause now, we can have some real fun!"
Really? What's cooking?

"Well, I know you've been following things..."

Trying, but with all the distractions...and now these complications, I'm just more comfortable here.

"Not to worry, old friend. Those things are soon in the past."

In the past?

"Ginny will handle it. Charlie, you know you can count on that girl."

Sure is special.

"The apple of your eye, huh, Charlie?"

If only you knew.

"But I do, Charlie."

You do? You knew me when I was her age. How can...

"I am more than you know."

But Ginny...

"Shush, Charlie. Ginny'll be there when the hour comes."

When the hour comes...?

"Time does draws near, old friend. Besides, we have another course before us."

Another course?

"Yes, but not as long. Still, the stakes grow higher."

And you want...

"I want you to stay close, Charlie."

Close?

Yeah. Watch, feel, learn. Get prepared.

Get prepared?

"Will you stop worrying, Charlie? This is going to be fun."

J ust got off the phone with Betty Paxton, Ginny." Laura stuck her head into the den. "Grandie took a bad turn last night."

"Oh, no! He really wants to see this race."

Laura hugged her daughter. "Dr. Winfree says he'll get a TV in his room when he gets out of the ICU. They just don't know when."

"Then I want to see him, Mom. I want to be in his room right after the race so I can tell him."

"Have you forgotten you're babysitting for the Cochrans tonight? You know this is their anniversary. Tina needs you there by four."

"But the race..."

"Watch it over there. And tell Grandie all about it tomorrow when we go in to visit."

"But Mom, when he saw Secretariat win the Derby, he was our old Grandie again!"

"Ginny, he's had a major stroke. It's worse than Dr. Winfree initially thought. He can hardly speak. Probably paralyzed on one side. I'm not even sure he understands us."

"He wants to see this race, Mom."

"I know. I know. Second leg of this Triple Crown thing."

"Yes. But there's something else. I could hear it in his voice. Like he can see..."

"Ginny! I'm tired of saying this, but girl, you need to focus on what's really important."

Patrons came to Baltimore's Pimlico Race Course not for history, or tradition, or elegance. Blue collar fans mostly, they had little interest in fancy clothes and stylish "hat parades." Or ogling a showcase of celebrities from film, music, sports, or politics. They viewed the races behind a massive, glass-fronted grandstand that had little architectural acclaim and boasted no "twin spires." Most preferred Schlitz and Miller to Chardonnay and mint juleps. Pimlico was where ordinary people came to place a bet and see the ponies run.

Except on Preakness Day.

For the second leg of the storied Triple Crown, all of racing flooded Baltimore on the third Saturday in May. The shortest of thoroughbred racing's three top contests at just a mile and three sixteenths, the Preakness favored the speed horses.

The 98th running featured but six entries. Talk on the street had Secretariat the overwhelming favorite. Many said he couldn't lose and they bet accordingly. Only Sham figured in the handicappers' musings. Trailing Secretariat by just two and one half lengths, Sham had run the Derby faster than any champion in history, save one.

The 1973 Preakness promised to be a match race. And on May 19, a mob of humanity flocked to see it. Nearly 63,000 strong, a record for Pimlico, race fans thronged the stands and swamped the infield, their energies building to a fevered pitch when the band played *Maryland, My Maryland* as the six horses paraded to post.

This time the start was flawless. Ecole Etage, in the sixth gate, took the early lead followed by Torsion and Deadly Dream. Sham, close to the rail, and Our Native followed. Secretariat trailed them all.

Many expected Big Red to make his move on the backstretch, but into the first turn he blew past Our Native and Deadly Dream, breaking to the outside with a stunning burst of speed. Ahead, Sham eased into third, waiting for the lead horse to tire. But Secretariat had his own agenda and surged past the entire field on the curve, thundering down the backstretch. Ecole Etage faded as Sham moved into second, trying to keep up. Into the far turn, the Kentucky Derby's top two finishers began their match race, going into the top of the stretch widening their lead on the rest of the field.

But Sham couldn't catch him and Secretariat won the second jewel of racing's Triple Crown, again by two and one half lengths. This time the great horse received a blanket of black-eyed Susans and had his racing colors painted on the weathervane of the Old Clubhouse cupola. Who said Pimlico had no history, no traditions?

Ginny and Laura visited Charlie the next afternoon.

"He's been sleeping most of the day," said Hannah Wilson, at the nurses' station. "But when I told him you all were here, he perked right up. Tried to talk, too. Even wanted a TV."

"Is he in any pain?" Laura asked.

"No, just weak. Confused a bit. Been mumbling stuff since he found out you were here. If you listen close..."

"Always a talker, our Grandie."

Nurse Wilson touched Laura on the arm. "Mrs. McGill, some days your grandfather's a real handful, but let me tell you, he's always a true gent."

Laura forced a tight smile.

"He's right over there." The nurse pointed to the bed near the window. "Should be awake."

Charlie saw them both and raised his right hand.

"Gin-ny! Laur..."

"How you doing, Grandie?" Laura bent over her grandfather's forehead. "I'm leaving lipstick."

Charlie nodded, his eyes sparkling.

Ginny leaned over his bed, beaming. "Guess what, Grandie!"

The patient struggled to raise himself but fell back, beckoning Ginny closer. "Just one...to go.

"You know?"

"It...was...won...der...ful..." He stared into her, weak but alive, taking her hand. "And again...by two...and a half."

Chapter Forty-Five

C harlie, I told you it was going to be fun."
Yeah, but not like this!
"Ahh! So you had a good time?"
Fabulous! I just didn't realize...
"No more confusion?"
Look, that was a long time ago.
"Not really, old friend."
Sure seems it. But tell me...
"Tell you what, Charlie? You know more about this than anybody."
That's not what I mean.
"What then?"
Why...I want to know why.
"Well, the troubles are back, Charlie."
Troubles?
"War."
A war consumed my parents. Changed their entire lives. Yet even with Mama from the North and Papa from the South, they still fell in love.
"And had you, Charlie."
And had me.
"They lived the life given them."
Yeah.
"But now it's back, Charlie."
And you're...?

"Wars wreck dreams, Charlie."

Dreams?

"Yes. Think of the lives lost, the destinies denied, the children who can never be."

I know it's tragic, but what's in the past... Look, you can't go back and change...

"War's indelible stain?"

Well, yeah. But...but what's your point?

"Do what you told Laura."

Huh?

"That part about changing history, Charlie."

Uhh...you mean...the day I realized...

"The day you began to see."

You...you're talking in circles. No one can go back and change the past.

"So...how about staying in the present...and changing the future?"

H annah, I'm putting Dr. Harrison on heparin. He's having a rough time swallowing those tablets, so no more Coumadin."

"Yes, sir."

"Just Heparin, parenterally from now on. Remember, subcutaneous, not intramuscular."

"Oh, Dr. Winfree, Betty Paxton called. Sounded urgent."

"I know what that's about. By the way, get me Dr. Harrison's prothrombin time before you go home. Lab should have it by three."

Harvey Winfree darted to the small office behind the nurses' station, closed the door, and picked up the phone. *Never liked this part of the job.*

Betty Paxton answered on the second ring.

"Checking in, Betty."

"Laura McGill's called three times about her grandfather."

"Yeah, I saw her last night. She's worn to a frazzle."

"Laura's frightened. Doesn't have anyone. Just her and Ginny."

"I know. Guess I need to prepare her."

"She needs a glimmer of hope, doctor."

Harvey Winfree sighed.

"Want me to speak to her?"

"No, Betty. I know you two go way back, but she needs to hear this from me. Charlie would have my hide if I pawned this off on you."

"Is...is there no hope?"

"He's 99 years old, Betty. Suffered an ischemic stroke to the right temporal lobe. Classic left hemiplegia. On top of chronic heart failure."

"What...are you going to tell her?

"The truth. That time's short. That her grandfather's not going to get any better. But that we'll make him as comfortable as possible."

SUPERHORSE! The word was everywhere!

With his string of impressive stakes race wins and record breaking victories in the Kentucky Derby and the Preakness, Secretariat stood on the threshold of winning the Triple Crown. No horse since 1948's Citation had swept America's three premier thoroughbred races.

No Triple Crown winner in a quarter century!

The hype on this horse had started early with one enthusiastic supporter declaring in print after the Sanford Stakes that Secretariat "swoops down on his field like a monster in a horror movie."

And from there with each win, Big Red amassed more and more fans. Not only was he fast, supporters styled him "gorgeous," "heroic," and "astonishing," admiring his white-starred forehead and distinctive three white stockings, his left front foot the chestnut exception.

But there was more to America's love affair with this horse.

In the aftermath of a divisive, inconclusive war, with more than 58,000 Americans dead in Southeast Asia; with the Supreme Court's controversial *Roe vs. Wade* decision on abortion splitting the nation along every religious, political, and economic calling; and with that troubling, daily headline of Watergate cracking from the shadows into the very foundations of democratic government, it seemed the country needed, wanted, indeed, demanded a hero.

Now, many believed they had found one!

In this "living locomotive," they could cheer for something good, honest, and pure. A competitor beyond the pale of ego, scandal, money, and war, Secretariat was "something special," they said.

Newsweek, Time, and *Sports Illustrated* agreed, each putting SUPERHORSE on the cover of their last issue going into the Belmont Stakes. This horse not only transcended sports, he captured the hearts and imaginations of a people hurting, but a people fervently wanting to believe.

In Goodness.

Honesty.

And Purity.

So they came to the Belmont, to this last race of the Triple Crown, hoping to see a real winner. They had no guarantees. But they believed.

And none more than a svelte, freckled, red-headed high school senior from Virginia, worried about an aged, dying country doctor and grieving for a father deemed lost on the other side of the world.

WALNUT GROVE
CHESTERFIELD COUNTY, VIRGINIA
JUNE 1886

"Charlie? Charlie? Where's that grandson of mine?"

"Coming Miss Jane. His mama's still getting him all dandied up."

Jane Harrison spied another carriage pulling up in the front yard of Walnut Grove. "Land's sake! Auntie, please go back upstairs and tell Alex the guests are starting to arrive."

"Yes, Ma'am. She's still trying to get that boy looking fine and proper for his birthday picture."

"Photographs! Oh gosh, yes. Nearly forgot. Tell her Payne's already out there with Mr. Cook."

"Yes, Ma'am." Aunt Hattie started up the steps as little Charlie Harrison's grandmother paused at the hall mirror.

Left my brush up in the bedroom. "Auntie, would you start the welcomes? I'll get Alex moving."

By noon, more than a dozen carriages crowded Walnut Grove's side yard. Charlie was everywhere, racing with young cousins and neighborhood playmates around the old log cookhouse, then scampering through the blackberry patch to play hide and seek along his secret trail, daring anyone to find him in his lair. When Sammy Goode did, Charlie fled across the East Meadow to the Water Cress Spring, yelling "Charge," followed by a troop of boys thrashing barefoot into the knee-deep marsh, snapping off cattails, eager young swordsmen all, swashbucklers in delight.

Children laughing and living life.

And to a photographer, these wannabe warriors presented a wonderful mess of mud, scratches, and soppy clothes.

Aunt Hattie watched Payne pick up the birthday boy and take him inside. *Another cheek-glowed child, Praise the Lord! Just like his papa! Course, nothin' like good discipline, Lord, to keep a boy straight.*

Twenty minutes later, squeaky clean and sporting new pants and a fresh blue and white shirt, Charlie rejoined his birthday picnic. As friends and family unfolded chairs and spread blankets under the shade of the walnuts, Alex Harrison kept tight rein on her rambunctious son. Guests savored pork barbeque on Aunt Hattie's sourdough rolls, and cole slaw and potato salad, topped off with watermelon and fresh cherry pie, all washed down with sweet tea and lemonade.

"So what do you really want for your birthday, Charlie?" asked his best buddy Henry Brown.

"Papa knows!" Charlie pointed toward the rebuilt stable. "Papa, you promised me I could ride him when I was old enough. And today's the day!"

"Think so, young man?" Payne Harrison's stern demeanor melted into a smile. "And so you shall. I see you're wearing our blue and whites."

Charlie stilled, his words quivering to a whisper. "Right...now?"

"Right now. Jasper's already got Twelve saddled out in the West Meadow. Just remember, he's not as fast as he once was."

"OH, BOY!"

Midst watermelon juice and cherry pie grins, everyone ran to the fence.

"But he's still faster than a cannonball, Mr. Harrison!" yelled Henry. "Charlie! You lucky dog!"

"Just...just a wild story, Henry. Besides, today's picture day." Payne Harrison patted the wide-eyed boy on the head. "OK, everybody close up."

Huestis Cook leveled his tripod, adjusting the large, black box atop it. "I need everyone to line up between the fence gate and...that fourth post to my right."

"Here?" asked Jane Harrison.

"Yes, Ma'am. That's good. Right there. Now you three young fellows bunch up a bit in front...that's it, right beside Charlie, and you Ma'am, thank you, I need you more toward the center..."

Posing took a few minutes, but Richmond's pre-eminent photographer soon had every attendee to Charlie Harrison's birthday picnic properly placed and smiling...with the birthday boy, of course, front and center.

"Now! Everyone stand very still while I count to three," said Cook.

Charlie's mob of friends and family hushed and froze.

"OK. Here we go." The photographer opened the shutter and held up a finger. "One...two...three! Got it!"

"How about the other shot we talked about?"

"Of course, Mr. Harrison. Need a little time to prepare, though. Can't do open lens with animals. They'll move and blur the image."

"Fine." Payne Harrison waved to Jasper out in the West Meadow. "Bring him up to the fence."

As the jockey dismounted, he handed Charlie a pair of leather riding gloves and a black tasseled crop. "Ole Twelve 'spects you to have these."

Huestis Cook waved his hand. "All set, Mr. Harrison. Get your son up in the saddle, step back, and we'll do it."

Payne leaned down. "Now Charlie, after the photograph, you can run him. But remember, Twelve's old. And don't touch his scar."

Alex hugged her son. "Hold the reins. But not too tight, Charlie. And remember this horse is the greatest horse your Papa ever owned."

"The greatest I ever saw," Payne Harrison whispered. Then with both hands he grasped his son by the waist. "Ready?"

Y ou know the rest, Charlie."
The old photographs...the picnic gathering. I'm...
"...the rider aboard Number Twelve."
But what went wrong?
"The photographer used flash powder. Instead of a time exposure, everything exploded in brilliant white."
But...
"The flash, Charlie. The explosion. It all rushed back!"
The war...
"With all its panic and pain."
And he threw me...
"An accident, Charlie. Everyone crowded in. Tried to help."
I couldn't breathe.
"Got the wind knocked out of you. Slight concussion. Dr. Morrissett was there and gave you a sniff of smelling salts. That and a tug on your belt and, well, although bruised and scared, you were fine."
But I didn't ride...
"Or remember."
Yet this tormented me all my life. I never...
"I know, Charlie."
I always feared I would die...out in that West Meadow.
"But you didn't, Charlie."
And now?
"You no longer have to fear."
But...how can that be?
"Because you're finally going to get that ride."
The one Papa promised me... Why?
"War, Charlie. It robbed your father, your mother. Everybody. You see, war ruins and destroys so many good things. So many good people. Scars and stains all of creation."
Papa rarely spoke of it.
"Your father sought perfection. And when he finally found it, the war stole it."
Stole it...
"He never saw his best horse run, Charlie. I mean...really go!"
But...

"Today's the day. Don't you see? It's the perfect things that endure, Charlie. Thwarted by war? Postponed by pestilence? You know of these things. You battled them all your life. For others. And you know too, ultimately, somehow, the good and perfect—and those you love—are just over the next hill, waiting. Because you believe."

Why do you tell me this?

"Because destinies cannot to be denied, Charlie. Even now, they wait."

They?

"It's time to go home, Charlie."

Home?

"Yes. All your life you've marveled at the heavens and searched the stars. Why, Charlie? What were you looking for, my friend?"

I...I don't know.

"Yes you do, Charlie. And it's OK to say it. Because this day you shall find it, speeding forth on the edge and into the light."

In the stars?

"Into the light, good friend."

The light...

"What were you looking for, Charlie?"

You wouldn't understand.

"Something you had lost..."

No...

"Someone you'd lost... All these years, you've searched for them. In Mizar and Alcor. And they twinkled back. And you believed."

You don't understand. So many nights, alone, out there in the garden. I got so close. I could...feel 'em!

"Because you believed, Charlie."

In Mizar and Alcor. The rider and the horse.

"Yes, Charlie. In Mizar and Alcor. And now they are calling."

MARTHA JEFFERSON HOSPITAL
CHARLOTTESVILLE, VIRGINIA
9 JUNE 1973

*A*nd *the Belmont is the Run for the Carnations!*
"Ginny, I'm going back up to Grandie for a bit." Laura pointed toward the elevator. "We'll grab supper after the race, sweetie."

"OK, Mom. I'll watch it in here." Ginny turned up the TV's volume. On this gorgeous Saturday afternoon she had the hospital's 4th floor waiting room almost to herself.

And it's roses in Louisville and back-eyed Susans in Baltimore. And if it's My Old Kentucky Home at the Derby and Maryland, My Maryland for the Preakness...

Just five entries graced the 105th running of the Belmont Stakes. At a mile and a half, this third and final race of the Triple Crown loomed as the most daunting. Few three-year-olds had any experience at this distance, lacking not only the stamina, but also the drive to sustain a winning pace for so long. Although position loomed paramount, knowing when to challenge the leader often determined the winner.

Fans touted the Belmont Stakes the ultimate "Test of the Champion."

Sidewalks of New York! Oh, so that's it. Ginny watched the five horses parade to post.

"...and you will see...and Secretariat being led...his number is two but he goes into the number one post," blared the TV.

Secretariat's on the pole. GOOD! Now Big Red, I'm counting on you! Long shot Private Smiles entered the second gate.

My Gallant in the middle. Then Twice A Prince. Both in the Derby. Starters moved to the last horse.

Sham! You, again. Don't dare think you can spoil this!

The last gate closed. America watched and held its breath, wondering if it was really true that there's no such thing...as a sure thing?

Ginny clenched her fists, knuckles white, eyes on the screen.

Grandie says I must see you run for real one more time.

The bell sounded and the five thoroughbreds broke from the gate.

He says there hasn't been a horse like you in a hundred years! He says you're magic!

This time he wasn't last. Secretariat broke tight along the rail and quickly surged to the leaders. Down the long Belmont homestretch for the first time, he caught and quickly passed My Gallant and Twice A Prince as a very determined Sham stormed into the lead on the outside.

Ginny watched, fingers to her lips.

You're going out too fast, Big Red!

Into the first turn, Secretariat and Sham thundered ahead, the duo opening a lead of six lengths, then eight on the rest of the field as they straightened into the backstretch. Eighty thousand fans roared, cheered, yelled, and screamed, jumping from their seats, waving their hands, and hammering their fists heavenward at the sight of the only two horses to ever run sub-two minute Derbys, battling for the lead and all but drowning out Chic Anderson's call of the race.

But Ginny McGill, watching alone in a hospital waiting room three states to the south, hung on the sportscaster's every word.

> "It's almost a match race now. Secretariat's on the inside by a head. Sham is on the outside. They've opened ten lengths on My Gallant who is third by a head with Twice A Prince fourth...then it's another eight lengths back to Private Smiles who is trailing the field..."

"You can't keep it up, Big Red!" Ginny yelled at the screen. "You're going too fast! No horse can run like this!"

But both did, stride for stride, leaving the field even farther behind, while Anderson called the race of his life.

> "They continue down the backstretch. In fact Secretariat's now taking the lead. He's got it by about a length and a half. Still Sham. Ten lengths back My Gallant, Twice a Prince."

Ginny could only stare, hands to her cheeks. *You've beaten Sham twice. Don't let him burn you out on the backstretch. You can't win like this!* But the inside horse wearing the number 2 continued to accelerate.

"They're moving on the turn now. For the turn it's Secretariat. It looks like he's opening. The lead is increasing. Make that three, three and a half. He's moving into the turn. Secretariat holding onto a large lead. Sham is second and then it's a long way back to My Gallant and Twice A Prince."

Then Sham faltered...broken, the match race over, while Charlie Harrison's granddaughter watched wide-eyed and in awe...

"They're on the turn. Secretariat is blazing along! The first three-quarters of a mile in 1:09 and four fifths. Secretariat is widening now! He is moving like a TREMENDOUS machine!"

And still the great horse surged. Pounding into the top of the stretch, Secretariat spread his lead to fourteen lengths. Then sixteen. Tight to the rail, he accelerated with a purpose that seemed bound beyond winning any race. Indeed, never had anyone—in the stands or watching the broadcast—seen anything like this. Never.

"But Secretariat is all alone! He's out there almost a 16th of a mile away from the rest of the horses! Secretariat is in a position that seems impossible to catch."

Now with a lead exceeding twenty-five lengths, this speeding horse was racing for something else.
And heading into the turn for home.

Young lady! Quiet please!" The blue-bunned matron who ruled the weekend 4th floor visitor's desk filled the doorway, arms folded and glaring. "This must stop! Get hold of yourself!"

Ginny quit jumping on the sofa and tried to straighten her hair. "I'm sorry! I didn't mean to... "

"Don't you know this is a hospital! There are rules..."

"Yes, I'm sorry...I'm really sorry. I promise to be quiet!" she yelled, skipping toward the door, bouncing to get out of the room.

"Girl! Didn't you hear me?"

"OOoops! Sorry," Ginny said, spiraling her voice to a hush. "I promise I'll be quiet." And then before the dowager could even blink, Ginny squeezed the woman's shoulders, kissed her on the cheek, and fled for the elevator!

OH, GRANDIE! THIRTY-ONE LENGTHS! THIRTY-ONE LENGTHS!

She sprinted from the elevator the moment it opened on the 6th floor and burst into her great-grandfather's hospital room.

"Grandie! Grandie! He won! He won! He won! You should have seen him! The Triple Crown! And a new track record! He ran the perfect race!"

An attending and two orderlies quietly exited the room as Laura McGill, hugging her grandfather's shrouded form, looked up at her daughter, weeping.

"I can come back later," said the senior resident.

They laid him beside his Nell.

Dr. Charles Harrison, 99, of Keswick, long time resident and Albemarle County physician, after a short illness.

Mourners gathered in the Macon's Ordinary flower garden he'd tended for half a century. It took a special permit from the County Health Department to open a grave so close to a residence. But a fifty-year-old family cemetery already existed, testified Dr. Harvey Winfree. And besides, this was Doc Harrison, Keswick's hero in that devastating flu epidemic.

Folks came from all over central Virginia. But not as many as one might have expected. A man who lives nearly a century survives his contemporaries.

Still, the Albemarle County Sheriff's department had to send two deputies to handle the traffic. Betty Paxton Barnes estimated 300 mourners. Cousin Mildred Blake, who rarely missed a family funeral, tallied 292 names in the funeral home registry.

"Your grandfather meant the world to me, my dear," she said to Laura the next afternoon. Both women hugged, dabbing at tears.

"There was only one Grandie, Millie. You of all people knew that."

Mildred walked into Charlie's old office, spotting something new on the wall. "Finally got his med school diploma framed?"

Laura smiled softly. "After he got sick, I found it rolled up with some old astronomy charts. He asked me to dig it out for him. Told me right where to look. Said he should have had it framed years ago."

"But you know, Laura, that wasn't him."

"Yeah. He really was from another time. Started off making house calls in a horse and buggy."

"And lived to see a man on the moon." Mildred sat down at Charlie's old desk. She picked up a pen and doodled across a pad of his letterhead stationery.

Charles Harrison, MD
Family Practice
Macon's Ordinary
Keswick, Virginia 22947

"And now Ginny graduates two nights after he's buried. Thank you, Laura, for letting me stay over for her commencement."

"You're family, Millie." Laura fought the catch in her voice. "Besides I need someone to lean on. Some days...some days, Millie." She looked down at the floor. "It's just that...that the Pentagon doesn't tell me much."

"Dear, dear, dear... Listen. You need anything, you let me know. I'm just a phone call away."

"We'll manage, Millie. Grandie provided for Ginny's college."

388

"So she told me. She favored Syracuse when I talked with her last night. But maybe it's Virginia Tech?"

"Got in both places, but right now the Orange men rule. I think a certain young fellow up your way wants to play baseball there next year."

As the hall clock chimed five, the backyard kitchen door opened. "Finished watering the flowers? Need to be at school in an hour."

"I'm on it, Mom," Ginny replied from the kitchen.

"Charles would be so proud of her," said Mildred.

"Don't know how many times I heard Grandie call her 'the apple of his eye.' He'd do anything for her."

"That reminds me. I keep forgetting a little box of stuff I found that belonged to Charlie's mother. Anyway, Ginny's graduation card is upstairs."

"All done, Mom." Ginny took off her softball cap and sighed. "It's so peaceful out there."

"I know. Grandie always loved it."

"Calling for clear tonight. Great night to stargaze. He always wanted to show me the..."

"Congratulations, graduate!" Mildred waved an envelope from the top of the stairs.

"Awwwwww!"

Grinning wide, Mildred Blake sauntered down the steps and handed the graduate a sealed envelope. "Spend it however you like!"

Ginny opened the envelope and read the card, finding a crisp $100 bill.

"Wow, Millie," she said after a hug. "Thanks!"

The Saratoga Springs native waved her off. "Work hard and play hard, girl. That's what your Grandie would have said. And believe in your dreams."

Chapter Forty-Six

P eople continued to call. A week after Charlie Harrison's funeral, those who had been unable to pay their respects interrupted a trip into town or stopped by on their way home from work. Some called ahead, but many just showed up, pulling into the old tavern parking lot as if the good doctor was still able to see them on a moment's notice, be it for a sore throat or a missed period.

Laura greeted them all, welcoming each visitor into her grandfather's old waiting room. She offered tea and coffee, listened and smiled to stories and jokes, and opened the gate to the backyard, dispensing thanks and embracing hugs when folks headed for their car.

The façade wasn't hard to maintain. People came, visited a few minutes, said good things about Doc Harrison, and left. "Please come see us," they added, as they got behind the wheel.

But when Laura retreated inside, she withdrew into her own grief, closing the door on a community moving on to other things. With the loss of her grandfather and the unknown fate that had befallen her husband, her life ebbed along as a sad series of endless, worrisome bothers. As always in grieving, it was the little things that stretched and frayed the fabric of getting on with life. Little things like a speeding ticket on Route 250. Forgetting a dentist's appointment. Or dropping—and breaking—one of her grandmother's dinner plates.

What's the purpose of it all, anyway?
Then there was the matter of sending her only child off to college. Ginny opted for Syracuse...with a double major in biology and education. She could always change, but for now, this, plus her summer job at Shadwell Veterinary Clinic seemed an ideal fit.

And on Monday, Wednesday, and Friday nights, she terrorized the Albemarle County girls' fast-pitch softball league with her humming curve and inside screamer. She blazed away as always, whipping the ball across the plate in a "white-hot blur," styled one astonished sportswriter. But Ginny McGill had gotten wild of late, noted others, walking in runs. Still, few players could hit her stuff—whether out of speed or fear—and by the third week in July, her team, the Sonics, was 13-2.

Her pitching the previous summer had already turned heads in Richmond. Early in May the manager of one higher-tiered team had come calling, asking if she'd play for them in the Greater Capitol league. Ginny yearned to go, but had only to look at her mother knitting in the parlor.

Maybe next summer, she replied.

Yet when she asked her mother about buying a car, Laura amazingly agreed to cosign the loan. Thrilled, Ginny picked out a bright yellow, secondhand VW Bug, making the $300 down payment herself.

Hank buzzed her for the details. Unable to attend Charlie's funeral, he had sent Ginny three white roses. "For you...and him." Puzzled by the words on the card, she placed the flowers atop Grandie's grave.

Indeed, it was partly the young man's language skills that captivated her. This guy could write. Hank Forsythe regaled Ginny McGill with all manner of tales in his letters, be it his 500 mile round trip hitch-hike to Niagara Falls with two buddies on Senior Skip Day, or his side-splitting account of the inebriated commencement speaker at his own graduation a week later.

Ginny thanked Hank for the roses and told him of Grandie's funeral. Softball was going OK, she wrote, but she'd hit a batter the other night, breaking the girl's forearm. Mortified, Ginny considered quitting, but when some ranting opponents screamed for her removal as a wild and dangerous pitcher, she wrote Hank of her resolve to stay.

Her next letter bubbled with chatty news about her Bug, about going to Syracuse, and about how much she loved working with animals, especially boxers and Jack Russells. "By the way," she asked, "anything on Big Red?"

"Left everyone in the dust last Saturday in the Arlington," Hank wrote back. "Wish I could have seen him. Won by nine lengths! Can you believe it? Any chance you can get up here in early August? He's running in the Whitney."

"Millie's already invited us," Ginny wrote back, "but I don't think I can get the time off. Playoffs and everything." She penned this afterthought: "I wish Mom would go. She needs to."

But Laura McGill didn't want to go anywhere. By the terms of Charlie's will, she received clear title to Macon's Ordinary with a substantial trust fund for Ginny and her education. Her husband's official status remained "missing in action."

"What to keep and what to heave?" she asked one Tuesday evening while going through a downstairs closet.

Ginny laid four of Charlie's old coats on the carpet beside a half dozen pairs of his shoes. "Salvation Army?"

"I guess. But this,"—Laura picked up a small box—"should be yours."

Ginny removed the top. "Grandie's binoculars! Cool!"

"Don't know about the old telescope, but those binoculars were out nearly every clear night in summer."

"...and spring..."

"...and fall..."

"...and winter."

Mother and daughter embraced in the quiet of the old tavern. There was much they might keep.

"Why was Grandie so interested in stargazing, Mom?"

"I wondered that, too. It's one of the first memories I have of him. Out there in the backyard, bent over that old telescope." Laura closed her eyes. "Ever hear him talk to the stars?"

"Mom, it wasn't the stars."

"Huh?"

"No. One night after Daddy drove us down to visit—don't think I was even in school—Grandie took me outside. I remember him peeking up at the sky, chatting away. Told me he was talking to Grandma Nell. Said she wanted to know how red my hair was. Well I didn't see anybody. And I was nine before I realized she was buried out there."

"He did that a lot, Ginny. That's why I wasn't surprised when Dr. Crawford mentioned his sleep talking."

"But Millie said he was yelling all kinds of weird stuff, shouting and arguing, then pausing as if to listen."

"Don't put much stock in that, daughter." Laura picked up Grandie's old shoe shine kit. "Can't toss this, either."

"But Mom, Millie said it seemed so real."

"Grandie wasn't well."

"But Millie said he sounded rational. Talked plain and clear about 'a West Meadow' and 'twelve of this or that' and something about 'finally getting a chance.'"

"We've all heard that 'West Meadow' stuff."

"But Mom, his intensity..."

"Ginny, your Grandie was quite the storyteller."

"I just know he made me promise to see Secretariat run again."

Laura turned from the closet and looked straight at her daughter. "As if that were practical, young lady."

"Mom, he's running at Saratoga...in early August?"

"So you leave your job, abandon your team, and drive up to Millie's?"

"I promised Grandie."

"You mean Hank!"

"It's not about him, Mom!"

"Then what is it about, Ginny?"

"Mom..."

"I'll tell you what it's about."

"Mom!"

"Hush, Ginny. This is about holding a job, keeping a commitment, and going to college. Is that clear, young lady?"

"Mom? MOM!"

"What?"

"Don't you ever dream about Daddy?"

T ake a little off, Ginny."
    "You sure, coach?"
"Yep. She can't hit you, so she's fishing for a walk."
"But I can blow it right by her."
"Listen to me. We only need one more out. But your screamer's starting to drift. I know you're all fired up, but you're going to walk her if you push the heat."
"Coach..."
"Ginny...slow it down. Nice and smooth, right across the plate. She's not going to bring that bat off her shoulder."

Ginny watched Coach Alvin Snead trudge toward the dugout. The left-handed hitter stepped back into the batter's box.

Oh, I could so cook this right by you! But OK, Coach, you win.

She brought the ball over her head, pausing, then downward, stepping toward the plate, planting her front foot first before releasing her pitch.

The batter never moved.

Sttiiiiirrrrkkkke Three!

GO GET GINNY, GANG! GET HER! SHE'S DONE IT!

Coach and teammates mobbed the pitcher's mound, hoisting their star pitcher on their shoulders and trotting her off the field. No one could recall the last no-hitter, much less a perfect game. A league first?

Perhaps. At least Ginny had stayed and pitched...instead of running off to Saratoga Springs and seeing SUPERHORSE get beat. That's right, beat... *upset* by a length in the 46th running of the Whitney Handicap by an unheralded horse named Onion.

Maybe Mom was right.

O f all the buildings on campus, Syracuse University's Hall of Languages impressed Ginny the most. Headquarters for the College of Arts and Sciences, the building anchored the center of campus "on the Quad," as students said. Slugging through freshman architecture in the labyrinths of Slocum Hall, Hank pointed out to

Ginny the details of the building's distinctive Second Empire Style, *all crafted in Onondaga limestone, by the way.*

But Ginny liked the building for another reason: Grandie. She found it just plain cool that the Hall was only a year older than her great-grandfather. Not to mention that the steps in front provided a convenient place to meet Hank for lunch after Western Civ on Mondays, Wednesdays, and Fridays. A week into the semester, they had the rendezvous down pat.

"But I promised Grandie!"

"Ginny, it's at Belmont again. Out on Long Island."

"So? We could have gone two weeks ago and seen him beat Riva Ridge in the Marlboro! And set a world record!"

"Sure, but you aren't way behind in Econ and Calculus like I am. If my folks found out…"

"OK. OK. If you aren't in this with me, fine. But I promised Grandie. And if I have to, I'll go by myself."

"Hold on! Not alone you don't. I'd love to see Big Red run, too, but I can't get free this weekend. He's in the Man O'War on Columbus Day. That's at Belmont. Maybe I can swing that."

"A three-day weekend. I promised Mom I'd come home then. First time back since school started."

"Well, what's the big deal anyway? You've seen Secretariat run before."

"I promised Grandie. You know how he went on about Big Red. Heck, we both did. Then after he got sick, he…I don't know. There's just something about this horse. Am I making sense?"

"Why do you think I sent you three white roses?"

"Well, I…"

"They're Secretariat's three white stockings. Grandie told me it reminded him of something. Just went on and on about it."

Ginny lifted her eyes to the ornate clock atop the Hall of Languages. "Did he ever mention 'twelve' of this or 'a dozen' of that?"

"Not that I recall. Golly, almost noon? Why?"

"Nothing. Probably just Grandie spinning another of his stories."

*S*o *what were you trying to tell me?*
Ginny raised the candle and ran her finger around the frame of her great-grandfather's medical school diploma.

All those years you helped people, all those long nights in vigil around some dying person's bed, tending them, listening to them breathe out their last hours. How did you do it?

Even as a little girl, Ginny had marveled at how quiet the old tavern could get. As if hiding secrets. Now as she listened in the pre-dawn hush, her attentions summoned only expansion cracks in the floor, ticks of the hall clock, and the stillness itself.

You...were trying to tell me something.

Despite the comfort of her own bed on this first Saturday morning in October, Ginny was up early. Given her long drive down from Syracuse and gabbing with her mother past midnight, she'd only gotten a few hours of rest before waking and lying there, listening and thinking.

If ghosts ever haunted this place, you ran 'em out years ago, Grandie.

But she was home, safe, warm, close to her mother and the things she knew and loved.

What, Grandie, what?

In her mind's eye, she sensed no pattern...only a confusing constellation of predictions and phrases, appeals and events...all tugging her toward...something. Something?

All right. You never followed the track, but you go to your first horse race in years and pick the top three finishers right off the bat. Luck? OK. But then you not only predict Secretariat winning the Hopeful, you nail his margin of victory as well. Wild guess?

Ginny stared out the east window toward the coming dawn.

And talk about confidence? When I asked you about the Derby, you already knew he was going to win! Same with the Preakness, only you were in that hospital out like a light for the entire afternoon. Yet you knew the margin of victory. And not a TV in sight!

The day's first rays speared brilliance across the horizon.

You always could tell a tale, Grandie, but this time it's different. Turns out Secretariat's not so special after all. Lost the Woodward last Saturday at Belmont. He's not invincible.

Ginny snuffed out the candle and closed her eyes.

So why should I see him run one last time?
She listened to the room's silence, knowing there'd be no answer.
Yeah, you always had me in the palm of your hand when you were telling your stories. You talked to stars and fought the flu. I knew you were Santa Claus even when you said you weren't. You showed me war and even said your mother had skipped a stone across that lake way back when. All the way across! And her wish had come true! Great stories, Grandie. Great stories.
Ginny opened her eyes, the morning sun playing through her red hair.
You didn't fool me.
But still she grinned.
Always knew you were just a Wrinkle Monster.
Daylight poured through the old tavern's wavy glass panes. A beautiful fall weekend beckoned. The leaves were peaking in upstate New York. Two more weeks and Virginia would glow in her own autumnal glory.
And now you're gone. And I need to say goodbye.
Ginny picked up the candle, but spilled red wax across the funeral home's soft bound visitor's registry.
Clumsy me.
She wiped at the wax, but smeared it across the book's cover.
All these people who paid you their respects.
She turned a page, then a second, recognizing about a third of the names. Some had left a few words after their signature.
Our sympathies and condolences...
Going to miss you, old friend...
A grand, warm, and compassionate man...
Journey to the stars, old friend...
The sage of Keswick...
Requiescat in pace, old friend...
Ginny pressed her fingers to the words.
Old...friend?
"Old friend!"
Oh my gosh! It's in the den!
But the small table drawer beside Grandie's easy chair was empty.
Oh yeah! He said it over there. 'Old Friend.'

Inside the second drawer of Charlie's walnut roll top desk, Ginny found the *Daily Racing Form's* Horse of the Year issue Hank had sent her. Beneath lay several ancient albumen prints atop the latched wooden box Charlie had brought down from the attic. Heustis Cook's stunning photography pulled Ginny straight into a world a century old. A world she'd never known. Penciled captions on the back identified each scene.

WALNUT GROVE, FROM THE PIKE, SUMMER 1886

What a great place to grow up! You had the whole world to roam and run.

CHARLIE'S 12TH BIRTHDAY PICNIC

Oh, Grandie!! Look at you! Your big day. Love your smile.

Ginny blinked back a few tears. *Such a cutie. And how about that shirt!*

She admired the image, for here he was, little Charlie Harrison on his birthday, wide-eyed but game, in the saddle astride one of his father's thoroughbreds. Photographer Cook had captured the essence of boy and horse on paper dipped in silver nitrate and coated with an emulsion of egg white and table salt, all in an instant with his powerful flash.

Ginny turned over the picture:

CHARLIE ABOARD NUMBER TWELVE

But...

She gawked at the cover of the *Daily Racing Form...*

...then back, in disbelief, at the albumen print.

Dark red chestnut, 16 hands, white star on the forehead with a descending streak.

Ginny went back and forth between the two images, struggling to reconcile what her eyes had unmasked.

And three stockings, with the left leg the chestnut exception...

She listened, hearing only her pounding heart.

"Promise me you will see him run again..."

What is this? My imagination? An echo? Or...

She couldn't be sure.

But Ginny McGill knew at that moment she had a promise to keep. She just didn't know why.

Hank was waving atop the ornate steps that stretched away from the Hall of Languages when she rounded the corner.

"Great weekend?"

Ginny ran up and gave him a squeeze. "Got back late last night, but it was so good to see Mom."

"Well, have you heard?"

"Heard what?"

"Secretariat set the course record for a mile and a half on grass..."

"You're kidding? At Belmont?"

"Yeah. I know. I know. We missed his world record in the Marlboro...and now this."

Ginny spun out of Hank's arms. Students crisscrossed the green in all directions, angling to class. "Couldn't have gone anyway," she murmured, looking at the ground. "I promised Mom."

"Ginny, I'm ah...already late for class. Catch you at supper?"

"Whatever." Ginny watched Hank until he darted around the corner toward Lyman Hall.

Now what?

The October chill promised an evening frost, perhaps flurries.

Just let it go.

But as she walked back to her dorm that evening after Chem Lab, she sensed urgency.

Probably in this alone. But I did promise you, Grandie.

A week passed. Then a second. Ginny plowed into freshman biology and chemistry, wrestling with the differences between DNA and RNA, and thinking Niels Bohr's theory of atomic spectra more a course in introductory Greek. But she got a 93 on her mid-term Western Civ exam and a B+ on her English Lit theme comparing William Butler Yeats to Dylan Thomas. Hank left for a great uncle's funeral in Albany on Saturday and returned Sunday evening to catch up on homework and two design projects. When Ginny spotted him in the library that night, he had three books open atop pages of notes.

It didn't help when he missed Monday's lunch "on the steps," then again on Wednesday. But her mother's letter the next day brought an interesting twist. *Let's do Thanksgiving at Millie's.*

"Great!" Ginny wrote back. "You know she's been after us to visit since Grandie died. And Mom, the break would do you good. I'll meet you there."

That settled it. The turkey and cranberry sauce would be in Saratoga Springs this year. She told Hank the next day.

But Hank had news of his own.

"Grades?" asked Ginny.

"Nah! Just swamped these last few weeks. But Big Red. Have you heard?"

Ginny held her breath.

"They've announced his next race. Woodbine, outside Toronto."

"When?"

"Sunday, a week. That's the good news."

The good news? Golly, what's the bad?"

"It's his last race."

*A*ll the way to Toronto?

Of course Hank wasn't going to let Ginny drive it alone.

All of Sunday morning on the New York State Thruway got them past Rochester, through Batavia, and finally into Buffalo. Once across the border with the day overcast and rainy, they heard more of Niagara Falls in the thundering, fog-shrouded gorge than they actually saw. By the time they exchanged currency and got back on the road, Woodbine's first race was over.

"He's running in the eighth, I think," said Hank, looking at his watch. "We need to keep trucking!"

But construction detours and intermittent sleet parlayed slow traffic and roadblocks into ten minute waits and unforeseen delays. Twenty minutes to post time, they pulled into the track's expansive parking lot and scrambled for the grandstand.

"Wait! Got to go back!"

"What for?"

"Grandie's binoculars. I left them on the back seat!"

Eight more minutes vanished and as they jogged up the steps, the call to post sounded for the Canadian International Championship.

"Look at those betting lines, Ginny!"

"Just get an open view of the track!"

Hank shook his head. "No time!"

Ginny never heard him, intent to grab any spot along the glass. But a mob of people five deep blocked all views.

Outside, leaden skies hovered, spitting snow and sleet. But bad weather deterred no one. Thirty-five thousand race fans crowded Woodbine, eager to see SUPERHORSE run his last race.

"Can't see anything in here," Ginny yelled. "Let's try lower."

"Better hurry." Hank pointed to a track monitor. "They're loading now!"

"Didn't come here to watch this on a screen."

"But we don't want to miss it, Ginny."

"We won't!"

The starting bell rang and the crowd roared.

Secretariat broke on the outside, going up with speed horse Kennedy Road and Presidial as they led past the stands for the first time. Around the first turn, these three moved ahead of the field, Presidial slipping back.

"Over here, Hank! Here!" Ginny wormed forward, elbow to armpit, peering into a partial view of the gloomy track. "They're into the backstretch."

"Which one is he?" yelled Hank.

Ginny brought up the binoculars but the raucous crowd jostled her away from the window. "Can't tell, darn it. Just can't see."

But those who could see recognized the second place horse in the blue and white colors approaching the half mile pole. And when Kennedy Road bumped the challenging Secretariat hard, all screamed foul, their disapproval roaring into amazement when the red chestnut surged into the lead anyway.

"How about that Big Red there, eh, girl!" said a man in plaid next to her. "Damn shame it's so rainy. Can't see whit out there, eh?"

"You got that right!" Once more Ginny tried the binoculars, catching Secretariat rounding into the top of the stretch headed straight at her. Kennedy Road trailed by six lengths.

"Here he comes, Hank! And he's flying!"

Men and women erupted, jumping and screaming and cheering for the greatest race horse they would ever see. Secretariat blazed around the final curve and into the turn for home, his muscled body angling parallel to the grandstands, exhaling great, visible gusts into the October chill...the "living locomotive" some had proclaimed.

"He's going to do it, Hank!" screamed Ginny. "Look at him go!" The Triple Crown winner thundered down the home stretch...

He's got it, Hank! He's going out a winner!

...and hit the wire five and a half lengths ahead.

OH, GRANDIE! GRANDIE!

Ginny pressed against the glass, watching Jockey Eddie Maple trot Secretariat back to the winner's circle.

Sure picked a nasty day, Big Red. But what now, Grandie?

Then she saw it...

Secretariat's post number. Two digits. A one, followed by a two. One. Two.

Twelve.

Number Twelve.

SARATOGA SPRINGS, NEW YORK
THANKSGIVING 1973

N ow this dish belonged to my great-grandmother."

Mildred Blake spooned herself another serving of cranberries.

"Charles' grandmother. And your great-great...great grand-mother, Ginny."

"How do you keep all that straight, Millie? Anything historic about that plate holding the cherry pie?"

"Laura, my dear, Grandpa Luke told me so many stories. About the Parkers and all their Boston doings. About going to the Springs. Old Tom Morrissey and his dalliance with a witch. Grandpa and Charles were a lot alike, you know." She picked up her Blue Willow platter. "Glad you asked. Now this came over on the Mayflower!"

"Come on!" said Ginny, "you're pulling my leg!"

Millie laughed. "But there're folks in these parts who'll tell you such trash! More turkey, girl?"

"No thanks, but I'd love another taste of those fried apples."

"Certainly, sweetie. Leah made them before she left this morning. Always perfect with cinnamon and brown sugar. Mind you, I always give Leah and Jamison the day off. Wouldn't be Thanksgiving without family in for dinner. Why when I was growing up, we'd always make our Christmas candles on Thanksgiving."

"They do the same thing in the Bitterroots," Laura said. "Women work on their candles Thanksgiving afternoon while the men ride into the mountains to cut down the Christmas tree. Harney always..."

Memories of the man she loved always lay just beneath a surface of aging Pentagon reports and second-hand accounts, all bravely cobbled together despite thinning dreams and forlorn hopes.

Last Thanksgiving, inside the venerable walls of Macon's Ordinary as he had done for nearly 60 years, her grandfather had pronounced the Thanksgiving blessing, sliced the turkey, and toasted invited friends. News from Washington and Paris pointed to an end of the Vietnam War. Fresh intelligence suggested her husband's survival in an enemy prison camp.

Two months later the war did end. And the POWs began to come home.

But not her Harney. Letters arrived from all over, expressing sadness, anger, fear, hope. Friends and family visited and called from Virginia and Florida, from Montana and New York, be they Harney's flying buddies or her Madison College suitemates, all expressing their concern, wanting to know, telling her they loved her.

And that she must keep believing.

Then they hugged her and said good-bye, returning to their own loves and concerns.

Nine weeks after the last prisoner of war left North Vietnam, Laura's grandfather, the oldest physician in Albemarle County, passed away. For a month, friends, acquaintances, and patients old and not so old came to pay their respects. Laura McGill struggled to keep the faith. But these good people, too, eventually took their leave.

Now on this Thanksgiving Day, Laura McGill found herself with only memories. Unable to fight back the tears, she stood up without a word, put down her napkin, and left the table without even tasting the cherry pie.

T hat *was* his last race, Ginny."
"I know. Just doesn't seem right."
"Syndicated for more than six million dollars. Too risky to keep running I guess."

Hank tossed back the softball. Mildred Blake's backyard was perfect for practice. Even in the off season, good athletes needed to stay in shape.

"No inside screamers, please."

"Shoot, Hank. Can't you handle my best stuff today?"

"Yeah, but not right now."

Ginny zipped two half speed pitches straight into Hank's glove.

"So. Woodbine was worth it?"

She halted her windup in mid-stroke, flipping the ball in the air and catching it behind her back.

How...how can I tell you what I saw? Or what I believe I know? Heck, I'm still not sure myself.

She stared back at the boy with the catcher's mitt.

I do feel something for you, Hank Forsythe. But I still ache inside. So does my Mom. You need to understand that. I need...time.

Ginny signaled screamer and let it rip, smoking the ball—CRACK!—with a vicious sharp break to the left!

"Hey! You angry or something?" Hank dropped the ball, threw down his glove, and began massaging the palm of his left hand.

Grandie, you want me to believe in a miracle. Yet as a doctor you knew the world doesn't work that way.

Ginny held up her glove. "One more?"

I know what I saw. But I can't explain it. Yet you believed. And wanted me to believe, too.

She burned the next pitch straight across the plate. WHACK!

Just show me why I should.

H ere, this is for you. I'm sure Charles would have wanted you to have it. Sorry, I didn't think to bring it down during the funeral."

"That's OK, Millie. I remember you saying you had something for him. What is it?"

"Just an old leather pouch my grandfather had. Got tucked away in things after he died. When Father came across it, he realized it had actually belonged to Charlie's mother."

"An old pouch?"

"Little sac for keepsakes. Knowing my grandfather, he probably put squirrel shot in it. Does feel like there's something inside. Anyway, after all these years, it's high time it got returned."

"I'd rather you give it to Ginny. She and Hank are coming in now."

Hank wrung his left hand on entering the kitchen. "More major league heat, Mrs. McGill. Big time ouch!"

Ginny shrugged. And smirked.

"My dear, your Mom thinks Charles would have wanted you to have this." Mildred held out a small, worn leather bag, laced tight at the top.

"Millie says it once belonged to Grandie's mother," said Laura.

"My great-great grandmother?"

"That's right. Maybe she kept jewelry in it. Anyway, here. It's yours."

"Awww, Millie, thanks. Hey...something's inside."

"I've never looked, but I'm sure it'll mean more to you than me, dear. Go ahead. Open it."

Ginny pried the laces and turned over the bag. A small stone wrapped in a yellowed, crinkled piece of paper dropped into the palm of her hand.

T he heavy morning mist lifted from the lake as the sun burned through the fog-shrouded hemlocks standing watch on the hills above. Autumn's crispness sharpened the air. Silence settled the shore, stillness smoothing the lake's surface. No wake from a fisherman's boat. No morning hikers. No one to impress. Hardly another soul venturing for fish, frolic, or fortune this quiet hour. Not even the loon's lonely call broke the approaching spell.

The lake is ours. And now I know!

Ginny McGill gazed to the other side. *There is peace here.*

She pulled the small, yellowed paper from her coat pocket and opened it one last time, careful of its brittle folds. Slowly, deliberately, she reread the words Angeline Tubbs had scrawled more than a century before.

> In way of beast and wager seen,
> Bold ruler, pocketed clean,
> A contest shorn of winner due,
> Something royal on tides adieu.

> Smitten 'gainst ye enemies sworn,
> A footleap fantasy 'tis now born
> Of carried stride this noble steed,
> And across the line, a prisoner freed.

> But two troubles—mixed and mighty—cling
> To fabric chaste midst flowers spring
> And garland mists as memory keeps...
> Askance perchance—thy epic sleeps?

> For a stunning triple looms driving hard
> On way to surge a challenge marred
> By war and fate from beyond the gloam.
> Yet all go awe when beast turns for home.

> A stone of legend thus speaks to dreams
> Sped on faith, and soaring, teams
> With a maiden's wish, vestal'd true,
> To a destined fate, and freedom anew.

The words were all there. Some from Grandie, others she'd seen with her own eyes. And a few...she'd always known.

Believe? Oh, Grandie, I do.

Ginny McGill stepped to the water's edge, eyes burning to the far shore. She reached into her pocket and grasped the smooth, contoured piece of granite. She judged its weight proper, the angle precise, and the tilt accurate. A scalloped hollowness coursed one side of the stone and she rubbed its smooth, weathered surface, curling her forefinger around the honed outside edge. *This is a good stone!*

Gripping it precisely—curved and contoured, balanced and tilted just so—she raised hand above head and paused, then swooped down with an underhand motion powered and precise, grinding to a halt with the stone still firm in her fingers.

That felt good! But I'll need my best inside screamer.

With practiced hand, she raised the stone overhead for the last time, scribing a high arc.

"I love you, Daddy!"

Ripping through in downward blur, Ginny McGill sent the stone speeding across the water in a sharp, clockwise spin, barely kissing the surface on its first touch before being spun upwards, streaking across the lake.

Down it came. Then up again.

And on and on it skipped, coursing straight and true.

This single stone.

Palm-sized.

Polished.

And perfect.

Dramatis Personae

A ngeline Tubbs lived, according to one contemporary, with *"her numerous brood of cats"* in *"a lonely, wretched hovel"* just north of Saratoga Springs. *"... she led a solitary life at home, and was considered a vagrant abroad - subsisting in part by mendacity, and in part by laying small contributions upon those simple-hearted and prurient rustic maidens who wished to peep far enough into futurity to learn something of their future husbands. ... Her lonely and uninviting habitation, however, was avoided by the good people in the region round ... Her general appearance was as peculiar as her habits of life were erratic and unusual ... simple-minded people did not scruple to declare her little better than a sorceress, who practised incantations and held familiar converse with the spirits of darkness ... Her features were sharp, sallow, and wrinkled; her nose high and hooked, like the beak of an eagle, while her sunken, coal-black eyes, whenever crossed in her purposes, or otherwise angered, flashed with the piercing and terrible glances of the basilisk ... Sometimes she was in the village, practising as a fortune-teller, by way of paying for supplies of food, which from fear would never have been denied her; but for the most part, her time was occupied in wandering about the woods, and among the hills - climbing from crag to crag over the rocks, and traversing the glens and ravines of the neighbouring highlands. ... Had she been mistress of the whirlwind, she could not have been more delighted with storms. She had been seen, her form erect and with extended arms, standing upon the verge of fearful precipices, in the midst of the most awful tempests, conversing, as it were, with unseen spirits, her long, matted hair streaming in the wind, while the thunder was riving the rocks beneath her feet, and the red lightning encircling her as with a winding-sheet of flame."* Tubbs died in 1865, the year the Civil War ended.

John (Old Smoke) Morrissey was born in Ireland on February 12, 1831, but immigrated to the United States with his parents at the age of two. A brothel bouncer, freight thief, gambler, and failed California gold prospector, Morrissey eventually channeled his ferocious fighting abilities into prize fighting, defeating Yankee Sullivan for the American Championship in 1853. Ingratiating himself into the patronage of **Commodore Cornelius Vanderbilt,** Morrissey became a gambling-house proprietor in Saratoga Springs, and with **William R. Travers, Leonard Jerome,** and **John R. Hunter,** founded the **Saratoga Race Course.** In 1866, with the backing of Tammany Hall and Boss Bill Tweed, Morrissey won a seat in Congress in New York's 5th Congressional district. Knowing only muscle for persuasion, and often declaring he *"could whip any man in Congress,"* Morrissey grew tired of Washington—and Tammany Hall's rampant corruption— after two terms. After giving testimony that would help send Boss Tweed to prison, Morrissey was elected to the New York Senate. He died of pneumonia on May 1, 1878, age 47, and at his funeral, with the state flag at half mast, the State Senate adjourned and joined 20,000 other mourners in paying their respects.

Major General Edward (Old Alleghany) Johnson was born near **Midlothian,** in **Chesterfield County, Virginia,** on April 16, 1816, and graduated 32nd in his West Point Class of 1838, taking five years to get through the academy's four year curriculum. Blunt and profane, suffering no fools, Johnson is profoundly linked to two of Robert E. Lee's bloodiest fights: Gettysburg's Culp's Hill, and **Spotsylvania's Bloody Angle.** Noted one enemy combatant at Spotsylvania: *"He always wrinkled his eyes and every time his eyes wrinkled his ears flopped. He cussed and swore dreadfully, worse than anyone I ever heard. Our officers told us not to kill him. He got a musket and knocked down 15 men before we could stop him."* Johnson was captured twice in 1864—at Spotsylvania in May and Nashville in December—and after the war was lost, rejoined his brother **Philip** at **Salisbury,** two bachelors engaged in farming what was left of the family estate. Ed Johnson died on March 2, 1873.

Lieutenant General Richard (Old Baldy) Ewell was born in Georgetown, D.C., on February 8, 1817, and graduated 13th in his West Point class of 1840. Noticeably less effective as a corps commander after losing a leg at Second Manassas, Ewell's performance at Gettysburg is often cited as one of the primary reasons the South lost that epic battle. He died near Spring Hill, Tennessee, on January 25, 1872, three days after his wife's passing.

General Robert E. Lee was born on January 19, 1807, at Stratford Hall in Westmoreland County, Virginia, the son of Revolutionary War hero Maj. Gen. Henry "Light-horse Harry" Lee and Anne Hill Carter Lee. Graduating 2nd in his West Point Class of 1829, Lee was brevetted three times during the Mexican War. After Appomattox, he accepted the presidency of Washington College (now Washington and Lee University) in Lexington, Virginia, serving for five years until his death on October 12, 1870. An iconic American figure, Lee is regarded by many students of the American Civil War as *"Caesar, without his ambition; Frederick, without his tyranny; Napoleon, without his selfishness, and Washington, without his reward."*

Lieutenant Colonel Orville Babcock was born in Vermont on Christmas Day of 1835 and graduated 3rd in his West Point Class of May 1861. Brevetted a brigadier general for his service during the war, Babcock became General Grant's personal secretary. His indictment in the Whiskey Ring scandal—a group of Republican politicians siphoning off millions of dollars in federal liquor taxes—contributed to Grant's administration being viewed as corrupt. Alleged involvement in trying to corner the gold market and being named in the Safe Burglary Conspiracy forced Grant to demote Babcock, who had managed to avoid conviction, to a lighthouse inspector. While on the job at Mosquito Bay, Florida, Babcock drowned during a storm on June 2, 1884.

Lieutenant General U. S. Grant was born on April 27, 1822, and graduated 21ˢᵗ in his West Point Class of 1843. Depression and loneliness, complicated by excessive drinking, forced his early exit from the army. Subsequent farming near St. Louis proved a financial failure. And his two-term presidency would be stained by corruption. But today, America recognizes cigar-lover Sam Grant as Lincoln's most effective commander and historians revere his *Memoirs*, written and completed just days before his death from throat cancer on July 23, 1885, as one of the 19th century's great successes in publishing.

Traveller, originally named Jeff Davis by owner **Andrew Johnston** of **Blue Sulphur Springs** in what is now West Virginia, stood 16 hands high. Eventually sold to Captain Joseph M. Broun for $175 by Johnston's son, **Captain James W. Johnston,** Broun knew that Lee was looking for "*a good serviceable horse of the best Greenbriar stock,*" and sold him to Lee in February, 1862 for $200. In Lee's own words, Traveller possessed "*fine proportions, [a] muscular figure, deep chest, short back, strong haunches, flat legs, small head, broad forehead, delicate ears, quick eye, small feet, and black mane and tail. Such a picture would inspire a poet, whose genius could then depict his worth, and describe his endurance of toil, hunger, thirst, heat and cold; and the dangers and suffering through which he has passed.*" As to the colt's appearance, Lee would "*only say he is a Confederate gray.*" Traveller died the year after his master.

Secretariat endures. A popular movie bearing his name, released in October of 2010, revisits his life and times. His sub-two minute Kentucky Derby track record remains untouched as is his 1:53 record time in the Preakness. Yet Big Red's 31-length victory in the Belmont—a world record on dirt for that distance that has not even been approached—almost defies belief, with many fans insisting it was the finest horse race of the 20ᵗʰ century. Recalled a member of the New York Racing Association who witnessed the first Triple Crown in a quarter century that day, "*It was like the Lord was holding the reins. Secretariat was one of His creatures and He maybe whispered to him...go. And that horse really went. It was really an almost supernatural event...it really was.*"

CPSIA information can be obtained
at www.ICGtesting.com
Printed in the USA
FSOW04n2235221216
28773FS